Don't
Let Go

ALSO BY
SHARLA LOVELACE

The Reason Is You

Before and Ever Since

Just One Day

Stay with Me

Don't Let Go

SHARLA LOVELACE

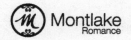

Montlake
Romance

Published by Montlake Romance, Seattle

www.apub.com

Amazon, the Amazon logo, and Montlake Romance are trademarks of Amazon.com, Inc., or its affiliates.

ISBN-13: 9781503944022
ISBN-10: 1503944026

Cover design by Eileen Carey

Printed in the United States of America

To Troy, my real-life hero,
who never lets go . . .

CHAPTER 1

I love red. It's my absolute favorite color.

I have a red car, a red coffeepot, have been known to have a red purse on occasion, and there is one accent wall in my living room painted a dark red. This was done both to make me happy when my daughter and I moved into my mother's old house and to spite my mother. Who hated red. Two birds and all that.

Certain times of the year, however, the color red gives me the willies.

The end of January, for example.

January—let's be honest—is a dead month. The hype of the holidays is over and people are back to work, slaving to pay off the credit card bills they just amassed. Resolutions have already been attempted and failed, for the most part, after the first few weeks. All there is, is cold. And wet.

In Texas, that wet cold is very rarely white. It's pretty much just gray. In fact, I've seen it actually snow—and stick—probably four times in my whole life. One of those times was when my daughter was in the sixth grade and the whole school district shut down for the three inches we got. Kids were having snowball fights on the playgrounds and the high schoolers had a snowball war on the football field. It made the local news.

Most of my winters have just been rainy, misty, freezing misery, with the occasional brisk pretty day that fools townspeople into thinking throwing a carnival in the middle of it is a grand idea.

The Copper Falls Winter Carnival is chaos, themed red in honor of the chili cook-off, and offset in white by the ridiculousness of a fake-snowflake parade. That about covers it.

They get giddy over this mess. Making floats for a parade that will kick off carnival rides in the icy rain and turn all their papier-mâché and Ivory-soap creations into paste. Every year.

Everyone except me. And my Nana Mae, who finds the festival and the whole snow thing in a town right off the Gulf of Mexico as silly as I do. Well, except for the chili part. That part is pretty good, and Georgette Pruitt from the flower shop usually makes the best one, if you could ignore the blinged-out snowflake hat she always insists on wearing.

But it isn't just that, either. And it isn't just the cold, rainy ick in the air and people progressively losing their sanity over a lame festival that essentially celebrates nothing. Or from having to watch my otherwise intelligent neighbors self-implode every year debating whether deer-meat chili is better than beef or trying to one-up each other with a hundred and one versions of fake-snow crafts for their floats. No, I think that's just extra icing for me.

I've had my own reason for the event to push me sideways every year. The cheesy festival and music and lights and red flyers on every street post; the smell of chili, cookies, and homemade candles; and the weeks preceding it when no one talks about *anything* else—those are just markers. Big obnoxious signs that hang that reason right out in front of my face.

And then, even that felt different this year. I felt lopsided.

I should have taken some time off from the bookstore to read or reorganize or clean out closets for the giant communal garage sale that was also part of the fun. Something brainless that didn't require thought or hand-eye coordination. I should have, but as usual, I didn't. And my nerves had about had it.

This particular morning was not a winner. Like a jolt from a dead sleep at two in the morning. That tends to mess you up a little, overly zealous neighbors or not. I cracked my knuckles and rolled my neck, trying to pull my foggy head together.

Bam . . . bam . . . bam-bam . . .

I clenched my teeth as the wall vibrated behind me, and I elbowed it back sharply in response. Another bam answered, sounding all too much like a cane against the thin walls that separated the bookstore from the diner next door. A cedar cane, in fact. One with a duck-head handle. I heard my heartbeat in my ears and took a deep breath to dial it back.

My wise old Cajun Maw Maw used to say, "Hide your crazy, girl. Ain't nobody wanna see that shit."

Maw Maw died of a heart attack at the age of sixty-two. My other grandmother, Nana Mae, who is neither Cajun nor known for being exceptionally wise, is still kicking at eighty-five and says it's because she lets all her crazy out.

As I rolled my head back and forth on my shoulders and listened to the snap-crackle-pop of too much stress, I started thinking that Nana Mae's way might be the smarter choice. Holding my Southern tongue and smiling through the melodrama of a moody teenager and the daily antics of the old Scrooge next door didn't seem to be good for longevity. Not to mention people who cared entirely too much about the logistics of papier-mâché. Maybe I should let go of a little crazy.

Bam . . . bam . . .

"Like—now!" I yelled through my teeth in the direction of the wall.

An elderly woman in an unfortunate Pepto-Bismol-pink pantsuit glanced up at me with disdain from where she sat in an oversized chair reading a paperback romance novel.

What, the *banging* was okay?

"Sorry, Mrs. Chatalain," I said softly, reaffixing my smile and sucking back my crazy.

My stomach growled, reminding me that it was lunchtime and that I'd forgotten my leftovers at home. I rubbed at my temples, which had drummed out a dull rhythm since I'd awakened. Something had me on edge. It was always my most difficult time of the year—I expected it. Waited for it. But still, something was different.

"What's with you, today?" said a voice to my left. My assistant manager, Ruthie, strolled from the back of the store looking all bohemian with her black beret cap and her hands tucked in the pockets of a long and well-worn black sweater. Her small frame looked lost in it.

I shook my head. *She's forgotten*, I thought. *She doesn't remember. But that's okay. Somebody needs to be normal for once.*

"Johnny Mack and his stupid-ass cane," I said under my breath, nodding toward the offending wall. "There's not one note of music playing anywhere in here today."

Ruthie chuckled. "It's his entertainment, Jules," she said with a wink before something else caught her eye. "Uh-oh, look who's coming."

I followed her gaze to the wall of spray-snow-frosted glass flanking the front of the bookstore, where a lone teenage girl with crooked hair was heading up the sidewalk.

"Damn it," I muttered.

The bell jingled as she pushed open the door and I watched Mrs. Chatalain raise an eyebrow at the girl's black smudgy eyeliner, dark shiny hair that was longer on one side than the other, and navy-blue T-shirt that said, "You laugh because I'm different. I laugh because you're all the same."

"Hey," the girl said, her mouth cocking in an endearing crooked grin that lit up her face and killed the *I don't care* mask that she worked so hard to maintain.

"What's wrong?" I said, standing up.

She frowned and shrugged, the frayed black backpack slung over her shoulders moving with her. "Nothing, why?"

"Why aren't you at school?" I asked.

She pointed to the giant clock across the street that was about to rattle the windows with its eleven o'clock toll.

"It's lunchtime," she said.

I closed my eyes and counted the reasons why I loved her as my pen slipped from my fingers and clattered from the counter to the floor. "At school, Bec."

Her face scrunched up. "They had gumbo today," she said simply. "Their gumbo sucks. Nothing like Nana Mae's."

"Not even mine?" Ruthie said with a head tilt and mock hurt expression.

Becca smiled. "Not even yours, Aunt Ruthie." She tilted her head to match. "Although I do really like when you make potato salad to put in it."

"Thank you," Ruthie said with a little curtsy.

I splayed my fingers wide on the cool granite countertop, letting the hard cold seep in. I probably needed to press my wrists against it. Or go stick my head in the break-room freezer. "You have to quit doing this, Bec. It's not an open campus. I'm tired of calling—"

"Okay, okay, I get it," she said, holding her palms up. I noticed there was something new drawn in black Sharpie inside her left wrist. Of course there was. "We're not doing anything anyway."

"The law doesn't care, baby."

She widened her eyes at Ruthie in the eternal oh-my-God-ness of it all. "Got it. But I'm here, so do y'all want to take me next door?"

Her face broke into a cheesy innocent grin that was so fake, it broke me.

Ruthie snickered at my side as I shook my head. "Girly, you really ought to be my blood. You've been around me too long," she said, walking around to hook an arm around Becca's neck.

That was true. Ruthie had been Becca's "aunt" since birth, and my best friend since kindergarten. She'd been with me through everything. *Everything*. And helping in the bookstore right alongside me since we were eight years old and my mother ran it.

"I do like your hair, I have to say," Ruthie said, fingering the lengths that were razor cut from just under her chin on one side to past her shoulder on the other. "Wasn't sold when your mom told me about it, but it works for you."

Bec's smile was brilliant, and she fluttered her eyes at me. "Thanks!" I smiled, humoring them both. "Ready?"

"I'm gonna go to the bathroom first," Bec said, dropping her backpack where she stood. "Theirs is kinda—ick."

I sighed as I stooped to pick up her bag. "Why don't y'all just go and bring me back something?" I asked Ruthie, gesturing toward our lone customer.

"Nah, I'll stay," she said, plopping onto the stool and grinning at me. "I brought chicken salad." Laughing at my expression—which I'm sure showed I'd rather be flogged—she continued, "Go fuss at him."

As if on cue, three short bumps reverberated through the wall. I sneered and gave her a knowing look. "Not a good time for that."

She frowned. "Why—oh." Her expression changed and her eyes got a far-off cast to them as she joined me in my retro journey. "That's right. No wonder you've been funky this week." She sent a glare toward the wall. "He probably doesn't even know anymore."

I licked my lips. "He knows. He always gets a little extra asinine right after New Year's." I looked away and reached behind the counter for my not-red purse. "Maybe I'll dump my food on his head or something."

"Oh, if you feel the urge, text me first," she said. "I'll run over there for that."

I laughed and shook off an involuntary shiver at the same time. Ruthie narrowed her eyes at me.

"What else?"

"What do you mean?" I knew what she meant. Ruthie could read me like a damn psychic. She knew me too well.

"Something else is going on." Her dark eyes narrowed to slits in her pale face. "You look all twitchy."

I scoffed. "I'm not twitchy."

"You're twitchy."

"Snowflakes," I said.

She shook her head. "This isn't a snowflake twitch. I know the snowflake twitch."

I blew out a breath and glared at her, not that it had one iota of effect on her. Ruthie was impervious to my attempts at badassery.

"Whatever," I said, looking away. "Just had a bad night."

"Did you have sushi again?" Ruthie asked.

I chuckled as I ran a hand through my hair, holding it back. "No," I said, glancing toward where Becca had disappeared. "I just—I had a hell of a time falling asleep, and then when I did—I dreamed about Noah." Her eyes widened just a little, then she crossed her arms as she set a smile right back on her face that made me laugh to myself. "Nice cover, Ruthie, don't play poker."

She ignored my snarky remark. "So, like, a 'Hey, look at me, I'm Noah, I'm an asshole just walking by' kind of dream, or like—a *dream*?" she said.

I picked up my pen, dropped it again, and squatted to grab on to it with both hands. "Not that kind of *dream*," I said, mimicking her drama voice. "It was just one of those—" My face suddenly felt itchy and I rubbed at it. "It was probably just because it's coming up. My brain trying to make it harder than it already is."

I pasted a smile on as Becca strolled up like a queen.

"What?" she said.

I shook my head. "Ready now?"

"Yeah, I'm hungry, let's go," Bec said.

I sighed. "Oh, yes, let's."

"Don't beat up Johnny Mack!" Ruthie called out, smiling back at Mrs. Chatalain and grabbing some mailers I needed to address and send out.

Bec's new hair swung in front of me as we walked outside in the breeze. To her credit, she could pull it off. To her detriment, I saw her dad's truck parked outside the diner and knew instinctively there would be drama.

I was actually a little intrigued that Hayden would be there, since Johnny Mack Ryan wasn't on his favorite list either, and I knew he wouldn't go to his diner on purpose. The old man's hatred for me spewed over onto everything, and my marrying Hayden three years after Johnny Mack's son joined the Navy and swore never to return—well, let's just say that expanded the toxicity to Hayden by association.

To my daughter, too, but that had different roots.

The aroma reached me before we even opened the thick wooden door, and my mouth was watering by the time we made it two steps in. I wished the smells came over to my side of the wall as often as the phantom music came to his.

The clock tower in the old courthouse across the street vibrated the tile under my feet with its announcement. The diner was still only half full, it only being eleven. The tide of office workers from the courthouse wouldn't hit till noon, and the contractors perpetually working construction down at the river would roll in around a quarter to one. Then it all would start up again for dinnertime at five. Johnny Mack did a booming business, in spite of his sour disposition. With his daughter, Linny, at his side keeping customers happy and laughing and spending money on his amazing dishes, people tended to overlook the snarls and sneers and griping from the chef.

Well, people except me. I had a little more trouble blowing him off. Maybe because his vitriol toward me wasn't just the snark of an old man. Because he used to love me like a daughter. Because it was personal.

Linny winked at us as we walked past the counter, and Becca patted the surface loudly as she passed. "Hey, Mr. Ryan," she called out.

I saw him shake his head, not even looking up from the food he was preparing as he grumbled something to himself.

"Got shrimp today?" she continued, and I had to smile in spite of myself. She didn't care that he didn't like her. She didn't even know why. She just enjoyed the hell out of goading him.

"Have a seat or move on," he said, his gravelly voice monotone and lacking the bite it usually had. "Mind your manners."

"Oh, her manners are just fine," Linny tossed back over her shoulder at him. "She just knows ornery when she sees it." She shook her head and rolled her eyes at me knowingly. "Did you have a call-in, hon?"

That would have been a grand idea. "No, we're"—I gestured toward some empty tables—"sitting." I was most definitely not interested in landing at the counter and getting scowled at. I looked for a table by the windows, but they were all occupied.

I saw Hayden at one, head bent over a stack of paper, and with a pretty woman in a suit. A working lunch. Or maybe the prelude to something else? He didn't see us, so I didn't do any jumping up and down to call attention.

"This is good," Becca said, picking a four-seater and dumping her backpack in an extra chair.

Closer to Johnny Mack than I liked, but then again, I needed to get over it. Normally I was able to mostly ignore him. It had been twenty-six years. Over two decades, living in the same town, working next door to each other, and putting up with his temper tantrums. I didn't normally feel such a strong urge to get away. Maybe it was the dream still messing with me; maybe I was being hormonal. Whatever it was, it had the little hairs on the back of my neck going stiff.

"Ugh," I muttered, rubbing at my neck and my arms.

"What?" Becca said, looking up from the plastic menu.

I shook my head. "Nothing, baby. I'm just wiggy today."

"You're wiggy every day," she said, perusing her choices like it was her last meal. "Last time I got the fried shrimp po'boy sandwich and it was to die for."

I plucked a menu from its resting place between the napkin holder and the condiments, not really needing it but looking anyway. I sighed at the red napkins in the holder next to the salt and pepper shakers. Linny already had it going on. Ruthie would be redding up the store soon, too. Frosted glass wasn't going to satisfy her. "I usually get the plate lunch. I think today is open-faced turkey with mashed potatoes."

"That sounds so boring."

"Not the way he makes it," I said. "It's amazing."

"Thought you hated him." She said the sentence in a completely disinterested tone, as if she were talking about the sky being blue.

I looked up at her. "I don't hate him. We just—"

"Don't see eye to eye," she said, nodding, looking bored. "I know. Can we get dessert?"

"No dessert with lunch, Bec, you know that," I said. "That fried shrimp you're having is bad enough, you'll never stay awake through class."

She was blowing out a sound of disgust before I even finished the sentence.

"Sorry," I said. "Have some yogurt tonight."

"Yogurt," she muttered. "Can we have real ice cream for once?"

I let it go. She was in a mood, and nothing I was going to say would make her happy, so I decided to keep the peace. Let her dad over there duke out every single battle. I chose mine. It was better for my sanity.

She bit her bottom lip for a second and closed her menu, which caught my attention.

"Something the matter, Bec?" I asked, closing mine, too.

I could see the gears working. There was a question percolating somewhere. She wanted something, or needed something, or had a world-shattering revelation to tell me. I didn't like those.

"Hey, ladies."

I turned at the familiar voice and fought the mixture of joy and annoyance. Especially when I saw Becca roll her darkly lined eyes. So much for an almost-moment.

"Hi, Patrick," I said, patting the hand he'd rested on my shoulder. Possessively, I thought. I patted it again to give him the hint to let go. My skin was jumpy enough without someone holding me down. "I thought you were working that site in Torrence?"

"It's delayed a few days, for permits and shit." He stopped short and glanced at Becca, touching her shoulder. "Sorry—stuff."

She glanced up at him hulking over our table, looking hot in a scruffy motorcycle-gang kind of way, and smiled tolerance before widening her eyes back to the menu she'd reopened. She'd met Patrick twice before. Once at the bookstore, where he was so painfully out of place he practically glowed. And then one awkward moment at our house, when Becca came home early from a night out with friends and we were walking down the stairs looking like we'd forgotten how to dress ourselves.

I nodded, and I couldn't help darting a glance over to Hayden's table, hoping he hadn't caught sight of us. Not that he cared, since we'd been divorced for almost seven years, but he was one to make comments that weren't supposed to mean anything and yet usually left marks. He was still deep in conversation with the woman over whatever was on the papers.

"So, maybe we can grab a bite to eat or something tonight?" he said, squeezing my shoulder again. "Or tomorrow?"

I knew exactly what that *or something* was, and as I let my memory travel the planes of his body built from years of site-construction labor, my stomach tingled.

"Tonight's not good," Becca said, replacing the menu. "I have a test to study for. I'll see if I can find something to do to be scarce tomorrow."

Even smooth-talking Patrick looked lost for words, and I felt the heat whoosh up to the top of my head.

"I'll call you," he said quickly. "Y'all have a good lunch."

I stared at her as he grabbed a to-go bag and bolted out of the diner.

"Becca, that was—" I began.

"Awkward?" she finished, nodding with a sarcastic smile. "You have no idea."

I rubbed at my face, wondering if I just needed to go home for the day. "What happened to *doing nothing*? And since when do you study for anything?"

"Since maybe I want to watch TV without hearing my mom bang Mr. Hardbody down the hall."

"Becca!"

It was loud. It was too loud, and drew the eyes of everyone in the place, including Hayden's. But never in my life had I been so mortified.

"Sorry, just sayin'," she said, at least having the decency to color up, herself.

"Sweethearts, how's it going?" Linny said then, appearing at our table with a smile and a wink and a significant girth pushing at her apron. "Everything okay?" she added in a quieter voice.

"It's good," I said, maintaining the glare at my daughter. "Becca just forgot her mouth for a second."

Becca's eyes landed everywhere but on me, and then she smiled up at Linny. "I want a Coke with lots of ice, and the shrimp po'boy. With fries," she added, not looking my way.

"Got it," Linny said, not writing a thing down, just winking at her. She looked at me. "And you?"

"I'll do the plate lunch. And hey, Linny?" I added as she nodded and started to walk away. "Please tell your dad to quit banging on the wall. I swear to you on all that is holy that there is no music playing over there," I said with a smile.

Linny laughed and wiped her hands on her apron. "I've told him again and again that I don't hear anything, but he ignores me." She nudged me with a finger. "But check him out today. He's almost giddy."

We both turned to see Johnny Mack grinning at a customer, and the feeling I'd had at two that morning settled over me like a chilled blanket, making me shiver again.

Why was he happy? And why did that make me feel like a caged animal? I had a bad feeling that this particular crazy was going to have to be held close to the vest. Maw Maw was right. No one was going to want to see this shit.

CHAPTER 2

Johnny Mack beamed. And if I'd learned anything in the twenty-plus years since his son left town, that was reason to put your guard up. He was conversing up a customer, his normal look of disgust replaced by— was that interest?

"I mean, he's still a grouch, but he's actually been nice to people today," Linny said.

I tried to shake off the heaviness I felt on my skin. "What's up with that?" I asked, frowning.

She shrugged. "No clue. He just keeps saying to watch the door. I don't know what the hell the door's gonna do, but if it makes him smile, I'm game."

"How's it going, Linny?" came a voice to my right, yanking me back to the real world. Becca's whole face crumpled.

While Hayden pulled up a chair, I looked around for the pretty lady in the suit, and she was nowhere to be seen.

"Another day in paradise," Linny said, winking at him.

"You putting your chili in the contest again?" he asked. "You know it's always my favorite."

Linny's cheeks flushed up as she chuckled and walked away. Hayden had that way. He could make women stutter-stupid with just a smile. Not like he was some hot *GQ* type or anything. He wasn't. He dressed it, but always a little messy, like maybe he needed a little help with that tie. With that shirt. With that belt. He wasn't really a guy to lust over at first glance, but he could have you with a five-minute conversation. I think he'd had me twenty-three years earlier with a "hello" and a slow dance. But then, as Becca had so fluently pointed out, I was evidently an easy bang.

"By all means, join us," I said sarcastically as I leaned on the table and forced that thought away. I suddenly felt as if the day was hell-bent on wearing me out.

"Hey, bug," he said, ignoring my zinger and focusing on Becca.

"Hey back," she said, smiling her crooked smile.

"So—did the hairdresser have to leave midway for a family emergency or something?"

Her smile faltered, and I wanted to throw sugar substitute packets at him.

"Yep, she did," Becca said, meeting his gaze. "So we only paid for one side."

Hayden nodded, I guess for once seeing that it wasn't worth the fight. "And you're okay with it?" he asked, turning to me.

"She's not eight, Hayden. She's a high school senior." I took a deep swallow from my water glass. "If having weird hair—"

"Hey!"

I ignored her indignation. "—is her worst sin, then I think we can count our blessings."

"Until I get my tattoo," Becca said, which managed to render both Hayden and me speechless for a second.

"Come again?" he said.

"When I graduate," she said matter-of-factly, holding up her Sharpie'd wrist. "Something here, don't know what, yet."

"Just nod, Hayden," I said on a sigh. "It changes monthly."

"This one won't," she said.

Linny swung back by with a basket of rolls and extra butter, because she knew Becca and I were butter whores. I slathered one up and took a bite, relishing the carbs.

A hand on my shoulder turned me around. "Did you get the e-mail?" said an elderly man with spinach in his teeth and a comb-over that never moved.

I blinked. "E-mail—um, I haven't had a chance to check yet today, Mr. Morrison, but—"

"It went out four days ago," he said. The spinach didn't move. "You are supposed to have your ad and payment turned in for the flyer by this weekend."

Of course I was. The all-important festival flyer. Priorities. "Okay, well, I'll—check in on that."

He patted my shoulder, shook Hayden's hand even though he probably didn't remember who he was, and then just kind of looked at Becca as he walked past.

"Am I purple or something?" she whispered.

"It's your aura," I whispered back, making her snicker. "So, what brings you to the dark side?" I asked Hayden, nudging him with an elbow.

"I was at the courthouse with a contract, so I figured what the hell. Hey, you know the old man didn't even give me a dirty look?"

"Linny said he's all happy for some reason," Becca said around her own bite of gooey roll.

"So who was the fancy woman?" I asked, unable to resist the jab and needing to distract myself from Johnny Mack's issues. "Dating lawyers now?" I asked with a grin.

Hayden turned to meet me dead-on, his hazel eyes twinkling. "Who was the crustacean? Dating bikers now?"

A full-on belly laugh started low and worked its way up, making me realize just how much I'd missed laughing like that. In spite of our differences, Hayden could always make me laugh. And this particular time of year, with the damp cold creeping in and the crispness in the mornings making the sad in me rise to the surface, I needed to feel that release.

"Touché."

I raised the roll to my lips, and the remaining chuckle froze in my throat as the door opened and in walked a couple. The small brunette woman was all in red and beautiful enough to make anyone notice, but it was the man.

A man I'd last seen as a seventeen-year-old boy. Unless you counted last night's dream. My skin went cold and tingly and my head felt like I'd been sucking helium. I felt the roll leave my fingers.

"Mom?" I heard Becca say. "Mom, what's the matter?"

"Jules?" Hayden's voice said in my ear.

But it was the eyes that traveled the room, looking nostalgic but wary as they took in every detail until they landed on me and stuck. I felt their weight. And went back to the last time we'd locked eyes.

The day I gave our baby away.

"Noah."

◆ ◆ ◆

Twenty-six years. A lifetime ago. And yet in that moment, with Noah Ryan standing fifteen feet away from me, I was suddenly the seventeen-year-old pregnant senior, holding his hand in the hallway and trying to get through the day. The swollen, hormonal girl at the Copper Falls Halloween picnic, leaving yet another fight with my mom to go meet up with my boyfriend and talk about visions of marriage. The waddling, back-gripping girl at Christmas, and the conflicted young woman at the cursed Winter Carnival, arguing with her fiancé by the river, going into labor and rushing to the hospital through tears. And then an empty girl, giving some very lucky couple a beautiful treasure, while the boy she loved left crying. Left town, left the country, left her completely.

For twenty-six years.

"There he is," sang Johnny Mack from the kitchen in a voice that was more upbeat than I'd heard maybe ever. The old man came around that counter with his duck-head cane, barely needing it as he held his arms open. "There's my boy!"

He wasn't a boy anymore. Gone was the lanky frame, and in its place was solidity and muscle. His dark hair was cropped short, with a smattering of something lighter. His face was more filled out, as was his whole body. And the black pullover shirt he wore loosely over jeans showed all of it. Dear God, the military had been good to him.

Johnny Mack Ryan's face broke into a grin as he embraced Noah, and Linny came running from the restroom.

"Jesus Christ, Noah!" she said, tears in her voice. "What the hell?" She nearly knocked her father over to get to him, and he laughed as she wrapped her arms around his neck. "You worm! Not telling us you're coming?"

"Dad knew," Noah said, and the sound of his voice after all those years sent ripples through my skin. I gripped my napkin like it could keep me together. "He wanted to surprise you."

She let go of Noah and shoved at her dad as he laughed a wheezy laugh I hadn't heard in decades. "You—ornery old goat!"

I realized I was still staring when Noah's gaze found me again. Something there hit me like a cannonball to the chest, and I forced my eyes back down to the half-eaten roll on my plate, listening to myself breathe. Hayden's voice reminded me that there were still people at my table.

"Julianna."

He only called me my full name when he wanted to get my complete attention, so evidently he'd been talking to me for a while.

"Yes?" I said, a little too loudly, my voice cracking. At the pause, I looked his way.

"That's him?" he asked.

Under all the turmoil whizzing through my head, I felt his true questions, saw them in his eyes. But I wasn't going to go there in front of Becca. I just nodded, not trusting my voice with all my insides turned to Jell-O, and then hating myself for acting stupid over a man from two decades in my past.

I felt Becca's gaze on me and chose to look past it. I intended to check out the fastest path to the door. I didn't care about the food; I'd get it from Linny later. I just needed to leave before my nerves got the better of me.

"Dad met Shayna when he came to Italy," Noah was saying, pulling my eyes back his way. "But, Linny, I want you to meet her." He reached back where the stunning woman was standing slightly behind him and gently pulled her forward, his hand going to the small of her back. "This is my sister, Linny, babe." The woman smiled warmly and extended her hand as Linny's large ones swallowed it. "Linny, this is my fiancée, Shayna."

Fiancée. My blood burned as the word bounced around. Oh, I was such an infant. Who cared if he was engaged, or married, or shacking up. People ran into old boyfriends and girlfriends all the time. The difference was that usually you saw them living life in the meantime. The last time I'd seen Noah—*I* was his fiancée.

I reached into my bag and pulled two twenties blindly from it, handing them to Becca. Knowing it was probably thirty dollars too much and not caring. She could call it a score.

"Go ahead and eat, baby. Visit with your dad."

"What?" she said, looking genuinely disappointed and breaking what I could feel of my heart. "Where are you going? We don't even have our food yet."

"Back to, um—something's come up," I said. "I need to go. You and Daddy have lunch on me."

"Um, I need to go, actually," Hayden said.

"Visit with your daughter," I said slowly, pinning him with each word. I turned back to Becca, who was looking at me like I was traitorous. "Eat your lunch. Box mine up. Drop it by on your way back to school."

"Wait, hang on," Hayden said, narrowing his eyes at her. "How are you out of school?"

"Have a good chat," I said, patting him on the back as I rose from my chair. I kissed Becca on the top of the head. "Loves," I said into her hair. Our trademark word since she was little.

"Loves," she said, although I didn't feel love. I felt her hate spewing out all over me.

Another parental-fail moment I'd have to own up to, but it was better than melting down in my chair. Fortunately, I managed to pass the happy couple on my way to the door without tripping on anything.

"Jules."

"Oh, shit," I said under my breath, turning around. At least I thought it was under my breath. By the expression on his woman's face, it might not have been. She was even more beautiful up close, I noticed, with no crinkles or zits and perfectly lined eyes. I forced myself to meet his eyes instead. "Yes?"

And that was a bad idea. He was two feet away. I could see the deep blue of his eyes, smell him. Feel the heat of his body. Okay, maybe not that, maybe that was just my anxiety and rage and anger and hormonal imbalance going ape-shit.

He opened his mouth to say something, but he looked nearly as floored as I felt. Why was *he* floored? He at least knew he was coming. He knew he'd see me eventually. I, on the other hand, was just fine with him on the other side of the world, and didn't realize that gap had closed. Especially not now.

He swallowed back whatever thought was there, and I didn't let myself analyze it. Not all these years later, when I couldn't even say I knew him anymore. I just nodded.

"Welcome home, Noah."

I was so proud of myself for forming words.

He just blinked and let himself be pulled back into the chaos as his dad stepped between us and turned his back to me, slapping him on the back as Noah's fiancée slipped a hand into the crook of his arm.

"Everyone!" Johnny Mack hollered out to the entire diner. His face was transformed from grouch to grin. "My son is here!" At the murmurs and curious looks from people who didn't know why that was holler-worthy, he waved his hands impatiently. "From Italy! Noah's home from the Navy. He's finally home!"

At the smattering of claps and amused expressions and *welcome home's* from the clientele, Noah smiled stiffly and visibly reddened. He still wasn't one for the spotlight, I noticed, as he backed up a step and put a hand on the back of the brunette's neck, eyeing the room. I felt the discomfort with him, backing slowly toward the door so my exit wouldn't be analyzed by any town gossips. As much as I wanted to bolt, I couldn't quit looking at him. It had been such a long time. Most of the people in there were too young to remember the juicy story or the boy who'd left Copper Falls to be a career Navy man. The few old-timers sitting around the lunch counter got up and shook his hand, as they remembered him and knew what he'd been—what he was. They'd kept up with Johnny Mack's stories of Noah's adventures over the years, when he joined Special Forces and when he made master chief.

"You here for a visit, Noah, or home for good?" Spinach Teeth asked him.

Noah took his hand in both of his and smiled. "I'm home, Mr. Morrison. I'm getting too old to keep moving around. I'm home."

I pushed the door open with my back and slipped out, welcoming the brisk breeze on my flushed skin.

"He's—he's home," I whispered, echoing the words. I leaned against the scratchy door for a moment, letting the crispness of the air cool me down. I blew out a slow breath and ignored an odd look from a passing couple. "It's okay," I said to them, smiling, squeezing my own fingers to stem the shaking. "It's okay," I repeated, softer, to myself. "Quit being a child."

I pushed off the door when I heard group laughter inside and started the twenty whole feet to my own door. Ruthie was laughing in her singsongy way as I pulled the door open and the little bell jingled overhead. Mrs. Chatalain was on her way out, a little gold sales bag held against her pukey pink outfit.

"Have a good day," I managed, holding the door open for her. "Enjoy your book."

"What kind of sale you going to have for the Winter—" she began, nodding back toward the inside.

"No idea," I said briskly. "What would you like?"

"Buy one, get one free would be nice," she said, squinting up at me.

"Yeah, it probably won't be that," I answered.

"Figures," she muttered, holding her bag against her as if it would block the wind. "Your mother would have done that for an hour or so," she said. "With hot chocolate or something."

"Good to know," I managed, what my mother would have done or not done being the least of my concerns.

A couple was at the counter finishing up a large purchase of self-help books when I went in, and the guy was flirting shamelessly with Ruthie as the woman laughed a little uncomfortably. I smiled as they left, swiped a sprinkled cupcake from a platter Ruthie had brought out, and landed in a nearby chair, suddenly spent.

"Anyone in here?" I asked, resting my head against the back with my eyes closed.

"Not now," she said. "That was a fast lunch. Becca already headed back?"

I lifted my head and focused on the cupcake, trying to unpeel the paper with fingers that had forgotten how to function.

"No," I said, the word coming out raspy. I cleared my throat and tried to push his face from my vision.

"Jules? Is everything okay?" I heard Ruthie say.

I set the cupcake down and closed my eyes, shaking my head just slightly. The air felt thick and quiet around me, the ticking of a nearby clock being the only sound. He was back.

"Jules?" she asked again, her voice coming closer as the curiosity beckoned her.

With my eyes shut and my other senses heightened, I heard the wariness and concern in her voice. I opened my eyes and stared straight ahead, blowing out a breath slowly. A tiny laugh bubbled up my throat that had nothing to do with anything being funny.

"Noah's home."

CHAPTER 3

Noah Ryan was my first love. He was my first everything. He was my first boyfriend, daring me to climb to the top of the monkey bars in the second grade and then kissing me square on the mouth when I did. He brought me special rocks he picked out and held my hand in the lunch line.

In later years, Noah would give me my first beer, first cigarette, and first real kiss during Truth or Dare. He was the first one to break my heart, then steal it again. He was the first boy to ever tell me he loved me, the first one I ever loved back, and the one I gave my first time to. We both did. Fumbling and awkward and passionate in the pouring rain one late April night, driven by young love and raging hormones, we learned what making love was.

And what making life was.

He wanted to marry me. In all his teenaged wisdom, he was ready to give up his lifelong dream of being a soldier and just stay here and be a family. My mother said no. My parents were devastated and mortified, of course. All the things you would rightly feel upon finding out your pure-as-the-driven-snow angel has given up the goods and gotten herself knocked up. They had loved Noah up until that point, but all that went out the window. My dad went lunatic crazy, his Cajun blood sending him to angry places he didn't need to go, but the thought of his baby being violated sent him past reason. It didn't matter how many times I used the words *consensual* and *in love*—I never got further than that. As soon as he'd hear the L word, he'd go off wanting to kill the boy that ruined his daughter.

That child would have been twenty-one years old when my dad died, and another year older when my mother followed him. In all those years, they never spoke of it to me—the grandchild they passed up, arranging for the adoption to happen the second it was born, with the records sealed. Not even nine years later when Hayden and I finally had Becca. It was easier for them that way, I supposed, pretending it never happened. I couldn't pretend that well. I had the memory of a son I'd never hold, and never know. And the image of Noah's tortured expression as he let go of my hand to see his son and they wouldn't let him. The sound of his pleading and the tears soaking his face.

I lost it for a while as well, but it was too late. The baby was gone. And then so was Noah.

And now here he was. Back in a town that had mostly forgotten. At a time I'd never forget. Stirring everything up again.

That was unfair, I thought, to think that. He wasn't to blame for what his presence stirred up in me. And I wasn't my parents. I did think about my baby boy on every holiday, every Mother's Day, and every time I'd see a young man resembling Noah. Every first that Becca had, I'd wonder about his. I wondered about his life, if he was nearby or far away, and if he loved dark chocolate like I did or licorice like Becca. If he had an artist's hand or a sniper's eye. But I especially devoted January 29 to him in my heart. His birthday.

Why would Noah pick now to make his grand entrance? Was he even aware of it? Was summertime not good enough? Or any of the other eleven months?

I sat in the dark after Ruthie left for the evening, soaking up the quiet and thinking way too damn much. I knew I needed to go home, but even though it had been mine and Becca's home for four years since I'd inherited it, today nothing felt like mine. Like I was going back to my mother's house to be judged again. The logical part of me knew that was silly, but logic wasn't playing a big part in my process.

The bookstore had been hers, too, but it was a business. The house just never felt like ours. I never felt it settle into our skin the way a home should. Growing up there, it had been structured and perfect and run with strict guidelines. Nana Mae always said her neck went stiff every time she walked into that house, and while she said it to be funny, I knew what she meant.

The bookstore was the opposite, and maybe that was my mother's way of releasing all her pent-up creativity. It was magical there. Free and flowing and musical. She always had delicious-smelling candles burning, something baking in the back kitchen to put out for customers, and happy music playing. She'd leave the counter to go read a storybook to a child if they looked interested in one. She talked to customers and within minutes knew exactly the book they would like or needed. She was Miss Mary Dee to the world of Copper Falls. The store breathed through her, and I used to love to watch her work. My friends were always envious of me for having such an amazing mom. But they didn't understand.

Miss Mary Dee was left at the store each night, and the mother I knew at home was someone else entirely. It was like she exhausted all her creativeness during the day and only had the rules of life left in her once she got home.

I pushed to my feet from the reading sofa in the corner, shelving a book someone had left out. The store still wove its spell on me every time I entered, but I didn't have her touch. I tried to keep customers happy, but I couldn't read them the way she did. There was still an oven in the back, but fresh cookies and cupcakes and other goodies were only made when Ruthie would find the time or make them at home and bring them in. And while Ruthie would light candles, I'd end up following behind her and blowing them out for fear we'd forget one and the whole place would burn to the ground.

And music? I snorted just thinking about it. Johnny Mack made sure we didn't have that. I didn't remember him banging on the wall when *she* played her soft jazz tunes back then, but he definitely didn't like it now.

I made another round through the back office area, snatched my jacket and bag from behind the mammoth old wooden checkout counter that I'd added a granite top to, and let myself out, locking the door behind me.

I had to pass the diner on the way to my car, but before I headed there, I couldn't help a sideways glance inside. It was dark behind the little white stringed lights Linny had painstakingly trimmed the window with. There was no one in there. I breathed a tiny sigh of relief, mixed with the dread I felt as I let my eyes drift toward the big gazebo that was located catty-corner from the diner. In a couple of weeks the gazebo and the whole park behind it would be blinged out in all manner of white and red, smelling of fried carnival food and all kinds of chili. But for now it was still green and serene. In general, I didn't have much reason to hang out down there anymore. The river was nice, and I'd bring Becca down there to feed the ducks when she was little, but it was tied to a moment that clamped down on my heart. I had a version of it on canvas in my living room, and that was all I needed. I only went in person once a year, and it wasn't that day yet.

Taking a deep breath, I wrapped my jacket around me and crossed the street. The dusky dark had the streetlights flickering on, and the ice cream shop down the block was still lit up brightly, serving hot chocolate and spiced tea.

I felt conspicuous as I passed the gazebo and reached the path that would lead to the river, as if everyone in town were watching me. As if no one had anything better to do than wait all year for me to go to the park.

The river wound into view among big beautiful cypress trees, and as I moved toward the bench I always inhabited, I stopped short, my steps faltering. There, sitting in the dim light, lit only by the low security lights along the water, was Noah. Sitting alone, looking down at something in his hands, he didn't see me.

He remembered.

Every centimeter of skin on my body tingled as the emotion welled up in my throat and burned behind my eyes. It was the last place where our baby had still been ours.

I closed my eyes and could smell the cold rain of that late afternoon, hear the music filtering over from the carnival rides. Noah and I sat on that bench and didn't care that the sky was leaking on us. We'd made that life in a storm, and then we were arguing about whether to keep it in the middle of another one.

"Please, Jules," he said, leaning over to lay his face on my stomach. I could feel the heat of his skin through my shirt. "Give us a chance. Don't let your parents do this."

"Look at us," I said, lifting his head and raking his rain-soaked hair from his face. "We're a mess, Noah. We live at home, we have maybe forty dollars between us, and we have to ride to school with your sister. We can't even pass algebra. What kind of parents can we be?"

"Ones that love each other," he said back, heat in his voice and his eyes. "That'll go to hell and back to be a family. I promised you I'd take care of us and I will, Jules. Fuck algebra."

"How?" I said.

"I'll make it happen."

I shook my head. "How are we going to pay for—"

"That's your mother talking," Noah said, jumping to his feet and

pacing. "That's that place they sent you to. It's not you." He dropped to his knees again in front of me. "Where are you, Jules?"

I blinked against the rain in my eyes and instinctively palmed my belly as the baby did a somersault. "I'm right here," I whispered.

He shook his head and took my hands in his. "No, you aren't. You haven't been for a while. She's got your head so filled with—"

"With things that make sense," I shot back. "You didn't see that place, Noah. The girls my age that looked thirty, just trying to get through the day."

"They're alone, you're not," he said. "You've got me."

"I want this, too, Noah," I said, my voice cracking. "I'd give anything. I live with it every day, feel it every day. This baby is depending on me right now and I'm scared to death. All I have to do is eat to make it happy, and still I'm scared to death." I placed his hands on the squirming movement of my belly. "Feel that?"

His eyes filled with liquid that had nothing to do with the rain. "Yes," he choked.

"How do we take care of that?"

He reversed our hands so that mine were back underneath. "Feel that?" he said, fat tears falling from his eyes. I couldn't breathe. "How do we walk away from that?"

I opened my eyes to realize there were hot tears rolling down my face. That was the last time our baby had been ours. Two minutes later, my water had broke, and I went into labor, setting off a comedy of errors to get to the hospital. And said good-bye to everything.

How do we walk away from that? Those words had haunted me ever since.

I swallowed hard, blinking my tears free to see his profile, and turned around. I walked as quietly as I could back up the path, thanking God I wasn't wearing heels to clack on the sidewalk.

Was he remembering that same night? Was he thinking about us? *Of course not*, I chided myself, wiping my eyes. He was back here with a gorgeous girlfriend and plans for the rest of his life. He wasn't concerned with the nostalgia of an old flame. That look on his face earlier had been totally natural. We both were a little taken aback for a second at seeing each other again for the first time, that's all. Had he stayed in town, we'd have become dulled to the other's presence after a while, as all breakups go. We never got the chance to dull. So now—twenty-six years later—we'd have to awkwardly do that.

My cell buzzed as I got to my car, and I checked to see a text from Becca.

Out 2 eat wth Lizzy & Darlene. Spnding nite with L.

I leaned against my car and steadied my breathing, still feeling the burn behind my ribs. *Why was he back? Why couldn't he just stay gone?*

I cleared my throat and shook the thoughts free. I had other issues. *It's a school night*, I texted back, in full words, rebelling against the text-speak. I remembered her troubled expression from earlier and felt a stab of concern and curiosity. And wondered what she was really up to. I remembered seventeen. Way too well.

They go 2 school 2, was her reply. *Quizg 4 the govmt test. L mom said ok.*

Quizzing, my ass. She'd forgotten she'd already copped to that. But too tired to pick that particular battle, and remembering I'd dumped her at lunch with her dad, and knowing Lizzy's mom was somewhat of a Nazi June Cleaver in workout clothes, stricter on Lizzy than I could ever be accused of, and would probably feed her a four-course breakfast in the morning and personally supervise homework, I broke my own rule and gave in.

Loves, I texted.

Loves :)

I got in, fixed my eyes, got my shaky nerves under control.

And called Patrick.

◆ ◆ ◆

Patrick was a guilty pleasure, unlike anything I'd ever done before. Never in my life had I had a one-night stand. I'd gone from Noah to a rotation of random losers to Hayden. After my divorce, I went solo for a very long time. Deciding that I was clearly not cut out for relationships, I focused on being Becca's mom. Once I did start dating, it was small-time. Only one ever got close to being serious, and when it did, I doused it. I wasn't looking for another husband, or even a significant other. So when Patrick sidled into my world with his no-strings-attached, let's-just-have-fun sexual whirlwind, I was ripe for the picking. And he was fun.

Fun.

Like taking off on a motorcycle and feeling the wind whip by at eighty miles an hour, just to stop and eat pizza and have sex in a field kind of fun. Okay, we really only did that once, but it was so outside my box that I'd never forget it. Ever.

We didn't talk about our personal lives, other than the obvious surface things, like he knew about Becca and he knew I owned a bookstore. I knew he had no kids and headed up a construction crew.

That about summed up what we needed to know to make small talk during rest periods. Because we didn't hook up for the stimulating conversation.

I crawled back in bed, propping up on an elbow so I could stare at him. The new morning light peeking through the curtain was just enough to highlight all I needed to see. One arm was thrown over his head, and his face was relaxed in sleep. He'd shaved for me because he knew I couldn't stand the scratchiness, but the darkness was working its way back onto his jaw.

Patrick exuded raw sex appeal. Anyone could say anything they wanted about his crude language and rough exterior—he was hot. And was a product of the life he chose. Construction guys don't worry about what wine goes with what entrée; they are just happy that there's wine. And they don't call it an entrée.

The sheet was tangled around him, a leftover result of the monkey sex we'd had around two. I traced a finger down his chest, in awe as usual of the muscle definition that continued into his abs. He was my age, roughly, or so I assumed. That was another thing we'd never actually defined, but although his body didn't look it, I felt like he was in his midforties.

He drew in a deep breath as the touch stirred him from sleep, and he opened his eyes slowly and blinked at me.

"Hey, beautiful," he said.

"Hey, yourself."

He wound a finger around one of my locks and pulled me to him for a kiss. I dropped a light one on his lips and he chuckled.

"You've already brushed your teeth, haven't you?"

I snickered. "Of course."

He nodded, eyes drifting back closed with a lazy smile. "Of course."

"Want some coffee?" I asked. "I just made some."

"Not just yet," he mumbled. "I'm gonna go see if I can hit this dream up again." I ran my lips lightly along his arm and then moved to his stomach, kissing the parts the sheet didn't cover. "Mmm, but if you keep doing that—"

"What will you do?"

"Probably not much till you make me go brush my teeth."

I gave his stomach a nip and laughed as I pushed off the bed. I was restless. I'd already had two cups of coffee and showered, and aside from being naked was nearly done getting ready for work. Two hours earlier than necessary. It was like my skin couldn't be still.

I eyed Patrick's flannel shirt where it lay over my chair in the corner and opted for my big floppy warm robe instead. As sexy as wearing a man's shirt felt, that struck an intimate chord with me that I wasn't interested in pursuing. I took the stairs softly, stepping around the creaky spots out of habit. Hearing the familiar ka-thump, I turned to see Harley, our pit bull, exit from Becca's room. The giant brindle-coated teddy bear slept in Becca's bed every night whether she was there or not. Although she could put on quite the guilt trip when she felt like the girl abandoned her.

"Hey, Harley-bear," I whispered, scrubbing her neck. She looked up at me with a doggie grin that warmed me like nothing else could. "Wanna go get some coffee with me?"

I ran a finger along the bottom of three framed photos on the way down. One of Becca, Mom, and me right after Dad died. Another one held Becca's school picture. And the last one was of me and my parents when I was around ten, with my weenie dog Duchess in my lap. It was there on the wall my whole life, was still there when I moved in, and was one of the few things I couldn't discard when I redecorated. Duchess was buried in the backyard, under a Texas-shaped pavestone in the flower bed.

I opened the back door for Harley, poured myself another cup of coffee, and turned the machine off so I'd quit, and then just—stood there—soaking in everything. The countertops were granite now instead of the original Formica. The blue-and-white-checked linoleum floors and shag carpet had been sacrificed for natural stone tile. While I'd changed everything I could afford to change and replaced the old furniture with our own, it was still my mother's house in many ways. I'd even arranged the furniture differently so it wouldn't feel the same, but it still came down to the same old shell with the same old ailments it'd always had. Creaky stairs. Noisy plumbing. And too many memories in the bookshelves.

That was another thing that hadn't changed much. In my mother's will, after leaving me her house, she'd requested that her books remain in the wall-to-wall bookshelves that stretched across the living room. By "remain," I took that to mean anywhere on those shelves, so I'd taken out all the knickknacks and shoved them all together on one side so that my books would fit. I thought it was fair. I mean, what a bizarre request.

Regardless, I complied, just like I always had. Feeling the jolt of memories that came attached to each and every book I touched. Each one had a story behind the story. And sometimes it was better that those stories stay right where they were rather than pull all my crap to the surface. I figured there would be time enough to deal with all that if I ever decided to remodel or sell. In four years it hadn't been a priority.

At the familiar scratch on the back door, I let Harley in and sank into the couch, curling my legs under me and pulling pillows onto my lap. She jumped up as if she were a little lap dog, the couch sinking where she planted herself, squirming half onto the pillows on her back. I chuckled as I rubbed her belly and all her taut muscles melted into mush, legs sprawled and head thrown back. Harley didn't know about her breed's reputation. Nobody told her she was supposed to be fierce. She thought she was born for belly rubs and bacon treats.

The room was dim except for the early light streaming from behind the curtains at the front window. It was quiet. Too quiet. It was odd, not having Becca there making noise and griping about what clothes she couldn't find or homework she'd forgotten to do. I was used to the chaos, and the lack of it had my ears ringing and my thoughts working way too fast.

A light knock at my door cut them off, and I set my mug on a nearby side table as I checked the wooden clock sitting on it. 7:35.

Harley contorted herself back upright and her ears went on alert.

"What, did you forget something, Bec?" I said under my breath. "Like your key?"

I got up shaking my head, the responsibility lecture already booting up in my head. Assuming it to be Becca, I opened the door unchecked,

·grateful I hadn't opted for Patrick's shirt. And felt every pore in my skin wake up. That last swallow of coffee sat in my stomach like mud.

Noah stood before me with tired eyes, hands crammed into the pockets of a black leather bomber jacket. His gaze took me in quickly, but I had the feeling he could have passed a test on what he'd filed away in those two seconds.

"Morning."

CHAPTER 4

Morning? Really? I opened my mouth to say something back, but nothing came out, so I licked my lips and fidgeted with my robe like a crazy woman.

"Too early?" he asked, as if that were a normal thing to say to me as well.

A laugh-scoff-snort thing fell out of my mouth, which I chalked up to rounding out the perfect start to the day. I coughed and cleared my throat.

"No, I'm—just getting ready for work." I stepped back so he could come in and held on to the door for dear life as I glared at Harley for just sitting there on the couch like a diva. Some guard dog. She should have had his leg chewed off by now. "Come in. There's still coffee if you want some." Oh, what the living hell was I babbling about?

Noah stepped in hesitantly, as if maybe he hadn't thought things out that far. Maybe he expected me to slam the door or not be home or God only knows what. He gave me a sideways glance as he passed me, and I caught a subtle whiff of soap and shaving cream. I stared at the door as I closed it, as if it had betrayed me, too, and then I turned on my heel and put myself in motion.

I walked straight past him to the open kitchen, trying not to really look at him. I knew he'd follow. He knew the way around my mother's house. My house.

Harley's curiosity finally got the better of her and she followed on his heels, making him turn around to check out the beast stalking him.

"Hey there, killer," he said, holding out a hand for her to smell him, and then scratching her ears. "Are you nice?"

"That's Harley," I said. "I'm afraid growing up with two women has made her a big wuss." I took a deep breath. "Coffee?" I asked again, opening a cabinet.

When he didn't answer, I turned around, and felt my heart slam against my chest. He was standing on the other side of the big island from me, where I'd seen him so many times before. Except he was a man now. With something in his eyes that resembled lost.

"What?" I asked, though not much of the word came out.

Noah shook his head and his expression cleared a little. "Just weird being back here, I guess. In this kitchen." He gestured with a small hand flick. "Seeing you here."

"I know the feeling," I said softly, turning back to grab a mug whether he wanted one or not.

"Linny told me you were living here again," he said. "Sorry to hear about your mom."

My hands shook as I poured the hot black liquid and turned to set his mug on the counter.

"Thanks," I managed to push out. "Sugar and creamer are right there," I said with a gesture.

"Black's fine," he said.

I nodded and headed into the living room for my cup. *Shit, Jules, breathe.* I planned to come back, but he followed me. *Shit.* The kitchen felt more stable. We could stand up in there. Have the island between us. The living room was cozy and said *please sit and stay a while.* Granted, I did have to go to work—in an hour and a half. *Shit.*

I licked my lips again and sat back down where I was earlier. Feet curled beneath me. Two pillows on my lap for security. I felt every centimeter of my nakedness under the robe and wished for more clothing, but it was big enough for him not to know that. I just thanked God for giving me the wisdom to get ready early and not be sitting here with wet hair or raccoon eyes. And then I mentally kicked myself for caring. He didn't. I wondered if his woman knew he was paying me a visit. Or if she even knew who I was.

Noah took his time in the room, his eyes not missing a thing. That was different. The old Noah was open and carefree. This one was wary and overtly observant, taking in the changes as well as the familiar. I saw him take note of the photos of Becca on nearly every surface. Of the abstract art on the walls, and then stop in front of one that I wished he wouldn't.

He had matured into an amazing-looking man, I noticed, not wanting to. Everything about his body was solid and powerful, like he took root wherever he stood. He looked comfortable in his own skin, like he could rock a tux as easily as the jeans and soft leather jacket and boots he currently had on. Not that I was picturing that at all.

"These are yours," he said without turning.

I took a deep breath. "Yes."

He nodded, still staring at the canvas. "I can tell. Do you sell them?" he asked, turning his head.

I chuckled. "No. Gave some away, but I've never tried to sell anything."

His eyes narrowed. "Why not? You have a gift."

The back of my neck prickled at the old topic. "Life doesn't always care what our gifts are. I have Mom's store to deal with." My store. *My* store.

He looked at me a few seconds longer, as if processing that, and then turned back to the painting. When he finally sank onto the sofa across from me, his gaze landed on me like it had in the diner the day before. Heavy and purposeful. I wouldn't give him the satisfaction of making me look away, so I lifted my chin, gripped my mug, and focused on the heat searing my palm. That was good. Pain was distracting.

The only sound was that of the nearby clock on the table, and the screaming tension between us seemed to amplify it. He seemed to be weighing out his words, so before the agony of silence stretched out any further, I decided to cut to the point.

"How've you been, Noah?" I asked, my voice wavering on his name. It sounded so odd to say it out loud. To be talking to him after so many years. Even Ruthie and I rarely brought the subject up.

"I'm good," he said. "It's nice to be home."

Home. "What drove that decision?" I asked, wondering where the words were coming from, because it certainly wasn't me. There was nothing in me capable of thinking out coherent questions at that point.

His gaze dropped to his cup. "Just been on my mind since I retired—"

"Congratulations—on that, by the way," I said.

He met my eyes again with a small smile that sent a tingle to my stomach. Damn it. I made a mental note not to bring about any more smiles. I didn't need to see him that way. Think of him that way.

Harley rounded the corner of the sofa he was sitting on and hurtled her big body up there with him, to his surprise—and mine. He laughed and rubbed her neck as she rested her head on his leg. *Traitor,* I said in my mind, trying to shoot her mental ice daggers. She turned her face so that she couldn't see me.

"Thanks," he said. "And Dad's getting old. Linny's not gonna be able to do everything by herself when he can't work in the diner anymore."

"You're gonna cook?" I asked.

He looked at me with something akin to playfulness, and I cursed myself again.

"I'm a damn good cook."

I held my palms up in my version of playing back, but I was beginning to sweat under that robe. "Hey, you want to come back here to be a short-order cook, knock yourself out."

39

He gave a small silent chuckle that didn't really reach the rest of his face and shook his head almost imperceptibly. "I—have other irons in the fire, too."

"Oh?" I asked. "What's that?"

He paused. "Private security."

"Ah." Made sense. His background was perfect for that. Secret soldiers that morph out of water are a good choice for security. But I was running out of nods and agreements and small-talk questions. It was going to come around full circle shortly, and I decided to make it now. "Why'd you come over here, Noah?"

The question barely made it out of my mouth. In fact, the last words were little more than a whisper, but he knew what I said. The intense look came back. The one that felt like lead, making the room feel lighter in comparison. Instead of answering, he picked up a framed photograph from the side table next to him. One with a smiling Becca and smaller Harley posing in the backyard.

"Your daughter?" he asked, not looking up from the photo.

I felt my chin tremble, and an unnamed old emptiness ached within me. "Yes."

"She's beautiful," he said. "Looks a lot like you at that age." His eyes made a slow trip to meet mine, and the weight of emotion in them pushed the air from the room. "Shayna's pregnant," he said. The words were slow and careful, as if he'd practiced saying them. "And I didn't want you to hear that from anyone else."

◆ ◆ ◆

My ears rang with the words, and I felt myself nodding as if he'd just told me he'd bought a new Crock-Pot. Pregnant. Noah and his new woman. Going to have a baby. That—that was perfectly fine.

"Con—" I stopped to clear my throat of the rocks that apparently settled there. "Congratulations. That's—wow, that's—really cool."

He looked at me for far too long, as if waiting for me to quit babbling and nodding and get to my meltdown. I wasn't going to have a
meltdown. I was a grown-up. And he had every right to have another
child. I had. And it would have probably ripped his heart out if he'd
been around to see me pregnant again, and married, raising a baby, so
my chest threatening to cave in was completely justified.

I focused on the way his fingers worked methodically on Harley's
neck, massaging, making her eyelids get heavier and heavier. She was
calm. I could be calm, too.

"So you're okay?" he asked, pulling my attention back to his face.

I scoffed. "Of course. How old is she?" As that fell out of my
mouth, I realized how it sounded. "I mean, in relation to you," I added
quickly. "I mean, I only saw her for a second, but she looks really young.
But—maybe that's how they make them in Italy." I laughed and was
dimly aware that I sounded insane.

Noah chuckled, his eyes staying serious and focused on me. I
knew without a doubt that I already hated that new trick of his. It was
unnerving.

"She's from Virginia," he said.

"Oh," I said. "I assumed—"

"She's a military brat," he said. "They were stationed overseas for
several years when she was young, and Italy was her favorite place. After
college, she went back."

Well, of course. Doesn't everyone?

"And she's thirty," he added. "In case you need to card her."

I smirked. "Cute."

He shrugged, a crooked grin working on one side of his mouth.
"What can I say?"

Warmth went from the center of my chest to all extremities on that
grin, and I promptly got to my feet and set my mug on the side table.

"Well, it sounds like everything's going your way, Noah. I'm happy
for you."

I wanted him to go. I needed him to go. Before I could really sink my thoughts into what he'd told me, and before my mouth overloaded my brain. Because it was about to. I could feel it all up in my throat. He gently moved Harley's head and rose as well, bringing him a little closer than I anticipated, and I backed up a step and crossed my arms as those eyes looked straight through to the core of me.

"It's really good to see you, Jules," he said softly. "You look good."

I bit my bottom lip and dug a thumbnail into my arm. Dear God, he looked good, too. Even better up close. That voice that went with the eyes—and the body, even buffed out and different, was still the same. But my thoughts wouldn't stop shoving their way to the surface.

"Why this month?" I blurted out, wishing for duct tape over my mouth. "Why now? You could have picked any other time of the year to come back home. March, April—July, even."

For a moment, the comfort left his eyes, and I saw the stricken, hurt boy I'd seen him as last. My stomach tightened at the memory. He glanced over his shoulder at the painting and then back to me, and I had the irrational urge to wrap my arms around him and comfort him.

"Yes, I could have," he said, the words barely more than a whisper. "But I didn't."

I thought of him sitting alone on the bench the night before and wondered if his perfect fiancée in red knew about it. Knew about us, knew the history she was moving into.

"I—" Movement to my left caught my attention, and I turned to see Patrick coming down the stairs in jeans and no shoes, buttoning his shirt. "Patrick!" I said, a nervous laugh escaping my throat as I realized I'd completely forgotten he was there. *Oh, holy shit.*

He stopped midstep on the stairway when he saw us, an unsure smile on his face as he looked from me to Noah and back again. Harley jumped from the couch and met him halfway, big tail swinging, clearly thinking it was a party. I was able to register that Noah looked as if he'd been slapped, right before my brain went on panic mode.

"Patrick," I said, backing up farther and mentally pulling myself back together. "This is Noah—Ryan. The—" I gestured with my hand as both men raised eyebrows at me. "The diner—?" I continued, praying for the rambling to stop. "That's Noah's dad. We grew up together. Me and Noah, not his dad."

Patrick narrowed his eyes at me and my psychotic rant and chuckled as he made it down the stairs and across the room to shake Noah's hand.

"Nice to meet you, man," he said as they did the manly grip thing. "Patrick Keaton."

Noah's face had shut down. I had no way of reading what he was thinking. "Likewise."

"Noah just retired from the Navy," I added, feeling for some inane reason that I needed to fill space. "And Patrick runs a construction contracting company."

Noah nodded and patted Patrick on the shoulder as he walked around him. "Again, good to meet you. Y'all have a good day," he said, setting his mug on the nearest table and making a beeline for the door.

I followed him, my heart slamming loudly in my ears. "Um, Noah," I said for absolutely no reason at all. Other than that things felt unfinished and I had the crazy guilty feeling of being caught cheating on someone. Which was truly nuts, considering I owed neither of them anything.

"Jules—" he said, turning to meet my eyes for a second. In that second, I saw the last traces of the kids we were and the intensity that had defined us. Then his expression cleared and he was the stoic adult again. "Thanks for the coffee."

I watched him walk down the steps, take a pause at the bottom to glance back at the porch, and then disappear behind bushes that were in severe need of grooming.

"Old boyfriend?" Patrick asked, standing right behind me so close I jumped.

43

"It's—" I blew out a breath and shut the door. "I told you, we grew up together."

A laugh rumbled in his chest, and I turned to face him and his beautiful eyes. The eyes that had originally seduced me at a pizza place, of all places, before they'd pulled me to a pitcher of beer, two ice cream cones, and sex on my living room floor. Everything about him was reckless and dangerous and not my game.

"You know what that tells me, beautiful?" he said while planting a kiss on my nose. "It says he was the first to spread those pretty—"

"Please don't finish that sentence," I said, putting two fingers against his lips.

He took my fingers into his mouth and nibbled them until I laughed and pulled them away. "So I'm right."

"Don't you have a site to go check on or something?" I said as he pulled me into his arms.

"Told you, there's a delay," he said. "I do have some research to do, though, if I can bum off your wireless."

I raised an eyebrow. "You brought your laptop with you?"

He dropped some kisses on my lips and let go gently. "When you never get to go home, babe, everything lives in the car with you."

As Patrick walked outside, I turned and walked the few steps to the nearest couch and gripped the back of it for grounding. My gaze fell on the painting across the room. The one Noah had zeroed in on like a bloodhound. A black-and-gray depiction of the park, the river, the bench. Our bench. A painting I'd done for my son, to mark his first Christmas, even though he'd never see it. One that even my mother had never known the inspiration for—but my only claim to a day I could never get back. I'd sat on that bench every day for weeks after Noah left, replaying the day, sketching and resketching the rough concept. Withdrawing into myself a little more. Praying he'd come back. But he didn't. And after I'd finished the painting, I stopped going.

◆ ◆ ◆

As I watched Patrick go through his quick morning routine, I realized I'd never thought much about his life before. I was trying desperately to now. I needed something to pull my thoughts away from Noah's revelation, and Patrick was outstanding in that capacity. He was all about distraction.

And what an odd life that would be, running a contracting company. In order to stay in demand, his men had to be available to go anywhere, and so did he. He was always mobile, always on the move to the next job.

That worked for me.

Patrick was so outside my normal realm of anything, so free-spirited and daring, that having him around there in Copper Falls all the time—actually *dating*—would have been horrific. We would have never made it past the pizza. Well, yeah. We would have. That night was a weak moment on my part, but there definitely wouldn't have been a second pizza.

I kept taking deep breaths as I got dressed, trying to find normal. It wasn't anywhere near me.

"Come on, fool, get it together," I said under my breath.

I pulled on a pair of worn jeans and my favorite soft fuzzy blue sweater. Not that it mattered that it matched my eyes perfectly or anything. Because it didn't matter. I couldn't care less whether Noah Ryan showed up in the vicinity of the diner or anything.

It was about comfort. I never wore jeans to work. I was adamant about professionalism. Not skirts like my mother always insisted on, but it was at least slacks.

Not today.

Today, moving up from my robe was a Herculean task.

Noah was back. He was engaged to be married. He'd come to my house. And his wife-to-be was having his baby. All this was within the same twenty-four hours. My carefully structured world was wiggling. To hell with wiggling—it was swinging around like a damn lasso.

I grabbed my keys from the bowl at the bottom of the stairs and then paused, remembering Patrick was still there. I leaned over to catch a glimpse of him sitting at the kitchen island with his laptop, eyebrows knitted together as he read.

"I have to go . . . you okay here?" I said. The shock of my own words tingled over me. Did I just give someone free reign of my house? What if Becca played hooky again and came home to find him there? "Um, I mean—"

Patrick looked up as I walked up behind him, a smirk tugging at one corner of his mouth.

"I'm done, beautiful. Don't worry."

"I wasn't," I said, attempting to cover with a savvy smile.

He closed up his computer and rose, brushing my lips with a soft kiss. "I know." He winked at me. "Come on, let's go kick this day in the ass."

Nothing sounded better than that.

◆ ◆ ◆

Knowing Ruthie would be at the store before me, lighting her ever-loving candles to get the place smelling good, I texted her that I would be late. I had a stop to make, two blocks from my house.

I pushed the doorbell button twice before remembering it was broken, and then knocked on the dark, blood-red door as hard as my knuckles allowed. Two stamped envelopes were clipped with a clothespin to the old metal mailbox that hung by the door, with Nana Mae's careful print written across them.

I heard Maddy, Nana Mae's five-hundred-pound cat, purring at the door before her owner got there. She was the one to look at me with disdain when the door opened. Nana Mae looked at me with a surprised smile.

"Well, hell, Julianna, what brings you over here?" Nana Mae said, her wrinkles morphing into different patterns with her wide-spread smile. "I was going to stop by tonight on my walk. What's the matter—the coffeepot broke?"

"Ha ha."

"Laugh all you want, girly, you never come by this early," she said, waving me in and nudging Maddy over with one slippered foot. She still had on her morning attire of a magenta-and-white floor-length velour robe, zipped up to the neck. Her long white hair wasn't twisted up in its usual bone clips yet, but hung loose down her back. She looked older like that, more vulnerable than the cocky put-together woman she showed the world. "Don't you have to open the store?"

I shrugged. "Ruthie's there. I texted her."

Nana Mae stopped midturn and narrowed her eyes at me. "What's wrong? Are you sick?" She let her eyes peruse me from head to toe. "You have jeans on, Julianna."

I blew out a breath and let a chuckle out with it as I shook my head. "I'm fine."

"You never go in late," she said, not moving. "Is it Becca? Something happen with Becca?"

I laughed and linked arms with her, guiding us to the living room sofa. Maddy beat us there, sprawling across a good third of it and daring me to move her. I let Nana Mae do that. I knew Maddy wouldn't bite her. When Nana Mae got settled, I curled up on one end with a pillow to hug like I was fifteen.

"Noah Ryan is home," I said. "Came in yesterday."

"Ah, hell," she said, sagging a bit. "Well, that explains a little."

"With a woman he's engaged to," I added. "And they're pregnant." The hand that was stroking Maddy paused mid-hover.

"Holy shit," she breathed. "Well, I'll bet the old man is beside himself."

"He was pretty happy."

"You were there?" she said, resuming her Maddy love.

I nodded. "Becca and I had lunch—sort of—at the diner when Noah and his new Barbie doll walked in. Johnny Mack was yelling it to the crowd."

That got me a look, but she didn't pursue it. I knew it was being catty, but I felt I deserved a few moments of it.

"So Becca—" Nana Mae began, looking down at Maddy with a frown creasing her forehead. "Sweetie, if he's back—the way this town talks, it's all going to stir back up again. I know you never told her, but you need to now."

My mouth went dry. Another fuel to my impending nervous break-down. "Yeah."

"Better to hear it from you than from someone else," she said, eyeing me sharply.

Noah's words. Again. Everything haunting me kept coming back to Noah's words.

"I wish Mom were here to take on some of it," I said, picking at a broken thread on the seam of my jeans. "She'd make it sound right. Logical."

"It was logical to her back then," Nana Mae said softly. "You know she did what she thought was right for you."

"I know," I said.

"But parents make mistakes, too."

CHAPTER 5

Tell Becca.

Hey, baby doll, you aren't really an only child, we have a secret kid stashed somewhere. What's he like? Don't know. Never met him.

That's every family's normal conversation, right?

I wanted to step in front of the nearest bus. If there were buses in Copper Falls. As odds go, I'd have better luck with a scooter on a hell-bender. In lieu of that kind of luck, I headed to work with uncharacteristic procrastination.

I could call in sick. I never did that, either, so Ruthie would think I was dying, but it wouldn't be such a bad thing to take a day off.

Yes, it would. I'd sit on my couch all day and picture Noah, and think and dwell and obsess myself into a state of doom. I needed to go; I was pretty sure we had a large order coming in, and it wasn't fair to put all of that on Ruthie. I could step outside my boundaries and park on the other side of the store instead of close to the diner like I always had. That way, I'd avoid potential encounters.

A plan in place, I turned down Main Street, approached the bookstore, and kept right on driving.

"You are such a baby," I muttered, making the block.

But spying the bank and knowing I needed to cash an insurance check and snag a little cash for Becca's lunches—assuming she actually stayed at school to eat—I pulled in and justified it as productive. I blew out a breath as I tugged my purse onto my shoulder and entered the lobby. I had to shake off this crap. This was crazy. Yes, I had a bucket of shit swirling around, but so did everyone else. I wasn't special. And this was my town. I was not going to go skulking around it like a scared bird just because my particular bucket might get stirred up.

I had to learn to live with Noah back in town, like it or not. And I had to tell my daughter things about myself that went against everything I'd ever preached to her.

And I could never eat at the diner again. Or wear red.

I rounded the corner toward the tellers and was stopped short by a huge donation display of a giant red kettle, the sign reading, "Help our local families. Give at the teller window."

"Show-offs," I said under my breath.

I started digging for my wallet as I stepped around the obnoxious kettle and right into a pair of arms and hands that I didn't see and wasn't ready for.

"Oh!" I exclaimed, my head shooting up. "I'm so sorr—"

My word was cut off as I looked up into Noah's face. Again. About four inches from mine. Damn it.

"—ry," I pushed out, as all the air left me.

Time stopped in those few seconds, and all the little nuances of his face that were new registered like files being tucked away. A tiny white scar above his upper lip. Another thin sliver of one through his left eyebrow. The little laugh lines next to his eyes. All new to me, and yet achingly familiar. The subtle scent I'd picked up from him earlier filled my senses as his eyes panned my face in the same three seconds. I wondered what he saw.

His face went neutral again as he dropped his hands from their hold on me and backed up a few inches. I could still feel the heat imprints on my upper arms.

"Sorry," he echoed.

I should have just gone to work. This was what I got for being a big lame wuss.

I shook my head and gripped my purse strap. "No—um—I'm just—" I pointed at the teller windows so I could shut up. "Going over there." I noticed he wasn't, and was kind of hovering around the desks. "What are you doing?"

"Opening an account," he said, nodding toward an empty desk. "Waiting to, anyway."

I nodded. Of course he was. That's what you do when you move to a new place and plan to stay. Forever. Noah and Shayna and the newest little Ryan.

"A joint one?" I blurted out, feeling suddenly like I was standing off to the side watching myself talk.

He smiled. "Not just yet."

Not just yet. "So don't you have to have an address or something?"

His eyebrows drew together slightly on that. "My dad's is fine for now. I just need to get a debit card." He looked around the room, probably silently begging the bank lady to come back to her desk and rescue him. "We'll start looking for our own place soon."

"Oh, good," I said, shaking my head at myself. *Oh, good?* Who was using my mouth?

Noah met my gaze again with that infuriating locked-in non-blinking thing of his, and as much as I wanted to look away, walk away, do anything that carried me away—I couldn't move.

"Listen, I'm sorry about just dropping by earlier," he said, backing up yet another step. "I don't know what I was thinking."

I shook my head. "It was fine—"

"No, seriously," he said, the hint of a smile at his lips. "I didn't take into account that you might have—someone there."

He ran a hand along the back of his neck on the last words, as though they made him itchy, and I closed my eyes, wishing to die.

"I didn't—I mean, I don't—" I stumbled, opening my eyes again. Of all nights to call Patrick. "That wasn't like that." I held my chin up, refusing to show weakness.

Noah's eyebrow shot up, carrying the tiny scar with it. "Okay," he said on a chuckle. He stepped forward again, and I reflexively crossed my arms. Holding my crazy in. "Jules, relax. You've had a life. So have I. We both have someone in our lives, that's normal."

"He's not a—Patrick isn't a *someone*." I blew out a breath, cursing myself for not just going to work. And for talking. Because making myself out to be a rent-a-whore was infinitely better than letting him think Patrick was my boyfriend. I smiled and looked at the floor, drawing in a huge breath before looking back up at him. "You know what, Noah? This is just going to take some getting used to—for both of us."

Noah let out his own breath, a relieved expression passing over his features. I'd saddled up the white elephant in the room.

"You're right," he said softly.

I nodded. "So—let's just make the best of it and go about our normal days."

He did a head tilt that signified a shrug. "Whatever normal is."

I smiled and ignored the shimmy in my stomach when he smiled back and dropped his eyes to my mouth.

"So, I'm gonna head over there," I said, pointing to the teller counter. "See you later."

"Later," he responded.

I told my feet to walk around him, and they brought me to my destination, where I was eternally grateful that no other customers were around. Because it took me a good minute or two to remember what I was doing and how to do it.

By the time I was done and turned around, he was seated in front of a petite blonde woman, one ankle resting on the other knee and his arm resting across the chair next to him. My knees nearly betrayed me at the beauty of him, so relaxed and confident, yet exuding raw masculinity as he chatted with this woman and smiled as she kept fingering her hair. Well, hell, of course she did. My God, he was positively edible.

I strode out with the intention of looking nonchalant and hoping not to trip over my own feet. When I looked his way and found him watching me leave, however, my throat closed up. I gave a polite smile, which he returned before turning his attention back to the blonde lady having sex with her hair.

I counted my steps back to the car. Thirty-seven. Thirty-seven steps to make it to a place where I could close and lock the door and have a nervous breakdown.

"Shit," I said, my voice quivering on the word as I hit the lock. "Crazy," I muttered, starting the car so the heat would blast through the vents. It wasn't all that cold, but I needed the heat and the noise to calm my blood down. One day at a time, I told myself.

My cell buzzed.

Where are you? From Ruthie.

Currently on a fast track to the loony bin, thanks, and you?

On my way, I texted back. Where I would stay from now on. Either the store or my house. Safely tucked where I could see people coming.

◆ ◆ ◆

"We need a night out."

I was shelving newly arrived books and arranging the new releases up front on the display table, listening to Ruthie sing along with the eighties music she'd set up at a ridiculously low volume with an iPod station in the middle of the store. Away from the wall to avoid Johnny Mack's cane. So far, so good. But the day was young.

The day might be, but I felt ancient. Like I'd lived three days before ten o'clock.

"Did you hear me?" Ruthie said, moving some books around in my wake.

"I heard you," I said, stacking more titles on the table. "We have that stupid party, don't we? The Chamber thing?"

"It's a meeting."

"It's after hours and requires a change of clothing," I said. "That's a party."

She made a huffing sound. "Whatever, that's not till next week," she said. "I'm talking like tonight."

I sighed. "I'm just not up for that right now. I don't need—"

"Are you crazy?" she said, picking up the books I laid out and rearranging them with plastic boxes and easels. "It's exactly what you need. Get out and live a little."

"I have Patrick for that," I responded, digging back into the box and smiling at an older gentleman carrying around an old used copy of a Jackie Collins novel. You just never knew.

"*Out* being the pertinent word," Ruthie said. "Someplace not in your house." She put down her props for a moment and pulled a hair clip from the mammoth pocket of her big black sweater. She twisted her hair up in two seconds and still managed to look adorable. "Come on, Jules, step out there with me. Eat, drink, talk to people who aren't me or Becca. Or your boy toy."

"And Frank's fine with you stepping out and eating and drinking and talking?" I asked, eyeing her.

She scoffed. "Frank loves it when I go meet my clubs and committees. He gets to eat crap out of a box and chili out of a can." She laughed and waved a hand. "He'll be fine. It's not like we're swinging on a pole, Jules, I'm just thinking of something like the Grille over in Katyville. Good food, good music—"

"Oh, I love their baked squash and peppered pork chops," said a woman standing nearby who I recognized as a regular from the courthouse. "And all their desserts are to die for."

"Mmm, the blackberry cobbler," Ruthie said, nearly salivating.

The woman sighed. "Now I have to talk my husband into taking me tonight." She laughed and touched Ruthie's arm.

"Well, maybe we'll see you, Tess," Ruthie said, shooting me a look.

"Tomorrow, okay?" I said, bringing her social endeavor to a halt. "I just want to get through the rest of this day and go home and watch TV in my sweats tonight. Maybe I'll even find something Becca and I can watch together for once."

"Nothing on Lifetime," she said.

I frowned. "Why? I love Lifetime."

"She hates it. Get on SyFy."

I groaned. "I swear we aren't related."

Ruthie and the woman who was evidently Tess laughed and headed to the register with a couple of books. I watched them, a little envious of the easy way Ruthie dealt with people. She had that way of connecting, of being so likeable that people just wanted to be around her. I mean, I knew I recognized that woman, but I couldn't have pulled her name out of the air if my hair was on fire and she owned all the water.

Ruthie was good at that. And she had something else, too. Watching her work the store, the customers, knowing what was right and how and when—it was a little like watching my mom back in the day. Ruthie had learned from the master. Why hadn't I?

A few minutes later, the store empty, Ruthie looked at her watch. "Lunchtime." She looked at me questioningly. "You want something from next door?"

I gave her a pointed look. "No."

She tilted her head. "I'll go pick it up."

I opened my mouth to say no again and my stomach grumbled loudly. "Maybe McMasters still has some tacos left?"

McMasters Meats was a butcher shop up on the next block that also served breakfast. I didn't hit it that often, but Becca did on her way to school. The bacon was droolworthy, along with the brothers who owned it, and right then that sounded wonderful. The breakfast tacos with bacon, not the brothers.

She gave me a lip curl. "From breakfast? Doubtful."

Crap. "Okay." Ruthie grinned and grabbed her purse from behind the counter, and I studied her. "You look too pleased. What are you doing?"

Ruthie frowned and did a little smirk, but didn't meet my eyes but for a second. "I'm picking up lunch."

"Don't say a word, Ruthie."

She looked at me like I was a loon. "What are you talking about?"

"If Noah is there, not a word."

She blew out a breath and did a little eye flutter like I didn't know what I was talking about, but I knew her. Given the chance, she'd bow up with her little five-foot-five self and tell Noah Ryan just where to go and how to get there.

Ruthie wasn't swayed by his smile or his eyes or the way he looked with his arms crossed over his chest. She was oblivious to all of it. Because once upon a time, she'd believed in him. And he'd let her down.

"I swear I'm screwed, no matter what I do," I said.

"Don't worry, Jules. Noah loves you," Ruthie said. We were taking a break out back of the store, holding a bucket of chocolate chip ice cream with two spoons. "He'll ride this out with you no matter which way it goes."

I rubbed my basketball belly and took another bite of the cold creaminess, feeling a little foot push against the side.

"Maybe," I said. "So why do I get the feeling that if I keep it, I lose my parents, and if I don't, I lose Noah?"

Ruthie waved a spoon at me, pushing glasses up her nose. "You're not losing anybody, silly. Everybody's on your side, even if it's different ones."

So much for that. And Ruthie never forgot it. Not with my mother, when I spiraled into a destructive mode afterward and she refused to acknowledge it, and certainly not with Noah, when he shocked the hell out of Ruthie by leaving me alone to deal with it.

She'd waited many years to give him a piece of her mind, and I could see the wheels turning.

"What's your order?" she asked, clear-eyed and ignoring me.

"I'm serious, Ruth Ann."

Her gaze turned deadly—if she could pull off deadly. "You call me that again and you'll get a scene over there worthy of the evening news."

I held my hands up. "Okay, okay, just—please don't stir shit up. I've already talked to him twice today, and I'm sure he's as tired of the subject as I am."

"Who cares how tired he is," she muttered. "Look at you." I looked down at myself in question and then back up at her. "One day back and he's got you coming in late to work, avoiding public places, wearing blue jeans to work—which I happen to like," she added, doing a little flair with her hands. "But that's beside the point. It's not *you*. You're cowering in your own town," she said. "*Your* town."

I blinked. "You're right."

"Damn straight I am," she said. "Once upon a time you thought you'd die without him. Then you thought you'd crumble into dust if you ever saw him again." She leaned forward at me, intending to be forceful. "Well, he's back. And you're still standing."

True. Although that crumbling part wasn't that far out of reach.

"So, your usual order?"

I looked at her and shook my head. "Get me a cheeseburger."

Her eyes widened in surprise and she chuckled. "Whoa."

"And fries," I added. It may not have been ballsy to anyone else, and it wasn't as good as going over there, but it was a step outside my carefully constructed, lined, and sealed box.

I was still standing.

◆ ◆ ◆

The cheeseburger only made me want more crap, so I figured that nachos would be a good follow-up for dinner that night. And the look on Becca's face when she came in was nearly worth the empty calories we were about to consume. She looked almost as excited as Harley, who was sitting at my feet, looking up at me like I was God.

"Are you dying?" she asked. "Am I?"

"Ha ha," I said, chopping up the lettuce. "Check those beans in the microwave. See if they're ready."

She dropped her backpack where she stood and headed that way. "Is there a reason for the madness?"

"Is there a reason for your backpack on the floor?"

She waved a hand as she grabbed a spoon to stir the beans. "I'll get it in a second."

"And if you'd just put it on a chair to begin with, you wouldn't have to get it, and we wouldn't—"

"Be having this conversation?" she finished for me with a sarcastic expression. "Oh, yes, we would. You'd find a way."

I sighed, already tired. "Becca."

"Hi, Mom," she said, turning. "Can we just do that? Do we have to fight?" Her gaze landed on my jeans. "Did you go to work today?"

I closed my eyes and sucked my readied comment back in. "Yes, I did. Hi, Bec. How was your day?"

"I passed my government test."

I stared at her. "There was really a test? Wonderful!" I said, grabbing the shredded cheese. "Sounds like a good day."

"Yeah, well, until Jill Bartlett decided to be a douche," she said, her shoulders slouching a little.

I glanced up. "And why is that?"

Becca shrugged and did the scrunch-up thing with her face that said the subject was about to be done. "Nothing. It was stupid."

"So tell me."

"I did tell you," she said, widening her eyes without meeting mine. She grabbed a plate from the cabinet and started building her nachos. "It was nothing."

"Nothing enough to mess up your day?" I asked, attempting another angle.

"Whatever, Mom, can we just eat?" she said, clearly done. And irritated.

"Yeah, *whatever*." I blew out a breath. "You bring it up and then get mad at me for it." I pulled the sour cream container from the fridge. "I swear, baby, you make me want to bang my head on the wall sometimes."

"Ditto," she muttered.

Well, so much for the relaxing girls' night at home. I tried again in the living room.

"Grab the TV trays and we'll see what's on."

She stared at me as if I'd grown horns. "We're eating junk food—and eating it in the living room?"

"Good Lord," I muttered, grabbing the trays myself. "You'd think it was the first time ever."

"First time in Nonnie's house," Becca said, setting her plate on a tray and settling herself on the couch next to me as Harley jumped up on the other side of her and stared. "We did it sometimes at the blue house, but never here."

I looked at her. "That's crazy, Bec, that was four years ago."

She held up her hands. "Just saying." She scratched Harley's chin. "I'll save you some," she whispered as Harley's tail thumped.

I frowned, thinking about it, wondering if she were right. We did have a more casual lifestyle in the old house she called the blue house. Hayden and I had leased it early in our marriage when it was painted a hunter green. He never liked it and painted it a sickly beige a few years later. When we divorced, I got the house, and one of my first actions as a single woman was to paint it whatever color Becca wanted. Thank God, her favorite color was blue.

When my mother died and left us this house, I thought it made sense to move here and sell our smaller one. I'd second-guessed that decision a hundred times or more since then. Especially when I'd hear Becca refer to it as belonging to my mother, or Nonnie, as she called her. Very seldom did she refer to it as our house.

"Well, this doesn't hurt anything," I said, turning on the TV and attempting to make light of it. "Give the table a break for the night."

I flipped through the on-screen guide as we ate, hoping I wouldn't have to resort to SyFy but willing to just to keep her there. Finally, I landed on a romantic comedy she'd liked when she was younger. "Yes?" I asked.

Her shrug was the best I was going to get, but the genuine laughs that came later were proof I'd chosen well. Becca's two major appendages, her phone and her journal, rested by her side, and every now and then she'd scribble something down or smile at a text. I couldn't help feeling a pang of envy toward whoever was pulling that reaction from her.

I remembered her being attached to my hip when she was little, always wanting to lay in my lap to watch TV, begging me to play with her hair. I missed those days.

I leaned sideways to bump heads with her. "Loves, baby girl," I said during a commercial break.

"Loves," she said, pulling the afghan from the top of the couch behind her and half curling into it as she leaned against me.

"You know, I'm going to miss this kind of thing when you go off to college."

"Eating on the couch?" she said, throwing her arms over her head in a contorted stretch I'd probably need help to get out of. "I'm pretty sure you can still do that if you want."

I smirked. "Cute. You know what I mean. It's been just you and me for a long time, Bec. I'm gonna miss you."

She shrugged and finger-combed her crooked hair back. "Well, who knows," she said, hugging a pillow with a lazy smile. "Maybe I won't go anywhere."

Tiny bells rang in the back of my brain. Ones that had been poised and ready to ring for months now over the lack of college application enthusiasm.

I licked my lips. "Meaning?"

"Meaning—maybe I won't go anywhere," she repeated, finding that broken record again.

"So, have you heard back from any of them?" I asked, fully aware of the answer since I got the mail every day.

"No, but it's early," she said. "Besides, there's always community college if nothing else."

I felt my eyebrows raise. "For an associate's degree, Becca. For summer courses. You can't get a master's or even a bachelor's degree there. For the level of teaching that you want—"

"Here we go," she said, pulling the afghan off and sitting up.

"Here we go?" I echoed. "It's a simple conversation, Bec, and a legitimate one. You graduate in less than six months."

"Totally aware of that," she said, nodding. "Believe it or not, they actually mention that once or twice at school."

"Don't get smart with me," I said, feeling the tide go out. "All I'm doing is asking what the status is on your college plans. A lot of kids already have it planned out by now."

"And—I don't," she said.

"I thought it was teaching."

"I don't know anymore," she said.

I frowned. "But it's always been teaching."

She rubbed at her face. "Oh, my God, Mom, have you ever been undecided on anything *ever* in your life? Has everything always just fallen in place for you?"

I blinked at her, stunned, before a laugh worked up from my chest. "Are you serious?"

"Whatever."

Becca stood and carried her TV tray back to its designated place as the show came back on, and headed toward the stairs.

"The show, baby, it's back—"

"I'm done," she said, waving a hand halfheartedly. "I'm—gonna go read or something. Supper was good."

I watched her trudge up the stairs in her socks, shoes probably discarded in the kitchen. I kicked myself for ruining the night with logic. I was already missing the good vibes and warmth of hanging out with her.

"I love you, Bec."

"Love you too, Mom," she said quietly before the house swallowed her up.

The photograph of her and Harley looked at me from the side table, and my eyes went to the park painting from there. *Has everything always just fallen in place for you?*

Wow.

I got up and walked upstairs, passing Becca's room and mine, going to a door that was seldom acknowledged anymore. I opened it, instantly breathing in the old familiar smells, as charcoal and paper and mostly dried-up oils wafted up into my senses. My art closet, easels hanging obediently on their hooks, drawers of supplies sitting unused, and huge portfolio envelopes of charcoal drawings leaned together in stacks.

I licked my lips as my fingers twitched, itchy to pull things out and explore. But to what end? Something else to fill up time I didn't have? I closed the door. I had a business to run now.

CHAPTER 6

A whole day with no drama.

No Becca tantrums—she got up and fixed herself some Pop-Tarts and headed off to school. No Johnny Mack canings. And no Noah sightings. It felt almost normal. And had me feeling just skippy enough to hit Ruthie up on her night-out offer. *Why not*, I thought. It had been forever since I'd been out to eat with anyone except Becca—well, unless you counted the pizza and beer with Patrick. I didn't count that, since it was really all just foreplay.

I even left work an hour and a half early so I could run some errands before I went home. And smiled at Georgette Pruitt when she flashed her new delivery of white carnations for her carnival parade float.

I got in my car without a second look at the diner, this made easier by the fact that I started parking on the other side of my building. Deciding to top off my gas tank, I slow-rolled into the station, turned down the song I'd just cranked up, and got out.

And enjoyed my peaceful feeling for about fifteen seconds into my fill-up.

The midnight-blue Ford truck that pulled up behind me at the next pump had a chrome grille so shiny I could have fixed my makeup in it.

I actually chuckled at that thought until the driver's door opened and Noah Ryan stepped out.

It was everything I could do not to groan out loud. I was so damn close.

He closed his door and glanced back inside to Shayna sitting in the passenger seat. "Hey, Jules."

I smiled politely, remembering the sort-of precedent we'd set at the bank the day before. "Hey."

Shayna opened her door then and stepped out, still looking adorable even without her chic red dress. She looked girl-next-door sweet in faded jeans and a hoodie pullover. I turned my focus back on the pump handle in my hand and thought of happy thoughts. I thought of Ruthie's cupcakes. Of Harley and her sweet face. And how—

"Babe, I'm gonna grab a drink, want something?" Shayna asked.

"Yeah, a Coke, thanks," Noah said offhandedly as he pulled a card from his wallet and fed the pump its magical numbers.

His words triggered a memory. Coca-Cola used to be the only soft drink he'd touch. *Coke's the real deal, Miss Ju-li-an-na*, his young smart-aleck voice reverberated in my head as I flashed on a second-grade elementary school moment. I'd bought a Dr Pepper from the "Coke machine," as they are all called in the South. And a young, cocky Noah, sweaty and dirty from playing touch football at recess, stood there with his seven-year-old swagger and dissed my choice.

"So," I said. "I like Dr Pepper."

"That's because you're a stupid girl," he said. "With a stupid name."

"Well, who asked you?" I said, scrunching up my nose. "You stink."

"Why's your name so long, Ju-li-an-na?" he said, his voice mocking.

I made a face and walked around him. "Why do you have dog poop on your jeans?"

He whirled around like a dog chasing his tail. "I do not."

I laughed, sitting cross-legged on the grass. "Made you look."

The glare I got was short-lived. He dropped to the ground in a lunge, as if he were practicing reaching first base. "You need a nickname."

I shrugged. "I have one. My dad calls me Jules."

Noah nodded and sat up, as if he had to give that some deep thought. "That's better. At least for someone who drinks Dr Pepper."

Wow, I thought with a start, there was something I hadn't pulled up in decades. I studied his profile as he leaned against his truck. Worn jeans that fit him like heaven. A blue sweatshirt with the sleeves shoved up on his forearms.

"Here you go, honey," Shayna said, walking between our vehicles to hand him the icy can. She glanced my way and did a double take, smiling curiously.

I saw Noah take the cue and his manners kick into gear. "Shit," I whispered, staring down at the pump handle. *Don't do it, Noah. Don't do it, Noah.*

"Jules," he began, and I raised my head with a smile as if I knew nothing. "I don't think I've gotten to introduce you to—Shayna."

I met his eyes and caught the pause, no matter how slight. He was going to say *my fiancée,* but his tongue flipped it just in time. In any case, I was glad. I wasn't sure I could have masked my reaction that well.

Shayna turned to me with an outstretched hand and a soft smile. "Hi. Shayna Baird."

Her long dark hair was shiny and perfect, even pulled back into a carefree ponytail with shorter pieces falling around her face. She didn't look thirty. Fresh-faced and dressed like she was, she looked like she could model for an outdoor magazine or a college catalog. When I pulled my hair up like that, I looked like I was scrubbing my toilet.

"Julianna White," I said, noting her firm handshake in lieu of the limp girly one I expected. Noah had said she was a military brat, so she'd probably been taught right.

"Nice to meet you, Julianna," she said, her eyes showing the slightest hint of wariness. She knew who I was. It was there.

"You too. Oh, and—call me Jules," I said, darting a look to Noah. "My full name usually means I'm in trouble—or my grandmother is hunting me down."

Shayna laughed. I laughed. Noah just looked as if he were stuck in a bad dream. My pump mercifully clicked off and I had something else to do besides stand there. She started making her way back around the truck, and the words came out of my mouth before I even knew they were there.

"Congratulations, by the way," I said, feeling all the awkward atoms of the universe descend upon our little fifteen-foot area. "On the baby—and the engagement." Noah's eyes fixed on me with a clear *What the hell are you doing?* look, and if I'd had one for *I have no fucking clue*, I would have used it.

Shayna's steps faltered, and I watched as she looked at him with questions before turning slowly back to face me. "Um—thank you," she said with a more pallid complexion than was just there seconds before. She covered with a smile as she looked at Noah again. "I didn't know it was public knowledge yet. I thought just family—"

Oh, son of a bitch, I wasn't supposed to know. I wanted to jump in my gas tank. Noah wanted to run over me with that truck—I could see it in his twitching jaw muscles.

"I told Jules yesterday," he said, meeting her eyes with that dead-on look I was learning to recognize. I didn't apologize, knowing instinctively that would sound coy and even more like Noah and I were in cahoots.

After a few beats of silent stare-down between them, Shayna looked away, fidgeted with her hoodie, and brought her gaze back to me.

"Thank you," she said with a smile carved from practice. Possibly from years of growing up as an officer's daughter and knowing when to be politically correct. "We appreciate it."

Oh, *we*. That was good. Very smart of her, staking her claim and making them a unit. I nodded and smiled at both of them as I closed my gas tank and "see you later'd" them. I got in my car and released a long breath with my eyes closed.

"Why, you idiot?" I breathed. "Why can't you just say hello like everyone else? Holy shit."

I started the car and pulled out, not wanting to look back, but I did. I couldn't help myself. And there they were, still standing in front of the truck, facing each other in what looked like an intense conversation. I'll bet it was.

◆ ◆ ◆

Becca was out the door within thirty minutes of walking in it, including a full wardrobe change, makeup refresher, and half a care what I thought about it.

"What do you think?" she'd asked when she came downstairs, spinning so that the mock chain-link belt she wore loosely around her hips spun at the ends.

"I think I got whiplash," Nana Mae said. "If I got ready that fast, I'd need to skip the going out and take a nap."

Nana Mae had walked over to surprise me with my all-time favorite dessert. The one thing I could not say no to. Mississippi Mud. So of course showering and getting ready for the evening had been temporarily delayed. Mud requires sitting and savoring, and Nana Mae and I were doing just that.

I laughed. "You look beautiful. Just try not to spin like that too much or you might take someone down."

She gave me a mischievous grin with narrowed sexy eyes. "Maybe that's my evil plan."

"Well, then stay under the radar."

She laughed, and I had the urge to snapshot the moment. For one precious second, we were clicking.

Nana Mae gestured to the big red plate with the yum on it. "Get you some Mud, Becca."

Becca eyed the plate as she plopped down next to me, and then snatched the remnants of my piece instead.

"Hey!" I said. "Get your own!"

"Just wanted a bite," she said around the mouthful. "Oh, dear God. Talk about evil plans."

"No kidding," I said, plucking another smallish piece of the gooey chocolaty marshmallowy nutty goodness from the plate. "There's nothing even remotely right about this."

"Yeah, well, I say live a little," Nana Mae said, holding her piece on a napkin away from Harley, who was eye level with it all and nearly trembling with hope.

"Are you driving?" I asked.

"Nah, Lizzy is," she said, reaching over me to attack Harley's head with love scratches. To her credit, Harley tried to enjoy it, but the smell of melted chocolate trumped love. "It's four or five of us going to the mall and a movie and whatever."

Ah, that *whatever* is what made my heart pitter-patter. On the upside, Lizzy was a better driver than Becca was and a straight-A student. I always wished she'd sprinkle some of her glitter on Becca.

"Home by midnight," I said as she rose, which got me more of the face I was used to.

"Oh, come on, Mom," she said, one hand on her hip. "I'm almost an adult."

"*Almost* being the key word."

"Everyone else gets to stay out till one," she said, a frown scrunching the top of her nose.

"Well, if Lizzy is driving all those *everyones* home at one, then how does *she* get home on time? Think of how considerate you're being," I said, reaching over to pick up that morning's newspaper from the end table.

Nana Mae snorted, and Becca just looked at me like I'd gone off the deep end. "Thanks."

"Bec, it's four o'clock," I said on a chuckle. "You've got eight hours. What on earth are you complaining about?"

She shrugged as she appeared to contemplate that, and then snatched up her bag at the sound of a car horn outside. "Bye, y'all," she said, giving us both quick head hugs.

"Check in, Becca," I reminded. "Is your phone charged?"

"Yes," she called over her shoulder as Harley bounded after her, thinking it was time to go play. "I know, I know, text you so you know I'm not dead—got it. Bye, Mom. Bye, Nana Mae."

And she was gone.

"It was better in my day," Nana Mae said, settling back into the couch pillows a little. Her brand-new sneakers glowed as white as her hair against her dark-green sweats. "When we'd leave the house, we left the grid. No cell phones to track you down."

"Same here," I said. "Although I had neighbors that were more efficient than any electronic device. Still do," I added, pointing. "Mrs. Mercer next door nearly called the cops the first time Patrick came over on his bike."

"That's because Kathleen Mercer sits in her living room bay window with binoculars every day," Nana Mae said. "I'm always tempted to turn around and moon her when I leave here, just to hear the scream."

I snickered. "Well, she used to wear out the phone, too. Mom knew every place I stepped a foot in before I ever got home."

"And you still managed to get yourself in a pickle," she said. Meeting her look, I felt the pull at my gut. "Knowing my daughter, I'm surprised she ever allowed you to have that boy in your room."

"Oh, he wasn't," I said as Harley came back to stare at the Mud, her big head resting on my knee. I chuckled—maybe a little more bitterly than intended. "Nothing ever happened in this house, I promise you."

Nana Mae patted my hand. "As I suspect you'll make sure is the case for Becca as well."

I paused, caught somewhere between then and now. "Well, yeah. Obviously I hope she isn't doing anything."

"And your mother hoped the same thing," she said. "Just as I did for her."

I scoffed. "I sincerely doubt my mother ever did anything that scandalous."

Nana Mae wiped her fingers clean of the sticky chocolate. "Well, no, she didn't get herself pregnant, if that's what you mean, but she certainly pushed her boundaries at times."

Curious. My mother pushing boundaries. "Like?"

"Like sneaking out at night, stealing her daddy's cigarettes, reading books she wasn't supposed to read and stashing them under her mattress." Nana Mae chuckled. "Or carving out old books to hide things like letters from boys—and her daddy's cigarettes."

I stared at her in amazement. Those things did not mesh with the woman I knew as my mother. "How have I never heard this before?"

She shrugged. "Never came up before, I guess."

"And *she* wasn't about to tell me," I said, brushing crumbs into my napkin. I got up to find a ziplock to store the rest of the Mud.

Nana Mae laughed softly as she worked to her feet as well. She scooped up the plate and followed me to the kitchen. "Of course not," she said. "Would you? *Have* you?"

I turned from my open cabinet and gave her a look. "No."

"Okay then, Julianna. Then don't be so hard on your mother." She laid her hands flat on the cold granite of the island and clicked her ring against it. "We don't tell our kids about our questionables, past or present."

"But you want me to," I said, setting the ziplock bag down.

Nana Mae picked it up and began moving the pieces of Mud cake inside it. "Only because your past has joined the present, my girl. And Becca deserves not to hear it from the gossip mill."

I watched her with her old, wrinkled, heavily veined hands placing each piece in carefully. Her nails were still painted perfectly every time I saw her, hair always smooth and tidy. Even in the days surrounding my mother's passing, Nana Mae always looked her best, sitting at her daughter's bedside day and night in full dress and makeup until the advanced cancer took her from us. So much like my mother in those little ways, and a complete opposite in others.

"What do you think Mom would say if she were still here?" I asked.

She didn't look up, just finished her task. "She'd probably disagree with me," she said softly. "But she always did have her own mind. Would swear the sky was green just to argue with me."

"You miss those arguments, don't you?"

Nana Mae met my eyes with a little wink before she looked away, but I saw the glimmer of emotion first. "Every day."

◆　◆　◆

"Stop looking at me like that."

Harley lay curled in a half circle next to my chair as I got ready, her head resting on the bath towel I'd discarded. Her little eyebrows kept alternating up and down as she looked imploringly at me, devastated that I was leaving her alone on a Friday night. After all, I was always the steady one, the home body. It was usually she and I watching Lifetime movies on the couch on Friday nights, while Becca either went out with friends or had them over.

Now, as I sat putting on my makeup with a sulky dog at my feet, I recalled my nights out at Becca's age and took a fearful breath. Not the time to think of those things. I knew what I was doing at seventeen, and it frequently involved steaming up the windows of Noah's car. But I couldn't put my indiscretions on Becca. My *questionables*.

She'd had boyfriends, but nothing that lasted long enough to get gropy to my knowledge. And most of her outings were with groups, so I always felt a little safer with that.

How could I tell her what I'd done at her age and ever expect any semblance of respect on that subject?

My cell buzzed on the dresser and I snatched it up to see Becca's name.

Checking in, Sarge.

Cute.

Ha ha, I texted back.

Then a picture text came in showing her in a royal-blue strapless body-snug dress that fit her like a dream—if she were twenty-two and lived in New York City.

At the mall. Wnt this dress 4 prom. It's on sale rt now.

I decided to put the phone down. Prom was still four months away, and I wasn't about to get in an argument of wills over a hoochie dress I'd never buy at any price.

I finished up the last attempts at making my wavy mess look cool, pulling back the heavy sides so that soft pieces fell around my face. I sighed, remembering Shayna's careless perfection, and wished I could be that fortunate.

Disgusted, I went to stare at my clothes. A dress? Jeans? I knew Ruthie would have some version of black going on. I could do the same and we'd blend together, or I could be bold and go for color. I remembered the hot red dress Shayna'd had on the day they arrived, but I didn't have anything that good.

And then I slammed my closet door, making Harley jump to her feet and look at me for her next move.

Damn it, I needed to stop! Here I was trying to live up to a woman more than ten years younger than me who I didn't even know, just because she was with a man I no longer had.

"This is crazy," I said to Harley, who wagged her tail uncertainly, not sure if we were going to war or if Mom was just having a loony moment. "This is going out to eat with Aunt Ruthie, it doesn't matter." She took a step toward me and I scratched her soft head.

I pulled a pair of dark jeans from a drawer, a black tank top, and a red—yes, *red*—gauzy see-through long-sleeved blouse. Kinda sexy without being overtly so. I wasn't looking to pick up anybody or find myself another Patrick. One was quite enough.

I grabbed my body spray and spritzed myself once and Harley twice. She didn't see the humor in it and promptly ran downstairs. I zipped up my black low-heeled boots and took one last look in the mirror.

When you are really young, you think of the midforties as so ancient, and that of course all of life's plans for you have long fallen into place. I twisted to see my backside and then back around to pose and pretend-walk.

Okay, maybe I didn't look ancient, thanks to good genes and hair color, but where were those life plans? Was I somewhere else when they were falling?

"Okay, Harley-bear," I said when I made it downstairs to the door. "Stand guard."

Which clearly meant something different in her language, because she jumped on the couch and wrapped her body around two pillows.

I was kind of envious of her evening.

◆　◆　◆

The Grille parking lot was pretty packed when we got to the other side of Katyville. Either we were at the happening place or all the other restaurants were closed. Circling around to the back, we managed to snag a parking spot. Music emanated from the walls as we approached the screened-in patio, a section clearly being avoided due to the cold.

"I can't wait to get some jalapeño poppers," Ruthie said as she swung one of the front doors open and the full volume of the music thumped into us.

"I just want a margarita," I said.

"We can do that, too."

The tables were mostly full, both high-stooled and regular, but the hostess wound us through them, past a large table of laughing women, to a small high table on the other side of the dance floor.

"This'll work," Ruthie said, settling herself on her stool. "Good view. Now, let's get something greasy and some alcohol to wash it down with."

She looked adorable, as usual. Her straight dark hair was pulled to one side and fastened so that it rested prettily over her shoulder. She wore black opaque tights with a fitted black tunic dress over them, and knee-high boots similar to mine. I knew it would be black. I hadn't seen her in color in probably fifteen years.

"What's Frank doing tonight?" I asked when our drinks came.

"Watching zombie movies," she said, licking the salt from the rim of her glass. "He saves those up for when I'm gone because I won't watch them with him."

We ordered food and I watched the dance floor, trying to remember the last time I'd been dancing. When Hayden and I were married? Possibly. I know we used to tear up a two-step when we were dating, and probably did later, too, but it was too far back to remember. I knew for a fact that I hadn't danced with anyone I'd dated since.

"Good God," I said. "I just realized I'm old."

"Just now?" Ruthie said, snickering over her drink. "I realize that every morning as I groan my way out of bed. Now, if I were independently wealthy or owned my own business so I could maybe or maybe not go into work—maybe I wouldn't have to groan so much."

"Is that a dig?"

"No!" she said with a wink. "I'm just saying. I dream big."

"What kind of business do you want to start?" I asked.

She waved a hand. "Oh, I have no idea, it's just something Frank and I have always talked about. We have the money, but the right opportunity just hasn't come bouncing along."

"Well, you'd be excellent at whatever you bounce into," I said.

"Why, thank you," she said with a little mock bow. "So have you sent in your sale ad for the carnival flyer?"

I narrowed my eyes at her, wishing I had lasers to go with them. "Seriously? That's what we're starting with?"

She set her drink down and held out her hands. "What, it's a valid question! One I get asked at least twice a day. I'm only asking you once."

"You know what?" I said. "*You* take it on this year."

"It was due today."

"And if I know you, you already have something cooked up and designed on the computer," I said.

She shrugged. "Just in my head."

"Well, knock yourself out," I said, sipping my margarita. "I pass the sales genius to you."

She laughed. "You're such a procrastinator."

"I'm totally not," I said, frowning. "I just—"

"Hate this festival," she finished.

"No," I said defensively. "I don't hate it. It's perfectly fine—and yeah, I'm lying, I hate it." I laughed, holding up my glass.

"It's okay," she said, some of the snark leaving her expression. She looked at me lovingly. "I understand why you hate it. But you could just have fun with it like everyone else," she said.

"It's a fake-snow parade in Texas, Ruthie. When's the last time you saw snow?" I leaned my elbows on the table. "I can tell you all three times for me. Kindergarten, senior year, and five years ago when Becca was twelve and the school let them out to play behind the gym."

"Exactly," Ruthie said. "It's rare, and therefore fun to be corny with it." She leaned forward. "Be corny with it."

I rubbed my temples. "I can't."

"That's because the senior-year instance was—"

"Ladies," said a male voice from behind me, cutting Ruthie off and making me jump in my seat. I swiveled to see Patrick smiling down at me and Ruthie smiling up at him.

"Hello," she said, tilting her head in amusement and darting a glance my way.

"Oh, crap, Ruthie—you haven't met Patrick, have you?" I said, startled as I realized that. She wasn't at the store the one time he'd come by.

"No, ma'am, I haven't," she said, widening her eyes with a *holy shit* look. "I've heard the name, heard the stories—"

"Ooh, I have stories?" Patrick asked, managing to look completely wicked.

"Oh, most definitely," Ruthie said, absently stirring her drink with her straw. "The—motorcycle trip alone was worth the time."

Patrick laughed, a deep sound that had my senses stirring. A nice feeling, but I wasn't there for that. I was out with Ruthie, for a girls' night, not trolling for sex.

"So, you," I said, attempting sultry. Sort of. By the look I saw pass over Ruthie's face, I assumed I failed. "What are you doing out here tonight?"

He nodded toward the bar. "Just picking up some quick dinner, and then driving to Austin tonight."

"Austin?" Ruthie said.

"My next job starts there on Monday," Patrick said, his hand resting on the back of my chair. "Have to go get set up this weekend and get my guys ready. Make sure everything works and everyone is there."

"You're gonna be a while, huh?" I said, meeting his eyes.

"Yeah," he said, a soft look playing there that had me thinking naughty things. "Probably till mid-February. I'll call you."

"Well, yeah, you can have phone sex," Ruthie said, her tone casual.

Patrick laughed and I stared at her. "Ruth Ann."

"What did I tell you about that name, Ju-li-an-na?" she said on a laugh. It was meant as an inside joke, a nod to our childhood, but it brought Noah back to the forefront, and I felt my stomach tighten up.

"Maybe we will," Patrick said, his tone half flirting with her, half promising me something hair-raising as he circled the subject back. He chuckled as he slid past my chair. "Be back in a little bit, beautiful," he said in my ear, sending goose bumps down my back as he headed for the bar.

We watched him together for a second. "God, I'm such a damn easy lay when it comes to him," I said.

"I can see why," she said, and then she thumped me on the arm. "You didn't tell me he looked like that."

"Like what? Hot?" I asked. "Yes, I did."

"No, I mean—" She circled her hands, looking for the right gesture. "Bad. Dangerous. Like he could—gnaw on raw meat or something."

A laugh tickled me at the visual. "I'm pretty sure he likes his meat cooked," I said. "Then again, it's never come up. We had pizza once."

"What kind?"

"Meat lovers."

Ruthie's look had me giggling like a schoolgirl. If a schoolgirl would be drinking a top-shelf margarita.

"So are you drunk yet?" Ruthie asked when we recovered.

"On half a margarita? God, I hope not," I said on a laugh. "Why?"

She licked her lips and peered down into her glass before looking back up at me with a very contemplative expression.

"I have something I need to tell you," she said, attempting a smile that I knew her well enough to recognize as placating.

"Is someone dying?" I asked.

"No."

"Okay then," I said, taking a deep breath. "Anything else is minor. What's going on?"

She took another swallow, and my skin tingled with anxiety I couldn't even name.

"Becca asked me how to get on birth control."

CHAPTER 7

I remembered being Becca's age. All too well. I even remembered thinking how enlightened and cool I'd be if the subject ever came up with my own kid.

I was a moron.

And all I could do with my decidedly uncool self was sit there and listen to my heart thumping in my ears. The music hovered in the background somewhere as I visualized Becca pregnant with her crooked hair, or taking an infant up to her room to feed it and losing it in the hovel that was her bed.

"Jules?"

My name broke through, and I felt Ruthie's hand on mine.

"Jules, are you okay?"

"She's having sex?" I said, my voice sounding scratchy.

"I don't think so," Ruthie said. "Not yet."

"Not yet," I echoed, covering my face. As I dropped my hands and met her eyes again, a different switch flipped. "Hang on, how do you know this?" I said, sitting straighter.

Ruthie tugged her bottom lip between her teeth, a telltale sign with me that she was uncomfortable. My head spun with the possible conversations.

"She stopped at the store today after school," Ruthie began. "After you left. And we got to talking while I was cleaning up."

Today. The day she flew in the door and got ready in a flash. Left with a group of girls. Wasn't it girls? She just said a group. Shit.

"Okay." The alcohol suddenly sat like acid in my stomach. The giant platter of loaded nachos and jalapeño poppers we'd decided to share arrived, and I grabbed one almost before it even landed on the table. I knew that feeling of curiosity and adrenaline and lust. And I knew where it could lead her if she wasn't clearheaded about it. "She's got a boyfriend? I didn't even know she was seeing anybody."

It occurred to me as I shoved a second one into my mouth that it was my second time that week to have nachos. And then it occurred to me that having such a meaningless thought at such a crucial revelation might mean I was losing it.

Ruthie eyed me as I pushed another chip loaded with shredded chicken, dripping cheese, and steaming beans in my mouth before she spoke.

"Anyway—she started talking about this boy she met—"

"Met?" I said, ceasing the chewing. "She's just met someone and she's already having this conversation?"

Ruthie smiled as you would at a frustrated child. "Calm down, Jules. This is why she came to me and not you."

And that was just the icy dousing I needed to jolt me into silence. I bit my lip to fight back the burn that started in my chest and crept upward. That was the crux of it. Becca had gone to Ruthie to talk about the most intimate of things. Something I couldn't have gone to my mother with, either. I blinked and swallowed hard as that reality pushed the burn up into my eyes.

"Okay," I whispered.

"I'm sorry," Ruthie said, grabbing my hand again, but I shook my head.

"It's okay," I said. "Go on, I'll be good."

She took a long swallow of her drink and glanced over to where Patrick was standing at the bar, chatting up the bartender.

"She met a boy, his name is Mark."

"Mark," I echoed. "From school?"

"I didn't ask, but I assume so," Ruthie said. "His dad is one of Patrick's crew."

My ears rang with the information. I'd seen Patrick with his crew before, most of them much rougher-looking than he was. A young version of that?

"And he's pressuring Becca for sex?" I asked, hearing my voice go up a little higher and louder than normal. At precisely the wrong time.

"What?"

The deep voice was behind me and louder than mine ever dreamed of being, and everything in me cringed. I turned just as Hayden stepped up to our table, looking at me all wild-eyed. With one look I knew he was at least three or four beers into a good buzz, but unfortunately still very coherent.

"No, no, no, no," Ruthie said, waving hands at both of us before something blew up. "Nobody's pressuring anybody for anything. Shit," she added, dropping her head for a moment. "This is out of hand. She was just asking questions is all."

"Who's the dad?" I asked.

"What dad?" Hayden asked. "And what the hell is going on with Becca? Why's she asking questions about sex?"

"You know, this was a private conversation," Ruthie said, glaring up at him.

"Not anymore it's not," he said.

I held my head together with my palms. "Hayden, it's okay that she's curious. That's normal."

It just wasn't okay that she didn't come to *me* with that curiosity. That she was going so far as to ask about birth control. That wasn't okay. But I wasn't fueling that flame in front of Hayden.

"I heard you say that someone was pressuring her—"

"I was just—" I stopped and took a deep breath. "It was my misunderstanding, okay? I was flying off the handle just like you are now." I turned back to Ruthie, who looked as if she'd rather chew a brick. "Who's the dad?"

"I think she said his last name was Wallace," Ruthie said quietly.

"Why does it matter who the dad is?" Hayden said.

"Back in a minute," I said to Ruthie as I got up to join Patrick at the bar before he could rejoin us. I was frazzled enough without Hayden getting in the mix. At the look on Ruthie's face for being left with him, I made a mental note to buy her another margarita.

"Hey, beautiful," Patrick said as I reached his side.

"Do you have someone working for you named Wallace?" I asked. Patrick's eyebrows raised just a fraction. "Um—yeah. David Wallace?"

"Lives in Copper Falls?"

The eyebrows lowered to a frown. "No, none of my men do. But I think a couple of them have ex-wives around here. Why?"

"Does he have a son named Mark?" I asked, feeling very much like a prosecutor and yet unable to stop shooting off the questions.

Patrick turned to face me fully. "I have no idea, Jules. We don't sit around comparing photos. What's going on?"

"My daughter wants to have sex with a boy named Mark and said his dad works with you," I blurted out, realizing somewhere in the places where logic lived that I wasn't anywhere close.

The eyebrows shot back up and he cleared his throat. "Oh. Well, I guess he probably does then." When I continued to stare at him, he gave me a questioning look. "Sorry?"

There was a pen lying on the bar, and I picked it up and started clicking it. "So what's this guy like?"

Patrick narrowed his eyes. "Babe, I'm sorry you're having to deal with this, but what does his dad have to do with it?"

"They learn it from somewhere."

He chuckled and winked randomly at the woman behind the bar as she handed him a to-go box of something that smelled wonderful. "They *learn it from somewhere*? Because he couldn't just be a normal horny teenage boy, right?" He squeezed my hand and took the pen I was furiously clicking, setting it back down. "Come on, Jules."

"Well, look what he sees," I said, refusing to be placated. "Y'all pick up women wherever you land. If he sees him screwing around all the time—"

"I'm gonna stop you right there," Patrick said, the jovial expression leaving his face. "Despite what you obviously think of me and my guys, we aren't traveling fuck magnets."

"I didn't mean it like—"

"Oh, I think you meant it exactly like that," he said, pushing off the bar with a fired-up coldness I'd never seen before. "Let me tell you something. We have a job to do. We work hard, eat crap food, sleep in cheap motels, and move on to the next job. What my guys do on their few off-hours is not my business, and what their *kids* may do damn well isn't."

"Patrick—"

"Look in your own house before you start pointing fingers, Jules," he said, turning to leave. "I didn't *screw around* with you all by myself."

"What?" I exclaimed, a little louder than I intended. "I wasn't talking about you."

"I am. Maybe *your* kid is the one watching."

At that, he left. I watched his back as he wound his way around the tables and pushed the front door open.

"Want something, hon?" the bartender lady asked me, pulling my attention back.

I blinked and held my hands against my stomach, feeling the stab to the gut that Patrick had just left there.

"Um, can I get two more margaritas on the rocks to that table?" I asked, pointing to where Ruthie sat looking irritated and Hayden stood hovering like a hawk.

I made my way back, feeling heavy and wrong and stupid. Was Becca paying closer attention to my actions rather than my words? She knew what we were doing; she'd said it out loud. The one time in my life that I'd allowed myself outside my own rule book was with Patrick, and that's when she decides to pay attention?

Ruthie just met my gaze with that universal silent communication all best friends have. She saw Patrick leave, she saw my face, my deflated composure. She knew how I felt. That was enough while we had an audience. Hayden, on the other hand, was still up on level four somewhere.

"Your boyfriend leave?" he said, a twitch to his jaw telling me that the word bothered him.

I knew that even after our years apart, he still cared about me. He'd always loved me more than I did him, and as unfair as that was, I'd married him anyway. Back then, I was damaged goods. Mourning the loss of a child that no one but Ruthie ever spoke of with me, and still carrying a torch for the love of my life. A love that had left me to mourn alone. To worry about him, cry for him, curse him, and sometimes hate him. It took Hayden two years to win me over completely, and although I never felt that all-consuming passion again, I assumed that was my fate.

He was cute and witty and smart and could always make me laugh when laughing didn't come naturally to me anymore. Hayden had found me in my darkest place and showed me the light again. That was enough. His controlling nature and lack of an off switch when he drank made it not enough.

I ignored his question and palmed my glass, sucking up what was left of my margarita and watching the dance floor. I needed the cold and the tangy citrus to cool my blood.

"I have the right to know what's going on with her, Jules," Hayden said, leaning into my line of vision.

As an upbeat country song filled the room, I met his eyes. "Let's dance."

He backed up a step. "What?"

"You heard me," I said, hearing Ruthie snicker to my right. I grabbed his hand. "Let's see if we still remember how to do this."

"What are you doing?" I heard him say behind me as I pulled him along.

I wheeled around to face him. "Trying to let off a little steam, Hayden. Trying not to be my mother." The burn hit the backs of my eyes, and I blinked back the impending flood. "She went to *Ruthie* with this. Instead of me," I said, trying to control the quiver that laced my words.

Hayden's eyes panned my face and went soft. He'd lived with me long enough to know where my head was.

"When's the last time you two-stepped?" he said finally.

"With you."

He rolled his eyes and smiled that smile that always made women look twice, making me chuckle to myself.

"Lord, you've got some rust to work out," he said.

"Well, get on it, then," I whispered, making him laugh as he pushed me out onto the dance floor.

Time fell backward a little as he rested his right hand against my neck to guide me and my feet remembered what to do. The song was quick, upbeat, and we fell into our easy rhythm almost immediately, sliding in and out and around the other couples that were taking it a little more conservative.

"Like riding a bike," Hayden said over the music. When I laughed, Hayden dared me with his eyes. "Ready to kick it up a notch?"

It was easy to have fun with him; he had that way of somehow knowing what I needed and making sure I got it. Even though I knew we both had Becca spinning around in our heads, he focused on spinning me. He pushed me away, keeping hold of my hand, and I turned in a circle alone and then around him, all the while making tracks around the floor. He whirled me back into his arms, grinning.

"Not bad, lady," he said.

"Let's spin," I said, grinning back.

We got our footing, and he winked down at me as his hand gripped the back of my neck tighter and we started spinning around the floor to the last part of the song. The other couples on the dance floor moved a little to the side to give us space, and as the song came to an end, clapped and hooted for us. I saw Ruthie stand up from our table and whistle.

"Wow," I said, feeling the heat from the rush and the spotlight rise up to my face. "That's been a while."

Hayden hugged me lightly, and as a slow country song came on, squeezed my hand. "One more?"

I hesitated, knowing how sexy and intimate a two-step waltz could be. Especially knowing how sexy he could make it. It might have been several years, but I wasn't losing my memory just yet. Not that I was afraid I'd suddenly jump into bed with him or anything, but I also liked keeping the lines clean between us.

"Come on," he said. "For old time's sake."

I narrowed my eyes at him. "Old time's sake, huh?"

But as Tim McGraw crooned "Please Remember Me," Hayden smiled and took that as a yes, pulling me close and moving us around the floor. I didn't fight it. It was familiar, and I guess something in me needed that normalcy, as bizarre as that was. Slow-dancing with your ex-husband probably shouldn't be normal, especially that way, with the combination of bodies moving slowly together in a close rhythm and legs going in between each other.

The lights on the floor had turned low, with little spotlights shining on the tables that flanked the dance floor, making those people glow a little.

He pulled me tight against him as we did a slow spin, his fingers going up into my hair and my face pressed into his chest, filling my senses with the same cologne he'd worn since I bought it for him on our two-year anniversary.

Something in my head rang out with warning bells, that I was maybe enjoying this too much and my clean lines were fogging up a bit. So when the spin was done, I pulled back a little and smiled up at him, noting the fog in his eyes as well.

He'd had me with a slow dance when we'd first met, and I was damned if I was going to follow up with it now. He pushed me out to do a turn, and I breathed a sigh of relief as I saw it in his face, too. The need for distance, accompanied by a grin that said he knew he'd gotten to me in that one moment.

I smirked at him. "Shut up."

He laughed and spun me around carelessly, and as I came around laughing, another pair of eyes sank into me from the edge of the dance floor.

The song crooned about remembering, and everything in those eyes remembered. My feet faltered as Noah stood there, dressed in all black like some stealth god, leaned against his table, arms crossed over his chest, with every possible nuance of hurt, anger, and defiance playing over his features. Even in the near darkness, it emanated off him like a glow stick.

Hayden followed my gaze and pulled me with him, my lungs filling with air as I realized I'd stopped breathing. How long had he been there? And where was—

As we made another turn, I saw her. Sitting at the table, watching him. As he watched me. His face was stony, his body taut with raw power. Like he was spring-loaded.

"Focus," came Hayden's voice just above my ear.

I stumbled and got my feet back on track. "Sorry."

We made it around the floor one more time, but Hayden managed to avoid passing them again, moving among other couples instead. I did notice that Noah had sat down, though, and I breathed a little easier.

"You okay?" Hayden said when the song ended and we walked slowly back to my table. The seriousness had crept back on him.

"I'm fine," I said, my voice husky. I cleared my throat and grabbed the new margarita that awaited me on the table. "Thank you, Hayden, that was fun."

"I mean, since he's back," he said, his eyes boring into mine.

"Who's back?" Ruthie said, even though she instantly looked around, knowing exactly who the *who* was.

"It's okay, Hayden," I said, trying to make light of it. "We're all grown-ups now."

"Really?" he said with a smile that didn't make it all the way up. "That's why you go numb every time you see him?" He thumbed at the dance floor behind him. "You nearly landed on your face."

"Let it rest, please?" I said softly. "Are you here by yourself?"

He looked at me one more moment, then shook his head. "With some buddies from work."

I patted his arm. "Well, go hook back up with them. Trash your ex-wife for thinking she could still dance."

When he finally left after ordering a beer, I sat down heavily. "Shit."

"So, where is he?" Ruthie asked.

"Fucking everywhere," I said, lifting my hair and fanning my neck. "He's on the other side of the dance floor." I shut my eyes tight against the memory of his heated expression. What the hell was that about?

"I assume he has his woman with him?" she asked.

I gave her a look and gazed off in their general direction. I couldn't see them through the wall of bodies between us, but knowing he was there made my skin tingle.

"Yes, and if I had to guess, I'd say she's probably pretty ticked off right now," I said, scooping up a loaded chip.

"Why?"

I shook my head. "I don't know, he just looked so—" *What? Lost? Pissed?* "She caught him watching us."

Ruthie's eyebrows raised a little over her glass. "Watching you—dance?"

I opened my mouth, then closed it. "It sort of got a little cozy for one little second there."

She set her glass down with a thunk. "With *Hayden*?"

"Don't judge," I said, grimacing. "It wasn't anything like that, just—there for about two seconds, things probably looked a little blurry. It was stupid and we both laughed it off."

"And Noah saw the blurry?"

"I'm assuming so," I said, rubbing my temples. "By the murderous look on his face, I'd assume something—" I stopped and blew out a frustrated breath. "Why would he be bothered with that?"

"Maybe he wasn't?" Ruthie offered, holding up a chip. "Maybe he and Preppy Girl Barbie had a fight and he's pissed at her."

I pointed at her. "They most likely did have an altercation earlier today." I gave the quickie version of the gas-station debacle.

"Well, there you go," she said. "If he was having murderous thoughts about you, that was probably why. So since he's actually trained to do that, you might want to steer clear," she said, giving me a cute smile and a head tilt.

I scrunched my nose at her in response and grabbed a jalapeño popper. "I can't believe I'm eating this crap."

"Neither can I," she said. "You've been binging all week. Are you pregnant?"

I stopped midbite. "Do you even know how not funny that is?"

She giggled. "Sorry."

I excused myself to go get some water at the bar. Everything from my shoulders up felt like it might ignite if I rubbed two hairs together. I wasn't sure if it was stress, anxiety, or just an unfortunate hot flash, but I was pretty sure I could conjure up fire if I really put some thought into it. Plus, the margarita was getting too sweet for me, and our waitress seemed to only remember alcohol.

"In a glass or a bottle?" the bartender asked.

I glanced down at the giant bin of ice and fantasized about plunging my head into it.

"Glass with extra ice, please," I said.

I felt him before anything else. Before sight or smell or words could come into play. I felt the pull of Noah Ryan at my right before he ever even spoke.

"Quite the little dancer you've become," he said, the deep familiar voice unsettling me as it did every single time I heard it. He caught the bartender's eye and held up his empty beer bottle and one finger. "And a Sprite with ice, please." She smiled like her life depended on it, completely ditching my glass of ice to get his needs taken care of.

I smiled into the mirror behind the bar, finding it safer to look at him that way than the five inches between us.

"Not really," I said. "Haven't done that in years."

"Where'd you learn that?"

I thumbed behind me as if that would clear things up. "Hayden, actually."

Noah glanced behind us and looked at me, making me look him in the eye. "Hayden," he echoed. My stomach went to war as a tiny flicker of humor passed through his blue eyes. "Is he another *not-a-someone?*"

I couldn't help the smirk that tugged at my lips at his memory of my description of Patrick. I chuckled.

"No, he's more like a used-to-be-someone." The woman behind the bar came back with his beer and filled a glass with ice that wasn't for me. "Hayden's my ex-husband."

Noah's left cheek twitched. "*Ex*-husband?"

"Yes." I drummed my fingers on the bar, wishing she'd hurry up with my glass of ice water.

"You dance like that with your ex?" Noah asked.

Like that. I grimaced as I cursed the fact that he kept catching me with my pants down. Someone squeezed in at the bar on the other side of him, nudging him sideways into me. I felt the heat of his arm through his shirt and my gauzy one, and my mouth went even drier.

"It—wasn't what you think," I said, pointing to my glass emphatically as the woman came back with the sparkly Sprite. Hearing my words, I realized I'd said something very similar about Patrick. Wanting to change the subject, I said, "I'm sorry, by the way, about today at the pump. I didn't know I wasn't supposed to know."

He shook his head. "It's okay, it was my fault."

"Hope you didn't get in too much trouble," I said, cutting another glance his way.

His face tightened a little and he handed the lady a ten and held up a hand to let her know to keep the change. "It's all good, Jules."

The woman grabbed my glass and stared at it as if she couldn't remember what she was supposed to do with it. "Ice water, please," I said, reminding her. She jumped into motion, smiling at Noah, scooping one scoop of ice into the glass. "Extra?" I reiterated, and she huffed out a breath as if that just put her over the top.

He could have walked on, but he didn't. He waited to walk with me. Why did he do that? I wanted to pour that whole glass on my head as I walked back to the table with Noah behind me. The look must have registered, because Ruthie clamped her lips together like she was ready to either laugh or beat him up. I reached for my chair to pull it out more, but it moved out of my hand as Noah pulled it out for me. I paused and met Ruthie's eyes, wishing he'd just go bring Shayna her damn Sprite and stay on the other side of the room.

"Ruthie," he said as I sat and he passed behind me.

She smiled up at him with a smart-assed head tilt. "Noah." She nodded at the glass and beer he held expertly in one hand. "No waitress on your side?"

His eyes flashed with the urge to spar with her. He picked up her drink and took a swallow straight from the glass, licking the salt from his lips as she shot him ice daggers with her glare.

"Nope."

He set down the glass with an almost-smile and walked around the outskirts of the dance floor till he disappeared behind all the groping bodies.

"God, he's such an ass," Ruthie said, grabbing a napkin to wipe his cooties off her glass. "It's like he's still seventeen years old in an old man's body."

I chuckled in spite of myself, chewing on ice to cool off. "You think he looks like an old man?"

She gave me a look. "Hell, no, he looks like he was carved from stone. Which is amazing, considering he left here looking like a pole."

"I guess the Navy finds things that weren't there before," I said. "He was supposedly a badass."

"Well, you just be careful," she said, seriousness back in her tone.

I frowned, trying to pull her meaning. "Of—?"

"Noah."

I started to protest, but then I took a deep breath and looked around. I knew what she was saying. "There's nothing to worry about, Ruthie. We're all adults now." Hadn't I just said that to Hayden? "And he's settling in here with Shayna." The words were rancid on my tongue.

"Mmm, yeah, I can see how settled he is," she said, sarcasm lacing her tone. "And I'm willing to bet she can see it, too."

CHAPTER 8

We'd had Patrick, Hayden, and Noah so far, and I felt better knowing there was no one else to crash our party. I was fresh out of exes—not that Patrick was an ex, although he probably qualified now. Ruthie's husband was hours into zombies and I couldn't see him dropping by the Grille.

Ruthie and I had gone out on the floor for a line dance I no more knew how to do than that last chip on my plate did. What I thought was a brilliant strategy of staying in the middle so that Noah wouldn't see me didn't really pan out. There weren't enough of us out there for anyone to hide, and he'd zeroed in on me like white on rice.

Not as heavily as before. Just with his eyes, on and off, as he chatted with Shayna. Then he'd look away and give her his full attention. Of course, I might not have noticed it so much if I weren't looking at him.

An old friend of Ruthie's stopped her on the way back to our table, and I kept going. The relative aloneness at the table was nice—in a way. I could regroup and adjust. I saw a few people I could go say hello to, but I didn't want to. My mind still reeled from the news about Becca, and the few times I saw Hayden, he looked more and more irritated. My guess was that his liquid cure-all wasn't working. Becca texted me twice with updates, one being a picture of the whole group of them. Two were boys, and I zoomed the photo up, studying them and sending them subliminal warnings. All I could think of was history repeating itself. It was not going to be a pleasant conversation with her, and every angle I thought up ended in a screaming fight.

A slow song came on, and as I glanced around to make sure Hayden wasn't gunning for me, I got an eyeful of Noah and Shayna on the dance floor instead. Wrapped in each other's arms, her head tilted back to smile up at him lovingly.

I was hit with a gut kick and a burn that set my whole chest on fire. I looked away and gulped down my third glass of water, refusing to watch that. *Look away, idiot. He's not yours to get possessive over.*

"Shit," I muttered, turning back in spite of myself. They were laughing about something, and he tucked a stray piece of perfect hair behind her ear. "Okay," I said, bolting to my feet, needing something to do.

I walked to the bar, my skin feeling like it had taken on a life of its own.

"Can I order food here?" I asked.

"Sure," the lady said. "Do you need a menu?"

I shook my head. "Dessert—what's the best you have?"

"The blackberry cobbler," she said.

"That'll work," I said, nearly bouncing on my toes. I couldn't be still. "Two of them, with ice cream."

I showed her our table and made my way slowly back to it, taking in the view and understanding with a start what Noah's expression had been about when he saw Hayden and me. Not that it made a bit of sense. We had nothing to be jealous about and no rights to each other—but at that one second I wanted Ruthie to come sit on me before I ended up yanking a pregnant woman out of his arms. I wrapped my arms around my middle as if that would ease the burn, but all that did was make me feel the trembling more. What the hell.

"Stop watching," Ruthie's voice said to my right as she perched back on her chair.

I jumped, startled, and twisted around to face her, feeling like an errant child. I grabbed a coaster and fanned myself with it.

"This is ridiculous," I said, emotional laughter bubbling up that threatened to turn to tears. "What is this? I'm forty-three years old, not fourteen. Why am I reacting like an adolescent?"

"Because that's where you left off," she said. "You two never got to see each other as adults. Or with other people."

I blew out a slow breath. "Well, this sucks."

"We can go, Jules," she said, chuckling. "We don't have to stay here so you torture yourself all night."

I shook my head. "No. You said not to let him run me away, and I'm not." I held up my chin and smiled at her. "Besides, she's pregnant, she'll want to go home soon."

Ruthie laughed. "Good point."

"By the way, we have dessert coming."

Noah being back in town was going to turn me into a hippopotamus.

An hour later when they were still there, my resolve began to wane. And as I left the ladies' room for the fourth time after fifty glasses of water and three margaritas, another slam to the midsection hit me. Yes, Noah and Shayna were on the dance floor again, but they already had been. I was getting immune to that.

It was the song that started playing.

"Oh, holy hell."

◆　◆　◆

I was never one to go wiggy over a song with an old flame. Hayden and I had a song, and I quietly recognized it every time I heard it and that was that. I even kind of remembered that Noah and I had an actual song we'd danced to at a high school dance once, but that one never really registered with me.

The day our baby was born was crazy. It was drizzling and cold and confusing. We'd just had an argument at the park, and when my water broke, we lost our minds. The scrambling we did to get to the car in what then became a downpour was insane. To this day I remember thinking the sky was crying for us. For the decision I hadn't completely made yet.

"Damn it, Linny's tank is on fumes," Noah said, pounding the steering wheel. "I meant to get gas before I picked you up."

"We have time—I think," I stuttered, trying to remember what I'd read in the book I'd checked out from the library. "No contractions yet."

Noah's right hand went to my belly, my rain-soaked T-shirt stretched across it. "I'll get you there safe, Little Bit," he said, his affectionate name for it making my eyes burn for the fortieth time that day. "We just need to get some gas first."

"I need my bag," I said. "I prepacked everything like the book said. I can't go to the hospital without my bag."

"We'll call your mom when we get there," he said, trying to see through the rain. "She can bring it."

"Or we can swing by my house, Noah, it's right—"

"No," he said, taking his hand off my belly and gripping the steering wheel with both hands. "Please, Jules, for once can we do something on our own without your mother? Can we do this on our own?" He darted glances at me between watching the road and pulling out of Copper Falls onto the highway. "She'll take over and push me aside, you know she will."

"Okay," I said, feeling unsure of everything. I'd never felt so unprepared and insecure in my life. The only thing I'd done right was pack that damn bag, and now I didn't even have that.

"Trust me, baby. Please?" Noah said, grabbing my hand and squeezing it. My hands felt like ice against his warm ones, and the warmth spread like honey through me. "Let me take care of you."

I squeezed back. "I do trust you, Noah. I'm just scared." I rubbed my free hand over my belly, where the baby shoved a foot against my palm. "This is all happening—like right now."

He shoved a cassette tape into the deck in the dash. "Listen to this, Jules. Really listen to it." He pressed a button to advance it a few tracks, and then grabbed the steering wheel to turn the car off the highway as a gas station came into view.

Tonight's the night we'll make history . . . honey, you and I . . .

"It's Styx," I said, cringing as a tightness grabbed hold of my midsection like giant hands squeezing. "I know this song—shit, Noah, something really is happening."

Noah's face was whiter than normal as he looked my way and swallowed hard. "Okay, baby, just—here, hold my hand. I'm stopping up here for gas and then just a few more minutes up the highway."

There was a line of cars waiting at the station, making us the third one back, and I closed my eyes and squeezed his hand as we sat in silence listening to Styx sing about how even when you think it's the worst of times, that taking on life together made it the best of times.

Another contraction pulled everything inward, like my body was trying to wring the baby out of me. I shut my eyes tighter, and the music filled all my senses as Noah inched the car closer.

"Ow, damn it," I said, hearing the tears in my voice. I didn't want to be scared. I thought I was good with everything. I thought I could handle it. But there with it happening, with it actually happening, I wanted to run. "Noah, hurry."

"I am," he whispered. I looked his way and he was breathing as hard as I was, probably just as scared. We made it up to the pump and he slammed the car into "Park" and jumped out. "Hang in there, Jules, I'll be right back."

He literally sprinted into the store, and I absorbed the sound of the rain pelting everything around me. I rubbed my belly and took breaths like I'd seen women do on television. I never took Lamaze—my mom said it was a bunch of bunk—but now I could see where it might at least be distracting.

Hot tears fell down my cheeks as I worked my fingers over the wet fabric and felt feet or hands or elbows or something small pushing my stomach into contorted shapes as whoever was inside rolled over.

"I want to be your momma, baby," I whispered, my voice shaking. "But I don't know how. Right now, I just want mine." Sobs worked their way up. "Do you know how much I love you?"

Noah ran back to the car and crammed the pump into the gas tank as fast as he could, pumping ten dollars in. Then he jumped in and handed me a roll of wintergreen Life Savers.

"I know they always soothe your stomach when you—" He stopped short as he caught sight of my face. "What's the matter? Shit, Jules, I'm sorry, I'll hurry." He jerked the car out of the parking lot and onto the feeder road on two wheels.

"No—it's not that," I sputtered. "I'm just—freaking out a little."

Noah blew out a giant breath as he got back on the highway. "Baby, I know. I know you're scared. I am, too." He glanced my way. "But it's just like that song. You think this is the worst right now, but it's really the best. I mean, yeah, it's crazy but we're—we're starting our own family here. Right now." He laughed out loud, sounding so proud. "My God, I'm about to be a dad." He brought my hand to his lips and kissed it, kissing the little engagement ring that adorned my finger. "And you're gonna be a great mom, Jules. Who cares that we're starting early? I'll stand with you and Little Bit till the end of time, baby."

"I know," I whispered, feeling the invisible hand squeeze my middle again. "Oh, God, this is so not cool, Noah," I said in a grimace as I automatically doubled forward.

Five minutes that felt like five hours later, we screeched into the emergency-room drive and Noah jumped out of the car and ran around. He opened my

door and took my hand, pulling me to my feet. His blue eyes glittered with
excited tears.

"This is it, Jules."

"This is it," I said back. I wrapped my arms around his neck for dear
life. "I love you, Noah."

"Always, baby," he said, hugging me back. "I'll always love you."

"Don't let go," I whispered.

"Never," he said into my hair. "Holy shit, look!"

I backed up and followed his eyes upward. The rain had turned into
snow. Oh, my God, snow was falling. Here.

Noah started laughing and cradled my face in his hands, blinking fast.
"It's snowing, baby, it's a sign. This is our miracle."

I blinked upward as Noah knelt and kissed my belly. "Our miracle."

I shut my eyes against the memory as I found myself on a darkened edge
of the room, gripping the back of a chair. It had been years since that
song spoke to me. I'd avoided it every time it came on the radio at first,
and then when I moved on to darker, angrier music to numb things, it
wasn't a consideration.

Over the years it was rarer to hear it, and when I did, I usually
changed the station and moved on. It wasn't part of the last-moments-
as-a-family montage like the painting and the bench were. It stood for
the black moments that made up my mind. And I didn't need to revisit
that to remember them.

A back-door exit caught my eye as a couple of women came inside
from what I assumed was a smoke break. That's what I needed. A smoke
break. Ruthie had left the table again when I looked, finding other people to talk to as I kept ditching her, so I made a beeline for the door.
Pushing through it, cold icy air hit my face, making me gasp with the
contrast of it.

I welcomed it—sucked in big gulps of it, hoping it would freeze up everything inside of me. Numb everything. As the door settled back in place, the song and its taunting lyrics were muffled. The dual visual of Noah and Shayna intertwined and Noah and I standing in the falling snow fizzled a bit with the icy wind. The cold and the darkness from no lighting wrapped around me as I sat in one of two old plastic chairs set out there against the brick walls. I felt like I could breathe easy for the first time that evening, and I leaned over, elbows on my knees, resting my forehead against my palms.

I considered myself a strong, independent woman. I never saw myself as weak or needy or weepy. I couldn't stand those types of women. But it was too much. Upside down and sideways. My head spun through zinging thoughts of Becca, Hayden, Noah, and that damn song, even Patrick and how I'd insulted him.

Hot tears burned my eyes, and I wiped them away as they turned cold on my cheeks. I had to get it together and quit this. I was better than this.

The sound from inside barreled out to me as the door opened again, and I tried to shrink against the brick in the dark, sniffing and wiping the wetness from my face. The aroma of beer and fried food wafted on the air.

"You okay?"

I wanted to groan at the familiar voice as he walked closer. I quickly wiped the remnants of my tears away and sat up straighter, feeling delirium coming on. I chuckled as I swiped under my eyes one last time.

"Do you have a GPS on me or something?"

Noah knelt directly in front of me, making my pulse jump up a notch. "I'm not that crafty," he said, his voice low.

"Yeah, right."

One shoulder shrugged slightly. "Well, maybe." Even in the dark, I could see the hint of a grin tug at the corners of his lips. "But, no. I just wanted to check on you, I saw you come out here."

After "The Best of Times" knocked you on your ass is what he didn't add on to that sentence. I was surprised he'd noticed me at all, all locked up with Shayna like he was. Or that there was the possibility he even connected the two. He might not remember that moment in the car at all.

"Of course you did," I muttered, running a hand over my face, feeling wrung out. "Is there anywhere that you won't be? Because I haven't found that place yet."

The grin left, and a coldness that had nothing to do with the air emanated off him.

"Yeah, here's one," he growled, pushing to his feet, and regret flooded through me.

"Noah, wait." I reached out before logic could form a plan and grabbed his arm, making us both suck in a breath as my hand slipped to his wrist and then his hand. We both stared at the union, and his fingers wrapped around mine. That breath fell right out of me. "I'm sorry," I said, the words barely making it out of my mouth. "I didn't mean—"

He slowly lowered back to one knee until we were eye level again, resting an elbow on my knee and not letting go of my hand. His expression was cloudy and troubled, his jaw tight, but all I could think of was the feel of his hand around mine.

"I know," he said, his voice gruff. He took a deep breath and closed his eyes for a couple of beats before they opened and burned into me. "This is harder than I thought it would be."

The proximity of his body, his arm on my knee, and his hand shooting heat through mine had me dizzy with the stupids. I needed order, structure, someone to tell me to hold the crazy in, because right at that moment we weren't grown-up responsible people. We were back in the place where we were us and knew how to be with each other, and I wanted to let everything sensible go.

"It's been a lot of years," I said instead, my voice sounding hoarse and scratchy. Trying to find the logic that had to be floating around if I could just snag it. "Everything got put away—doors locked up tight." I paused and watched his eyes go soft. "But now you fall out of the sky and knock all those doors open. And suddenly I'm not sure where I am half the time."

It was ballsy to admit that. It put me on very uneven ground. Shaky and vulnerable and wide open for him to scoff and blow me off and leave me looking like a fool. I never put myself in such a precarious position, and I couldn't imagine why I was being so foolish now.

I felt his thumb move across my hand, and warmth shot to all kinds of places it shouldn't. He looked down at my hand in his with something I could only describe as heaviness.

"I know the feeling," he said softly.

I was getting light-headed, and I hadn't had near enough alcohol to justify that. I needed normal back. I needed to not want to wrap myself around him and do things we'd regret.

"Why are you out here with me, Noah?" I asked, knowing the direction I needed to go to get us back thinking right. "You have a pregnant girlfriend—" I stopped and licked my lips, feeling the burn in my chest again and refusing to allow it. "A pregnant fiancée out there," I corrected. "Sitting alone, not able to drink, while you come track me down. That can't bode well for your evening."

He let go of my hand and scrubbed at his eyes, and I immediately missed the contact.

"Probably not," he said.

Lighten it up. "You know, those pregnant emotions are—"

"I know," he said. "I remember the emotions, Jules. I've had a pregnant fiancée before."

Everything left me. All the words of wisdom, patience, sadness, chemistry, even anger—it all left me. I had nothing to say back as my lips moved but thoughts were whisked away with the icy cold. I shivered, realizing I hadn't even felt it since he'd come outside. But the whiplash changing from the earlier tender moment was quite palpable.

"Yes, you did," I whispered finally. "At least up until the pregnant part was over."

I saw the flash in his eyes, felt it as he pushed away from me and to his feet.

"Not my doing."

"Really?" I said, rising to my feet as well. I stepped away from the chair to put some space between us. "Because I'm pretty sure I didn't leave to go sail the ocean blue—"

He walked slowly into me, backing me to the bricks until I gasped. He braced one hand against the brick wall. "You have no—idea—what I did," he said, just inches from my face, his voice low and raw.

"No, I don't," I whispered, my voice shaking. Under the circumstances, I thought that was pretty remarkable. I held my chin up, refusing to back down even when he was so close I could have licked him. "And whose fault was that? You knew how to find me. *I* never left."

"You didn't have to," he said. "Your mother did it for you when she convinced you to bail on us—" he said, his voice clipped. "To bail on *our son.*"

My entire body went hot, my skin prickling with the fire from a million tiny flames. The conversation we'd never had over twenty years earlier was boring into me with what I knew to be hard blue anger, but in the dark just looked black.

I pushed against him, hoping he'd move, but it was like attempting to move a boulder. Blinded through a shimmer of tears, I pushed up so that our noses nearly touched.

"And you bailed on *me*," I said through my teeth.

My heart pounding in my ears, I stepped under his raised arm and pushed past him, yanking the door open and letting the warmth and barrage of sound sensations envelope me. I swallowed tears back and made a beeline for my table, wishing for crap to eat. I nearly sang with joy to see a bowl of cashews on our table, and Ruthie walking back to join me.

"You okay?" she asked, mirroring what Noah had asked me earlier.

"I'm fine," I breathed, knowing I wasn't. Knowing that she knew I wasn't, too. I dabbed under my eyes with a napkin and grabbed a handful of nuts, not even caring for once if they'd been freshly opened or if five hundred other patrons had pawed through them.

"Noah just walked back in the same door," she said warily.

"Yep."

She nodded and I saw her gaze follow him before returning to mine. "Didn't go well, I'm guessing?"

I closed my eyes and blew out a slow breath to return my heart rate to normal. The heat radiating off my skin would take a little longer.

"Doesn't matter," I said, fanning myself with a coaster and forcing a smile. "So tell me about you and Becca's conversation. What did you say when she told you that?"

Ruthie's eyes widened in surprise. "O-kay. When did we get back here? I thought you wanted to talk about anything else."

I pushed another handful of nuts in my mouth and proceeded to talk around them.

"Turns out, it's the sanest subject of the night."

◆　◆　◆

The girl had freakish stamina. When I was pregnant—both times—I had trouble staying up past eight o'clock. She looked just as perky at eleven as she did at seven, whereas I was fading, big time.

I was ready to go—had been since that little exchange outside—but I refused to let a pregnant woman outlast me. I didn't care if she was thirteen years younger.

While the people-watching was interesting enough, including a brief wardrobe malfunction from an inebriated couple groping on the dance floor, the crowd began to thin. The only-here-for-dinner crowd was falling out to go catch a movie or have sober sex, while the true partiers were holding out for the drunken variety.

Or in my case, holding out for a Sprite-drinking pregnant woman to leave.

"Um, what's—" Ruthie began, narrowing her eyes to something across the room. "That can't be good."

I followed her gaze through the handful of remaining dancers on the floor and my stomach twisted up. "Oh, shit," I said, pushing off the stool.

Hayden had approached Noah and Shayna's table and appeared to be asking them both questions with a grim expression. Shayna visibly backed up a little, looking wide-eyed.

"Hang on," Ruthie said, patting the table at my side. "They're men. They have to do the whole dick-swinging thing. Just wait—"

Her words were cut off by our unified gasp as Noah stood up quickly, putting the two men in that unmistakable stance.

"Shit," I said, my feet already propelling me forward. I could hear Ruthie behind me muttering curse words as we wound our way through the oblivious gropers, reaching their table just in time to hear Noah ask him to leave.

CHAPTER 9

Judging by the edge to his voice filtered through his teeth, it wasn't the first time he'd made that request.

Hayden was laughing in his face. And stupid drunk.

"Hayden, what are you doing?" I said, rounding the table to get to him. "I'm sorry," I mouthed to Shayna, who smiled politely.

"Jules!" Hayden said, his eyes lighting up like we were all at a party. "We were just talking about you."

"I'll bet," I muttered.

He slung an arm around me and I tried to use that to move us both along and away from their table, but it didn't work that way. Noah's eyes were dark and menacing, and I could only imagine what Hayden had mouthed off about.

"Did you know that these two are having a baby?" Hayden said loudly. "That's fantastic."

"Let's go, Hayden," I said, trying in vain to move him. He was surprisingly solid for a drunk.

"Just like we had a kid, Julianna," he said, his words slowing. "Although I'm sure your kid'll be perfect," he said to Shayna, who darted a glance from me to the table and back to Noah. "Not like our daughter.

I mean, she used to be. When she was born and had all that hair and perfect little fingers," he said. I stared at him, mortified. "But now she wants to chop her hair sideways, dress like a freak, and have sex with God knows who."

"Hayden!" I pinched him in the side, hoping he'd feel it. He didn't. "Y'all, I'm so sorry." I felt my eyes well up.

"Jesus," Noah muttered, shaking his head. "Have some dignity, man. Go home."

"But yours won't be like that, sweetheart," Hayden said, leaning toward Shayna, who scooted back more. "Because Jules just had me. You've got Superman here." Hayden clapped Noah on the shoulder with his hand, which Noah shoved off with a jerk of his arm. "What could be more perfect than the man everyone wants."

I closed my eyes, wishing the floor would swallow him whole.

"No one could ever live up to you," Hayden said, refocusing his eyes on Noah. I got the distinct impression he'd just forgotten about Becca in that split second and was on another course entirely. "Not the perfect Ghost of Noah Ryan Past," he continued on a chuckle. "Didn't matter that I stuck around to raise *my* kid—"

Everyone moved at once. Noah stepped forward with lightning speed and I tried to move between them. Shayna's stool scooted backward as she jumped to her feet. Ruthie hopped sideways to get out of the way.

Hayden had the idea all mixed up in his riddled state, and I knew it, and Noah knew it, but it triggered something primal that was already touchy.

"Noah, don't, he's drunk," I yelled, turning my back to him and pushing against Hayden, dimly aware that we were developing an audience. "Stop this, damn it!" I yelled up into his face.

"Let him come, if he's such a badass," Hayden slurred, wrapping an arm around my neck possessively. Even drunk I could feel every muscle in his torso tensed and tight, wound and ready for a fight. It was an old hurt with him, his insecurity over Noah. His feeling that I never gave my heart to him completely. I thought it was a buried subject. Clearly, not so much. "Maybe I'll show you once and for all the difference between a real man and a memory."

As he said it, I felt Noah's body against my back.

"You don't want to go there, buddy," he growled.

"Hayden—" I pleaded, but my voice was cut off as he pushed Noah back, jostling me in the process. His arm around me tightened and I wrestled against him. "Hayden, stop it!"

As Noah moved forward again, Hayden's awareness of me morphed into more of an annoyance—something in the way of what he wanted. His grip on me turned into leverage to fling me aside, and like something in a slow-motion action scene I saw an empty table coming my way. Or more like it saw me coming its way.

Ruthie yelped as I crashed into it, and it probably looked and sounded worse than it was, as silverware and a metal napkin holder banged to the floor with me.

That was it.

In time that didn't seem possible, Noah lunged at Hayden and spun him on the spot, wrenching his arm behind him and planting his face on the table. With his other hand he yanked Hayden's head up by the hair so that he was sure to see me, and leaned down, his face contorted with something unrecognizable to me.

"That your idea of a real man, asshole?" he growled into his ear, his voice seething. "Throwing her around?"

Ruthie and Shayna rushed to either side of me, taking an arm.

Hayden's eyes slowly adjusted on me, still reeling from the shock of moving so fast and not seeing it coming. I saw the dawning in his expression.

"I'd never hurt her," he said, his voice cracking.

"No, you just wear her like a trophy," Noah said, barking in his ear. Which wasn't really true, but my current position on the floor wasn't the place to pipe up on that. "Beat down her dreams so far that she doesn't even remember she had them."

What? My head spun, wondering where that came from.

"Was that just your thumb on her?" Noah hissed in his ear. "Or did you join forces with her mother on that?"

I scrambled to my feet ahead of Shayna and Ruthie's helping hands, the words burning in my ears.

"Noah, I'm fine," I said. "Let him go."

He yanked on Hayden's hair a little harder, pulling his head into an awkward position. "Feel like a real man now? Get your point across?"

Hayden's face was blood red, and there were angry tears in his eyes. He was too drunk to really know the scene he'd caused, but not drunk enough to not feel the embarrassment.

"Noah," I repeated, which fell on deaf ears. I wrapped both hands around his arm and tugged, putting my face right next to his. "Noah!"

His head jerked in my direction, and the eyes that met mine were glazed over. Realization hit a second later, and he stood upright again, moving me behind him with one hand before releasing his grip on Hayden.

"Are you okay?" he asked under his breath, and I nodded.

Hayden jerked upward and stumbled sideways, searching for dignity and anonymity at the same time. I grabbed his arm and turned him around so we could walk away. All I wanted was away.

"Don't bitch about your daughter or trash her in public," Noah said, his voice thick with simmering aggression. Hayden tensed and paused midstep but didn't turn around to face him. "Be glad you've gotten to know her at all."

Heat flashed from my neck to my scalp on the stab, and I looked away as his gaze landed on me.

"Let's go find your buddies," I said to Hayden, wondering where they'd been for the floor show.

He pulled his arm free, refusing to look at me. I knew he was horribly humiliated, and horrified that he'd pushed me down. Even in his current state, he was coherent enough to remember that. Never since I'd known him had he ever gotten physical with me, and I'd definitely seen him a lot worse off.

"They left," he grumbled.

"They left you here?"

He shook his head, running fingers through hair that was sticking up in all directions. "I met them here."

I blew out a breath. "Well, you aren't driving." I glanced at Ruthie and she nodded. It was time to call it. "We'll take you home."

Ruthie took over walking Hayden out while I paid our bill. When I chanced a look toward their table again, Shayna was picking things up to leave as well, and Noah wasn't around. She looked distracted and distant. I walked back over there and smiled politely the way I'd come to expect from her, and she touched my arm.

"Are you okay?" she asked, sounding genuine.

I nodded. "I'm fine. I'm—really sorry he came to hassle you. He's going to be so mortified tomorrow when he remembers this."

She shook her head with a smile. "You don't have to apologize, Jules. It wasn't your fault."

Kinda was.

"Well, it was my ex-husband being a douche, so—"

She smiled but her eyes didn't, and the hands that shouldered her bag trembled a little. "Well, Noah didn't have to rise to the bait, either," she said. "That was his choice."

I raised an eyebrow, remembering the flash reaction. "I've never seen Noah get so—" I stopped. "But then I've never seen him be an adult before, so what do I know?" I said, attempting a chuckle that fell short.

"He has a hot fuse," she said. "I'm sure the military created some of that, but he also has a lot of baggage." She looked down and palmed her still-flat belly and then looked back up at me with those same distracted, distant eyes. "And he wears that baggage twenty-four-seven, so I'm used to it pissing him off on occasion."

I wasn't sure what she meant by that, but something in me wanted to put her at ease. She looked troubled. And was *likable*, damn it.

"Well, I'm sorry that Hayden ruined your evening." And me. And Noah's baggage. I glanced around at the crowd that was left, wondering if any of them were regulars at the diner. God, Johnny Mack would have a field day with gossip like this. "Hopefully Noah's dad won't get wind of it and this can all die down."

She chuckled at that. "He's quite the character."

There was a definition.

"Quite."

"You know, even Noah thinks he's acting weird," she said. "I told him that he's just been gone too long to know."

"Exactly," I said, moving as I spoke. I spotted Noah coming from the restroom and didn't want questions. Or advice. Or resolutions. Or pity. I didn't want any more conversation with him, period. "He's just odd. That's all there is to it."

She laughed, and that time it was real, transforming her face into rainbows and sunshine. I said my good-bye and made my way to the door around the long way so that I wouldn't pass him. I caught his look across the room anyway. I couldn't read it, but it lit my skin up.

But he wasn't walking to me. He was walking to Shayna. I had to admit, I could see the attraction. She was genuine, and sweet, and beautiful. And impossible to despise.

I, on the other hand, was walking to the car to bring home my drunk and slightly obnoxious ex-husband. I was one lucky lady.

He was leaned up against Ruthie's car when I got outside, with his arms crossed and his lips in a tight line.

"He wouldn't get in," Ruthie said, throwing her arms up. "I give up. He's too big for me to shove in, and these heels aren't spiky enough to poke holes," she said with a smirk and a head tilt.

"Get in," I said, leaving no room for argument. "You're going home. I'm going home. This night has officially kicked my ass."

"I didn't mean to push you, Jules," he said, his voice belying his stony expression.

I met his eyes, and they looked worried. "I know," I said. "But if you'd just kept your mouth shut it would have never come to that."

"I had to meet him."

I sighed and closed my eyes, disgusted. "And a handshake and a hello wouldn't do it for you?" I rubbed at my face and opened the front passenger door since he was leaning against the back one. "Get. In."

He gave me one last imploring look and got in, all his puffed-up-ness deflating in defeat.

I got in the back, and Hayden was snoring before we even made it to the highway.

◆ ◆ ◆

My eyes felt gritty and heavy, the result of staring at my bedroom ceiling instead of sleeping. It had crisscrossed beams that made a cool pattern, but not that cool. My brain just wouldn't shut down.

Becca had made her curfew, which normally would have me feeling all kinds of happy toward her, but I wasn't finding the happy. Not with her, not with her dad, not with Noah. Not even with myself when I thought about how unfair I'd been to Patrick.

He wasn't an emotional attachment—no, I didn't allow myself those. But I did like him. He was funny and witty and fun to be with. He was a good guy, and I'd been a real bitch. I wasn't proud.

Becca, however, kept coming back to the forefront. Most of the night I'd spent working out the scenario. Working on my initial approach. It wasn't going to go well, I knew that instinctively, and once she was pissed, she would tune out everything else. Therefore, anything I needed her to soak up had to be up front.

Becca, I love you. There's more to protection than birth control. Condoms protect your life.

Yeah, no.

Do you love this boy? Because having sex will affect all of you, not just your body.

Becca was a savvy girl, and unfortunately had inherited my ability to spot bullshit from a mile off. While all of my points were valid, none of them completely covered my real agenda in the two actual sentences she might hear. Which was basically *Having sex before you're ready and with someone you don't actually love or even know all that well just to get it over with is a bad idea, and, oh, yeah, you can catch a life-threatening disease or end up pregnant with life-altering decisions at the age of seventeen.*

Deep breath.

If only I could do that. Write it in a card, or better yet, text it to her. That would increase the likelihood of it being read.

I swung my legs down and rubbed my tired eyes, thinking orange juice sounded good and knowing we didn't have any. I wondered if I should send her to the store before she got angry with me or just do without. She wouldn't be up yet anyway, since it was only eight o'clock on a Saturday.

I trudged downstairs to make coffee and was surprised to see her curled up on one of the couches, pillows piled around her, reading a book.

"You're up early," I said.

She looked up with a yawn. "Had a scary dream so I thought I'd come down here and read."

I felt the old heart tug. "And the pillow brigade?"

She grinned. "My protection against the evil forces."

I laughed, heading around the kitchen bar to the coffeepot. "I remember the days when you'd come jump in bed with me after a nightmare."

"Don't think I didn't consider that."

It was an easy morning, no animosity, no drama, no attitude. Why did I want to go and ruin that with parenting? I rounded the kitchen island to get the coffee going, knowing full well she hadn't been that helpful.

"So, what are you reading?"

Becca held up a copy of *The Great Gatsby*.

I raised an eyebrow. "On purpose?"

"For school," she explained. "Supposed to be done by Monday."

I chuckled. "And you started it—?"

"This morning," she said on a sigh that lent itself much better to the attitude I knew would be coming.

"Ah. Good luck with that."

I got the coffee gurgling and just stood there, not quite knowing where to begin. Yes, I did. Of course I knew where to begin, I just didn't want to begin. I was operating on no sleep and too much drama and wasn't in the mood to dive off into a battle of wills. Not that there was anything saying I couldn't wait to battle it out later. I didn't have to kick off the morning with it.

I perched on the armrest of a sofa, not wanting to invest in complete comfort till I had my steaming mug in my hand.

"So, how was your night?" I asked. "Didn't get to talk to you last night."

She raised her eyebrows, mocking me. "Yes, I beat *you* home, missy."

I chuckled and rubbed my eyes, remembering the drama of bringing Hayden home and how he kept hugging me and apologizing at the door.

"Yeah. Regular party animal."

"Did you and Aunt Ruthie have fun?" she asked, deterring off of herself.

I opened my mouth and closed it again. "Sort of," I said, finally. "At times."

"What does that mean?" Becca said on a laugh, setting the book in her lap.

"Well, the night had its moments," I said. "Good and bad."

She gave me another haughty look. "Sounds like you *were* a party animal."

I shook my head and laughed quietly. "No. Not those kinds of moments." I wasn't about to tell her that her dad got stupid drunk and tried to brawl it out with my high school boyfriend, or any other highlights for that matter. "What did you and your friends end up doing?"

Becca shrugged and picked her book back up. "Went to a movie, walked around the mall, just stuff."

Just stuff. Love that.

"Get anything at the mall?" I asked, knowing how to find the details if I wanted to.

"Yeah, that little kiosk by the food court with the leather stuff and jewelry? They had bracelets two for one, so I couldn't resist." She grinned and held up her wrists to show off two beaded and braided leather strips. I got up to look closer and smiled.

"Cool," I said. "Very you."

"That's what I thought, too," she said, smiling to herself.

I kissed her forehead and messed up her hair before I headed back to the kitchen for my coffee, batting around my options. On the one hand, I didn't want to ruin a good mood. On the other, being a parent sometimes just had to suck.

"Are we donating to the clothes drive this year?" she asked as I came back in.

I sighed, feeling that familiar Winter Carnival annoyance like a fly buzzing in my ear. Only this year, more so. I attributed that to Noah's return, stirring up things I'd pushed down for years.

"Do you have clothes you want to get rid of?"

"Only so I can make room for new," she said with a cute little grin.

"Well, as long as your priorities are in place."

"I was asked to help with a float this year," she said. "Lizzy's mom and dad are doing one with their four-wheelers, like, I think they're connecting them or something."

Of course they were. The Cleavers. On four-wheelers.

"Oh, cool, that'll be fun," I said, pretending it would be.

"Why haven't we ever done that?" she asked. "We could have done something with Dad's truck."

Because I'd rather be buried alive. "I don't know, Bec, I guess we never jumped on it in time." How old would she be before that excuse stopped playing? "Go through your clothes and get me a bag if you want to donate."

She shrugged. "Okay."

I sank onto the couch next to her with my coffee, sitting sideways to face her while pulling a pillow on my lap. Comfort moves. She put her book down again, looking at me questioningly.

"So, I heard that you have a new boyfriend," I said, a small smile in place, hoping to nail that let's-talk-girl-stuff ambiance.

The change in her eyes, however, told me I didn't. Or that girl stuff wasn't a place she wanted to go with me, at any rate. I saw the walls come up.

"Did you?" she said, her voice edgy.

"Yes, and don't be mad at Ruthie," I said, tugging on her oversized T-shirt.

"Of course not," she said. "Why would I be mad when someone lies to me? Can't imagine."

"She's looking out for you, Bec," I said. "She felt that I needed to know what was—"

"If I wanted to talk to my *mother* about it, I would have," she said, tossing her book on the coffee table. "I thought I was talking to a friend that I could trust."

I licked my lips as the dig hit home.

"Aunt Ruthie *is* a friend, Becca, but she's also an adult who knows that sometimes you have to make tough choices to take care of people you love."

"Well, she won't have to worry about that anymore," Becca said, pushing the blanket off her lap and swinging her pajama-clad legs down. "I'll keep my crap to myself."

"Becca—"

"Seriously, Mom," she said, facing me with the most mature expression I'd ever seen on her. "Of all the people I thought I could trust to keep their mouth shut, it was her. Now I have nobody."

I flinched. "Excuse the hell out of me? You have plenty of somebodies, Becca. You have Ruthie, you have Nana Mae, your dad, your friends—*me*." I narrowed my eyes at her. "You always, always and forever, have me."

"Only if I'm saying what you want to hear," she said quietly.

"That's not true," I said, my mind frantically pulling at itself, wondering if it was. Something was eerily reminiscent.

"Whatever, Mom," she said, getting up.

"Becca, please, sit down," I said. At her look, I gestured to her seat.

Instead of sinking back down, she walked around the coffee table to the opposite sofa and sat, pulling her feet up to her chest and gazing absently at nothing.

It was going well.

"Like it or not, sweetheart, you aren't an adult yet," I said, adjusting my position to face her. "There are things I need to know." At her silence, I took a swallow of coffee, relishing the burn on the way down. "Like who this boy is?"

"I'm sure you already know that," she said flatly.

"How long have you been seeing him?" I asked.

She closed her eyes and gave a tiny head shake, as if she couldn't believe the conversation. Seeing as I'd felt that way the night before, I didn't care.

"A couple of weeks."

"A couple of weeks," I repeated. "And you're asking about birth control?"

She rubbed her face and kept her hand partially covering her eyes. "We aren't talking about this," she said, as if to herself.

"Oh, but we are," I said, her attitude spiking mine. "Do you know that safe sex isn't just about avoiding pregnancy?"

"Fully aware, actually," she said, still resting her face in her hand. "There are these balloon thingies. I think they're called *condoms*."

I swung my feet down and set my mug on the table with a thud, causing a tiny splash to spill over the edge.

"You have some nerve talking to me like that, little girl," I said, her mouth setting off my ire the way it always did.

"I'm not a little girl, Mom—"

"Oh, when you get snarky with me like you think I'm your equal, Becca, that shows me just how little you still are," I said. My tone brought her hand from her face, and I saw the tiniest worry over what she might lose in her eyes. "You want to be treated like an almost-adult, act like one."

Both her hands went to her face on a deep sigh, then she dropped them. "Fine, what do you want to know?"

"Why keep this boy a big secret?" I asked.

"He's not."

"Really? Then why not bring him over here? Introduce him."

She scoffed. "So you can put him through the Spanish Inquisition? No, thanks."

"I don't do that."

"You totally do that," she countered. "You do that with my friends that I'm *not* going to make out with, so God help the ones I do."

"Becca," I said, trying to keep my voice calm and rational. "You are considering something far beyond making out. Something that should be special with someone you love."

"Oh, my God, Mom," she groaned. "Are you seriously trying to sound like an old woman?"

I gaped at her. "Are you seriously trying to be a brainless twit? You want to throw yourself away just to say you've done it?"

"Jesus," she muttered, pressing her forehead against her knees. "I don't want to do anything. I was just asking some questions in case it came up."

Right.

"Well, if he's someone you'll consider falling into bed with if the subject *comes up*, why don't you bring him around?" I asked, knowing full well that wouldn't happen. Especially not now.

"So you can ask him a million questions?" she said, raising her head. "Hover over us in case we accidentally kiss? Have a meltdown if we go upstairs to watch TV?"

"Oh, you won't go upstairs," I said, sitting back and pulling my feet under me.

"Well, of course not," Becca said, melodrama now in full gear. "Because that's rule number 553 of the Julianna White Book of Etiquette. Never, under any circumstances, have a boy in your room. His sperm might jump out and infest you!"

I dropped my head into my hand. "Becca—"

"You must have been a dream child for your parents," she said. "Did you keep a log of your gold stars, too?"

I looked up and stared at her, feeling my skin create a million goose bumps. "No," I said quietly. "I was no dream child. And I'm not expecting you to be. But when I find out that you are talking to someone else about sex when I didn't even know there was a guy in the picture, and then you tell me it's only been two weeks—baby girl, I worry. Somewhere along the way, you got the idea that sex is all physical."

"Oh, my God, Mom," she said, rising to her feet. "No, I don't. But that's what you hear because all you hear is you. This is exactly why I didn't come to you." She gestured around her. "I didn't want a lecture on love and birds and bees. I'm not stupid, Mom."

"I never said you were stupid."

"No, you said I was a brainless twit," she said, snatching her book from the table.

Of all the things I've said in her life, that's what she remembered. "Bec—"

"I'm not a five-year-old, either," she said. "If you'd actually listen to me, and hear me for once, you'd know that—yes, okay, maybe I'm asking questions and I'm interested, but I'm also not an idiot. If I was an idiot, I wouldn't be asking about birth control."

I met her gaze and let a few beats pass. "I just don't want to see you do something foolish and ruin your plans, baby."

Becca let out a long breath and shook her head, walking up the stairs. "Whose plans, Mom? Mine or yours?"

CHAPTER 10

Saturdays were always my biggest days at the store, and at this time of year it jumped up to chaotic at times. Ruthie did a children's story time right before lunch, so many moms could bring their kids for an outing of stories, lunch at the diner, and dessert at the ice cream shop just down the sidewalk. Also, since everyone else with normal jobs had Saturdays off, many of them saved their holiday shopping time for the weekends.

And that was okay.

Normally.

Today, I wasn't in the mood. I knew Noah was next door, having seen his truck parked out front, and that knowledge sat like acid in my stomach. Too much had transpired the night before, and not just the fight. The moment we'd had on the back patio had stirred my blood and gripped my heart, making me relive it on long loop over and over.

You bailed on our son.

And Becca had me irritated, both at her and at myself. The things she'd said had hit home, about being the perfect dream child with all my rules, and about my plans versus hers.

Dream child? Pregnant at seventeen was hardly a dream child, but she didn't know about that. I still didn't know how I'd gotten that lucky, having grown up in the same town, but basically time dulls memories and no one cared much about two dumb kids who got themselves in a pickle. Especially when the child never showed up. Made it easy to forget, I guess. For them.

Nana Mae kept bending my ear about telling Becca, though, before someone suddenly grew a memory, and she was right. I knew she was right. The latest topic, however, made that a little awkward.

I had followed the rules before all that, though. Mostly. But they weren't mine. They were my mother's. Her way of keeping control and order in the life around her, and I guessed I'd grown up to do the same.

Sitting at her counter, in her bookstore, selling one gift certificate after another and watching her customers mill about while Ruthie acted out *Brown Bear, Brown Bear* in the corner amid a mob of little people—and letting that realization settle over me like a blanket, my skin prickled all over. Whose life was I living? Mine or my mother's?

Whose plans, Mom? Mine or yours?

My clothes suddenly felt heavy and hot, and I got up and headed to the back break room for a bottle of water. I got the water, but the leftover Mississippi Mud in the fridge caught my eye as well, and I unwrapped the cellophane-covered plate and pulled out a gooey piece.

"Mmm-mygod," I mumbled around it as the heavenly comfort food excited my taste buds and put me in a chocolate state of Zen.

I heard it from the kitchen. The unmistakable sound of a cane against a wall. My Zen moment melted away with the chocolate down my throat, and I chugged the water on my way out to the sales floor.

Bam-bam.

Feeling like everything inside me was riding on the edge, I fisted my hand and banged back. Pictures rattled on the wall around me and a bronze sign with the saying "No better peace than right here" clattered to the floor. I heard Ruthie's voice halt abruptly, and I turned to see her staring at me along with fifteen sets of little eyes and many of the parents.

"Sorry," I said.

Bam.

That was it. I set my water bottle down on the counter and walked right out the front door, the bell jingling madly behind me. The brisk air hit me full-on, making me suck in a chestful of the cold, thick air, but it felt good. I wanted it to chill everything in me and freeze over.

Noah's truck was gone, and I felt an odd mix of massive relief and the twinge of disappointment. When I pulled open the heavy diner door, warmth hit me again, coupled with the mouthwatering aroma of fried chicken.

But I wasn't there for that. I couldn't show weakness.

I smiled briefly at Linny as she looked up from taking an order, and she winked at me. I walked right up to the counter and stared at the top of Johnny Mack's head as he bent over the grease pits. I was determined to stand there until the force of my will made him look up.

"Hey, Jules," said a voice to my left.

I jerked my head to see Shayna sitting alone at the lunch counter, smiling at me with tired eyes. Some of my ire fizzled down, but a large part of it just started a whole new swirl of uncomfortable.

"Oh—hey," I responded, not moving at first. I glanced back at Johnny Mack, who hadn't budged, and then back to her.

The polite thing to do would be to go talk to her, especially after the night we'd had and the fact that she had been very nice then, too. Everything inside me battled as I wished her not to be so damn nice.

She looked girl-next-door pretty in a long denim skirt and matching jacket, and tall brown boots. It made me fidget with my own boring Ruthie-inspired black sweater and tank top over a black wraparound skirt and leggings. Maybe I felt the all-black would help me disappear. Maybe I wanted to feel as confident as Ruthie. But as I walked closer to Shayna, I felt like an old woman or a school librarian next to her freshness. I could have looked that good thirteen years ago, but I didn't then, either. I was just as boring then.

"Did you have the fried chicken?" I asked, for lack of anything more rousing to say. "It's really good."

"I did have a piece," she said. "With the grilled veggies—really good."

One piece. Great, she ate like a sparrow, too.

She looked sideways at Johnny Mack. "I saw him banging with his cane," she said softly. "That's your store on the other side, right?"

I blew out a breath. "Yes, and he's driving me up a damn tree with that."

"Why does he do that?"

I shook my head. "He says he hears music," I said. "We hardly ever play any music. My mom used to, years ago, but I don't play anything. Linny doesn't even hear it," I said, raising my voice to reach him. "He's off his damn rocker."

I saw his mouth tighten, although he didn't look up, meaning he'd seen me from the get-go and had chosen to ignore me. The muscles in my shoulders tightened into tiny balls as the old hatred spurned by hurt burned deeper into my chest. I took a deep breath and turned away, facing Shayna full-on. I wouldn't let him goad me, not even with his haughty silence, not in front of her.

"So how is everything going?" I asked, with not a clue in hell where I was going with it. She could take that fifty different directions, and I just hoped she'd pick one.

"Good," she said, fiddling with her coffee cup, giving me nothing. Great. "Your ex make it home okay last night?" she asked, her nose crinkling on a cute smile.

I groaned. "That's a memory I'd like to erase. For everyone."

Shayna laughed and pushed her cup away. "Don't sweat it. We all have crazy exes."

"And that's the sad part," I said. "He's not. He's always been the stable one, emotionally. I've never seen him be so idiotic before."

She licked her lips, looking at the counter before meeting my eyes again. "I think maybe it was seeing Noah."

And there it was, the giant elephant.

"Probably," I said quietly.

"More decaf, hon?" Linny asked as she moved down the counter with a pot in each hand.

"No, thank you," Shayna said, holding up a hand.

Linny questioned me with her eyes and I shook my head that I didn't need anything so she could keep going. I couldn't have any of these conversations around her; I never had in all these years. Not once did I ever talk to her about her brother, or giving up the baby, even though she always remained nice and chatty with me and even sent a beautiful card when Becca was born. It was like an unspoken agreement between us. We'd talk about Johnny Mack being a dick, and we both knew why, but we didn't go there. And it was like Noah never existed.

With him back now, I knew she was keeping a bit of a distance to avoid conversation that might go past "Hello" and "Here are the specials," and that was okay. I didn't know what to say, either.

"When he first came to the table, I thought it was an old friend of Noah's," Shayna said, bringing me back. "But when Noah went into his—glazed-over mode," she said with a gesture at her eyes, "I realized it was the guy you'd been dancing with earlier."

My stomach churned with the uncomfortable air that settled around us. "What did Hayden say?" I asked.

"Oh, he introduced himself, we did, too, it was all fine until he made some comment about me keeping Noah on a tight leash."

"Oh, my God," I said into a hand I'd raised to hide behind.

"Yeah, it pretty much went downhill from there."

I dropped my hand. "Shayna, I am so sorry."

She chuckled silently. "It's okay, Jules. I'm a big girl."

"I know, but—" I stopped and breathed in deep and let it out. "I know you have probably been swamped with Noah's past since you crossed into Copper Falls, and it keeps landing on you at every turn."

Sharla Lovelace

She laughed out loud, transforming her face into stunning again. "Very true."

"You handle it so damn well," I said. "I want to grow up and be you one day."

She giggled again and touched my hand. "Never fear, I'm not as secure as I look."

"Well, then you fake it like a pro."

She tilted her head, her face morphing into a mask of professionalism. "My daddy taught me to smile through pain, never to give your hand away, and shake hands like a man."

I raised an eyebrow. "Wow."

Her face relaxed back into reality. "Yeah, my dad didn't have any boys."

I laughed out loud, realizing I felt truly relaxed for the first time in a week. Damn it, this girl could actually be my friend. If she weren't— something else. The thought sent my gaze to her left hand, and my mind flew back in time to a piece of string that turned into a tiny gold band with a sparkly chip on top. Shayna sported a white-gold ring with a large square-cut diamond and smaller ones headed down the sides. It was gorgeous. And expensive. I wondered if he'd tied a piece of string around her finger first.

"So speaking of boys," I began, feeling braver in our conversation. "Do you know what you're having?"

The light in her eyes faded instantly, although the smile remained tacked in place. One hand rested against her belly protectively. I remembered that feeling.

"Not yet," she said. "Not sure if I'm going to. I'm kind of old school like that. I want the surprise."

"I did, too," I said, thinking only of Becca. I didn't even let myself go anywhere else. "I know what you mean."

"So—how was it when you were pregnant?" she asked, meeting my eyes with an odd look. For a hair of a second I wondered if she *was*

126

talking about the other one. Noah's. I opened my mouth, but it went dry as my heartbeat sped up. "I mean, was the dad all involved in it or was it mainly just you?"

The strange question took me off guard even more than my fear of which pregnancy she was talking about. I licked my lips so they'd function again.

"Um—yeah, he was very involved, wanted to know everything, feel every kick." Both times. I remembered Noah kissing my belly good-bye every day. Hayden spooning me, sleeping with his hand palming my stomach, holding both of us. "I was lucky," I said, never realizing that before.

"Yes, you were," she agreed.

I couldn't get a read on her mood, but it had definitely shifted. "Well, I'm sure you have that, too," I said, pushing to lighten the air. "Just keep him up on all of it, because they don't have the advantage we do, of our own little personal dance party going on twenty-four-seven. They just get to look in the window."

Shayna smiled again, chuckling at that as she looked down thoughtfully. "Good point."

"You may want to ask mommy advice from someone who values the role," said a scratchy voice to my right.

We both turned to see Johnny Mack standing behind the counter in front of us, having come around from the kitchen without either of us noticing.

"What?" I breathed.

Without looking at me, he wiped his hands on his apron and patted Shayna's hand. "You care about family, honey. This one doesn't. She throws one kid away and never thinks of him again while she raises another to be a heathen."

My eyes filled with instant tears and every molecule of my body lit up with a blaze of heat. His image swam before me and all I could hear was my own breathing. I couldn't even look at Shayna. I felt her grip my hand, and I blinked the tears down my face.

"Don't say things like that," I heard her say quietly.

"Honey, you don't know—" he began, again pretending I wasn't there.

"What's wrong with you?" I whispered, my voice too shaky to go louder. "You don't talk to me for years, and then you go spewing poison like that."

"I'm still not talking to you," he said, focusing on Shayna. "I've fixed your screwups."

"You've done *what*?"

"I'm not talking to you," he repeated slowly, looking me in the eye for the first time. "I'm telling Shayna what I know—"

"You don't know anything," I said, not recognizing the raw gravelly tone coming from my throat. I pushed away from the counter. "And how dare you insult Becca like that, you miserable old fuck. You aren't even lucky enough to know her."

"I don't need to," he said, leaning over the counter, his wrinkled face older than I remembered noticing. "I have real grandchildren to get to know. My blood."

I backed up, noticing Shayna's shocked face drain even paler as she stared at Johnny Mack. I was oblivious to the tears running down my face.

"Rot in hell, old man," I said, the words choking me even as my hatred for him overwhelmed me. Once upon a time I'd loved him like a father. He'd treated me like his own. It broke my heart and hardened it at the same time. "And you bang on that wall one more time," I said through my teeth, pushing forward again, "and so help me, I will personally come over here and rip everything off of yours. *Do* you hear me?"

He grabbed a towel and began wiping down the counter as if I'd never been there. Sobs bubbled up and I turned and bolted through the door, pushing a lady out of my way and barreling straight into Noah's arms.

"Whoa," he exclaimed, wrapping his arms around me to stabilize us both before looking to see who he'd caught. "Jules, what's—"

I broke free without speaking and pushed past him.

"Jules, wait, what's wrong?" he said, following me.

"Leave me alone, Noah."

If I'd only had my purse with me, I would have headed straight for my car and driven home. In lieu of that, I yanked open the door to the bookstore and prayed he'd stop.

He didn't, and the barrage of questions trailed behind me all the way to the break room, the swinging door bouncing in his wake. I whirled on him, adrenaline sending a new wave of hot tears over the edge.

"You're not allowed back here," I said, my voice shaking with anger.

"Deal with it," he said, looking at me with exasperation. "What happened over there that's got you so upset? Surely, Shayna didn't—"

I laughed, a bitter sound I didn't even recognize. "Are you kidding me? Shayna is like the nicest person on the planet. I didn't think it was even possible to be that good."

A tiny look of relief passed over his face. "What, then?" he demanded.

I scoffed, remembering the horrid words and trying to shove the burning sob down that wanted to split me in half.

She throws one kid away and never thinks of him again . . .

It won. A noise of pain escaped my throat, and I hissed in a breath to quell it.

"Ask your father," I spit out, turning away.

I headed for the fridge, wanting to stick my head in the freezer, but the grip on my upper arm stopped me.

"I asked you," he said roughly as he spun me around.

We both inhaled sharply as we landed together and found ourselves nearly nose to nose. I blinked tears free, bringing Noah's face into perfect focus. His quickened breath felt warm on my face, and all the hard lines of his expression dissolved when he searched my eyes.

"Shit, Jules," he said under his breath, so softly it was nearly inaudible.

One of his hands went to my face as if on autopilot, and I shut my eyes tight as the warmth of his hand against my cheek and hair nearly broke me. I could smell him, feel him, and I didn't dare open my eyes to look at him. He'd see it.

"Noah, don't," I whispered through broken breaths. I reached up to pull his hand away, but then the other side of my head was cradled as well, and all my strength melted away. My grip on his hand stayed where it was, and I could feel the slight tremble. Or was that me?

I didn't open my eyes until I felt his thumbs move across my cheeks, wiping away tears, and it hit me in the chest like a wrecking ball. He looked like someone had beaten the crap out of him from the inside. His eyelids were heavy, like a man who hadn't slept in days. The turmoil radiating off of him was palpable.

That, plus the feel of his hands in my hair, the closeness of his body, so close I could feel him breathe, it was almost too much. His eyes went to my mouth, and for a second it was like ropes were pulling us together. I could nearly taste him.

"What did he do?" Noah asked finally, halting the forward motion, his voice hoarse and strained.

I shook my head as much as I could inside his hold. I wasn't going to pit him against his father, and I didn't want another fight. "It's my battle with him," I said. "It has been for years. He just"—I stopped to pull it together as the burn jabbed at me again—"crossed the line today."

"I'm sorry."

"You don't need to be."

Everything in me wanted to wind my arms around him and pull him the rest of the way in, to feel his lips come down on mine, but I shoved that thought away. That was from a lifetime ago. The old us. Before a baby and parents and an ocean and two decades separated all that we were. I grasped his hands instead to pull away gently and backed up a half step, still holding on.

"We can't help who our parents are," I said.

A look that felt like an eternity passed between us, full of so many things I couldn't read and yet couldn't look away from. Then he slowly pulled his hands from mine, running them over his face and up through his hair as he walked around the tiny break room.

The moment was broken, but something had shifted. The walls that weren't really walls but more of a respectful barrier had gone wiggly. From last night's moment on the back patio to just seconds earlier, the push-pull thing between us had taken on a life of its own.

My feet had taken root in the cheap carpet when he touched me, but I refused to stand there like a stunned statue. I refused to let Noah see what he could still do to me. Forcing myself into motion, I made it to the fridge, swiping the tears from my too-warm face on the way. With shaking hands I grabbed two waters and held one out to him, thinking he might need the cold as much as I did.

He stopped by the sink and took it from me, leaning back against the counter and draining half of it in two swallows. He took a deep breath and crossed his arms, letting his gaze fall on me again like there were a thousand questions to ask. There weren't. He looked like he felt safer over there, but the room wasn't big enough for me to share that opinion. The mere six feet separating us seemed like two, and it was as if all the air had been sucked from the room.

"Why are you still here, in this store?" he asked finally, holding up his hands quickly. "And don't take that wrong or get mad at me. It's just a question."

Just a question. I was learning that nothing was that simple with him now. I wanted to ask him why *he* was still here in this store. Like, instead of next door with his woman.

"Why did you come back to Copper Falls?" I asked.

He narrowed his eyes and paused for a second. "Family."

"Ditto," I said, tilting my head like Ruthie would. Like she would likely come in and do any minute after watching Noah follow me back there. "I'm here because my mother wanted me to take this on."

He shook his head. "It's different."

"How?" I said, laughing. "Because it's me and not you?"

"No, because I came back on my own," he said quietly. "No one wrote up a map and a guidebook and demanded I follow it."

I felt my jaw muscles tighten, my shoulders following close behind. That was good. Angry and closed off was better than emotional and wanting to dive under his clothes.

"Once upon a time, you were my best friend, Noah," I said, keeping my voice low and nearly quiver-free. He blinked and pulled in a long breath, telling me I'd hit a nerve. "But you've been gone a long time. I don't pretend to still know you like I used to. So don't judge my life like you've been here to see it."

There was another of those pensive looks of his, and I had to look away to keep from getting pinned to the floor again. I drained the last of my water and tossed the bottle in the trash, finger-combing my hair back. I needed to stay in that mode. No more damn tears, especially not in front of him.

"I'm not judging you, Jules," he said. "Or I'm not meaning to come across that way."

"Well, you're failing, then."

He pushed off the counter and came to stand in front of me again, crossing his arms for a sense of distance. Or possibly to keep from touching me. "No disrespect to your mom, but she and I never saw eye to eye."

"Really?"

"Really," he said, his voice harder, rising to my bait. "She worked you like a puppet back then, and—" He breathed in and out as if weighing his words. "I guess I always hoped you'd get out from under her one day."

I felt my chin tremble, but it wasn't from sadness, it was from my blood boiling.

"She died," I said through my teeth. "I'm not under *anyone*."

He shook his head just slightly, his eyes boring into mine. "Twenty-six years and you're still here doing her bidding. Running a store you wanted no part of, giving up on what made you—"

"How dare you," I seethed, pushing forward, not caring how close that put me. "You come back here after all this time and dare to tell me where *I've* gone wrong. You told me last night that I didn't know the life you'd lived, well right back at you, babe." My voice quivered with anger this time, and I didn't care. "Everything I've done since you left has been on me. Every choice, every path I've chosen has been alone. Even when I was married, I was alone in my own head. You think you had to go overseas to be alone with your pain?" I poked him in the chest. "I was in a whole damn town full of people and was completely by myself."

He grabbed my hand when I poked him, eyes flaring. I got the feeling that people didn't dare do that to him. Well, then he shouldn't have come back, because I didn't give a rat's ass at that moment about his aggression or pride or who he was in that other world.

"What happened to art school?" he pushed.

"Jesus, why do you care?" I breathed. "And why do you remember that?"

He used my hand to pull me in to him, jaw muscles twitching. He looked intimidating, but I was too torqued to let him mess with my head like that. I held my chin up higher and glared right back at him, pushing back the turmoil I felt in my own core at being held tightly against him. That didn't matter.

"I remember everything," he whispered through his teeth.

"Well, if you were so damned concerned about where I'd land"—I pulled my hand free and pushed at him; it only pushed me back instead—"then what kept you on the other side of the world?"

The thin white scar above his lip twitched. My heart sped up as I realized what the new thing was about him that made me so crazy. The softer he looked and spoke, the higher his engine cranked, so that talking up close and personal felt like a lightning show.

"Maybe I couldn't stand to see everything ripped apart," he said. "It was easier to start over."

"Easier," I repeated, smiling. "How convenient for you."

His blue eyes went dark. "Don't go there."

"Oh, you already did," I said, moving back to lean against the counter where he'd previously been. I gripped the edges so he wouldn't see my trembling. "You don't have the market on self-righteous anger, Noah. I've got a little of that myself. You followed me in here, and you're welcome to leave if it's uncomfortable now. If it's *easier*."

I knew I was playing with fire, even as the words fell out of my mouth. I expected to see the rage I'd seen the night before. Maybe he'd come pin me to the counter and yell at me. Maybe he'd storm out and leave and not come back. He didn't do either of those things.

Instead, his face went stony, and he took two slow steps in my direction before stopping and shoving his hands in the pockets of his jeans. It was an odd tack, and while initially bewildering, I saw the barely restrained energy pulsing through him. What was intended to be a casual stance of nonchalance was given away by the tightness in his shoulders and arms and a tiny twitch by his right eye. He focused on my mouth instead of my eyes and looked like he was ready to either chew me up or kiss me, and that thought was the one thing that did make my knees go weak.

"I'm listening," he said slowly, robotically. He'd flipped a switch somewhere.

"I'm done," I whispered. I truly had nothing left. Between Noah and his dad I felt like I'd just run ten miles in the sand with boots on.

His head moved almost imperceptibly, and just as he was about to speak, the door opened slightly. Ruthie stood halfway in, one eyebrow raised in question as she looked from me to Noah and back again.

"Everything okay?" she asked.

He never turned around, never took his gaze off my face, and as I met his eyes I realized it might never be okay.

"It's fine," I said.

She nodded slowly and backed out, not looking entirely convinced. I wasn't, either. But I was too tired to do the leaving. He needed to go.

"Noah, it's been a shitty morning and looks to be an equally dismal afternoon," I said, rubbing at my face. "Can you just go?"

"Tell me about after I left," he said in a low, toneless voice.

I wanted to scream.

"No."

I pushed off the counter and made to walk past him, choosing to leave if he wouldn't, but he reached across my middle to stop me, holding me at my waist.

"Please." His face was still a mask, but his eyes looked different. Haunted, maybe.

"It doesn't change anything, Noah," I said, taking his hand off my waist but suddenly unable to let it go. It felt right, holding his hand, his arm, like in that one second we were who we used to know. It was disconcerting, and I averted my eyes. "It doesn't change how you feel about me. You feel like I bailed, I feel like you did, and your dad thinks I'm the Antichrist. None of it matters now." I squeezed his hand. "I may have signed those papers, but it's not like I wanted to. And you left me to deal with the fallout of it all by myself, with a daily dose of your father to make damn sure I paid the price."

I let go of him and went back to the fridge for another water bottle, not offering him one this time. Not even looking at him. I couldn't get through even the summarized version if I did. I put the icy cold bottle on the back of my neck, closing my eyes as the cold chilled down my blood.

"My parents pretended it never happened," I said, keeping my eyes shut. "No one talked about it, no one grieved with me but Ruthie. The days went by in my house as if he never exis—" I swallowed back tears, determined not to cry again. "Even when Becca came along years later, everyone acted as if it were the first time, even my mother. She gave me pregnancy tips like I'd never been there before."

"Did Hayden know?"

The thickness of his voice, heavy with emotion, pulled me out of my reverie, and I opened my eyes. His face was tight and his eyes reddened as if he were fighting tears himself.

"Yes." I looked away and twisted the cap off my water. "He pulled me out of a self-destructive place, and I loved him for that. I always told him the truth."

"Which explains last night."

I let out an exhausted breath. "Not really. He's never acted like that. I'm sorry," I said. "He just—" I swallowed hard against the guilt that always danced there. "I learned early on not to count on anyone but myself, and I guess he had too many years of being on the losing end of that."

I took a deep breath and held my head up as I watched his expression change. He turned and walked slowly to the door, stopping before he reached it and putting his hands on his hips like he knew he needed to keep walking but couldn't. My chest burned with that same need to stop him.

"I'm done with this, Noah," I said to his back quietly, thankful he wasn't looking at me. "I really don't want to talk about it anymore. I've got my own problems, and you have a second chance at fatherhood sitting right next door."

He nodded, not turning around, and pushed through the door as I took a deep breath and sagged against the counter. There weren't any more tears. I was just exhausted. Mentally, emotionally, and physically spent.

I covered my face with my hands, still seeing his face—his eyes—in my mind. So close I could have kissed him three different times. *Shit, shit, shit.* Everything we used to be in another lifetime was still there, pushing and tugging and teasing. It wasn't just my imagination. I'd seen it in his eyes as well.

I had to stay away from him. That was all there was to it.

CHAPTER 11

I needed normal. Like, in a big way.

I needed to just come to work, do my job, go home, argue with Becca, go to bed, and do it all over again the next day. Well, Becca's piece of that pie was still covered, but not in a comfortable way. And what wasn't in the pie, but basically the whipped cream on the side—no pun intended—was Patrick. Or someone like Patrick. Someone to feed that adult side of me that didn't require major maintenance or deep feelings.

Unfortunately, I'd probably burned that bridge, and I felt bad about that. Not for me, but for him. He was a good guy and treated me like a queen. He even had started to pick up on things—little things that were important to me. Like a boyfriend might do. Which put him back in that maintenance category that probably needed trimming back. Just maybe not in the manner I'd trimmed it.

And now, with the current change in tide, I wouldn't have been satisfied with the side of whipped cream anymore, anyway. I wanted more pie. The original pie.

I was screwed.

Ruthie kept eyeing me for the next hour as I pulled extra copies of older titles from the shelves and loaded them into a box for donation to the library. My mother used to make a big event of that, advertising for people to come drop off their used books, making little stickers to attach to the insides of the books that said, "Donated with love and sparkles from Book Enchantment."

I just couldn't get into all that. Ruthie would if I gave her half a chance, but I didn't have the patience. I needed to stay busy and not hover and obsess over Becca's life, and not think about mine at all. Anything was better than what wanted to invade my thoughts.

"Hey, did you turn in an idea for the store decoration?" I asked, completely not caring whatsoever. And she knew that.

"Yes, ma'am," she said with a wink.

"And?"

"And I'm on it," she said, haughty little head tilt in play. "Don't worry about it."

"Works for me," I said, already not worrying about it.

"Are you okay?" she asked when I tossed the box on a chair. She stopped me and made me look at her. "Seriously?"

I swallowed and nodded. "Yes." Then I shook my head. "No. But it's okay."

"I worry about you," she said, her dark eyes soft.

A small smile relaxed my face muscles. "I know. I'm good, I promise. I'm gonna go—" I pointed at the box and lost my train of thought as I gestured toward the door.

"To the library?" she asked, squeezing my arm.

"That would be it."

"Yeah, you're good, all right," she said with an eyebrow cocked. Conceding, she let out a sigh. "Headed over there right now?"

I grabbed my purse and balanced the box on one hip. "Good a time as any."

"Because there's an awesome old rocking chair over at the Brass Ass I want you to look at when you get a chance."

I blinked. "A rocking chair."

"For story time," she said. "It's beat up, but Frank can restore it and make it look really cool."

I nodded. "I thought you hated that place."

The Brass Ass was an antique-slash-resale shop on the other side of town. They were annoying. They had a brass donkey on the lawn.

"I do," she said. "I like the barn better, but the rocker can't help where it ended up."

The barn was an actual old barn turned into a junk business the next block up and run by the Barneses. Old Tin Barnes. Too cute for me, but Ruthie had an antique fetish. And Copper Falls was proud of its discards.

"Okay," I said, palming my keys. "Brass Ass. Rocking chair. Is there more than one? Do I need a guide?"

"Nope, just the one," she said. Her eyes searched mine, though, always seeing too much. "I can go rip some ass, I'm telling you," she said.

I smiled. I wasn't feeling it, and I knew she knew that, but I smiled anyway. "No ass ripping necessary. It's all fine."

"Didn't look fine."

"Appearances are deceiving," I said, walking toward the door. "If you really want to rip somebody, though, go cut Johnny Mack's tires or something."

"Really?"

I gave her a look over my shoulder. "No."

"Whatever you said to him, by the way," she said as my hand landed on the door handle, "he looked ready to lose it."

I stopped, knowing the *him* wasn't Johnny Mack, and stared out the window to the trees behind the gazebo.

◆　◆　◆

It took me a few minutes to get on the highway and drive the few exits down to the Katyville Public Library, the same highway that took me everywhere. Including two trips to the hospital to give birth. The radio crooned a love ballad, and I stabbed at the button with my finger. The next station's DJ made a comment about an hour of eighties music, and I snapped the power off, rubbing a temple to ease the dull headache coming on.

It wasn't worth my sanity.

When I pulled into the library's parking lot, I avoided the side area that was closer to the building but so cramped that it was difficult to get your car out unscathed. Choosing the longer walk with a heavy box, I pulled in and parked.

Just as I was tugging the box from the backseat and fighting a snag against the door, all my senses took note of a dark-blue truck with shiny chrome trim pulling in next to me.

"Seriously?"

I didn't think I could take another Noah encounter just yet. It was going to go badly. Furious at the turn of my day and trying to stomp back all the sensations that kept attacking me every time he made an appearance, I yanked one last time to free the box of books.

And out it came. Knocking me off balance as the box toppled and all the books scattered on the pavement around me.

I will not cry. I heard the door open and shut, and I pulled anger from every cell in my body to help overcome feeling like a weak klutz. I braced myself for his voice, but what I got was significantly lighter.

"Jules?" It was Shayna. "Oh, my Lord, let me help you."

I looked up in surprise as she hurried to kneel beside me and pluck the books up as the wind riffled their pages. Shayna driving Noah's truck around—like a couple. *They are a couple*, I chided myself.

I was struck with relief, gratefulness, and then guilt as I remembered her fiancé's hands in my hair earlier, wiping my tears and coming so damn close to kissing me. I doubted she'd be on her hands and knees in a skirt helping me if she knew about that.

"Thank you," I said, tossing an armful into the box, no longer caring if they were straight. "God, it's been a day."

She blew out a breath and shook her head, little pieces of hair blowing into her face. "I know, I'm so sorry."

Oh. No. She had no idea. Johnny Mack's insults were a distant buzz in the back of my head, spurring my headache on. That had been bad, but what had my heart pumping pain into it was Noah.

"I couldn't believe—" she continued. "I mean, I know you said something about him the other night, but that was just—uncalled for."

I nodded, choosing not to let my emotions be pulled back in again. "You'll find that he doesn't have a filter, Shayna, he just says whatever is there." I forced out a chuckle. "You'd think I'd be immune to it by now."

I felt the pause.

"You and he were close once, weren't you?" she asked, grabbing one more wayward paperback hiding behind my tire.

My first reaction was to lie and make some off-the-cuff remark about how no one could ever be close to Johnny Mack Ryan. But something about Shayna made me feel that I could be honest. In some things. Things that didn't involve me wanting to undress Noah and lick him.

"A million years ago," I said on a laugh, scooping my hair out of my face. "Before—" I said, glancing her direction. "Well—before. He used to make cookies for all Noah's friends when we were young, and they had the good backyard with all the trees, so it was kind of the place to be."

We rose at the same time, and I saw the questions in her face before she asked them.

"And when you were together?"

I nodded and smiled over the pinprick to my midsection. "It was good until it wasn't. Why?"

She blinked a couple of times, appearing to ponder that. "Because if he'd always been mean, he wouldn't have the power to hurt you."

I chuckled and looked at the pavement. "Very true." I shifted the box of books onto my hip and started walking, wishing for a subject change as she fell into step beside me. "So what brings you over here?"

She laughed lightly and grinned a little sheepishly. "I wanted a book."

I raised an eyebrow. "I know a closer commute."

Her laugh grew melodic. "I know, I'm so crazy. But I didn't know if it would be awkward—me coming over there."

I scoffed. "I take everyone's money equally," I said, making her snicker again.

"Well, I'll keep that in mind," she said. "Now if Noah would just relax."

My stomach clenched and I gripped the box tighter. "What do you mean?"

"I mean, he's so paranoid we're going to end up in the same room or something," she said. "Like we're gonna compare notes."

I laughed, but it was an uncomfortable laugh, and I felt he might be right. Just talking about him with her was giving me the willies.

"And he's been so moody the last two days. Today when he got to the diner he was somewhere else completely, not listening to anyone, so I dropped him at home and told him to have a beer and tell me how to find the library," she said. She held up her palms as if to justify. "He'd do that a lot when he was working, so it's not new to me. Everything was classified and everything ate him up until it was done. But, my God, we're just sitting here in this sleepy little town, what could be so damn stressful?"

My mouth opened and closed, and I turned to focus on the doors ahead, spotting Becca's little blue Chevy parked on the side. Where all the cars were jammed together. A new irk joined all the rest in my brain as I thought about her not telling me she was going anywhere, parking where I'd specifically told her was a guaranteed fender bender, and Noah's apparent mood change after our encounter. I felt a sweat breaking out.

"Well, coming home is probably an adjustment," I said, turning to face her before we went in. "He's about to be a dad—and a husband." And I said that with not a bit of stutter.

The light left her face. "Yeah."

I was taken off guard by that and wasn't sure how to respond. It wasn't like we were best friends or anything tight enough to dig around. She wasn't Ruthie. I couldn't threaten to take her mixer away if she didn't spill the goods.

I bit my lower lip. "You okay?"

"Yeah," she repeated, distracted. She twisted her fingers together and averted her eyes. "Can I ask you a question?"

Oh, shit.

"Okay," I said, not actually feeling okay about it. Her face said it wasn't going to be okay. It wasn't going to be something innocent like who cut my hair or where I got my necklace.

Her eyes met mine, blinking fast. "Do you think things really happen for a reason? Like—you know—every purpose under Heaven and all that?"

Wasn't what I expected. "Um, yeah, I guess so." My mind reeled, looking for the reasons behind that question. "I've always kind of had to believe that, it got me through some rough times."

"That's what I mean," she said, her pretty face going serious. "I worry about stuff like that. My mom's always been one for 'Give it to God, things happen like they're supposed to,' and all that, but—"

She stopped, and I was intrigued.

"But what?" I asked.

"What if I'm not making the right choice?" she asked, her voice fading at the end and the color in her cheeks fading with it.

I blinked and pushed down the feeling of impending shock that wanted to land on me before I even knew what she really meant.

"About what, Shayna?" I asked.

She licked her lips and her eyes misted. "About marrying Noah."

◆　◆　◆

It felt as if all the air in my lungs was sucked out with a vacuum cleaner. Oh, my God.

I stared at her, trying not to look shocked or disturbed or confused as hell. I must have pulled one heck of a bluff if she was able to admit any reservations about her relationship with Noah to me. It went against all brands of woman code to show weakness with your man's ex. Then again, I realized, she was new to town and alone except for Noah, and I was probably the closest thing she had to a friend in Copper Falls. That just proved how truly twisted up the situation was.

"That's just nerves," I said on a whisper.

"I don't know," she answered with a forced smile as she dabbed at her eyes.

"You've got double-duty hormones going crazy, too, so don't let your mind mess with you like that," I said, wondering where the words were coming from. "And my ex-husband's floor show probably didn't—"

"We were about to break up again when I got pregnant," she blurted, two heavy tears breaking free from her eyes. She instantly sucked in a deep breath and blew it out slowly like the words had been strangling her. All the color came rushing back to her cheeks.

And probably to mine, as well.

"Ag—" I stopped and cleared my throat. "Again?"

"Jesus," she breathed, covering her face with her hands. "What is this, true confessions day?"

My box suddenly felt like it grew in poundage, and I shifted it on my hip. "Let's—go inside, Shayna," I said, pulling the door open. "We can go sit down."

I needed the seconds to pull my head together as well. Okay, pregnancy before marriage happened all the time; that was no shocker. It had been the same with me, and Noah was trying to make sure he did it right this time. That explained him revisiting so much of our history, too. It probably felt like déjà vu.

But being about to break up—again—that was a whole new head spin.

"No, I should just go," she said, looking back toward the parking lot, her eyes looking troubled again. Probably that woman code slapping her in the face.

"Come on," I said, guiding her in. I pointed at a group of couches and chairs in a far corner. "Let me go turn these in and I'll meet you over there."

"Mom, what are you doing here?" said a voice behind me.

I wheeled around and handed Becca the heavy box. "Hey, Bec, help me out a second."

"This is your daughter?" Shayna asked, swiping quickly at her eyes.

I smiled. "Yes, this is Becca." I put my arm around her neck and squeezed her in a hug that I hoped she was smiling for and not looking tortured. "Bec, this is Shayna Baird. She's—" How to explain? Becca didn't even know Noah. "She's Johnny Mack's son's fiancée."

Shayna chuckled and shook Becca's free hand, and I was proud of myself for not choking on the word.

"Nice to meet you," Becca said, very polite. "I didn't know Johnny Mack had a son. Thought it was just Linny."

I saw Shayna's eyes dart to me for a split second and then she did her practiced smile. "He's like the prodigal son returning."

Becca laughed and then gestured at the box on her hip. "Reason?"

"Bring that up to the counter for me, please," I said. "Those are donations from the store. Why are you here, by the way?"

"Lizzy had a book on hold for a project, and I said I'd meet her here before we go to the mall," she said, just as the blonde and perpetually cute Lizzy walked up.

"You're going to the mall?"

"I texted you all this." At my questioning look, she rolled her eyes. "Okay, I was going to text you all this. I forgot."

"Who's going?" I asked, still fixated on the image of her hooking up with the mystery Mark.

"Me and Lizzy," she said slowly, with the tinge of last night's argument still blanketing her as well. "There's a shoe sale at Epic, can I have some money?"

"No!" I said. "You just got three new pairs of shoes and a pair of boots at Christmas."

"Then I'll buy some boots for you and we can share," she said, cheesy smile in place as she looked hopeful.

"Right, like I'm gonna want to wear your boots," I said. I pulled three twenties from an inner pocket of my purse. "Consider it toward your birthday."

"Hey, Ms. White," Lizzy said with a sweet smile.

"Hi, Lizzy, good to see you," I said. "Shop smart, Becca."

"Sixty dollars? That's all?" she said, eyeing the bills with dismay.

I scoffed. "If you need more than that for shoes, it's not a sale, Bec. Make it work."

"Don't argue," Lizzy whispered.

"Fine," she said, hugging me briefly. "Oh, by the way, they invited me over for a big barbecue thing later, that okay?"

Of course they did.

"That's fine," I said as she turned to make a beeline for the counter with my box. "And be careful leaving the parking lot since you parked—"

"In the pit of hell, I know," she said, waving as she kept walking. "I will."

I took a deep breath, watching them walk away, Becca's dark shiny lopsided hair swinging over a baggy hoodie jacket and jeans she could have painted on.

"Can't wait," Shayna said with a smirk.

I chuckled and shook my head. "Yeah. Luckily they start out sweet and unable to talk so you can fall in love with them before you get that."

I pointed in Becca's direction. Shayna laughed out loud, some happiness coming back into her face. "Let me go get the receipt for this and I'll meet you over there."

When I rejoined her in the corner, she had her game face back on, and I wondered if she'd had a chance to dial it back and change her mind. I would if it were me.

"She's beautiful, Jules. Stunning, actually."

That warmed my heart. "Thank you," I said, sinking onto a couch sideways to face her. I had the oddest sense of a repeat performance since I'd just talked to Becca the same way the night before. Hopefully the outcome would be better. "She has the potential—if she keeps her mouth closed."

"I can imagine it isn't easy being a single mom," she said, leaning an elbow on the back of the couch.

"It's not, but Hayden helps. When she lets him," I added. "She's making us both crazy right now."

"I remember feeling so under my dad's thumb," Shayna said. "I'd do anything just to give him a shock. One time I came home with a nose ring and a dog-collar necklace."

"Holy shit."

She snickered. "I know, it was hideous, but I was just trying to spread myself out a little. Once he let up, I wasn't interested in the weird stuff anymore." She hesitated a beat and tilted her head. "Your daughter doesn't know, does she? About Noah and—everything?"

Everything. I shook my head. "There hasn't been a reason for her to know. It was all before her time."

"And the longer time goes on, it's harder to do," she said, her voice going softer at the end. Guilt settled in my belly, but there was something else there in her tone. Something that maybe wasn't about me.

Shayna picked at a perfect fingernail that didn't need picking, but I knew it was so she wouldn't have to look me in the eye as the real conversation came up to queue.

"It was really good in the beginning with me and Noah," she said,

148

and I dug my not-so-perfect fingernails into my palm. "Of course, it always is. And it was for a long time. I think it was after I moved in with him that things started going south."

I remembered the same thing with Hayden. "Moving in changes a lot of couples," I offered, feeling a little like a therapist on the clock. "Nothing to hide behind anymore."

"Exactly," she said. "He'd—I don't know—he'd get in these moods."

"Moods?"

"He wasn't active in the field anymore, but he was still in top-secret clearance, and the man leaves nothing at the office," she said. "Every funk that went down there with any of the teams would be all over him for days, and when that was over, there would be nightmares."

"Reliving," I said.

"Yes." She scooped her hair back and let it fall. "But all that was okay." She looked up and met my gaze. "I was in love. I would put up with anything."

I swallowed hard and nodded. "So what happened?"

She looked back at her fingers. "He couldn't commit. Couldn't say the words. I wasn't in it for a casual roommate, I wanted the whole show. Love, marriage, family. So we broke up and I left."

"Understandable."

"Oh, but I was miserable," she said on a chuckle. "I couldn't stand it without him. I started going out with anyone who would ask me just to stay busy. I had no filter, it was—bad. One guy wouldn't give up when I called it off, and started stalking me."

"Oh, my God!"

"Yeah, I was so stupid," she said. "If I would have been thinking right, I wouldn't have started up with him in the first place."

"So, what happened?" I asked.

"Noah heard about it from a cop friend of ours that I'd reported it to, and he tracked the guy down." At my apparent questioning look, she added, "It's different in Italy, Jules. A lot of things go beyond the police."

I blinked. "Are you saying—"

"I'm saying I have no idea," she said quietly. "Noah has connections everywhere, Jules, and in that world, a phone call solves a problem in a second." She shrugged. "I don't know what happened and I knew not to ask, but the guy never showed up at my door again."

I rubbed my arms as the goose bumps traveled up and down. It was a side of Noah I never knew about. The dark side he learned on the other side of the world and kept hidden behind those very guarded eyes.

"We ended up deciding to give it another shot after that," she said, looking off at nothing in particular, something worrying her expression. "He retired, so I moved back in, thinking things might be different. We tried, but—"

She shook her head, still looking off, and I felt her pain.

"And then you found out you were pregnant," I said, keeping my voice soft.

She nodded. "He was so happy," she said on a whisper, tears filling her eyes. "I know he loves me, but it never felt like it was enough. He was always so haunted by not knowing his son, I think it's honestly the only thing that could ever fill that hole in his heart."

My chest felt like it would cave in with her words, and I swallowed hard against the burn that wanted out.

She blinked her tears free and swiped at her cheeks, then rested a hand against her stomach. "I felt like this baby could be our saving grace," she said. "Like everything happens for a reason."

Oh, God, she believed that. That holding him with a child would work. I shut my eyes against the sick irony of it all. He left one woman for giving a family away and was trapped with another woman to keep one.

"I just want to give him that," she said, wiping her cheeks free and trying to blink back the rest. "That zoned-out look he gets when he looks at all those pictures. I want him to have what he missed."

I was still breathing through all that she'd told me when something didn't sound right. I went back a few beats and dug till—

"What pictures?" I asked.

"Of his son," she said, as if that were clear.

It wasn't.

I narrowed my eyes and smiled, sure that I had misunderstood. "What pictures are you talking about?"

She frowned, like I wasn't talking sense. "He had all those pictures his dad sent through the years framed and taking over a side table like a shrine."

"Pict—there are pictures?" I said, feeling the words leave my mouth but not really hearing them.

Her frown deepened from confusion to concern. "Jules, why don't you know this?"

There was an odd ringing in my ears, and my fingers felt numb, most likely from the lack of breathing on my part.

Noah had photos of our son. *Noah had photos of our son.* "I don't know," I said, getting to my feet. "I have to go."

CHAPTER 12

I had no memory of leaving Katyville or coming down the highway. It was like I woke up in front of the diner, having gotten there on autopilot. My eyes were hot and dry, like I had used all the liquid up and I was just going to fry from within.

My heart was thundering in my chest and in my ears. *He had all those pictures his dad sent through the years framed and taking over a side table like a shrine.*

How was it possible? How did his dad get them? How could he?

I could go ask the source, I thought, glaring through the diner window all decorated in shoe-polish snowflakes. Linny's contribution. And I would, but Noah was first. He never said a word about photos, and I was driven to find out why and see them for myself. It was a physical ache pulling me to Johnny Mack's house.

Shayna was probably right on my tail, or burning up Noah's phone, but I didn't care. She could watch me rip Noah a new one and then follow me to the diner to get to the truth.

I skidded into Johnny Mack's driveway and had a foot outside before the key was even turned off. I poked at the doorbell three times, then three more for good measure. I'd just started rapping on the wood with my knuckles when the door swung open.

Damn it if he couldn't make me pull in an extra breath, even as pissed off and crazed as I was. Standing there fresh from a shower, barefoot, in gray sweatpants and an old faded Navy T-shirt, his frown turned wary as he saw my face.

"Jules, what are you—"

"Where are they?" I asked.

The frown came back. "Where are—what?"

"The pictures of him," I spat, walking in uninvited and pushing past him and his warm aroma of soap and sexiness. "Where are they?"

"What are you talking about?" he asked, closing the door and following behind me. "Look, Shayna told me what my dad said, and I'm sorry. I talked to him about it already."

I paced the living room I hadn't seen in over twenty years, noting that everything was still in the exact same place. Every piece of furniture, every photograph. Even one of Noah and me at the junior prom, me holding my flowers in front of my nonexistent bump. I was surprised he left that one out. It was like stepping back in time. But there was not one new photograph of a boy. Not anywhere.

"Jules," he said. "Did you hear me?"

I wheeled around to face him. "You had framed pictures of our son in Italy."

Noah blinked and physically moved back a step. "Okay."

I scoffed. "Okay?"

He held his hands up. "What do you want me to say?"

"What do I want—" My heart was pounding so hard I thought I might pass out. "Are you kidding me? Where are they?"

"They're packed up. I don't have a place to live yet, remember?" he said. "What the hell is going on with you?"

Why was he so calm? He wasn't even trying to hide it or deny it.

"Noah," I said, braving the distance and grabbing his T-shirt to get his attention. His sharp intake of breath told me I'd gotten it. "How do you have photos of him?"

He looked down into my face with the same look Shayna had given me. Like I'd lost my mind. "The same way you do." When I just shook my head, he blew out a frustrated breath and pulled free of me. "Hang on a second."

He disappeared down a hallway to what I knew must still be his old room and came back seconds later holding his wallet.

"Look," he said, flipping to the photos. "It's the same ones—"

I sucked in a breath as a face that looked like the male version of Becca when she was little, only with blue eyes, smiled back at me with no front teeth. It swam in front of me as tears reasserted themselves and came forth with a vengeance.

"Jules?" he said, his tone changed.

"Oh, my G—" I choked, taking the wallet from him and touching the photos gingerly as I turned them. "Oh, my God, my baby."

I didn't realize I was backing up until I met with solid wall, and once I did I started sliding down it.

"Whoa, whoa," Noah said, jumping forward and grabbing me by the upper arms. "Hold on, come here."

He attempted to pull me to him, but I pushed back. "Why?" I breathed, turning another and another as the boy got older.

"Seth, 5th grade" was marked on the back of one with neat blue pen.

"Seth?" I choked. "His name is Seth? He has a—oh, my God." It was too much. Suddenly the nameless, faceless little boy I'd mourned for and prayed for the last twenty-six years was a fleshed-out person with a name and a life, and it made the loss even more grueling. "He's beautiful," I breathed.

Noah didn't have them back to back, I realized through my haze, so he could see the years. Ninth grade, eleventh, a cap-and-gown picture, a snapshot of him standing next to a pretty girl, looking less like Becca at that point and more like Noah. And the last one, in a policeman's uniform at an academy graduation, looking very much like Noah, grinning next to two other guys. Men. He was a man now.

"Why—how?" I pushed out. "Where did these come from?" I sucked in a shaky breath. "And why didn't you tell me?"

"My dad sent them," he said. His hand came to my face and tried to lift my chin, but I jerked my face away, not wanting to look away from the little boy I'd last seen when he was two minutes old. "You have these, too."

"No!" I yelled, the sound more of a wail. "I have nothing!" At his shocked face, I pushed him back and walked the room, pressing his wallet to my chest. I gulped in air, unable to get enough, like something was pulling the oxygen from the room. "How did he do this?" I asked, turning to face him, begging with my eyes.

Noah's face showed a myriad of reactions—confusion, disbelief, questions. "I don't understand," he said, more to himself than to me.

"The adoption was sealed, Noah. No contact. How the hell did he get pictures, and"—a sob took over my throat—"I've been here all along. How could he not show me—"

My knees threatened to give way again, and I spurred myself into motion before the feeling could win. Before I'd let this agony overwhelm me, I had to get the facts. Walking straight to the door, I opened it and headed to my car, Noah's wallet still held against my chest.

"Jules, wait," Noah said, springing into action behind me.

"I have to talk to your dad."

"I'm coming with you."

"I don't need you," I said, wheeling on him on the sidewalk. "I have a twenty-year-old beef with him that's about to come to a fucking head right now."

Noah's eyes flared anger that I felt had more to do with my saying I didn't need him than what I'd said about his father.

"You don't need to drive," he said, his voice low and commanding. "Give me your keys, let me put some shoes on, and wait your ass right here."

I felt the muscles in my face, my neck, my whole body twitch with adrenaline.

"Fine," I said, slamming my keys into his hand.

I walked around to the passenger side while he glared at me, and then he turned back into the house. I got in and felt the cold quiet sink in around me, my breathing being the loudest thing. I pulled Noah's wallet away from my chest and started at the beginning. A faded photo that was marked "Seth, 6 months." Just six months after I'd seen him last, it was the closest in resemblance to the baby I remembered.

"I loved you," I whispered, sobs shaking my body again. "I always loved you."

The driver-side door opened and Noah got in, grimacing as his knees crammed against the steering column. He adjusted it and shut the door, giving me a look before he started the engine, an odd expression taking over his features.

"What?" I asked.

He shook his head slightly, almost as if that motion, too, were inside his own thoughts.

"The last time we were in a car together, you were crying then, too." His eyes met mine. "You'd already made up your mind." I looked away, unable to bear looking at him as he said that. "Jules, I didn't know you didn't have these pictures, too. I wondered when there was nothing at your house, but then—and now with what you told me this morning about your parents pretending it never happened." He rubbed at his eyes and raked his fingers back through still-damp hair, making his short cut stick up in little dark spikes. "It all makes sense now."

"It's about to make more," I said.

I turned back to the pictures, running a finger over the last one, the one of Seth in a policeman's uniform.

"That's the last one I ever received," he said, starting the car and putting it in reverse. "That was about four or five years ago. I guess once he hit twenty-one, they stopped sending."

Seth looked so much like Noah in that photo, it was like turning back time.

We were quiet on the drive to the diner. He was right—it was weird being in the car with him again, seeing him at the wheel. Weird and oddly right.

"Who told you I had photos in Italy?" Noah asked finally when we turned onto the street that flanked the river.

"I was talking to Shayna at the library," I said.

He looked at me with a raised eyebrow. "You two get along too well."

I would have laughed at that another time. If my world hadn't been upended and the diner wasn't rolling into view. Instead, every moment of every day that Johnny Mack Ryan had tortured me with his indifference and ugly words came to the surface and spread over me like a giant shield of armor.

Georgette Pruitt was headed up the sidewalk in our direction, looking purposeful and colorful all in purple. Lord.

"Can I have my wallet back?" Noah asked as he pulled in a spot and parked.

"No."

I got out and marched to the door, not caring what my drowned-rat face looked like. Not giving any thought to whether I had dried snot down all my black clothing after the day from hell that had barely made it to one in the afternoon.

Not caring if Noah was with me or stayed in the car. What I had to say was between me and his father, and probably a diner full of people. So damn be it.

"Jules, I need to talk to—" Georgette called out, upping her steps to catch up to me.

"Go see Ruthie," I said, waving her away.

"No, it's about the Chamber party," she said, like that made things different. If I had to hear one more thing about flowers or floats or snowy things, even in a party atmosphere, I was going to do something unladylike.

"Ruthie," I said, already swinging open the door.

I saw him immediately. He was out of the kitchen and behind the bar, refilling coffee during a lull. Good. He'd have plenty of time to give me his undivided attention.

Johnny Mack looked up as I walked in, a scowl clouding his face when he saw it was me before he looked away. Long-buried hurt freshened by recent events stung to the bone.

I slammed Noah's wallet down on the counter, pictures facing up. "Explain."

He let go of a deep sigh, sounding exhausted. "Maybe you should explain what you're doing with Noah's wallet."

"I gave it to her," Noah said from behind me.

Johnny Mack looked up, surprised. "What the hell are you doing with Julianna Doucette?"

"It's White now," I said. "Been that way for twenty-something years now, did you miss the memo?"

"Dad, I told you," Noah said, his voice carrying that dark demanding something that made people listen. "Enough of this."

"You have that sweet Shayna now, boy," Johnny Mack said. "Don't go messing—"

"I could give a shit who your *boy* is with now," I said, my voice rising enough to turn a few heads. I tapped the photos in the wallet. "We're not here for that. I want to know why you have these."

"Not your business," he said quietly.

"Not my *business*?" I said, scoffing. "He's my son."

Johnny Mack shook his head. "You gave up the right to call him that—"

"I said enough!" Noah said, making me jump. He came up to the bar beside me and splayed both hands wide on the counter. "Stop being an ass, Dad, it's beneath you."

Johnny Mack's expression was priceless. Like Noah, not too many people talked to him that way. I watched his jaw muscles work, and he sucked in a breath through his nose.

"I always assumed Jules had these pictures, too," Noah said. "Why on earth didn't you—"

"I know why you didn't share them with me," I said, cutting Noah off, tears burning my eyes and throat again. "You've made that quite clear through the years."

I felt Noah's hand come up to the back of my neck, and I watched Johnny Mack's eyes narrow as he took it in as well. Just the fact that it bothered him gave me courage.

"How could you hate me that much?" I asked, my voice dropping to almost a whisper as I braved out the question I'd wanted to ask for years. Emotion shook my words as they left my mouth. "Do you even remember loving me?"

He looked like he wanted to chew barbed wire as his eyes made a quick dart around the room. "You threw that away when you let that boy go."

"I was *seventeen*," I said, louder than I intended to, tears tracking down my cheeks. "Doing what my mom and dad said was best to do. I didn't want it that way, but I was too scared to say no. They sent me to that god-awful place to show me what being a teenage mother would be like, remember? I was fifty different kinds of terrified."

"I would have helped you," he said, sudden emotions coming to his face, mixed with the old anger.

"Until I told *you* no about something," I said. "Until I pissed you off. You're no better than they were. So I did what I did. And everyone left me." I moved away so that Noah's hand would drop. "I lost my son,

I lost Noah, my parents went into denial, and you spent the next twenty-six years making damn sure I paid for my sins." I slammed a fist on the counter in front of him. "And how dare you insult my daughter today."

His mouth worked and then clamped shut before he sighed with irritability. "I was out of line with that comment earlier, I apologize," he said, staring at coasters on the counter instead of looking at me. It sounded forced, but I didn't care.

"Jules said the adoption was sealed, Dad," Noah said, laying a hand on his open wallet. "How'd you pull that off?"

Johnny Mack grabbed a bar cloth and wiped the length of what he could reach, then gave up with a sigh, rested his hands on the cloth, and met my eyes. "Your mother gave them to me."

◆ ◆ ◆

For the first time in years, there was no animosity in his eyes. No hate. Just—a giving up of sorts. Giving up my mother. Throwing her under the bus. It wasn't possible. My mother was controlling and had done many questionable things in the name of "taking care of people," but it was too far outside the realm of belief.

I shook my head as every nerve ending in my body woke up. "I don't believe you."

Johnny Mack shrugged. "That's your choice, but it's the truth."

"How?" Noah said, moving closer to me again. As if he sensed my impending breakdown.

Johnny Mack met his son's gaze and then looked off into the diner, avoiding my hard stare.

"Mary arranged that as part of the adoption," he said. "That correspondence and two copies of photographs a year would be sent to her, and her only, until he was twenty-one." He darted a look my way and then just as quickly feigned interest in his rag. "She always gave me the second one. I sent them to Noah."

The trembling started at my core, like all warmth had left my body. I gripped the counter to stem it, but it just got worse.

"Why—" Noah began, his voice hoarse. "Why would they agree to that?"

"Mary set up a trust in his name in exchange for it," Johnny Mack said, not looking at either of us.

"No," I whispered. "That's not—" I shook my head, unable to believe that she would have done that to me.

"Why didn't anyone tell Jules about this?" Noah asked, voicing the question I couldn't seem to push out of my mouth. "Or me, for that matter? I didn't know any of that. Dad!" he yelled, when Johnny Mack didn't answer, making the old man jump and turn to face him. "Why?"

"Because Mary didn't think she could handle it," Johnny Mack said with a snarl to his voice and lips. "Okay?" He turned and looked me dead in the eye with both irritation and pity. "I didn't want to say that out loud, but there, you feel better knowing that? She made me promise not to tell you about the pictures or anything related to the boy. She said it was better for you to move on."

My stomach roiled against its contents as every muscle contracted. I grasped Noah's wallet and backed up, running into a customer who I heard offer apologies but I couldn't see. All I could see was Johnny Mack's face, looking at me with something related to remorse, as if saying it all out loud somehow finally highlighted the insanity of it.

Better for me.

I sucked in air as what felt like my mother's final blow knocked the wind from my chest, and as I turned for the door, I suddenly felt weightless. Blackness tinged the edges of my waterlogged vision, sounds of chatter started to echo, and as I reached for the knob it disappeared.

Arms caught me, wrapping around my middle.

"I've got you," came Noah's voice against my ear. He held me tight against him, one arm around my waist and one holding my head as sounds started coming back into normal tones. "Just breathe, baby, I've got you."

Sharla Lovelace

He called me baby, I thought, my woozy thoughts swimming around in the delicious aroma that was Noah.

"I need to go—home," I managed to say as my feet felt solid floor again.

"We're going," he said, lifting my chin to look at my eyes. "Are you okay to walk to the car?"

I blinked and nodded and pulled gently away from him, feeling the odd mix of my body coming back to life as my soul shut down. It was the last straw, the last thing my mind was willing to take on, and my heart felt like it turned cold in my chest.

"Noah," Johnny Mack said from behind us. "There's something I need to tell you. I was going to make it a surprise, but now I think I should tell both of you—"

"Save it," Noah snapped before he led me out the door.

He put me in the car and we drove in silence to my house. I had nothing left. No more tears, thank God; I was completely out of those. Nothing but betrayal and rage coursed through me as we passed the houses I'd seen all my life. As we passed the old one I'd shared with Hayden. That's where I should have stayed, I realized. I should have sold Mom's house when she died and stayed where we were. Away from the negativity and rules and controlling influence that her house still held over me.

She had ruined my life.

We pulled into the driveway, and I stared at the house I now despised with everything in my being.

Noah's phone sang "Love Shack" and he hit the button to silence it.

"Shayna?" I asked, and he nodded. "You can call her back."

He texted something quickly. "Told her I'll call her back later."

"I should have brought you home," I said, not recognizing the hollow sound of my words, my voice.

Noah shook his head and handed me the keys. "I'm not leaving you here alone," he said, his tone leaving no room for argument. "I'll walk the two blocks later if I have to."

My phone buzzed from my purse and I dug it out to see Becca asking to spend the night with Lizzy. Not a shocker. And probably a good idea, considering my mood.

"I'm not good company right now," I said, eyeing the house as if my mother were standing on the porch.

Ignoring me, he got out and walked around to my side, where I still sat, and opened my door. "Come on."

I swung my legs out and stood, letting him shut the door behind me as I walked up to a place that didn't feel like mine anymore. Not that it ever really had, but I was at least making headway. Now none of that mattered. My mother still lived there. Working me like a puppet, just as Noah had said.

I unlocked the door, hearing and feeling him behind me, and heard the ka-thunk of Harley jumping off the couch.

"Hey, my Harley girl," I said as she wiggled over to me, swinging her giant tail. I felt love and relief seep back through for just a second as her unconditional love melted my heart a little. I knelt and buried my face in her neck. "You and the girl-child are the only things that make this home," I mumbled.

Standing as Harley then made her way to Noah to get bonus points, I kicked off my shoes and looked around the room at all I had done to try and make it our home. It was lipstick on a pig, as Nana Mae would say. Nothing changed the guts of the thing. I narrowed my eyes as I scanned the room with a different perspective.

Somewhere in these guts were photos of Seth. Hidden away because I couldn't handle it. I clenched my teeth together at the anger those words fired up in me. Photos and *correspondence*, whatever the hell that could be. But how? We'd gone through every possible drawer and file, both at the house and at the bookstore, when she died. And then many of the older pieces of furniture had been put to the street in favor of ours. I couldn't imagine what I could have missed—

My eyes landed on the bookshelf. Or rather, my mother's corner of it. The section I never really touched, but pretty much just jammed together to make room for my own things.

Walking slowly to it, I stared, adrenaline boiling my blood as I remembered my mother lying in a hospital bed telling Becca and me that she loved us and never mentioning one word about *Oh, by the way, there's something kind of important you might want to find.*

"That bitch," I whispered.

"Jules," Noah said.

"No, Noah," I said, hearing the shake in my voice as the irony spread through my system like poison. "My mother sent my son away, cutting all contact for me but holding on to it for herself." I turned to face him, my whole head feeling like the top of a volcano. "For herself. She still had a grandchild, but I couldn't be a moth—" My words gave way as my chest pushed the air from my lungs. "She gave it to your dad to send to you on the other side of the world, but couldn't share it with her own daughter, right here in the same house."

He just met my gaze and didn't say anything. There was nothing to say.

"She knew his name," I said, the rage bringing tears back to my throat. "For years I've wondered how your dad could hate me so much, and now I have to wonder how my own mother could have had so little fucking faith in me."

Noah moved toward me, but I turned around. Turned to stare at her books and her beloved atlases and precious antique glassware. All collecting dust because I never did more than hit it with a feather duster. I never liked being around it. I always assumed that was due to so many unresolved, unfinished issues with my mother. Or my own guilt over the resentment I felt. Whatever the reasons, I left her things alone.

I pulled a book out, flipped through it, and set it on the floor. Pulled out another one and did the same. Again and again, thick atlases and small books. I moved the glassware to other shelves, and Noah silently picked up the books and began making stacks as I pulled faster and faster, not caring about what they were. Harley sniffed each one tentatively and would then look up at me with her little forehead creased like she wanted to understand the game but wasn't catching on.

I kept tossing and Noah kept organizing, and if he didn't know what I was doing, he didn't say. And although I originally didn't want him there, I found myself glad to not be alone.

It didn't take long.

Two thick volumes on astronomy stuck together as I tried to pull one out. Rather grossed out, thinking something nasty had bonded them together over time, I tried to pry them apart to no avail.

"What the hell?" I said, garnering Noah's attention.

"What's the matter?"

"These are stuck, they're—" I stopped short when I picked them up with two hands and felt the movement within. I stared at the books in my hand, looking closer at the seam between them. Bound with superglue.

My Nana Mae's words about my mother's teenage rebellion sung softly in my ear: *carving out old books to hide things like letters from boys—and her daddy's cigarettes . . .*

"Oh, my God," I whispered, fighting against the burn that wanted to take me under.

CHAPTER 13

"Jules, what is it?" Noah asked, coming to stand beside me, his hand resting on the shelf as he looked down.

I opened the hard cardboard cover, and there it was. My past, my big never-talk-about-it secret. All the things I was never trusted to handle.

A large cavern had been carved into the two books, leaving only an inch of paper around the edges. In the hole were photographs and letters, and something that appeared to be bank statements.

"Son of a bitch," Noah breathed.

I put a trembling hand inside and pulled out a handful of photos. One fell free and I knelt to pick it up. My breath caught as I saw it wasn't one that was in Noah's collection. It was of a man and woman, smiling, holding an infant.

My infant.

A noise escaped my throat, and the book box and other photos slipped from my hands. Noah dropped to one knee when I melted into a sitting position.

"What?"

I held out the picture, one hand over my mouth as if that would hold all the crazy in, and I heard him swear under his breath.

"That had to be—"

"Right after," I finished.

The image swam before my eyes and I kept blinking it clear, needing to see the people that raised my child. That taught him to say *Mommy* and *Daddy* and how to ride a bike. That kissed his hurts and hugged him through his successes, and made him a man.

"Fuck," Noah said, rising in one movement and walking away a few steps, running fingers over his eyes. His breathing was louder, and I looked up to see him go stand in front of my painting, bracing one hand on the wall. "I've never seen them before," he said, his voice low.

"Well, I guess my mother didn't quite share everything, huh?" I said, tears coming freely once I finally let them have their way.

He drew in a long, labored breath and blew it out slowly, running another hand over his face before he turned back around. When he came back, he slid his back down the wall and sat facing me. I sat cross-legged in my black leggings and wraparound black skirt, not caring. After a long look, he picked up the box and positioned it between us. We each pulled things out and explored, reading letters written in longhand from Seth's— mother. We touched crayon drawings and read his first poem. We looked over more snapshots of Seth and another boy, presumably a brother? Noah hadn't seen those, either, and we looked until there was nothing left.

I leaned over onto my elbows with my face in my hands.

"I'm sorry, Noah," I said into them.

He was only a foot away and pulled my hands from my face. "For what?"

"This should have been our family," I said, though very little sound went with the words. I was so tired, so wrung out, that even crying was too much effort. "My mother took that away and I let her do it." My chin trembled, although I felt dried up. "We could have been a family."

Noah's eyes looked exhausted, too, like he just wanted to sleep. He sat against the wall in his sweats and T-shirt with one knee up and the other leg sprawled out.

"Come here," he said, putting his knee down.

The look on his face told me not to argue. I scooted up so that my cross-legged position had my knees resting on top of his. It was kind of intimate, and him still holding my hands didn't help.

"You have a family, Jules," he said, his voice soft but his expression still haunted by all that we'd seen. "Everything happens the way it's supposed to happen." He squeezed my hands tighter. "You had Becca. Seth's parents got to raise a great kid they wouldn't have otherwise."

"And you?"

A stricken look passed over his face before he glazed it over, burying it forever. "I got to—make the world a safer place for them."

The stab to my heart was physical, and I winced.

"I used to think about you when I was out in the field," he said. "You and Seth." He looked down at our hands. "I'd imagine what he was doing. What you were doing—" At my look of doubt, he added, "Yes, even though I was angry, I still thought about you."

The scar in his eyebrow twitched as he frowned. I wanted to smooth it, touch his face more than anything in the world right then.

"You two were what kept me human," he said in a whisper. "When what I was doing"—he stopped and his whole face tightened and his eyes went dark—"wasn't very human."

He cleared his throat and forced his expression to clear.

"I'd think about the moment he was born," he said. "Your face."

"Oh, Lord," I said.

He smiled and moved a lock of my hair out of my face, temporarily stopping my heart. "It was beautiful." He held my hand up between us and held tighter. "You had my hand in a vise, begging me not to let go. I promised I wouldn't," he said, the smile in his eyes fading.

"And then you did," I said under my breath.

He inhaled slow and deep, nailing me with that thousand-mile stare of his. "And then I did." He looked physically pained by that admission.

"I'm sorry I left you alone, Jules. I swore to be by your side and then I left you to carry this by yourself."

I gave him a small smile. "Everything happens as it's supposed to happen," I said, and one side of his lips spread into a smile that turned my insides to a churning ball of energy.

I lost my resolve not to touch him with that smile, and I moved my hand softly over his cheek. Noah sucked in a breath and closed his eyes when I touched him. My breath quickened at the new rush of adrenaline that shot through me, and the look of surrender that heated his eyes when he opened them sent a new burst of nerves buzzing through my belly.

Both his hands came up to my face. "I'm sorry," he said.

"Sorry?" I breathed, confused and spinning.

Pulling me to him as he leaned in, he nodded. "I can't hold this in anymore."

Noah's mouth landed on mine with a sweet hunger that made my bones feel as though they left me entirely. Energy pulsed through me like lightning at the feel of his mouth, the taste of him, his hands twisting into my hair. It was like I'd been starving for him and one taste triggered everything. My hands went up into his short hair, pulling his head in deeper and bringing a low rumbled growl from his chest that set me on fire. I couldn't get close enough.

As if he felt the same need, he pulled me into his lap, my legs straddling him as he shoved my skirt up so that I'd fit against him better. Our foreheads pressed together and the tears that filled his eyes stung my core. Suddenly my lungs, my eyes, my throat—everything burned with the emotion of needing him so badly I couldn't breathe. His arms moved up my back and pulled me so impossibly tight that when I wrapped my arms around his head and he buried his face in my neck, we clung to each other as if our lives depended on it.

I felt his hot tears on my skin, and it brought all the injustice of the years we lost to the surface. Nothing felt more right than being intertwined so tightly we were one, rocking slowly, desperately clinging to each other.

The only thing that pulled me from that embrace was my need for his mouth. I was shaking when I held his face in my hands and saw the rawness in his eyes. I landed back on his lips, exploring his mouth, tasting the salt from our tears.

He dug his fingers into my back as his mouth trailed down to my neck, sending tingles to all the important places. His hands moved from my thighs slowly back up to my hair, lighting up every inch that they passed.

"Oh, God, Noah," I part whispered, part moaned, as I felt him hard against me and moved my hands over his shoulders, his back, his head again. I couldn't get enough. "I can't stop touching you," I breathed.

"I know the feeling," he said, shoving my sweater jacket off my shoulders and landing there with his mouth, tasting his way up my neck. Reflexively, my thighs squeezed and I arched against him, making him moan against my skin and dig his fingers into my hair. His kisses went lower, playing at the swell of my tank top neckline while holding me firmly against him, driving me mad.

A tiny voice in the back of my mind was screaming to be heard, telling me to stop. Telling me that it was a bad idea. Telling me that my heart couldn't take another Noah heartbreak.

But the rest of me was louder. Every cell of my being went on full alert as his hands moved over my body and I felt his need matching mine. I held his face against my chest and moved against him as his breathing grew ragged and he grabbed my ass and rode it with me. He let go and slid his hands up over my breasts to my face, searching my eyes as we both breathed as if we were racing. As if sensing the runaway freight train we'd climbed on was about to jump the tracks. The intensity hit me to the bone, filling me with a need that burned my eyes.

"Jules."

I saw everything in that one second, everything he couldn't say, everything he'd ever felt.

"Don't let go," I whispered.

Noah blinked back emotion, and when his mouth sealed over mine again it was solid, real, like a promise. He explored my mouth, pulling me deeper and deeper, my mind exploding with the thoughts that this was Noah. That I was kissing Noah again. Touching him.

"Hold on to me," he said against my lips, gripping me against him with one arm.

I wrapped myself around him as he lifted and pulled his legs under him, picking me up a little awkwardly and dropping me on the rug.

I pulled him down with me. "Nice move."

A smile curved his lips. "I'm slowing in my old age."

He dove into my mouth once more, hungry, needing. I wound my legs around him and pulled him down to me, craving the weight of his body on mine. He was so much more solid than the last time I'd held him like this. Tighter, harder. His kiss turned possessive, pinning me to the floor, taking my breath away with his ardor. Making me dizzy with my need for more. I tugged at his T-shirt, wanting skin, and he lifted so that I could pull it over his head.

God, he was glorious. I wanted to lick every inch of his torso, but my current position under him didn't allow that, so I settled for a shoulder as my hands kneaded his back. I didn't get much of that, however, as he was on a mission. Torturing me in a delicious rhythm, Noah dragged his mouth down my neck back to my breasts, lifting my tank top and sinking his face between them. His mouth made love to my cleavage while he pushed between my legs in a slow, pulsing tease. My little black leggings and his sweatpants didn't provide much in the way of restriction, so the mock lovemaking had me gasping for breath within minutes.

His fingers worked one thigh up and down until he'd cup my ass and grind himself into me. It was insane, the power he had over my senses. He had me almost blind with desire, digging my nails into his back with each thrust. Then he moved down, kissing my belly and untying my bunched up skirt in seconds, following his hands with his mouth as he pulled off my leggings in one move and kissed his way back up one thigh.

"Mmm, Jules," he murmured against my skin.

I arched and grabbed his head as he lingered over my lacy panties, his hot breath on the fabric nearly finishing me off.

"Noah," I breathed, barely able to form the words. "Please."

He could have yanked them down and had his way with me, but he didn't. Instead, he made the trip back up, kissed the inside of each breast, and then moved to suck a nipple through the straining fabric of my bra, grabbing my leg and pushing himself against me again.

I groaned and moved with him, feeling him tremble against me.

"Keep doing that," I said between breaths, "and you'll undo me. I'm so close."

"I've been undone for three days," he growled against my neck.

His next thrust put us face-to-face. His hands framed my face and his eyes bored into me with that look of his that turned my insides to mush. I was hopeless for him. Again. And I was ready to give him everything again. I raked my nails down his back to his ass, pulling him with me on the next one and sliding his sweatpants downward.

Just as his cell phone rang.

With "Love Shack."

◆　◆　◆

Everything froze.

Our eyes locked as the song played out, neither one of us moving a muscle, like that would hide us from the woman behind it. As it fell silent and reality seeped into every breath, there was a five-second moment when harsh awakenings landed hard. Noah closed his eyes and rested his forehead against mine, letting go of my leg as I pulled his pants back up and let my arms fall to the sides.

I was mortified.

We broke our own rules. I had given in, heart, mind, body, and soul—again. To a man who wasn't mine to give them to.

"I'm sorry," Noah said, under his breath, not lifting his head. His skin was hot against mine, or maybe that was just me projecting my own shame.

My body still ached with frustration and didn't want him to get up. I wanted to stay wrapped up in him. But more than that, my heart ached over the walls I'd let him knock down.

"Oh, my God," I whispered. "I am not this person. I'm not this woman."

Noah lifted his head from mine and rolled to the side, making me instantly chilled and vulnerable. I sat up and pulled my tank top down, scooting backward to lean against the back of the couch and pulling the afghan into my lap. Noah watched my movements with a narrowed gaze, leaning on one elbow.

"What woman would that be?" he asked, his voice low and controlled.

I covered my face with my hands. "One that sleeps with a pregnant woman's future husband." I shook my head. "I don't do this. I don't even *almost* do this."

He sat up facing me and pulled a hand away, holding on to it.

"Is that all it felt like to you? Sex?" he asked, raising an eyebrow. "Because I was in a very different place."

I closed my eyes and clenched my jaws tight to fend off the hurt in my chest. Remembering the connection we'd just had and the total surrender of my heart, the tender places in there that hadn't been touched in twenty-six years. My hand fisted at my stomach like I could hold it all in if I pushed hard enough.

"Yeah, that," he said, putting his hand over mine, making me open my eyes to look into his. "That right there."

"Noah," I said, my voice choking on his name.

"I know."

Minutes that felt like slow motion passed as we sat and breathed and wallowed in misery.

"She's become my friend, Noah," I said, wiping my face with the afghan.

"I know," he said again. "And I feel like the world's biggest fucking prick right now. But it doesn't change—" He closed his eyes and ran his free hand over his face, squeezing mine tighter. "It doesn't change that I've thought of nothing but you since I got back to town, Jules. Last night, it was everything I could do not to pull you out of his arms on that dance floor."

The memory of his eyes on me, raw and angry, made me swallow hard. I had to stay resilient.

"Shayna's a good person," I said, hearing the shake in my voice and begging God to take that away. I was tired of crying. I was tired of feeling weak. "She doesn't deserve this."

"I know."

"Your baby doesn't deserve this," I managed to add, the words coming slow and deliberate. The burn fed through me, and I prayed for the numbness to come. It had come before; it could do it again. "We have to live in this town together, Noah."

He closed his eyes and nodded, looking beaten down.

"We can't let this happen again," I said, the last word having to be choked out.

He opened his eyes slowly, fixing me with that unblinking gaze of his. "I'm sorry about the pictures, Jules. And my dad. And"—he gestured behind him to the box and other pictures on the floor—"your mom. I'm sorry about everything you've had to deal with. But I'll never be sorry for getting to find out a little more about my son today." He took a deep, shaky breath and threaded his fingers through mine. "Or about this."

All I could hear was the echo of those warnings that had been yelling at me earlier. The ones I'd ignored while Noah Ryan was feeling me up.

"I know that makes me a dick with Shayna," he continued. "But having you in my arms again—"

"No," I said, cutting him off. Not wanting to hear more words that I'd just replay again and again later. "It can't—" I looked away and clenched my jaws tight to hold back the pain that wanted out. The tears that somehow found a way to flow yet again. I pulled myself together before looking at him again. "I can't do this again, Noah."

"Do what?" he asked.

"You."

He blinked and searched my eyes for more, but it really just came down to that.

"You don't know all the details with me and Shayna, Jules," he began. "We don't have what you think—"

"It doesn't matter," I said. "What you have is a child. Everything you've ever wanted."

"Not everything," he said under his breath, his whole body teaming with tension. I could see his muscles twitching in his neck and shoulders, and his still being shirtless wasn't helping me.

I couldn't think like that. "I broke—everything today," I said. "Every promise, every rule, every—"

"Promises to who?" Noah demanded.

"Myself," I said, bitter laughter bubbling to the surface. "I've spent two decades living behind lines I never crossed. Twenty years of holding back, not giving my heart completely, not even to my husband. Not *ever* wanting to feel crushed like that again. And fifteen minutes with you blew all that away."

Sharp emotion flashed in his eyes before he pulled it back. "Because you gave me your heart."

The memory of that embrace and the tears in his eyes stabbed me in the chest. That would have been the moment. "I don't know how to be with you any other way," I said.

"I don't, either."

My chest felt so tight it was hard to pull in air. "You need to go, Noah," I added, softer. I tried to pull my hand free but he wasn't letting go. I pleaded with my eyes. "Please."

"I don't want to let go," he said.

He spoke so softly I barely heard him. But those words coupled with the devastation in his eyes nearly buckled me.

"You have to," I said, wondering where the words were coming from. "Your family's at home."

Your family. I saw it hit the mark.

He looked down at our hands, and when I pulled mine free, he didn't resist. Taking a deep breath to stem off the stab that sent through me, I got to my feet. It was easier to keep moving, and I tossed the afghan aside and quickly pulled my castaway leggings back right-side out and stepped into them. It was acceptable enough without fumbling with the skirt and sweater; I basically looked ready to go to the gym. I found his shirt and handed it to him as he rose, ignoring the flutter in my stomach at the full-standing, shirtless view.

"Thank you," he said, not looking at me. He tugged it on in one movement.

"Need me to drive you—"

"No, I'll walk," he said. His tone had changed. He'd gone under, shutting it down. That was a move I understood all too well. "I probably need the walk," he added, attempting to soften it some.

I crossed my arms and rubbed them, feeling chilled, and when our eyes locked my heart broke for the eighty-third time that day. It was unreal to think that we'd just been entwined in each other's arms only moments earlier, and I ached for it.

The second ringing of his cell broke the moment. I vowed then and there to never listen to "Love Shack" again.

"Bye, Noah," I said, hearing the wobble in my voice.

I lifted my chin to help counteract it and turned to walk into the kitchen, waiting for it. When I heard the front door open and close, I gripped the granite of the island, focusing hard on the cold, wanting the frigid rock to ice down my blood.

It wasn't enough, however. Short of diving into a lake of ice, nothing would push back the fiery pain that threatened to engulf me. I'd let it in. I'd let *him* in. In the days since his return, I'd broken every personal rule and boundary I'd ever set for myself.

I gulped for air as the sobs came, and I didn't fight them. I was tired of fighting them, tired of crying so much. That wasn't me. But it felt like I'd spent the last week holding it all in.

I grabbed a Coke from the fridge and held it to the back of my neck as I walked back into the living room. I stopped short, staring at the floor by the bookshelf. Books were everywhere, papers and pictures lying askew. And the rug where we'd nearly done the deed. How much worse would that have been? Or would it? Did it really matter that we hadn't finished?

I couldn't remember the last time I'd let love into sex. With Hayden, of course, but even in all those years of marriage—not heart-and-soul kind of love.

Noah had pulled that from me with a kiss.

"Shit," I cried, dropping to my knees on the rug and letting whatever needed to come, come. I curled up in a ball like I'd done so many years ago. All the brokenness seemed to come at once, like moths to light.

Harley bounded down the stairs a half hour later, pausing when she saw me on the rug, as if not quite sure what to do with that. Lord, I'd forgotten about Harley once we got started. She must have decided she didn't want to watch and bolted for Becca's room.

She padded down the last few steps and wagged over to me, licking my face and probably wondering if all this floor activity was some new game. She sprawled on the floor for a belly rub, her legs splayed wide.

"Slut," I said, my voice still thick with crying.

She didn't care. I lay down next to her and rubbed her till her head lolled to the side and her eyes closed. I envied her that. The ability to shut it all down, whenever and wherever. I buried my face against her side and let myself float.

The front door opening was unplanned.

I jumped at the sound and movement and light streaming in, not to mention Harley's full-flail awkward attempt at getting her feet back under her to get to Becca.

"Mom?"

Blinking my swollen and salt-logged eyes open, I saw a hazy Becca.

"Shit, I must have fallen asleep," I mumbled.

"On the floor?" she said, kneeling beside me. "Are you sick?" She peered closer at me. "Are you drunk?"

"Oh, God, I wish," I said, grabbing my head as the crying headache took root.

"What happened here?" she said, looking behind her. "Why are all the books on the floor?"

"Why are you home?" I asked, sitting up and suddenly realizing the near horrendous situation we'd have had if she'd walked in like that an hour earlier.

"Came to get different clothes," she said, distracted. "Mom, what's going on?" Leaning over, she picked up a photograph of Seth when he was around her age. "Who is this?"

I took a deep breath and scooted over to where the majority of the pictures lay in a pile.

"That's—" I began, my heart picking up speed. "Your brother."

CHAPTER 14

"My what?"

Becca froze midlean, dropping the photograph like it stung her.

Yeah, this was going to be fun. I rubbed at my cry-swollen eyes and pointed at the floor.

"Pull up some rug, Bec, I have a story to tell you." She looked at me like I'd lost my mind, still frozen in her awkward position. "Sit," I said.

"I don't have a brother," she said. "I don't have—" She shook her head and smirked at me. "Seriously?"

"Please, sit down," I said again, needing a calm heart-to-heart and quickly realizing that opportunity had come and gone. My eyes filled with tears again—how that was possible, I didn't know.

Becca scoffed and stared at me, bracing herself on the wall as if she needed proof of reality. "You're serious."

Her gaze dropped to the photos on the floor, and I watched a mixed look of horror and hurt cross her face as the family resemblance registered. I pushed to my feet, her shock pushing away the rest of my day. I needed to make this okay for her. I tucked an errant piece of longer hair behind her ear and smoothed the rest, my heart thumping loudly in my ears.

"Baby, we need to talk."

"You think?" she said, tears thickening her voice. "You—did I miss something? Like you being pregnant, maybe? I mean—how do you have another kid my age?"

"He's not your age," I said. My tongue felt thick and heavy. "He's twenty-six."

Her gaze shot up to meet mine, and it broke my heart.

"Twenty-six," she said, just above a whisper. "What's his name?"

It felt odd to answer that question, it still being so new to me. "Seth," I said, wrapping my brain around the sound of it.

She nodded and glanced back down. "And—I didn't know I had a brother named Seth because . . ."

I knelt to scoop everything up. "That's what I want to talk to you about, Becca. Let's go sit down—"

"No."

I stood up, my arms full of photos I was itching to look through again myself.

"What?"

She blinked tears free and whisked them away as if embarrassed to let me see it. Like I'd never seen her cry before. A bitter laugh came out like a cough.

"Lizzy is waiting outside in the car, Mom. I just came in to change clothes. And find you asleep—on the *floor* with Harley—clearly on a crying hangover. And now I have a brother?" she said, her voice progressively louder. "What the fuck, Mom?"

"Becca!" I exclaimed, stunned by the sound of that word coming from her.

"Really?" she said, tilting her head in a very Ruthie-like manner, gesturing in circles at the photos at her feet. "My *language* is what disturbs you most in all that?"

Hide your crazy.

The pounding in my skull stepped it up a couple of beats. "Go tell

Lizzy to come back in an hour. I'm sorry this is dumped on you like this, but that's the kind of day it's been."

She widened her eyes. "The kind of day? I just saw you at the library a couple of hours ago, Mom. Delivering books. Talking to some lady. How do you go from that to—this?" She pointed to the mess in my arms. "How is this okay?"

"Okay?" I asked. I looked at the floor and back at her. "Look at me. Do I look okay to you?"

"But why now?" she said, waving her arms. "How could you not tell me my whole life that I have—where is he, by the way?"

"I don't know."

She laughed as more tears fell. "You don't know?" She scooped her hair back and let it fall. "Really?"

"Really," I echoed. "I never even saw these pictures until today," I said, irritability bringing my own burn back to my eyes. "My mother—" I took a deep breath and let it go. "My mother had these hidden away."

Becca's eyes narrowed, disbelief all over her features. "Why would she do that? Why wasn't he here? Why would Dad let—"

I was already shaking my head, trying to reach for her, but she pulled away. And backed up a step, pointing a finger at me.

"Dad wasn't the dad, was he?" she breathed.

My throat felt like it was closing up. Nothing was going like I'd hoped. Not that I'd hoped for any of it. I'd hidden my life in a box just like my mother had.

"No."

"Oh, my God," she said, raking her fingers through her hair. She turned and headed up three steps before turning back to me, disgust contorting her features. "You cheated on Dad?"

"No!" I exclaimed. "It was years before I met your father."

Her shoulders sagged. "Years before?" she said, bewilderment adding to the gamut of emotions on her face.

181

Then it cleared. The knit between her eyebrows smoothed as I watched her wheels turn and everything I'd dreaded worked out in her head. She did the math. Nana Mae was right. I should have told her long ago. When she was eight and having a mysterious brother would have been cool, and I wouldn't be a horrible troll.

"If you had a kid twenty-six years ago," she said. "You would have been eighteen."

Oh, my math-challenged baby girl. My chin trembled, but I refused to have yet another breakdown today. I held my head up and tried my best to keep up the parent role, although I was beginning to feel more like the child.

"Seventeen."

She drew in a shaky breath and shook her head. "You're such a hypocrite." With that, she wheeled around and stomped up the stairs.

"Where are you going?" I said, my voice cracking.

"To change my clothes," she said, disappearing over the top and slamming her door.

"Shit," I muttered, pressing my palms against my pounding temples. Harley sat on the bottom step, looking upward, and I lowered myself to the one above her. "This went well, don't you think?" I asked her.

I needed to tell Becca the whole thing so she'd get it. So she'd understand my choices and my reasons—but who was I kidding? She wasn't going to understand those things. Ever. You had to live it, and even then I wasn't totally clear on it. And I never wanted her to have to make the decisions I'd made.

Two minutes later, changed into all black—clearly the wardrobe choice of the day—and eyeliner fixed from her momentary emotional slip, Becca came charging down the stairs. Her expression was cold and glazed over.

"I have to go," she said.

"You're not leaving right now, Bec," I said, sitting there with Harley like we were some sort of wall.

"The hell I'm not," she said, her face never breaking its mask.

Oh, how she knew what buttons to push to piss me off. I rose in one move, and even Harley seemed to catch the mood. She got up and headed out back through her doggie door, not wanting any part of the scene about to ensue.

"I told you we need to talk," I said.

"I told you I have plans."

"You don't tell *me* anything, Becca," I said, raising my voice. "And you don't talk to me this way. As long as you live in my house—"

"Then I won't," she said, glaring at me. "I'll go live with Dad."

My blood felt like it was on fire. The classic manipulative tool in every divorce kid's arsenal. She'd never played it before.

"Go ahead," I said softly. "But be damn sure of your decision, because you only get to use that card with me once."

Her eyes glazed over again. "Whatever. I don't care what you say anymore."

"Becca Ann, I know you're upset right now," I said, trying to rein my own anger in. She knew how to light me up and seemed hell-bent on pushing me to the limit. "But you watch your mouth. You are not my equal, young lady. Remember your place."

"And what is that?" she yelled. "Only child? Second child? Daughter to a lying hypocrite?"

Fire blazed hot in my brain and my hand came up before I could stop it. The smack across her cheek made us both suck in our breaths. I felt like my eyes were as wide as hers as we stared at each other in disbelief, neither of us breathing.

I'd never hit her before. Not like that. Not in anger. She'd gotten swats on her hands or bottom when she was little and being disciplined, but I'd never slapped her like that.

Her eyes filled with tears again as she palmed her cheek, and everything in me broke. The day descended on me with the weight of a tank, crushing any resolve I had left. A sob escaped my throat and I gripped the stairway railing.

"Go," I choked out, emotion taking over me.

She didn't move, just stood there, shocked and crying silently, holding her cheek. I shut my eyes and clamped a hand over my mouth, wanting the stairs to open up and swallow me. To take me away somewhere dark where I could come apart in solitude, where I wouldn't have witnesses and couldn't wreck anyone else's lives.

"Leave," I said through my fingers, my sobs pulling the last bit of energy from me.

Finally, she moved. Slowly, robotically, she stepped around me, sniffling. Walked out the door, closing it behind her with a click.

The silence rang in my ears as I sank to my knees on the steps and let it rip me apart.

◆　◆　◆

I woke to the sound of the dead bolt clicking into place and opened my eyes. Or tried to. They were so swollen and glued together that it took prying one open with my fingers to do the job. I rubbed it to focus better and hit the button to light up my phone.

Ten minutes after midnight.

"Becca?" I called out, my voice hoarse to my ears.

A hazy form stopped at the foot of the stairs. "Mom? Why are you on the couch?"

I struggled to sit up as my feet were tangled under the afghan, another blanket, and Harley's back end. Becca's voice got her attention, however, and she jumped off the couch still groggy, nearly face-planting into the floor. I guessed that as long as a burglar was quiet and didn't talk, Harley would sleep through it.

"I must have fallen asleep," I said, pushing myself upright. The side table lamp was on, illuminating the stacks of photos and letters I'd been looking through all evening. Five Dr Pepper cans were lined up next to them, as well as a bag of chips and a nearly empty package of Oreos I hadn't even known we had.

"Well, I'm home," she said, turning back to the stairs.

"I thought you were spending the night at Lizzy's," I said, trying to rub both eyes open.

Actually, I didn't know what she was going to do. My fear of her never coming back home after that escapade had me breathing a sigh of relief that she was standing in the living room.

"Didn't feel like it," she said.

Her voice sounded down.

"Come sit down?" I asked.

I heard the sigh I couldn't really see. "Mom, I'm tired."

"Just come sit," I said. She couldn't possibly be more tired than me. I felt like I'd been to New Zealand and back. By paddleboat. "Please?"

Becca trudged around the couch and landed next to me with a long exhale. She looked my way for what was probably intended to be just a quick glance, but then she did a double take.

"Jesus, Mom, what happened to your eyes?"

"Told you, it was a bitch of a day," I said. "This is why I don't cry."

Her eyes fell on the stack of Seth's photos next to me, then down to her lap and back at the stack. "Any Oreos left?"

I reached back for the package and shook it. "A few." I handed it to her and she shoved her hand inside.

"You really just see all that today?" she asked, nodding her chin at the photos.

"Yep."

"How'd that happen?"

There was still snark in her voice, but a little remorse, too. That was her way of fixing things. Talking around them.

I rubbed at my face, too exhausted to start up the fight again. "Do you want the long version or the summary?"

She met my eyes and then looked away. There was still hurt in her eyes, and my stomach tightened.

"CliffsNotes is fine."

I took a deep breath and let it out slowly. "He was put up for adoption the second he was born, my fiancé left town, and my parents pretended it never happened. Now the guy is back, I found out he had photographs—today. He said they came from his dad. I approached the dad and he told me they came from my mother." Becca's eyebrows rose at my rambling summary, and I gestured toward the pictures on the table. "Hence my raid on Mom's part of the bookshelf."

In the dim light, I watched her eyes glisten and she blinked it back, averting her gaze to stare straight ahead.

"Why did you keep all this from me?" she whispered, but I could hear the shake.

I opened my mouth to tell her that it was to protect her, but I realized we were past the point of either one of us believing that.

"It was so before your time, Bec," I said, the pain and guilt and rawness wrapping around my throat, choking the words as they came out. "A really, really difficult time for me. Something I don't talk about—with anyone. I guess I hoped you'd never have to know that—"

"That you weren't perfect?" she said.

"That I made horrible choices," I said, tears rising in my throat. "You called me a hypocrite and you're right. I did the very thing I'm begging you not to do, and I was in love and thought it was all okay, and then I had to choose between—" I shut my eyes tight against the words that nearly came out. I was about to say *choose between my mother and my love*. Oh, holy fuck, no wonder Noah had left me. What I'd convinced myself to be a responsible decision, he'd seen as betrayal. I sucked in a shaky breath. "I had to make choices that I couldn't take back. Like never knowing my son."

I felt her eyes on the side of my face, but it was my turn to stare straight ahead. I couldn't look at my daughter and say these things aloud.

"I never want you to have to make choices like that, Bec," I said. "Things you can't undo. Like painting over a mistake—it doesn't change the mistake underneath."

"I'm not a painting, Mom," she said. "And I'm not your personal do-over experiment."

"I know that."

"Then quit trying so hard to fix me before I'm broken," she said, whisking tears off her cheeks. "Okay, so you screwed up and you don't want me to, I get it, but I'm not you. Let me figure things out for myself."

I looked at her, trying to be so grown up, trying to process so much information at once.

"That's really hard to do, baby."

"Well, give it a shot," she said, her old sarcasm seeping back in. As annoying as that was, it was a good sign. She sniffled and wiped under her eyes again. "So you were engaged at seventeen?"

The memory of Noah replacing the string with his little ring he'd worked so hard for sent a pang of regret through my core. We could have been a family. *You had a family, Jules.* Now I'd pushed him away again so he could have one.

"For a little while," I said, forcing the words out. "He was going to marry me."

"God, it's like watching a movie, Mom," she said. "Like I've been in this family all along, the stupid one that didn't know anything. Do you know how crappy that feels?"

"I'm sorry," I said, inhaling deep and letting it go. I reached for her hand, and she inched it away. "Becca, I'm sorry. That's another choice I made, and maybe not the smartest. But it's not like knowing would have helped you."

"Who was the guy?" she asked, making my head spin with the direction change. "Wait." She turned to face me. "Linny's brother just came back from somewhere. Mr. Ryan was making all that noise over—"

I nodded before she finished. "Yes."

Her wheels were turning again, and all I could do was hang on.

"That's him?" she asked. "And that lady at the library—you said it was his fiancée—oh, holy crap."

"Fun, isn't it?" I said, rubbing my eyes.

Becca's gaze landed on the photos again, and she leaned over me to pick one up. One of Seth around thirteen years old, braces on his teeth. "So Nonnie had all this and didn't tell you?" she asked. "Why?"

The laugh that came out wasn't really a laugh but just exhaustion making noise. "That's the question of the day."

I looked down at the photo in her hand, and then at her profile. At the crazy hair framing her face, the eyes that had evidently cried the eyeliner off before she'd even gotten home. Still so innocent and young, no matter how many ways she tried not to be. I took a chance and swung an arm around her, pulling her head over to me.

"Things happen as they're supposed to, baby girl," I said, kissing her hair. "I thank God for giving me you." I heard a sniffle. "And I'm so sorry about earlier."

I knew that slap would haunt me forever.

"Me too," came a squeaky response.

I didn't hold any naive opinions that all would be rosy, but just for one tiny moment, curled up on the couch with my girl in the middle of the night, I took a deeper breath than I had in a week.

CHAPTER 15

Hayden looked as if he'd aged ten years in a day, sitting in my kitchen, staring into his coffee like a whipped puppy.

"I'm giving it up, Jules," he said. "I mean it this time."

I sat on a stool across the island from him, nursing a third cup of coffee, still in the black leggings and tank top from the previous day. I'd added an old hole-ridden sweatshirt I'd inherited from him when I was pregnant with Becca. It had seen better days, but it was a comfort thing, and if I was pathetic enough to keep on the clothes I'd nearly made love to Noah in, then my ratty sweatshirt was right there in the running.

My head pounded from the crying marathon; my eyes were gritty and my throat was raw. Hayden's face had lit up with concern when I'd opened the door, thinking I'd fallen on my face when he'd pushed me down at the bar. It's always encouraging to know just how bad you really look.

I knew what he was there for. It wasn't the first time. Hayden was a binge drinker, not a constant one, but when he'd decide to tie one on— well, there wasn't an off switch. There'd been many mornings such as this, full of apologies and promises and good intentions. And I'd learned long before that time faded them. His good intentions would fall in a hole somewhere, and four or five months later we'd be right back here. Sitting in a kitchen, drinking coffee, talking about how things would change.

It didn't matter that much anymore, since he always stayed on the straight path around Becca, but old habits die hard.

"I know, Hayden," I said. "It's okay." My whole face itched with salt overload. "Want a Pop-Tart or something?" I slid off my stool and opened the fridge. "I think I have a can of biscuits in here somewhere."

Harley jumped up from her full-body sprawl at my feet, her ears perking at the mention of Pop-Tarts.

"I'm fine, Jules," he said, running a hand over his face and up through his hair. "I'm not here for you to feed me."

"Well, that's about all the brain power I have right now, so I'd grab it if I were you," I said, opening the freezer to look for bacon. Found it. Closed the door. Not energetic enough to deal with oil.

"I know you don't believe me," Hayden said, his words bouncing off my headache like they were playing Ping-Pong.

"I always believe you," I said, finally finding the biscuits and deciding I wanted them. To hell with anyone else. I'd eat all five. Maybe share one with Harley. Thank God it wasn't an eight-count can.

"And I always let you down."

On that one, I turned. "Hayden, let it go. Please."

He met my eyes. "I can't."

"Yes, you can," I said, holding the cold biscuit can against my right temple. "It's not about me anymore. You want to quit? Quit. But it's for you, not for me."

"And if I'd actually got it together years ago?" he said, sitting back in his chair. "We wouldn't be sitting in your mother's kitchen talking about how it's not about you."

I closed the fridge and walked-slash-shuffled over to him and leaned against the granite feeling really damn tired of hearing how many things my mother still owned. My kitchen, my house, my son.

"It's my kitchen now," I said. "And stop it. We are where we are because—we just couldn't make it work." I pushed off and walked to the end table, scooping up a handful of pictures in one hand and coming back to spread them out in front of him.

Hayden's eyebrows came together as he leaned forward again, moving his coffee cup out of the way as he picked up and set down a photo or two.

"What's this?"

"My what-ifs," I said, bringing his gaze to mine. My breath caught in my chest as I said the words. "My son."

His expression sharpened as he focused on me harder, looking at the photos more closely and then back at me in question.

"Holy shit, Jules. You have pictures now?"

I shook my head. "My mom did."

His wide-eyed expression slowly moved back into a knowing frown borne of experience. He'd known my mother well. "What did she do?"

I gazed upon my little boy at various stages of his life. Stages it would have meant the world to me to be a witness to. "Arranged a trust for him—not a bad thing—but in exchange she got regular pictures and updates." I smiled, and my face felt as if it might crack. "Which she shared with Johnny Mack under another arrangement—that I never be told."

Hayden closed his eyes and rubbed them.

"His name is S-Seth," I said, still having trouble with knowing that. Feeling like somehow I should have just magically sensed it, and known he was a Seth, instead of being told my own son's identity.

"Shit," he whispered, squeezing my hand.

"I could play that damn what-if game for the rest of my life," I said. "With him, with you, with Becca."

"With Noah Ryan," he added.

I faltered in my spiel, the sound of Noah's name putting his face right in front of me. The last expression I'd seen on his face before I'd told him good-bye yesterday. *God, that was only yesterday.*

"I can't live like that anymore, Hayden," I said, recovering. "Obsessing over how I'd do things differently—especially with Becca. All I can do is try to do it right, now." I touched his arm. "You too."

He looked down at my hand and back at me.

"What's going on with Noah?" he asked, his voice low.

God, if I could just cut that name out of everyone's vocabulary, my insides would have it so much easier. As it was, the quiver that started at my center and worked outward at every mention of his name, every memory of his face, every relived second of being wrapped up in him yesterday just mere feet from where I currently stood had me a jittery mess.

I let go of him and walked back around to my coffee, deciding I'd had enough caffeine. "Noah and Shayna are getting married, Hayden," I said, trying to pour the words down the drain with the cold coffee from my cup. "They have a baby on the way."

"I didn't ask what's going on with them," he said. "I'm asking about Noah and you."

"There is no *Noah and me*," I said point-blank, turning back to him. "Never can be."

"Your eyes say different," Hayden said, his voice soft, and maybe a little sad.

I widened them as much as I could. "Bullshit. My eyes aren't open enough to say anything," I said with a smirk, tossing a dishrag at his head.

He gestured toward the pictures spread in front of him. "Becca know?"

I nodded, sighing heavily. "She does now."

"How did that go?"

The memory of me slapping her face as she called me a liar and a hypocrite seared through me. "We've had better moments," I said. "But I think it's kind of okay now."

There was a pause as Hayden stared at the pictures, though I had the impression that wasn't where he was at all.

"Jules, I remember the things I said—about her, about you. I—"

"Stop," I said, laying my hands flat on the granite. "Seriously, stop."
His eyes flashed. "I threw you on the floor."

"And you're lucky I don't kick your ass for that," I said, trying desperately to lighten the tone. "Now quit with the pity party and either pretend it never happened or make a change."

"What never happened?" Becca said on a yawn, shuffling into the kitchen in Mickey Mouse sleep pants and a Snoopy T-shirt, hair sticking up everywhere, looking like a ten-year-old with boobs.

"Nothing, monkey," he said, pulling the worry inside. He poked her in the side, making her flinch and grumble something incoherent.

She blinked sleepily at him, as if it just dawned on her that his being there drinking coffee in our kitchen was out of place.

"What's up?" she asked.

Hayden shrugged. "Just came to talk over some things with your mom."

She looked wary, cutting a look my way. "Like?"

"Like not your business," he said with a wink.

I knew what she was thinking—that I'd told him about the whole birth control conversation. Truth be known, he probably *was* heading to that topic next if he could manage to get the hell off of Noah, but I would deflect that. Becca didn't need to know that I'd told him. Nothing would have ever been the same between them.

I did a minuscule head shake to let her know that wasn't on the table, and her face relaxed. She picked up my forgotten biscuit can and her gaze fell on Seth's photos.

"You making biscuits?"

"Sure," I said, turning on the oven.

Becca picked up a picture of Seth holding a puppy. "Hey, Dad, while you're here, can you help me make a giant snowflake?" she asked.

Hayden blinked. "As in—"

"As in there's a big piece of plywood in the garage I can use, and your jigsaw is here, and—"

"Boy, do you have good timing," I said, smirking at him.

"Why do you need a snowflake?" he asked, his eyes going back and forth between us. "Oh, don't tell me."

"I'm helping with a float for the parade," she said.

"Oh, thank God," he said, giving me a look. "I thought for a second there your mom had crossed over to the dark side."

"Ha."

Becca grinned and grabbed a mug from the cabinet. It was kind of normal again. Or at least a new version of it.

◆   ◆   ◆

It did my heart good to see Hayden and Becca work on something together and bicker over the details like they used to. Who would do the cutting and what exactly the design would be, and whether one side matched the other. I really didn't think anyone would be measuring as it rolled down the street, but they didn't want my input.

Two hours later Hayden emerged, dusted with sawdust. "Well, I wasn't planning on staying this long, so I have to go," Hayden said, fishing keys from his pocket. "But I'll be back later to help her finish."

"Thank you," I said. I knew, even with his complaining and groaning, that he secretly loved doing all of that with Becca. Kept him in the family, made him feel needed, and I didn't have to do it. Double score.

"You're welcome." He turned to go and then turned back. "Later, Bec!"

"Bye!"

She'd already flopped on the couch with a book.

"You do have some white paint and some glitter or something, right?" he asked.

I bit my lip. "Umm, doubtful."

"Never mind," he said under his breath, taking the steps two at a time. He paused at the bottom and turned back around again. "Be careful, Jules," he said. "Whatever happens with Ryan—just, don't get hurt, okay?"

Probably too late for that.

I lowered to sit on the steps after he left. It was nice out—cold, but nice. Sunny, blue sky and rare, non-muggy air. Nice enough to leave the door open for a bit, and Harley took the bait. I heard her toenails on the wood as she slid into a prone position next to me.

"Hey, Harley-bear," I whispered, sliding my fingers into the soft fur at her neck. She instantly rolled to one side, probably figuring I was a sure thing for a belly rub.

I was pretty much a sure thing for anything not requiring thought. My brain, heart, and everything in between was fried. I would be strong and resilient and firm of resolve tomorrow. And every other day after that, as I watched Noah and Shayna embark on a life together with their new family, all up in my carefully crafted and protected world. I would be okay. I now had pictures of my son to help—and hurt—me. And a new reason to despise Noah's dad. I couldn't even think about my mother. My mind wouldn't let me go there yet, and that was okay, too. I probably didn't need to hate her, and right at that moment I couldn't make that promise.

Tomorrow. I'd put my walls back up tomorrow. They'd been with me for two decades, so one day of Noah yanking them down didn't scatter them too badly. I'd rebuild. Be a hard-ass again and never let anyone close enough to threaten that. Ever again.

Tomorrow.

"Can we go get some paint?" Becca said, padding outside in socks, still in her sleep clothes. She crossed her feet and landed Indian style next to me, leaning over to bury her face in Harley's neck.

I ran two fingers under my eyes, not realizing I'd teared up again. "Later, okay?" I said, the thought of going anywhere revitalizing my headache. "Or I'll give you some money and you can go get something. Or you can see what your dad comes back with?"

I saw her slump a little. "Okay."

Mother of the year. I was mother of the freaking year.

"I think I'm going to take a little walk down to Nana Mae's for a bit," I said. "Want to come?"

Becca shook her head and stretched. "No, thanks. That cat stalks me, I swear."

"Yeah, Maddy is a little unique, that's for sure."

She pulled her bottom lip between her teeth. "Isn't Mr. Ryan's house on that same street?"

I looked away, unwilling to cop to thinking the very same thing. "No, it's the one before. But I'm going the long way."

After scooping up all the Seth pictures from the kitchen, I put them in a big envelope and slipped on some sneakers.

"Wanna go to Nana Mae's, Harley?" I said, making her stop mid-step toward her doggie door and look at me. After a second's pause, she turned and went on through. She didn't like Maddy, either.

It was faster to go down Johnny Mack's street, since Nana Mae was on the far corner of the next one, but I refused. I power-walked past it without even looking sideways, and then strolled up the next street to her house. She was outside crawling in her flower beds, in winter when there were no flowers, in bright-orange yoga pants and a long-sleeved University of Texas T-shirt. Only my eighty-five-year-old Nana Mae.

"Hey," I said, my sneakers sinking into her soft, plush lawn. Mine was never that good. My house, either. Then again, I didn't have three yard guys and a maid service on my payroll.

Nana Mae turned slowly from her crouching position in the dirt and smiled.

"Hey there, sweet pea!" She backed out on all fours. "Hang on a second and I can look at you face-to-face."

"What are you doing?"

"Well, I planted this little cactus garden over there." She pointed with an elbow as I grabbed the other one to help her up. "Then I saw a couple of weeds sprouting up, and, you know."

"It's January, Nana Mae."

"It's cactus, Julianna, it doesn't care," she said, grunting to her feet.

"You pay people for this," I pointed out. "So you don't have to crawl around on your knees anymore."

"I like crawling around," she fussed. "And if I wait on them, it all goes to hell."

"You're hopeless," I said, giving her shoulders a squeeze.

"Yeah, well, I'm breathing," she said, brushing off her pants and rubbing her hands together to knock some of the dirt loose. "What's up?" she said, gesturing at the envelope in my hand.

I felt the smile leave my face and then tried to pull it back. I had pictures of him, finally. Something to show for the child I gave birth to, for the years of wondering. I should be happy. But all the crap surrounding them just felt life-sucking.

"Let's go in so you can clean up," I said, holding up the envelope.

"Uh-oh," she said. "What did I do?"

I laughed. "Nothing you've been busted for yet. Come on."

When she'd washed up and settled onto the couch next to Maddy—who glared at me for interfering once again—I opened the envelope and laid everything out on the coffee table. Nana Mae frowned and pulled her readers from the top of her head, peering through them.

"What is this?" she asked. "Cute little—" She stopped and gasped, looking up at me over the glasses. When I didn't say anything, she narrowed her gaze over them again, looking closer at one of them as she picked it up. One that looked very much like Noah. "It's the same boy, here as a man. Oh, honey, is this—?"

"Seth," I said, clearing my throat of the lump that had risen there. "I found out that his name is Seth."

"Oh," she exclaimed, her voice soft as she ran fingers over each of them, very much as I had. "What a beautiful boy." She shook her head as her eyes filled with emotion. "So much like Becca when she was little. How did you get these?"

I bit down on my lip. She was my mother's mother. But she looked up at me with true questions in her eyes and I couldn't lie to her.

"Mom had them hidden away," I said. "In a carved-out book."

I watched the words hit her with surprise, then make her sit back a fraction as she thought it through. Slowly, she shook her head, not wanting to believe what I might be saying, even before I'd said much of anything.

"There's more than this," I said. "Letters and drawings and stuff."

"Why?" she said, the word barely making sound. "Why?"

I swallowed. "Evidently she set up money for him in exchange for updates and stuff."

Nana Mae blinked rapidly. "But—okay, but what about—how did you find out about it?" She stared down at all the captured moments of his life, held forever on photo paper and Polaroids. "Did you just—I mean, why was it hidden?"

Her rapid-fire randomness was exactly how I felt.

"She didn't think I could handle it, so she decided—"

"Oh, my God," she mumbled, putting a hand over her eyes.

I took a deep breath and continued. "To keep it under wraps."

"How do you know this?"

"Johnny Mack."

Her eyebrows shot up and she shoved her glasses back up on top of her head. "Say what?"

"Noah had pictures all along, sent from his dad, who got them from Mom."

She narrowed her eyes as if I'd spoken Russian. "What the hell?"

"Shayna told me that Noah had pictures."

"And who is Shayna?" she asked.

"Noah's—fiancée." I licked my lips and swallowed hard at the word.

Nana Mae sighed and sat back on the couch, studying me in that way of hers that always rattled me. "Of course. And she's talking to you why?"

"Because I'm her—only friend here, I guess. I don't know. Anyway, she told me that and I went to ask him—"

"To ask Noah?"

"Yes. And he said that his dad sent them, so we went to the diner—"

"Just you and him?"

"Yes! Will you quit?" I said, getting flustered. "And Johnny Mack told me the rest. Mom gave him copies and swore him to secrecy. So we went back to my house—"

"Just you and him."

"Oh, my God," I said. "Are you really doing this right now?"

She scoffed. "Are you really getting all pinked up and bothered that I'm pointing it out?"

I felt the damning heat on my chest and neck. "This is about what Mom did," I said.

"Yes, it is," she said. "And that'll come back around to play. But first, I want to know why you're hanging out so much with the very people you need to avoid."

"I'm not trying to hang out with anyone, Nana Mae," I said. "I work next door, I live two blocks away, we do business in all the same places. What am I supposed to do—leave town?"

"No, sweet pea, but he doesn't need to be coming over to your house, either," she said. "You do have a door."

I blew out a breath. "I walked the long way today so I wouldn't pass the house." I sounded like a defensive teenager, but that's where I felt she was putting me.

"Good girl," she said. "So, back to the pictures. You—and Noah—went to your house, found her stash, and had sex."

My eyes flew open wide. "No!"

"Really?"

"Really." But I had to look away. Down at the pictures. Something to keep her from seeing everything else.

"Jesus, girl, don't you learn?" she muttered, putting her glasses back on and peering down at the photos again.

She wasn't fooled, and I felt the hopelessness of the night before pulling at me again.

"I told him good-bye again," I said, my voice sounding as empty as I felt. "He has a second chance at getting a family."

"Well, it is all about him," she said under her breath before glancing up at me over the rims. "Oh, crap, I know that weepy look."

I jerked my chin up. "You do not!"

"The hell I don't," she said. "I may be old, but I still have my memory, and this"—she wagged a finger up and down at me—"is you, twenty years ago over the same guy."

I stood up and reached for my pictures, Maddy raising her head to hiss at me over the quick movement.

"Oh, get over it," I hissed back.

"Where are you going?" Nana Mae asked.

"Home," I said. "I came to show you your great-grandson. Not get put on trial."

"Sit back down," she said, putting a hand on my arm. "I'm sorry, Julianna." When I didn't move, she pointed at the chair. "Sit?"

With a sigh, I sat and covered my face with my hands.

"I didn't sleep with him."

"But?" she asked.

"I was about to." I brought my hands down. "I'm pathetic."

"No, sweet pea, you're in love," she said. "God help you. And that's something you haven't seen in a really long time."

"I can't, Nana Mae," I said. "I can't do this. He's taken. And I actually like the woman. She's so damn nice it irritates the crap out of me."

"Then steer clear," she said. "Because she'll pick up on the sparks, believe me."

"Hayden tried to fight him the other night," I said, scooping my hair back. "Think he picked up on a few, too."

"Oh, Lord, I would've paid to see that." She sat back again, taking a photo with her and sighing deeply. "Oh, Mary, what the hell did you do?" she said, more to herself than to me.

I was quiet, letting her go where she wanted with her thoughts. I knew how it felt to want to shake your daughter senseless. Feeling that after their death must be heart-wrenching. Parents should never outlive their children.

"She didn't tell you, either," I said, finally.

Nana Mae shook her head and dabbed at her eyes. "I'm sure she knew I'd disapprove. That I'd tell you." She put the picture down, her face twitching with sadness and anger. "Some things about your mother I swear I never came to understand and probably never will."

"I'm sorry," I said.

"Me too, sweet pea."

CHAPTER 16

I sat in my car on the other side of the building, hiding again like a big fat coward. I'd made it through an entire day post-almost-sex-with-Noah, but that wasn't saying much, considering I'd never left my house or my make-out clothes.

It was Monday. A new day, a new week. Showering today had stripped my armor and my courage, and so while I'd come in early to hopefully avoid him—and checked out the front to make sure his truck wasn't there yet—I still felt the need to sit there and recharge.

"Grow up, Julianna," I said, blowing out a breath.

I got out and smoothed down the dark-green sweater dress I'd worn—just in case paths might cross after all. Because in all my determination to avoid him, I was supremely twisted in my need to look hot. For my ex-boyfriend that I'd turned away while still needing him to see what he was missing.

Women are messed up.

And as I rounded the corner of the sidewalk, I nearly sucked my tongue down my throat as Noah and Shayna got out of his truck, parked right in front of my damn door.

"Shit—son of a bitch," I muttered, fighting the urge to turn around and run back to my car. But we were only twenty feet apart, and the heeled boots I'd just had to wear gave me away.

They both turned. Shayna with a smile and concern and already moving in my direction. Noah, looking like he'd just been hit with a stun gun. He stopped where he stood, his eyes glazing over. That was his way, and how it would be for us going forward. Protection by way of shutting down. Boy, the next twenty years were going to be a real riot.

Damn it, if I'd just not been such a wuss and gotten out of the freaking car when I got there.

Look away. Look away. Don't make eye contact.

"Hey," Shayna said, reaching me as I got to my door. She grabbed my hand in her gloved one. "I heard about everything, Jules, I'm so sorry."

Everything? I sincerely doubted that. She wouldn't have been holding my hand if she had. She'd be breaking my fingers.

"Thank you, it's—it's all okay now." Which was a lie. Nothing was okay. Things might very well never be okay again.

Shayna reached back for Noah and pulled him from where he'd taken root in the concrete. I saw him shove his hands into his leather jacket pockets.

"Noah said you were really upset, Jules, I'm so sorry I told you like that. I didn't know—"

I was already shaking my head. "No, no, not at all, Shayna, you didn't do anything. And thanks to you I have pictures now." I smiled at her. "It was a rough day, yes. But something very precious came out of it." I pressed a hand against my stomach and held my chin up. "It's a day I'll never forget."

I heard a sharp exhale come from him, and he coughed to cover it. "I'm going in, Shayna," he said, his voice sounding tired. Like maybe he didn't sleep, either. "Glad you're feeling better, Jules."

At my name, my gaze shot up to meet his. In that one second, he faltered. I saw the rawness of our connection before the walls came back and locked into place. I blinked and jerked my eyes away.

And saw Shayna staring at him, her eyebrows slightly pulled together like she was studying a painting.

"Y'all have a good day," I said quickly, turning to unlock my door before anyone could study anyone. "Shit," I whispered under my breath as I pulled the door open and slipped inside.

The quiet darkness enveloped me, and I let it. I walked farther into the dark of the store, away from the invasive light of the windows, and sank into a soft chair. I'd forgotten how much I loved that—getting there before Ruthie and just soaking up the quiet. I'd let her open up for—I didn't even know how long it had been. It was never an official decision; it just sort of became the norm.

I felt it, the heaviness of the days. The strength of will I was going to have to muster. I should have never let myself go there with Noah. God, what was I thinking? There was no ignoring him now. Just seeing him on the sidewalk had made my knees weak. How the hell was I supposed to go about daily life?

The door jingled, making me sit up.

"Jules?" Ruthie's voice called out. She sounded wary and a little concerned.

"I'm here," I said, swiping under my eyes as lights started powering up. I hadn't even realized I'd teared up, but hell, of course I had. That's all I did anymore.

I knew I had some hell to pay with her, too. I'd left to bring books to the library on Saturday and had never come back, never checked on her chair, leaving her with cryptic texts that I was okay but out till Monday. She was going to string me up. And not for taking a day off.

"You're here early," she said, rounding a bookshelf to find me. "And what the hell is up?"

I laughed. "Oh—so much to tell you, so few days left in the year."

"Summarize," she said, a hand on one hip.

"My mother was the Antichrist, she hid photos of my son right under my nose, gave them to Johnny Mack in a secret alliance, his name is Seth, Becca knows about him now, Shayna and Noah are only together because she's pregnant, and I nearly slept with him."

I saw her eyebrows raise. "Holy fuck. All that in two days?"

"One," I said, rubbing my temples. "Yesterday was a recovery day."

"Jesus, how do you nearly sleep—"

Her words were cut off by the door jingling again, and we both leaned over to tell whoever it was that we weren't open yet. But it wasn't a customer.

"I'm sorry," Shayna said, rapping her knuckles on the open door for additional warning.

I was on my feet in an instant. "No problem, what's up?"

"You—need to come over there," she said, pointing at the wall between the diner and me. Her face was as white as a sheet, and her eyes looked glassy, even though she smiled. "To the diner. You need to come with me."

I frowned and little alarm bells went off in my head. Was it a showdown? Did she know? Or was it something else? Something about her expression was very, very off.

"What's wrong?" I asked, already walking forward.

"Just—" She turned and held open the door.

"Shayna, what's the matter?" I said, cold fear creeping up my legs.

Ruthie linked an arm with mine and walked out with me, probably getting the same sense of not-right. We followed Shayna, watching her take a deep breath as she pulled open the diner door for us.

Ruthie held my arm tighter as we entered, ever the protective one. But I searched Shayna's face as we passed her. Looking for signs of what we were walking into so I could layer up more walls. I steeled myself for Noah, knowing at the very least he'd be part of the equation, but I didn't see him right away. Customers were milling, but that was it. Not even Johnny Mack or Linny was in sight. I frowned and looked back at Shayna.

"What's going on?"

"In the back," she said.

"In the back?" I echoed, my feet halting of their own volition. I hadn't been behind the kitchen since before Noah had left town. "I don't go in the back, Shayna."

Undeterred, she walked past me and grabbed my hand, dragging me behind her.

"What the hell?" Ruthie muttered, balking, but I tightened my grip on her. Wherever I was going, she was coming, too.

Shayna pulled us through the kitchen to a back hallway, where I knew a break room similar to mine existed. Next to the office. She pushed open a door that wasn't completely closed, and I heard voices. Laughing voices, and Linny sniffling. Johnny Mack's wheezy guffaw.

When we entered, all heads turned to us. Linny's eyes were red, as were Noah's, but the glazed-over look was gone. He was nothing but exposed emotion. He looked like me a couple of nights prior.

Johnny Mack's expression changed slightly, from gleeful to cautious.

"What are they doing here?" he asked. Not as mean as before, I noticed. Just a question.

Noah shook his head. "No—Jules should be—" He looked at Shayna with immense gratitude. "Thank you," he whispered.

Her eyes watered, and my stomach knotted at the clear intimacy between them. I didn't want to see that. I didn't want to be around him or them or any of this.

"I have no idea," I said, letting go of Ruthie and crossing my arms over myself. "Why *are* we here?"

Just then, the door from the bathroom opened, and another younger man stepped out. All eyes went from us to him, and he looked around a little nervously under the weight of the attention. He had a polite smile, if slightly standoffish. His dark hair was cropped short, his eyes were dark blue, and when they landed on me, my heart slammed against my ribs.

"Sweet Jesus," I whispered.

I'd know him anywhere. Even though I'd only seen him in pictures the day before yesterday, and in person when he was only minutes old.

Noah's hand was on my back, pulling me with him.

"Jules, meet—"

"Seth," I finished with him, the sound barely registering in the room.

◆　◆　◆

The cry came at the end of my own, and it was like something out of a movie. My wail of pain and release that melded with the angry scream of something pulled from comfort into bright light and cold.

It was beautiful. It was horrible. It was over.

"It's a boy."

The doctor's voice was remote, as if he already knew this wasn't your normal happy delivery. There were no congratulations. Through a haze of pain I started to panic. To second-guess. What had I done?

"Wait—" I breathed, but no one heard me in the ruckus.

"It's a boy!" Noah yelled, fist-pumping the air. "Yes!"

He was crying and laughing at the same time, kissing me, standing up to stare in awe at the creation I hadn't seen yet, and then kissing me again.

"A boy," I echoed, my voice scratchy and raw from the screaming. I tried to sit up or move to see him, but my body wouldn't work. Damn epidural. I felt the burn of tears at the back of my throat as the frustration began to seep through my skin.

"You did it, baby," Noah said, over and over. "You did it." He laughed again. "Nearly broke my damn hand, but you did it. He's beautiful."

"He's—" My voice broke and I squeezed his hand as hard as I could to get his attention. My baby's cries were ripping at my insides. "Noah, I need to see him."

"You will, Mommy," he said, his blue eyes dancing with so much love it broke my heart. He moved the sweaty hair from where it stuck to my forehead. "Be patient, they're doing their thing." He kept looking over to the table. "God, he's amazing."

"We're cleaning him up," said a nurse to my right.

I reached for her with my other hand and gripped her arm as if it were the only thing holding my sanity together. "Please," I said, begging her with my eyes. "Please." My voice cracked and fresh hot tears burned tracks down my cheeks.

The woman's eyes went soft. Compassionate. Oh, God, she was going to help me. She patted my hand and placed it back on the rail as she nodded. I watched her face as Noah rambled in my ear about names and baseball and bicycles, lifting my head with great effort to watch her speak to the other nurse and doctor tending to my little boy.

Impatience lined the doctor's face around the mask as he turned back to look at me, but my angel nurse put a hand on his arm and said something else. Whatever it was made his expression relax, and my heart jumped as he nodded.

Noah's voice brought me back to him as he wiped my tears. "Don't cry, love, the hard part is over. We've got this."

We've got this. I met his eyes. They were so happy. So intent on making this happen. On being a family. "Noah—I'm—" I couldn't finish. My hot tears built to sobs that shook me from head to toe, and I had to look away from him.

"Jules, what's wrong—look, here he comes!"

The angel nurse appeared at my right, holding a bundle of screaming redness wrapped in a blue blanket. Her badge said her name was Courtney. And Courtney had tears in her eyes.

"I have to hold him," she said. "But you can look."

I'd always thought newborn photos were hideous. They always looked like little alien creatures, and I never understood why anyone ever thought those babies were attractive.

Mine was beautiful. He had a head full of dark hair and his face was all scrunched up, mouth trembling, bare little gums gleaming in the light. He was the most gorgeous alien I'd ever seen. I was in love. I lifted a hand and ran my fingers tentatively along his cheek, on skin so velvety I almost couldn't feel it. "Oh, my God," I whispered. "My baby."

I was in love with my little boy. And my heart stuttered in my chest.

"I can't—" I gasped. "I can't do this."

Noah didn't hear me. He was crying and kissing my hand. "I love you, Jules," he said, his voice shaking. "I love our new family. God, he's so—"

My mother's voice resonated outside the door, breaking through my baby's cries. The door opened then, and she was there, loose untied scrubs hanging on her and a mask held to her face.

Oh, God, I'd forgotten about my mother. Evidently someone had called her. By the look on Noah's face, it certainly wasn't him. And the look on her face as her eyes landed on the baby made my skin go cold.

"No," I said, instinctively wanting to shield him. From her, from me, from all that was about to go down. He wasn't going to know me. Oh, my God, he would never know me. What the hell did I do?

"What are you doing?" she said, looking at Courtney. "I had instructions not to—"

"Mom, no!" I croaked. "I need to see him!"

"Let her hold him," Noah said then, his tone different. Wary. Protective.

Courtney looked from Noah to my mother, but not back to me. "I'm not supposed—"

"You weren't supposed to even do this," my mother said, rounding the end of the bed. "It's cruel."

"I'm sorry," Courtney said, backing up with the baby. "She just wanted to see him."

"Let. Her. Hold him," Noah repeated, his voice strong in the room. "She's his mother. I'm his father. Let me hold him." I tore my eyes away from my son to focus on Noah's face. His eyes were narrowed on my mother. "You weren't invited in here."

"Noah," I said.

"This isn't your business," he continued. "This is our family." He turned back to Courtney, who was slowly walking back to the doctor and nurse, cooing at our crying infant. "Why can't we hold him?" Noah stepped in front of her, holding out his arms to take him.

"Because he isn't yours," my mother said.

Noah started as if he'd been slapped. "What?"

"No!" I cried. "Mom, look at him!"

"What do you mean, he's not mine?" Noah said, his voice clipped.

Mom ignored him, looking away from his glare. "Julianna—that doesn't help anyone."

"Look at him!" I screamed.

Reluctantly, she blinked rapidly and turned to peer upon my son. Her grandson. Her family. Slowly, the hand that held the mask to her face lowered, and I saw the quivering in her mouth. I saw her eyes fill. I saw it. There was hope. She'd fix it. She'd tear up the—

"He's beautiful," she said, her voice uncharacteristically unsteady. Slowly, she turned back to me and whisked tears off her cheeks before they could render her weak. "He's a beautiful boy, sweetheart. You gave him life. Now it's time to say good-bye."

"The hell it is!" Noah said, spurred into motion. "That's our son."

"No!" I cried again as the other nurse opened the door and Courtney walked through it. She looked over her shoulder before she disappeared, compassion filling her eyes. "No, wait!" I couldn't catch my breath, it was coming in gasps.

Noah surged toward the door and the doctor blocked him, holding him in a full body hold as Noah turned into a charging bull.

"You can't take my son!" he screamed, his voice hoarse and tinged with panic. "What the hell are you people doing?"

"I changed my mind—Mom, I changed my mind. Go fix this. Tear it up. Tell them it's off, we're gonna—"

"Changed your mind?" Noah said, spinning around as if he'd been shot. "Changed your mind about what? Tear up what?" He was shaking his head in disbelief, and my mouth couldn't form the words. "I didn't sign anything," he said slowly.

"You're not of age," Mom said.

He stared at her for a long moment before dragging tortured eyes back to me. "We talked about this, Jules. We—we—settled this." The shock and realization and horror settled into his face, looking exactly like I felt. "What did you do?"

CHAPTER 17

Everything I ever thought I would say left me. All the words. All the justifications. *He would never know me.* And he didn't. The last time I'd seen him he hadn't seen me—his eyes weren't even open yet. Now a man stood before me.

My son smiled nervously down into my face, as he would any other stranger he just met.

I did that.

Noah was somewhere behind me; I could feel him. His presence was powerful back there, like he was waiting to catch me again. Ever available to be my rescuer. But the face I'd seen when I walked in didn't look powerful. He looked like I imagined I did.

I wanted to hug this beautiful man-child in front of me, but I found myself stuck. Did I have that right? Was he a hugger? Would he stiffen and recoil if I did?

Instead, I stood there awkwardly, trying to stem the new tears that insisted on pushing forward, and I reached out with one hand. Touched his arm. He was real and solid, and something about that released everything.

Fat tears rolled down my face as I laughed and cried at the same time. "It's so good to see you again," I managed to say.

Seth smiled and took my hand in both of his. "It's good to finally meet you."

Yeah. Well, there was that.

"How did you—how are you here?" I asked, hoping he wouldn't let go. I was holding my son's hand, and every possible nerve in my body was aware of it. Holding his hand for the first time.

Seth turned to Johnny Mack and smiled again before looking back at me. "Mr. Ryan looked me up."

I glanced at Johnny Mack, who met my eyes for just that one second before blinking away. He looked him up. *I have real grandchildren to get to know. My blood.* Ah. Got it. How cute.

He looked him up for himself, or probably as a gift for Noah. Had Noah and I not reconnected, if Shayna were the protective jealous shrew she should be instead of being so damn nice to me, would I even be standing there?

Yes. Because Noah would have done the right thing.

"In all honesty," Seth continued, "the timing really worked out because I signed up on an online list last year." He gave a boyish shrug that tugged at my mommy heart. "I figured it'd be nice to know where I came from. In case there was anybody with eleven toes or insanity that hits at thirty or something."

Everyone laughed. And it felt wonderful. I swiped tears off my cheeks and let myself laugh, watching my amazing boy stand there with everyone staring at him like he was under a microscope and still talk with ease and make a room full of strangers laugh with no problem.

"Well, no extra limbs that I know of," Linny said, sniffling loudly. "But the old man has serious sanity issues."

Johnny Mack reddened and tried to look good-natured in spite of the fact that nothing in him could ever be that. Seth chuckled and continued to stand there as I realized we needed to do something besides stare at him in the little room.

"Um," I began, profoundly. "Do you want to go sit down? Go next door to the bookstore—it's mine, we can do that," I rambled. "Or forget the store, I'll close it for the day. We can go to my house and—" Wait. No.

"I think staying here at the diner is fine," Johnny Mack piped in.

"And what, cram everyone in a booth?" Linny said, fixing him with a look. "Let them go, he'll be back."

Seth looked amused at the tug-of-war over him. "Hey, I'm just grateful to be here. To meet everyone." He held his palms out. "I'm here today and tomorrow, so there's no rush." He looked at me and then to Noah, as if we were the deciding votes. Which I guess we were. "Whatever you want to do. Wherever you want to go. It's probably gonna be weird anywhere, so don't stress."

Damn good thing he was the grown-up in the situation, because I felt like neither of us were.

"Noah, Jules has the right idea. Why don't the three of you go over to her house so you can just be comfortable and relax," Shayna said, her hands on his arm. "It's okay," she said reassuringly as he looked down at her in surprise.

But I knew what that look was, as the same sense of *oh, shit* permeated my brain. Why had I suggested that? Going back to my house? With Noah. In my living room. Where we almost did the deed just two days ago. No, we needed Shayna there, because that made it infinitely better. Always better that the pregnant fiancée come along—the one whose phone call stopped us from the primal monkey sex on the rug.

"Or we could go back to your dad's house," I said quickly, meeting his eyes and pretending he was someone else so Shayna wouldn't see it. My stealth skills were toast. "If that's better."

Noah nodded, looking spent. "Probably so."

"Well, then I can just go—" Shayna began, looking uncertain.

"You don't need to go anywhere," I said. "You stay with us."

Her face relaxed and she smiled a thank-you to me that didn't quite reach her eyes. Nothing had. That was something I'd learned about her in the short time I'd known her. She wore her worry there. And something was chewing on her. Was it me? Did she know? Surely not. Or maybe she was beginning to suspect since Noah and I were wearing our crazy like neon signs. Then again, maybe that was my own paranoid guilt waving at me, and she just had a lot on her plate. Like being unsure about marrying Noah.

"Let's go," I said, leading the way, needing to move and needing to stop looking at him even more.

Ruthie dabbed under her eyes and stopped me to throw her arms around my neck. I felt the weakness come into my bones as everything in me just wanted to drop to the floor and sit cross-legged across from her and unload all my woes like we did when we were girls. But there was no time for that now.

"I've got the store," she whispered. "Go."

"Thank you," I breathed.

On the sidewalk, I turned back to Seth, struck once again with the Noah resemblance. "Do you—have a car? Want to ride with me?"

"I've got my truck over here," he said, probably grateful for the breathing space for the fifteen seconds it was going to take to get to the house. "I'll follow."

"Good," I said, turning down the sidewalk and then spinning around with a hand up. "I don't mean good, like good, I just meant—"

"I got it," Seth said, laughing and getting into his truck with a wink.

"Of course," I mumbled, smiling as I turned around and walked toward my car on legs I couldn't feel. I passed Shayna and Noah getting in his truck and refused to look that way. I was going to his friggin' house; I'd see plenty of them there.

I shut my car door and plugged my keys in, watching my hands tremble. I gripped the steering wheel and squeezed my eyes shut. My breaths got choppy, and I knew what was coming. I pressed my hand against my mouth to push it back.

"Oh, my God," I whispered, sucking in sharp breaths against the burn. "I just met my son."

◆ ◆ ◆

Seth cased the place very much like Noah had when he'd come to my house that first morning, hands in his jacket pockets and eyes soaking in every detail. He of course went to the photographs first, and I wondered what that felt like. Looking at photos of a family that you should have been part of but weren't. His photos were in another house, with another family.

Noah explained each and every one, named grandparents and cousins and told funny stories that had been captured of him and Linny. Shayna and I sat on two separate couches and listened as Noah danced around every one but the prom picture of us. Until he did. Or Seth did, actually.

He picked it up and turned to me with a smirk that made the skin on my back tingle. He looked so much like his dad in that moment it was surreal.

"Nice hair," he said, holding it up.

Noah laughed and I scrunched my nose. "It was the eighties, baby, what can I say?" I held a hand out for it. "Let me look at that."

Seth walked it over to me and sat on the arm of the couch like it was entirely normal for us to look at something together. I stared up at him for as long as I dared before he could catch me and it would get awkward. Then I blinked my vision free and focused on the dusty framed picture that was starting to show some age.

A skinny Noah with a hideous tux and a head full of shaggy dark hair smiled back at me, his arms wrapped tightly around a dark-haired girl with a secretive smile. She held flowers in front of where I knew

Noah's hands rested protectively. I knew what that smile was about. We'd just found out about the baby and hadn't told anyone yet. It was still our little secret. Before the rest of the world had a chance to weigh in. God, we looked so young, and in love.

"You were there," I said softly, my voice barely more than a whisper. I pointed to the flowers. "Right there."

"You were pregnant then?" Seth asked, his voice warm over me.

"We'd just found out," Noah said, walking closer but still keeping a safe distance. "No one knew yet."

"It was still just ours, then," I said, not looking away from the picture. From the moment in time—probably the only one caught on film—when we were happy and in love and full of romantic ideas of what having a baby would be. "Before parents found out." I pointed to Noah's huge grin. "See? How happy he was? My dad hadn't threatened to castrate him yet."

Noah laughed, a hearty sound that made me look up in spite of myself. An invisible hand squeezed my heart as our eyes met, but I didn't look away this time. *Memorize this moment, Jules. For this one tiny microsecond, the three of us are together again.* He saw it, too. As his gaze flickered between Seth and me, the rawness came to the surface. My own eyes filled, and I finally had to look down and blink it away.

"Was this your senior year?" Seth asked.

I shook my head. "Junior." I cleared my throat of the huskiness. "We weren't together for—"

"I left town," Noah said. "After—after you were born." He sat on an ottoman across from us, and I glanced over at Shayna. She looked like an island over there by herself. "I went to stay with my uncle in San Antonio and finished school there. Signed up for the Navy, and all that."

"Your father sent you away?" Seth asked, a frown on his face.

"No, it was my idea," Noah said, looking down at his hands. "I had to get away. I couldn't be here. Couldn't just—go back to school like nothing ever happened." He sat up taller and inhaled slowly. "Never planned on returning, but life changes things sometimes."

"When did you come back?" Seth asked.

"Last week."

Seth laughed. "Seriously?"

"Seriously," I echoed as Noah looked at me so intently that I couldn't look away or blink or anything. My fingertips went numb.

Noah looked down at his hands again, releasing me from that damn freeze-glare of his, the haunted memories still sitting on him as he mentally replayed everything. I felt Seth's gaze on me, and my skin felt like it was a thousand degrees as he put a hand on my shoulder.

"Did you leave, too?" he asked.

"No," I said, unable to look away from Noah's face. "My parents let me stay home sick for three days and then—" My words stuck in my throat. And then what? What was I supposed to say?

That I stopped caring or eating or talking to anyone? That I lived on angry music and alcohol and whatever drug I could find at the moment? That I pushed away everyone and everything that resembled what normal used to be? Anything that required feeling. My friends, my art, books, life. Until Ruthie reached down deep and yanked me out of my own self-imposed hell. And then there was Hayden.

"—I managed to graduate, let's just leave it at that," I said, handing the picture back to Noah.

Seth was studying me, however. Damn it, he had that Noah thing.

"It wasn't your idea to give me up, was it?"

"No," I said, the word coming out on a heavy breath.

Noah got up and put the picture back in its place on the table, and Shayna rose to stand next to him. The picture of love and solidarity.

"My—my parents made all that happen," I said. "My mother, mostly. She—thought it was the best thing for me." Oh, that was a nice way to put it.

"She was a coldhearted micromanaging shrew that arranged a deal with your adopted parents to get photos of you," Noah said, his voice even. "That she then kept hidden in a box and took that secret to her grave. Jules didn't see them until day before yesterday."

My mouth dropped open and Seth's eyebrows lifted.

"Well, okay then," I said softly. "Now you know the true guts of it." I touched his hand. "I'm sorry, Seth."

He squeezed it back and got up to take Noah's place on the ottoman, facing me. "Don't be," he said. "I mean, yes, be sorry for what you've given up, I understand that. But don't be sorry for me." Seth smiled, a little apologetically, and it reminded me of Becca when she was in trouble. "I had good parents. A good childhood. You gave me to great people who loved me."

My chest burned hearing those words. *I loved you, too. Every day.* "I'm so glad to know that," I whispered. "I can tell they did a fantastic job with you."

"And they were always honest with me. With me and my little brother. They adopted Shon three years after me. They told us even when we were little that we came from other mommies' tummies," he said with a smile. "And you showed me a picture of that."

Before I could stop myself, I reached out and touched his cheek, rough in one spot where a razor missed and very different from the velvetiness of the last time I'd done that. To his credit, he didn't flinch or pull away.

"So tell us about you," I said, needing to lighten the heaviness of the room.

"I'm boring," he said on a chuckle, relieving some of the tension. "Seriously." He pointed at me and Noah simultaneously. "Business owner with a crazy mom—no offense."

"None taken," I said with a laugh and little head bow. I had to laugh. What else could I do?

"—and a Navy SEAL?" he continued. "My life is very sedate compared to yours."

"How'd you know all that?" Noah asked.

"Mr. Ryan told me," Seth said. "Well—you added the crazy-mother part."

"Glad to fill in the blanks," I said.

"So, what do you do, Seth?" Shayna asked, speaking for what I realized was the first time since we'd arrived. She still wore that look of hers. The one that made her appear not totally in the room with us.

"I'm a police officer," he said. "Just made detective, actually," he added with a smile that lit up his face. "Youngest in my precinct."

"Sedate?" I reached over and patted his hand. "I don't think so! That's amazing, Seth, congratulations!"

Noah crossed the room, beaming, holding out a hand as Seth got up on instinct. "That's awesome," Noah said, gripping Seth's hand in that manly thing guys do. "You should be so proud. Your parents—" He faltered, and I saw the struggle in his eyes. "They must be over the moon."

Seth smiled and glanced back at me as if to gauge his words. I forced any sadness from my face—he didn't need that burden. I wanted him to feel free to say anything and not feel awkward.

"They are," he said. "My mom threw a big block party and forced all her neighbors to bring food. Even got her pastor to come over and bless me."

I laughed. "Sounds like something my Nana Mae would do—Nana Mae!" I sucked in a breath and looked at Noah as if he could possibly understand me. "Oh, my grandmother has to meet you!"

"Your grandmother is still alive?" Seth asked.

"Yes, I'm not that ancient, thank you," I said with a wink when he reddened. "And Nana Mae is eternal. She will love you." My breath caught in my throat. "And Becca, my daughter."

It was my turn to look at him with apology in my eyes. How do you look into the eyes of a child you gave away and tell him you kept the next one? He blinked a few times, and I would have given anything to be in his head, viewing those thoughts. Or then again, maybe not.

"I was going to ask if you had any other kids—if I had any siblings," he said finally. "Wasn't sure how to bring that up."

"You bring up anything you want," I said. "Coming here like this— that's a pretty brave thing, baby. Even for a grown, big badass police detective." Seth laughed, and I focused on the smile in his eyes instead of Noah's right behind him. Seth's were safer. "There are no taboo questions. Nothing off-limits."

"Okay," he said.

I took a deep breath and stood up so we were all on the same level. "You have a sister—a half sister. She's seventeen going on thirty, and her name is Becca."

"Sounds like fun," he said.

"Everyone should be tortured with teenagers at some point," I said.

"Oh, I get that," Seth said. "I see more than I want of teenage drama in my job. Or I did as a beat cop, anyway."

Seth glanced to Noah, and I saw the hollowness enter Noah's eyes as he tried to fill it with Shayna. He put an arm around her and pulled her to him. "I never had any other kids," he said. His eyes met mine instead of Seth's. "But Shayna and I have one on the way now."

I swallowed hard as Seth congratulated them and hugged Shayna. That was my life now. How it was going to be for a friggin' eternity. I almost wished Patrick was back next to me so I could introduce him as my boy toy and get the edge back.

Wow, that was mature.

"So, who do I meet next?" Seth asked, bringing me back. "Or what is next?"

I smiled. "This is your show. What do you want to do?"

"I have no idea," he said with a boyish grin that made him look much less grown up. He held his hands out wide. "Honestly, I'm winging this. And that is so far outside my box, you have no idea."

I raised an eyebrow. "A planner, are you?"

"To the core."

I laughed and moved before I could think about it. "You come by that honestly," I said as I hugged him.

His hesitance made me freeze and pull away. "I'm sorry," I said.

Maybe he wasn't a hugger. Maybe he wasn't a demonstrative person. Maybe he wasn't that comfortable with meeting his parents yet—no. I had to stop that train, cold. We weren't his parents. We gave him life, but his parents raised him.

"No, it's okay," he said, looking troubled. Or maybe embarrassed. "I'm just still nervous, I guess."

"Totally understandable," I said, wanting to stick my head in a freezer to chill the heat coming off my face.

"Why don't we go grab some lunch at the diner," Noah said.

I knew he was trying to diffuse the awkward turn of conversation and help me out, but he was suddenly standing too close for my heat-infused brain to handle gracefully.

"Lunch is good," I said, backing away from him a step and knocking into the coffee table. Loudly.

Noah grabbed my elbow to steady me and ended up pulling me closer in the move. I bit down on my lip as I looked up into blue eyes that darkened with memory and cursed my body's automatic reaction to him.

Not. Mine. To. Want.

That needed to be filed away under stupid things never to do again. Regardless of all the things his face was telling me.

"I'm good," I said, smiling to prove it. "Just clumsy. Let's go."

CHAPTER 18

Lunch was a blur. I couldn't tell you what was said, other than Seth's favorite food was french fries. I don't think I even dogged that. Ruthie would have been proud.

Words were like background noise, humming along to my thoughts and my chewing. To the visuals as I stared at the two men across the table. Linny got us a booth by the bar so she could frequent it, and Noah and Seth sat across from me and Shayna.

It was brutal. And all I could do was shovel food in so I'd have something to do with my hands. Not only was it surreal to see my son across from me, grown up and talking about the world with my mouth and Noah's hair and eyes and everything else, but just seeing the two of them sitting together—it killed me. They were so alike. Not just in looks but even mannerisms and personalities. Already joking like best buddies that had hung out for years. I'd taken that away from both of them.

Even though I knew now that Seth had a happy life and probably brought incredible joy to the family that loved him, I felt a severe hit to the gut that we missed it. That Noah never got to teach him to throw a ball or swim or ride a bike, like Hayden had with Becca.

And then there was the constant work of avoiding Noah's eyes. It seemed that every time I looked his way, he'd be looking at me, and we'd stick like that for a few seconds, turning my insides to a shimmying mess. I'd shove more food I couldn't taste into my mouth and stare at my plate like it was food from the gods until Shayna would occasionally pipe in with something, and then I'd catch Noah smiling at her and want to throw it all back up. It was the longest meal of my life.

"So, if you want to go back to your house for a while," Noah was saying, as sound went with the look he was giving me, "I'll swing by later."

"What?" I said. He was coming over? All nerve endings went on sweat mode.

Noah looked at me questioningly, and I looked back and forth between them for clarification.

"You can have him to yourself for a little while," Noah said slowly. "And I'll pick him up later to go get some dinner and a beer."

"Oh!" I exclaimed. "That sounds great. Absolutely." I wondered if Seth would want to start drinking early. Since my baby boy was now suddenly past drinking age. My brain needed massaging. And something to do. So I grabbed my phone.

"Put your heads together," I said, not even letting myself think about it first. We needed new pictures of him. The look in Noah's eyes as he looked at me for the photo was a sacrifice I'd have to make when I looked at it five hundred more times that night. Right.

"Good idea," Shayna said, pulling her phone out to click away as well.

Noah chuckled. "Good luck over there," he said, nudging Seth.

"Hey," I said, tossing a carrot at him. "Be nice." Food fights were progress, right?

"Just saying, if your daughter and grandmother show up, he'll have three generations of women on his plate."

"Ha ha," I said. "I so hope you have a daughter, so you can truly have all that testosterone handed to you in a pink teacup and tiara."

Both men laughed, Noah's face and body relaxing. For that one tiny second, even for me, it was easy. Till he looked at Shayna and frowned.

"What's wrong?" he asked.

I looked at her and she'd gone white. Like gray-white. "Shayna?" I said, touching her arm.

"I'm okay," she said, smiling it off but not too convincingly. "Just feeling a little puny is all."

"Can I get you something?" Noah asked, grabbing her hand. Six inches from mine. Not that I noticed. At all. "Need to go home?"

"Hey, y'all go ahead," I said. "We'll head to my house from here."

Noah paid the check and I didn't miss the look of enormous relief that came over his features when Shayna got up and we weren't side by side anymore. Guess it was a little wiggly from his side, too.

He slapped Seth on the back. "See you later, bud," he said.

Knowing him, he'd thought about that since we'd sat down. What to say to sound nonchalant. He couldn't say *son*, and *Seth* was so two hours ago. *Bud* would work. Perfect mix of affection and respectable distance.

I also didn't miss the slight hesitance in his step as he passed me and the melting look he gave me. I ran a hand through my hair and waited for the feeling to come back to my tongue. Damn him and those looks.

Of course, if I hadn't been looking up at *him* . . .

Yeah.

"You ready?" Seth asked, a hint of a knowing smile playing at his lips.

"Sure," I said. "A stop or two first."

We ducked into the bookstore for a bit so I could introduce him better to Ruthie. She cried again, hugged him whether he wanted it or not, and gave him two fresh-baked peanut butter cookies and a book to take with him.

That's what made her Ruthie.

I called Nana Mae, but there was no answer, so I left her a message.

"I figure you're probably out walking, so call me when you get this, or come by the house. And just so there's no cardiac arrest involved, I have more than pictures now." I glanced at the man in my passenger seat. "Seth is here. In person."

"Makes me sound famous," he said. "Like Pink. Or Usher."

"See, I would have gone with Sting or Madonna," I said. "Maybe Cher. But I'm old."

"Touché."

"And you are famous to us," I said. "You've been the secret on the shelf for too long. You coming out to shine makes it the best day ever."

Seth took a deep breath and exhaled slowly. "I'm glad. You never know what reactions might be." He raised his eyebrows as we turned into a residential section. "I read so many horror stories online about meet-ups gone wrong. I nearly turned around and drove back home the second I got here."

"Seriously?" I said, feeling the tug at my insides. "But you said Noah's dad got in touch with you."

"Yeah, but that was just a grandfather. It wasn't you or Noah." I stopped to meet his eyes at a stop sign. "He wanted to surprise his son. That could have gone twenty different ways."

"Wow, you're right," I said. "I bet that was scary. Thank you for not going home."

Seth smiled, a little crooked, and the Noah of two decades ago peeked out. "Yeah, I'm glad I didn't."

I faced forward and continued driving, determined not to get mushy. "So, Detective," I began, trying to lighten the subject. "I don't see a wedding ring on your finger. Anyone special in your life?"

And my attempt at lightening was probably the most awkward thing ever to come out of my mouth. All these years, he'd been a baby. A child at most. Here he was a man, and I was asking him if he had a woman. I might as well check his wallet for condoms while I was at it.

A sigh laced with a bit of frustration came from his side of the car. He raked his fingers through his short hair.

"There was."

I opened my mouth and closed it again. *Don't be awkward a second time.* It was a harmless question but might not be to him. Might be huge. Might be too personal to talk about with someone he just met a few hours ago.

"I was engaged, actually," he continued, canceling out my self-flogging. "For a whole four months."

"I take it it didn't end well?"

"No," he said on a sigh. "Best way to kill a good relationship is to put a ring on it," he said, smiling at his joke. But the smile didn't reach his eyes. "We were together for three years before that. We should have just dated for life."

"I'm sorry," I said. "I hate to hear that." I was. I wanted to go beat up the girl that hurt my baby and made his eyes look like that.

"It's all good," he said. "I should have known it was too easy with her. Too good to be true."

"There's something to that," I said. "Sometimes it's the harder relationships, the complicated ones, you have to fight and claw for that have staying power. May give you gray hair and bruises, but, you know."

Seth laughed. "Probably one of the things that spurred me on to find where I came from. I needed a diversion. And a connection." He paused and looked my way. "I'm really glad this went well."

"Me too," I said, rounding onto my street. Becca's car was in the driveway. At one in the afternoon on a school day. I blew out a breath. "Hold on to that thought, babe."

"What's wrong?" he asked.

"Not sure, but my Spidey sense is all twitchy."

I pulled next to her little blue car and got out, staring a hole in the front door as I approached it. The door wasn't locked, and we were greeted to a dancing Harley as she viewed Seth as new love. He instantly went to one knee and got acquainted, all the while absorbing the room in seconds.

"Becca?" I called.

The thump from above didn't give me a warm fuzzy. Then her door squeaked open at the top of the stairs.

"Yeah?"

Yeah? Seriously? "Becca!"

A sigh that had an audible eye roll with it traveled the stairs. "I'm coming."

The door closed, and she headed down, her steps quick. Her lopsided hair swung out to the side as she came into view and opened her mouth to argue, but whatever words she had at the ready stuck there when she saw Seth petting Harley. She glanced at me in question.

"Why are you home?" I asked.

Her eyes went back to him. "Why are you?"

"Becca."

Thank God she still had respect for "the tone." I didn't use it often, wanting it to be the sound of doom that would stop her in her tracks when I really needed it. This qualified. She straightened up and fiddled with the railing in front of her.

"I wasn't feeling well," she said.

"Are you sick?"

"Might be."

"The school didn't call me," I said.

"Well, I just—" She paused and her eyes darted to Seth again. He stood up, causing Harley to climb his leg in protest.

"You just came home without telling anyone," I said, rubbing my forehead. When would it stop?

"It's not a big deal, Mom," she said. "You make too much of it."

"Actually, truancy is a big deal," Seth said, causing her head to snap in his direction again. "Sorry," he said, raising his hands to me in apology. "My thoughts get away from me sometimes."

"And you are?" Becca said, coming down the last three steps with what I guessed she thought was sudden seniority.

"Seth," he said, holding out a hand with a half smile on his face. "Nice to meet you."

Becca's mouth fell open. Boy, I was glad I'd told her, as she looked at me and back at him again. "Like, Seth? *That* Seth?"

He chuckled. "There I am being famous again. Yes, that Seth."

"Oh, holy shit," she said under her breath as she walked forward slowly and took his hand. "You're my brother?"

My heart slammed against my ribs. God, what a sentence and what a sight. I never in a million years expected to look at the two of them standing in the same room. I almost stopped being mad at her.

"That's the rumor," he said softly, a smile playing at his lips.

"I just found out about you two days ago," she said.

"I just found out about you two hours ago."

Becca laughed, and even as that put my heart at ease, I saw Seth's eyes narrow a little.

"So, do you have any other brothers or sisters?" she asked. "Like, that you grew up with?"

Seth's eyes glazed over a bit. "I did," he said. "I had a little brother who was adopted, too. His name was Shon."

"Did?" she asked, picking up on something I hadn't.

"Yeah, he died six years ago," he said, averting his eyes.

"Oh—" I said, my chest contracting. The pain in his expression was palpable. "Seth, I'm so sorry."

He nodded and put his hands in his pockets, a self-protecting gesture that made him suddenly look younger.

"It was a stupid accident," he said. "He was—"

A thud from overhead halted his words.

"What was that?" I said.

Both hands were out of his pockets and he was at the base of the stairs in insta-cop mode in two-point-five seconds. I would have followed, but I was watching Becca. And she wasn't startled. Her glance upward wasn't questioning or scared, it was panicked.

It was *busted*.

"Who's upstairs?" I asked.

My tone was calm, and in that moment I was very proud of my control. Seth stopped his progression midstep and looked at me.

"Nothing!" she said defensively. "Nobody."

Her worry over where Seth was standing, however, told otherwise. As did a second thump and the subsequent creaking.

"Becca, who is in this house?" I repeated. The tone was making a comeback. "Alone with you. In the middle of a school day and work day when you didn't think anyone would be home."

"Mom, it's not like that," she said, holding up her palms.

"Please tell me what it's like, then," I said. "Before I go find out for myself."

"Mark, come down!" she yelled upward, darting one look at me and then at the floor.

"Mark," I whispered, closing my eyes. Not because I was being nice. More because my rage had taken the power of speech away.

"Mom—"

"Becca Ann White," I began, not caring anymore that Seth was seeing all this. So damn be it. "What is the rule on boys in this house?"

"Downstairs, I know—"

"And what about when I'm not home?" I said, hearing the rise in pitch.

"No one at all."

"And during school hours?" I said. No—I yelled it. I did.

Her eyebrows dipped into a frown. "During school hours? There's not a rule for that."

"Exactly!" I said, walking closer and enjoying the look on her face that questioned my sanity just a little. Good. She needed to worry. "Because you are supposed to be *there*."

"O-*kay*." The death glare.

This was why wild animals sometimes eat their young.

And the boy still hadn't made an appearance. "Mark!" I yelled. "The stairs aren't that hard to find, young man. Please get down here."

"Oh, my God," Becca said, her eyes filling with angry tears. "I hate you right now."

"Well, good," I said under my breath as a little piece of my soul broke away. "I'm doing my job. What the living hell are you thinking, skipping school and bringing him here?"

Feet appeared in my line of vision. Big sneakers, followed by baggy jeans and a jersey sweatshirt. The face it was all attached to looked worried. Well, at least he was that smart. He paused at the bottom as Seth stared at him for a beat before letting him pass.

He stood next to Becca, who did nothing but glare at me through her tears. Disgusted, I thrust my hand into the boy's hand.

"I'm Becca's mom, by the way," I said. "Since you are too rude to step up, and she's too rude to introduce you, I'll do that myself."

Becca's mouth fell open, as if she couldn't believe I could still shock her. Mark mumbled something including his name and how nice it was to meet me. I think. Out of the corner of my eye, I saw Seth grin and look away. I wondered if his—mother—had ever had to do the same.

"Mark, I would've liked to have met you a different way, but since I didn't, let me fill you in. Becca isn't allowed to skip class. Don't know if you are, but she's not. You aren't allowed in her room. Ever."

Echoes of my mother's voice rang in my head, but I was too far gone to think about that.

"You will respect those things, and keep all your personal property in your pants, and we will get along just fine."

"Mom!" she yelled, tears fully streaming down her face, black eyeliner coming with it.

"Ma'am, I'm sorry," Mark said, his words barely heard over Becca's carrying on.

"You can go, Mark," I said.

"I drove," Becca said through her sobs.

"He looks like he can handle a six-block walk, Becca," I said. "Mark, have a good day."

He wheeled around with big eyes and briefly squeezed her hand as he passed. Didn't make it three more steps, however, before Seth deftly plucked an object from the side cargo pocket of the baggy jeans.

"Don't think you're quite old enough for this," Seth said.

A stainless steel flask. Joy. Becca's face contorted as if she'd seen death up close and personal.

"Unless you have lemonade in here—" Seth unscrewed the top and sniffed. "Whoa, most definitely not lemonade."

"Hey, that's mine," Mark said, attempting to bow up with whatever he had under the three-sizes-too-big clothing.

"Really?" Seth said, holding up the flask. "Yours? You bought this yourself? I'm impressed. You must have one hell of an ID."

"I'm twenty-one," Mark said.

Seth laughed. "Yeah, I can see that. Why don't we call the school and see if maybe they have something different."

"Shit," Mark muttered. "Okay, it's my dad's. Just—can I have it, please? I'll leave."

"Sure," Seth said. "Kitchen?" he asked me in passing. I pointed, and he walked around the corner, leaving a perplexed kid in the entryway. I heard the sound of liquid going down a drain, and then he was back. "Here you go," he said. "Tell your dad he has good taste."

"You have no right acting like this," Becca said. "You're not family."

To his credit, he only faltered a second. Me, on the other hand—I saw ten shades of red.

"You're right," he said, putting a hand on my arm before I could say a word. "But I am an officer of the law, so . . ."

"You're a prince," Becca said, acid dripping from her tone.

"Yeah, I get that a lot," he said, opening the door for Mark.

When he closed it back, I focused on Becca. On her hate, her embarrassment, and my own disappointment and absolute mortification that the meeting with Seth went so sour.

"Drinking, Bec?" I said, my voice cracking. "Seriously?"

"We hadn't even had any yet," she said.

"Yet," I echoed. "Where's your head?"

Her fists went up in her hair, like she wanted to pull it out. "Oh, my God, I wish I was anywhere else but here!"

"You were supposed to be. Clean yourself up and get back to school," I said, feeling all the inflection go out of my voice. I was so angry that she'd blown my trust. Again.

She swiped at her face, essentially just smearing black around. "Are you kidding me? There's like an hour and a half left."

"Then you'd better hurry it up," I said.

She narrowed her eyes and scoffed and wheeled around in disgust. "I can't believe you," she said on her way up the stairs. She stopped, and I had the feeling something profound was coming. "You humiliated me today." Or that.

"Ditto," I said through my teeth.

Becca glanced at Seth and back at me. "Yeah, I'll bet. Awfully high and mighty on the subject of boys, aren't you—since your stellar example of restraint is standing here?"

I felt all the blood drain from my face, and the quiet was deafening. I saw it—the moment that passed through her brain when she knew she'd gone too far. I had a fleeting thought through the pounding in my ears that that was at least proof she still had a conscience. Then I turned and walked to the kitchen.

I pulled two glasses from the cabinet and started to fill them with ice when I heard footsteps behind me. Heavier footsteps than Becca's. Slower.

"I have sweet tea, water, and orange juice," I said, opening the fridge. I stared at the pitchers without seeing them and grabbed one of them without feeling it in my hand.

"Sweet tea is fine."

I turned to look at my son. A man. Standing in my kitchen. Not too many days back, I was in awe of seeing his father occupying that same space. It was surreal.

He pointed at the pitcher I was holding. "That's fine," he reiterated.

I looked down at it and realized it was the tea. "Okay," I said, pouring into both glasses.

"You okay?" he asked.

"Of course," I said. I wasn't. I was numb. I was standing in my kitchen, talking to my son. Talking to my son. A miracle of all miracles. And I was mortified and horrified and distraught. Where had I gone wrong with her? How could she talk to me that way? How did it get this far?

"Juliann—I mean—" Seth stopped and let out a wary breath. "I just realized I haven't called you by anything yet. What do I—"

"Most people call me Jules," I said. "Your gran—" Yeah, I was doing it, too. "My dad gave me that nickname when I was little and it stuck."

"Well, Jules, you don't seem okay," he said, pulling up a nearby stool. "And that would be okay if you're not. You don't have to pretend anything. That was pretty intense."

"Intense." I sank onto a stool and buried my face in my hands. "I am so sorry you had to witness that," I said. "That thing you said about never knowing how these things are going to turn out—well, I guess I just made your case for the dark side."

"Not at all," Seth said, resting his elbows on the counter. "Y'all have been great. And Becca'll come around. Was she upset about me when you told her?"

I shook my head. "Not about you. I think she was kind of intrigued by the idea, actually. It was my keeping it from her all this time that hit her buttons."

"Why did you?" he asked.

CHAPTER 19

Why did I? I listened to my breath going in and out. "I don't know," I said. "I told myself I was protecting her, but that wasn't it. I think it was just more of my mother's voice saying to keep it all quiet." I looked him in the eye. "I have no good answer for that."

"Understandable, too," he said, pausing. "Can I be honest with you?"

"Absolutely."

Seth averted his gaze, studying his hands. "She's a rebel. She's testing boundaries." He met my eyes. "Shon was like that, too. Me—I was probably an easy kid, but Shon was hard to follow sometimes. He was always bucking the rules."

"That's Becca," I said.

"My parents were kind of sticklers about rules, too," he said, blinking his gaze down. "And being the one usually watching the showdowns, I always wanted to ask them to back off a little."

"I thought you said everything was good," I said, feeling a frown dip my eyebrows.

"No, no, it was," he said. "Our house was normal—but normal has chaos, too."

"True."

"And it seemed like the more my parents cracked down, the more Shon fought back."

Our eyes met for a long moment. "What happened to him?" I asked.

"He got in some trouble," Seth said, looking into his glass as though the story was in there. "I tried to help him, but he needed a different kind of help."

"What kind?"

"Money to pay off debt—at nineteen years old," Seth added, bitterness entering his voice. "He got mixed up with bad people, and then thought drowning his problems in a bottle would stop it." He looked at me. "It did."

"Oh, God," I whispered.

"So he got behind the wheel after partying one night, and ended up dead," Seth said, upending his glass and draining the tea.

"I'm so sorry," I said.

"I was twenty-one," he said. "Just finishing up college. It's part of what pushed me to join the police academy."

"How did your parents handle it?" I asked, unable to imagine losing a child that way.

I'd lost one, too. But I knew he was still breathing. And then the most awful realization hit me. I hadn't known, not really. I guess my mother did, but I didn't. Shon's birth mother—she probably had no idea.

"Like you'd expect," he said. "It was hard to leave them after that, but they wanted me to go after what I wanted, so I did."

"Do they—" I stopped and took a sip of my untouched tea, then got up to refill his glass. "Do they know you came to find us?"

"My dad does," he said. "My mom—she'd probably be okay with it, but I just didn't want to put that on her yet. At least not till I had something to tell. After Lisa bailed on the wedding and all—she would have just worried."

I smiled. "She sounds like we'd have a lot in common."

"You're very similar, actually," he said on a chuckle. "Eerily so."

Becca came into the room, looking somber and clean-faced. "I need a note to get back in school."

"What was your plan?" I asked.

"Hadn't thought that far," she said, nothing in her eyes. Nothing in her expression. She handed me a pen and piece of notebook paper. "Just—please write whatever you're gonna write."

She knew me. She knew I'd write something like, *Please let Becca White back in school today, she was stupid and skipped class without my knowledge.*

She knew that because it's exactly what I would have done. As I looked at the trouble in her face and heard Seth's words, however, I paused.

I looked at the blank page with its rumpled edges, pulled from some dark cave of her backpack, and started writing. When I handed it to her, she snatched it and walked off, but stopped at the doorway as she started reading. She turned back around with a question in her eyes.

"Really?"

"Consider it your freebie," I said. "With the school, not with me."

It would be a little while before we were good again. Her gaze darted to Seth and then to the floor, and she nodded and walked away.

"What did you write?" he asked.

"To excuse her for a family emergency and that she'd be back the next day," I said, wishing I could put my head in my glass. My face felt on fire.

Seth's eyes widened. "Wow."

"Yeah, caving's not really my thing," I said, rubbing my forehead. "And I'm not sure how smart it was. Especially after her mouth over-loaded her brain like that."

"Did it hurt?"

"Massively."

He laughed. "Why'd you do it?"

"I don't know," I said. "Maybe your story about your brother. Maybe some things I've been thinking about my own mother." I looked at the empty doorway where she'd just exited. "I just know something has to change."

◆ ◆ ◆

We spent the next few hours catching up on twenty-six years. I told him his birth story—the one Becca described with such flare. I told him about Noah and me, and my parents, and Noah's dad. About the animosity and the drama. Spent some detail on my mother—as fun as that was—and I showed him the pictures I'd found after Noah returned to town. We made plans with Nana Mae to maybe hook up the next morning, at which point I hoped he'd get a different perspective on my mom. I just couldn't go there yet.

"Wow," he said, flipping over one of his childhood drawings—a particularly good depiction of a squirrel. "I never knew about any deal for a trust fund," he said. "My mom showed it to me when I turned twenty-one, said that my biological family had set it up. Honestly, I didn't give it a lot of thought. I just left it there."

"Well, it's not going anywhere."

He looked down at what was essentially his life in pictures. "I guess my mom had secrets, too," he said. "Maybe all parents do. Do you?" he added.

I smiled sadly. "Not anymore."

"What does Becca like to do?" he said, the turn of subject taking me off guard.

"Um—she writes," I said. "Carries a notebook with her everywhere. Other than that, she's attached to her phone twenty-four-seven."

"Do you mind if I go spend a few minutes with her before Noah comes?" he asked.

It was endearing and hurl-worthy at the same time, because I'd managed to forget that Noah was coming.

"Sure," I said, grabbing our glasses and heading to the sink. "Good luck!"

"Well, then again, I'm a boy," he said. "Am I allowed up there?"

I wheeled around to give him a look, and he started laughing, pointing at me.

"I wondered what your *mom look* would be," he said. "Sorry, I couldn't resist."

I bit my lip and instantly dialed back whatever might be glowing in neon across my face. "Boy, I'll bet you were fun," I said, tossing a dishrag at him.

He laughed and ducked and headed up the stairs, as I stood there and soaked in the five-second normal mother-and-son moment we'd kind of just shared. My chest tightened up and my eyes filled, and I blinked it all away while I rinsed our glasses and put them in the dish-washer.

◆　◆　◆

When the doorbell rang an hour later, Harley and I both jumped. It had taken me probably forty-five minutes of that to relax and quit peering up the stairway and finally sit down with a book. Not that a single word had registered with me. Harley was in my lap—or part of her was—and the tension had started to unknot itself.

At the sound of Noah arriving, however, I felt my neck turn back into an intricate web. I could make some chiropractor very wealthy. Especially with the added fun of Harley using my torso as a springboard.

"Jesus," I groaned as she pushed off and I took my time getting up.

On the one hand, it was nerve-wracking with the two of them up there talking about things I didn't know. I'd been ready for Seth to come down for thirty minutes. And *God*, what a control freak I was!

But on the other hand, Noah coming meant Seth had to leave, and I could spend weeks living off the joy of that afternoon. Something I never, ever thought I'd do—hang out with my son.

Noah coming also meant Noah was coming. And would be standing outside my door looking like—I opened the door—yep, looking just like that.

Hands in the pockets of his leather jacket, over clothes that I now knew packaged a dream body, warm and solid. A hooded gaze that absorbed me just as well in my green sweater dress and bare feet.

Shit, he looked like sex dipped in chocolate.

Harley must have entertained that thought as well, because she went straight for his crotch.

"Hey," he said, deflecting her like a pro.

"Hey."

I knew he was thinking about the last time he'd walked through that door. Two days ago. *God, that was only two days ago?*

"Is he ready to go?"

I laughed nervously, the moment striking me as one of many of Hayden picking up Becca when she was younger.

"Yeah, *Dad*, he probably is," I said, holding the door open and standing aside so I could smell him as he walked by. Multitasking. "He's been upstairs with Becca for an hour. Hopefully he's still in one piece."

"How did she react?" he asked, his eyes falling to the rug of sin.

"Oh, it depends on the day, evidently," I said, willing to do a jig just to get his eyes off that spot. "Possibly the hour."

Then he turned to me, pinning me with that look of his, and I was thinking the rug wasn't so bad. I could hear my blood move. His hand came up within inches of my face, and then snapped down, his fingers closing in. He stepped closer and fought his hand again like he couldn't stand not to touch me.

"S-so—how's Shayna?" I slurred like I was having a stroke, which wasn't completely out of the question.

He blinked but otherwise didn't look away. "She's fine. This how it's gonna be for the rest of our lives?" He pointed between us. "This?"

"Yes," I said. Sort of. Or I mouthed it, really. But as closely as he was watching my mouth, I was pretty sure he caught it.

"You aren't the only one that hasn't been able to love anyone, Jules," he said under his breath. "And I've tried. Shayna's the only one to come close, but—"

"Don't." My mouth went dry and my palms started to sweat.

"There's only one woman that ever fit that bill."

"And I betrayed that," I said. "I know. And *you* walked away from it. Together we set a chain of crap in motion, Noah. Twenty-plus years of baggage and lost time."

He stepped closer and reached for my face again, his eyes tortured. "I can't—"

I grasped his hand to stop him, but the touch took my thoughts away like they were dust. I inhaled a little gasp and closed my eyes, squeezing his hand to my chest for just one second. Just one second. Don't let go.

I smiled and pushed the hurt away, opening my eyes and lowering his hand. "Yes, you can. We can." I let his hand go, wanting to back up a step, but my feet had glued themselves to that damn rug. My voice sounded oddly high, probably because the words were complete bunk. I didn't believe them any more than he did, but someone had to make a stand. "You have obligations now. And she doesn't deserve less than all of you."

There were sounds of life above our heads, and Becca's door opened. Noah shook his head slowly—more to himself than to me.

And "Love Shack" rang at his hip.

"Oh, that fucking song," I muttered under my breath as I spun around to put some space between us. I walked across the room, finding nonexistent things to pick up as I gulped air. Harley followed me just in case, her nose twitching in interest.

Noah grumbled something I couldn't make out as he silenced the phone and the kids came down the stairs. *The kids came down the stairs.*

Did I actually just think that? I really must be stroking. I turned to see Becca leading the way as Seth followed. Neither of them were really kids anymore, especially not Seth, but still. It was a moment.

I pasted on a smile and joined them, and Noah held out a hand to Becca. She stared at it like he was offering her a firecracker.

"Haven't officially met," he said. "I'm Noah Ryan."

She took his hand with a small smile. "Becca White. Wow, you two really do look alike."

Noah beamed, whether he was aware of it or not, and Seth smiled.

"And you favor your mom," Seth said, of course registering with me right away that he hadn't said just *Mom* or *our mom*, but that was just my crazy peeking out. "Except for this side," Seth continued, batting at the long side of her hair. "So, do you start leaning this way after a while?" he asked, cocking his head to one side. "Maybe walk in circles?"

"Ha ha," she said, punching him in the arm and then aiming for his head, for which he was too quick. She may have acted put off, but I saw something different in her face. Something needy.

"Coffee tomorrow?" Seth said, looking at me.

Oh, he drank coffee. I loved him even more.

"Absolutely."

"What time are you up?" he asked.

I'll get up at three in the morning if you ask me to.

"Seven?" I said. "I don't have to be at the store till nine thirty."

"See you then," he said with a nod.

"See you then," I echoed.

Noah's phone went off again, just as I was standing next to him again. Jesus, it was like she sensed the proximity. He hit the button, his jaw tight.

"She's not much of a texter, is she?" I asked.

"Oh, I like that song," Becca said.

"Yeah, I used to, too," I said. Out loud. Unintentionally. "Have fun tonight," I added quickly, putting on a smile.

Seth hooked an arm around Becca's neck and hugged her, then me. For real. On his own terms this time. He smiled down at me, so grown up, and of course I teared up. What the hell else did I do anymore?

I swatted at his chest and laughed as I swiped at my eyes. "Go on," I said. "Y'all get out of here."

Seth backed up and then Noah's hand was squeezing mine like it finally won the battle. Noah looked down at the union like he was surprised, and then let go, looking up at me with a sadness.

"Bye," I whispered. It was all my brain could muster. And the kick to my gut felt like much more.

◆　◆　◆

When the door shut, the only noise was Harley's tail thumping against a metal vase. I turned to see Becca standing with her arms crossed, not quite looking at me. I wasn't up for that showdown again. Not just yet. I wanted to know how it went with Seth, but we weren't in that place. So I walked around her to my favorite spot on one of the couches, sat with a pillow in my lap, and opened my book.

Slow footsteps faded upward as she went to her room, but to my surprise the sounds came back down again. I glanced up from the pages I again wasn't reading to see her sit tentatively on the opposite couch, notebook and pen in hand.

"Mind if I sit in here with you?" she asked.

I shook my head as all the strings of my heart yanked at the same time.

She scooted back and arranged herself to be cocooned with pillows and an afghan, then opened her notebook and hovered her pen for just a second.

"He's okay," she said, not looking up. One corner of her mouth twitched upward as if she were remembering something funny. "Seth's okay."

"Yes, he is," I said.

"I like him."

"I'm glad."

It wasn't an apology, but it was her version of working up to one. She met my eyes for the briefest of seconds and then started scribbling madly in her book. I focused on the pages in front of me and let the words seep in.

◆　◆　◆

The next morning started with a ring of my doorbell that I expected to be Seth. I had coffee ready, as well as biscuits and honey. Just in case. Not from scratch or anything; let's not get crazy. And I figured that serving him a sliced apple probably wouldn't have screamed *motherly*.

The view I received when I opened the door was even better. Nana Mae, arm in arm with a grinning Seth. Her with big fat tears in her eyes, a photo album, and a big bag of donuts. She understood mothering a lot better than I did.

"Look who I found outside!" she said, her voice trembling with joy.

We had a sugar feast, went down a deeper rendition of memory lane, and fought Harley for the donuts and biscuits, although I suspected that Seth was sneaking her bites on the side.

Becca got ready early for school and actually stuck around for a bit before leaving. Granted, the contraband food didn't hurt. There still wasn't conversation of any real quality between her and me, just the obligatory morning necessities about lunch money and homework, but that was on her this time. She was going to have to throw the first flag. Truancy, boys in her room, and alcohol, all in one day—my mother would have stroked on the spot. I was doing pretty well, I thought. It dawned on me to call Hayden. He would think I should. Which was precisely why I didn't.

Nana Mae and Seth left together, her insisting that he come over and help her get some things down from the attic. She hadn't been up in that attic in over five years, maybe more, but I kept that little detail to myself.

I plopped onto the couch after they were gone and leaned over onto a pillow so Harley and I could be eye to eye. Also because I honestly could have fallen asleep like that. Meeting Seth the day before, wondering about his dinner with Noah (that I had not asked one word about over coffee, I was proud to say), on top of Becca's antics had put my brain on overdrive. It just wouldn't shut off.

I was mostly ready for work, anyway. Ready in a very going-casual-today kind of way. Jeans again. How far I'd fallen. My mom would have grimaced. And on that note, I wondered what Ruthie would say if I showed up in my robe.

At any rate, a few minutes of lazy time couldn't hurt, and Harley was closing her eyes as well as I scratched her favorite spot under her chin. It was one of those comfortable moments when you feel that pull into the black hole, when—the doorbell rang again.

Harley jumped, her closed eyes now wide in panic as she ran to the door and sniffed once and took up her barking medley. I groaned and pulled myself off the couch, wondering who had forgotten what and when my door had become so friggin' popular.

And opened the door to Shayna. Before I could even register that something was off about her—the crooked and straggly ponytail, the red puffy eyes and no makeup—she came running in past me.

"Um, what's the matter?" I asked, shutting the door.

A new wave of tears flooded her eyes and streaked down reddened cheeks.

"Is Noah here?"

What? Guilt, panic, and major backpedaling flooded my brain. "Here? No! Why would he be here?"

She took a deep breath of something that looked panicked, and yet a little relieved at the same time.

"Noah's gone."

CHAPTER 20

Noah's gone.

The last time I'd heard those words they were coming from Ruthie, as she had burst into my bedroom breathlessly. She didn't have a car yet and had run all the way from the diner. She flopped across my bed where I was curled up in hiding, and heaved like she'd been chased by rabid dogs.

I remember how my hand had gone straight to my belly at the sound of his name, it still being soft and mushy and not quite shrinking yet. Drawings littered the floor—my practice drawings for what would be *the painting.*

He's gone—like, really gone, she had said. *Moved to his Uncle Gerard's in San Antonio and joined the Navy! Linny was crying about it.*

Linny didn't cry back then. That made it real.

Everything went sideways after that.

Shayna standing in my living room looking like she'd just done a running of the bulls and lost, telling me those same words, made my throat close up.

"What do you mean, he's gone?" I said, the words falling off my tongue like someone else was saying them. Echoing like déjà vu.

She held her hands over her face and sank onto the arm of the nearest couch. Near the rug. *Too near the rug.* It was sick that that was what spurred me into motion, but I rushed forward and guided her around to sit on the couch. Where neither of us could see the place where I'd nearly banged the father of her child. Although technically he was the father of my child, too.

"He left," she said tearfully. "Sometime last night."

"Last night?" I repeated. "No, he was with Seth last night."

Why would he leave? His son was here, she was here, his baby was here. *I'm here.*

"After that," she said, sobs making her breaths come in jerky little gasps. "When he finally came home. During the night sometime after we—I thought he'd gone to sleep."

"Why finally?" I asked, knowing I sounded too interested but unable to stop. "What do you mean, *finally?*"

"I had to tell him," she said. "I couldn't stand it anymore."

"Tell him what?" I asked.

"As soon as he left the house to get Seth, I knew," she said. "I couldn't wait. I called and called. Was going to tell him to come home early, but he wouldn't pick up."

"Love Shack."

She was talking like a zombie. Like I wasn't in the room and she was just unloading her burdens to the air. And it was a little bit freaky. Shayna was the most calm and together person I knew besides Ruthie. Or at least as much as I could tell in the week I'd known her. And she was unraveling in front of me.

"I knew it was a horrible time, but I just couldn't—" Her voice trailed off.

"Couldn't *what*, Shayna?" I asked, my patience waning. Becca was still swimming around the front of my mind, and my ice was already thin these days. It didn't take much.

"I couldn't keep up the lie anymore," she said, whispering the words. "Not after seeing him and his son together. I had to—had to come clean."

My skin tingled. She had my full attention now. I couldn't ask another question; I just waited. I wasn't sure I really wanted to know anymore.

"The guy I told you about?" she said, looking at me for the first time since she'd arrived, her eyes red-rimmed and swollen. "That stalked me?"

"Yeah?"

"His name was Thomas," she said in a whisper, as if someone might hear. "The baby is his."

◆　◆　◆

You reach a point where you think there can be no more surprises.

Shayna's words pinged off the walls like they had nowhere to land. I shook my head.

"Don't say that," I said, my voice gone husky.

"It's the truth," she cried, her whole body crumpling.

The baby wasn't Noah's. Holy shit, that information should have been liberating. Those *obligations* that were anchoring him—fading away. But it wasn't like that. It was—oh, dear God, that baby wasn't Noah's. And all I could think about was him hearing her say those words and the horror he had to have felt of seeing another child yanked away.

I hadn't realized I'd sat until I found myself springing to my feet.

"Wh-why?" I asked, pacing and swiping at the tears that came unbidden. Oh, my God, Noah had to be devastated. And gone. "Where did he go, Shayna?"

"I don't know," she said.

"Did he take his truck?"

"No."

Okay. That was good. He couldn't leave the country on foot, at least. I wheeled around.

"Why would you do this?"

"I didn't," she said imploringly. "Not on purpose. We were already back together when I found out I was pregnant." She shut her eyes and held her palms against her temples. "I thought it was his—God, I *wanted* it to be his. He—he was so happy."

I could picture his joy. Hearing that news again. And not being seventeen and still in high school.

"He got down on one knee and proposed," she said, looking down in front of her like he was there. "I wanted it, Jules. I wanted the fantasy."

"You knew—"

"No, I didn't," she breathed. "Oh, I should have. I know that. But I wanted to forget about Thomas and his psycho mind games." Sobs racked her body again. "I believed in me and Noah. I bought into the thought of our little family."

I remembered believing in that once, too. So did Noah.

"Then I had my second appointment, and—" Shayna closed her eyes again, pushing new tears forward. "When they said how far along I was, I wanted to die. All I could think of was, how could I take it all back now?"

"Pretty much like you did last night, I expect," I said.

"And he was crushed!"

"Yes, Shayna," I said, wanting to throttle her cute little neck. "He moved across the planet for this. For you. To raise his child around family. Told everyone he knows. Again," I added, feeling sick.

"I thought it would work," she said, the sobs stealing her breath. "He would love me again. We would be happy." She took a deep breath and wiped at her face. "Then we came here."

I shook my head. "Don't do that. You can't blame the town for this going south. You had to know it would come back somehow."

Shayna met my eyes. "I'm not blaming anything. I'm just saying this was the beginning of the end, coming here." She laughed bitterly. "We came here for a future together, but there is no future here. There's only past."

I looked down, knowing instinctively what that meant, and I couldn't argue with it. She reached for my hand.

"I'm not dogging you for that," she said softly. "I'm just saying— it is what it is. I thought that what we had was enough until we came here. I mean—he holds people at arm's length, he always has. I assumed that's just the way he was, but—then we came here. And there was a difference. He looks at me and sees the sweet love affair we've had. He looks at you and sees an entire life he's missed." She looked away. "You are everything to him, and I don't think he even knew that until he saw you." Her eyes fluttered. "He will never look at me that way, Jules. I could give him ten babies and it wouldn't change anything."

"I'm sorry," I said, rooted to the floor. And I meant that. Regardless of what she'd done, no woman deserved to have to fight a losing battle for their own man.

"I know," she said. "And I wanted to hate you," she said on a teary chuckle. "I tried to. But God help me, I ended up really liking you."

"I know the feeling," I said, squeezing her hand back. Trouble crossed her features again, and it was time to move forward. "Shayna, what did he say?"

"Nothing," she mouthed.

Oh, holy hell, that was bad.

"Did you tell him who it was?"

"He knew," Shayna said. "And I don't think it was even about that. All that mattered was that it wasn't Noah."

Emotion choked me, and my chest felt like someone was squeezing it. "Did he get mad?" I managed. "Cry? Yell?" Anything besides the stare of the dead that I'm sure she got a load of.

She closed her eyes for a few seconds. "He just—went away. Like he was still in the room, but only on a technicality."

"And then he left?"

She shook her head. "He turned on the TV."

"Oh, geez."

"He does that when he needs to zone out about something or unwind, so I let him be," Shayna said. "I went to bed. Johnny Mack was already in his room. When I woke up at four this morning, he was gone." She grabbed my hand again. "His phone is off and I've been looking for him since sunup. I didn't know where else to go."

I met her eyes and remembered her question when she'd arrived.

"You thought he'd come here."

Her puffy eyes blinked and looked down. "I looked everywhere else first, but honestly I thought he'd be here."

I shook my head and looked at my door. "If he's feeling betrayed by women right now, I would be the last person he'd want to talk to." I got up. "He's not gonna walk forever. It's chilly out there."

"Please help me look for him," she said.

"Shayna, I have to go to work. Ruthie can't run my store indefinitely."

Which was a lie. She could run it better than I ever could and was probably doing twice the sales already. But I did need to actually make a full day. Something I hadn't done since Noah landed. And I would. Right after one little stop.

"Go home," I said, holding out a hand. "When he wants to be found, he will be. I'm sure he has some steam to work off."

◆　◆　◆

My thoughts were racing as I parked in front of the store. There was no reason to hide around the corner anymore. Hell, he was the one hiding now.

My head said to walk straight to my door, go in, do my job, give Ruthie a very deserved earful to catch her up, and wait on the sidelines to hear how Shayna and Noah's dilemma played out. That was my place, as her friend, as his friend, not to jump all up in the middle of things. It wasn't for me to worry over where he disappeared to in the middle of the night. Or what their fights were about. Or whether or not he was in pain and feeling like he'd been sucker-punched in the gut. Again.

Shit.

I let my steps veer down the sidewalk to the left and let the sound and smells envelope me as I entered the diner. A quick glance around didn't produce Noah but did give me Linny.

"Hey," I said, approaching the counter as she went back behind it. "Is Noah here?" I asked quietly, my eyes automatically darting for signs of Johnny Mack. I knew from experience that he could be ready to pounce at any time, his recent mood improvement notwithstanding.

"No, and Dad's in the back, so relax," she said with a smirk. "Never seen him so happy, though. That Seth is a godsend. Did you have a good day with him yesterday?"

I smiled, and for a second everything in me warmed. "I did. He's—he's better than all my dreams made him out to be."

Her eyes got a little misty. "I'm so glad. Noah seemed happy, too. I think he really needed this."

"Have you seen him this morning?" I asked.

Linny blinked and shook her head, narrowing her eyes a bit. "You okay, honey?"

"Yeah, I'm good," I said. Probably a little too enthusiastically.

Linny put down a stack of menus she was carrying. "Jules, I know all this has had to be pretty crazy." Her eyes went soft in her round face. "And by that, I don't just mean Seth."

I took a deep breath and let it out. "I know."

"You and I never really talked about it," she said. "It seemed like you wanted it that way, so I guess over the years—"

"It got easier to just pretend," I said. "I know."

"What a couple of stupid women we were," she said.

I laughed. "You're right. We need to remedy that."

Linny tilted her head. "So in the spirit of that, how *are* you, now that the prodigal son has returned?"

There was that feeling again. Like an invisible vacuum was sucking the air from my lungs. All I could do was smile and hope it was believable.

"Every day is a new day."

Linny chuckled. "If I see my moody brother, I'll tell him you were looking for him—or no?"

I opened my mouth to say yes, then closed it. "Just tell him to go home," I said. "Shayna is looking for him."

◆ ◆ ◆

Go to work. Those were the words I had for myself as I walked back outside. Where it started to drizzle. *Just walk*, I told myself. *It's right there—the door is right there. Ruthie will be so proud.*

It wasn't my business to worry about Noah. To think about his feelings or how hurt and angry he might be. We had an arrangement. Or I did.

And this was the thought that steeled me as I walked. Right off the curb, across the street, past the gazebo, and onto the path leading into the park. Where I knew with almost absolute certainty, if he was still in town and hadn't hitched a ride back to Italy, that he would be.

The drizzle upped to a really steady sprinkle, and I cursed as I wrapped my jacket tighter and apologized to my hair. At least I'd had the good sense to wear jeans and loafers, but too much more wetness and I'd be jonesing for my boots. Not to mention an umbrella.

And then there he was.

I recalled Noah's first day back in town when I'd come upon this very same sight. Him sitting on our bench, staring off in the distance and lost in his own thoughts. I'd been paralyzed with shock and flashbacks and had crept away like a mouse.

Amazing what could change in a week.

I slowed as I approached him, watching the droplets soak into the wood of the bench while they rolled off his leather jacket. That was fitting and matched his stony expression. Nothing reaching him. Nothing touching him. And my heart twisted in my chest. I wanted to cradle him in my arms and take the hurt away. Show him how to feel again.

Problem was, some of that hurt was on me. Shayna had just reactivated it.

He didn't move when I sat beside him, and I realized it was exactly how we'd sat many years earlier. On another rainy day. I felt my phone buzz in my jacket pocket, but it could wait.

"I'm not good company right now, Jules," he said.

"Well, good thing I didn't come here to hang out then, huh?" His hand moved over his face and then his hair. "Shayna's looking for you. Been out here all night?"

"No, I just—landed here eventually." He let out a heavy sigh. "This is where things used to make sense."

"I know."

The silence felt loud as we watched the rain hit the water in front of us. How many times had we sat there just like that in our younger years? It was a happy place then.

I chanced a look at his profile, and he'd gone hard again. He hadn't shaved, and it made him look tired and fierce at the same time. Walls and chains went up and made his eyes cold blue stones in a face locked down tight. Untouchable and unbreakable. I had a feeling he'd made good use of that in his career.

The wet cold was doing a job on me. I could feel the shivers coming on, and I pulled my jacket tighter.

"You should go, Jules, it's cold," he said, his voice tired.

"Coming with me?"

"No."

"Then I'm good," I said. I had no clue what I was doing, but suddenly I knew I wasn't leaving him.

He sighed and wiped rain from his face. "This doesn't involve you," he said.

Yeah, that kind of stung and gave me a twitch, but I shook it off with the raindrops. "Doesn't really matter what it involves, does it? I'm here supporting a friend."

"Which friend?"

"What?"

"You here to plead Shayna's case?" he said, still staring ahead.

I frowned. "No. But she wasn't an evil troll in this, either. Her heart was in the right place. She wanted to raise this child with you."

He shook his head. "I have to figure out what I'm going to do." His voice was toneless, emotionless.

"As in?"

"As in what the hell am I doing here?" he said. "I was an idiot for coming back to Copper Falls. I swore I never would."

There was that twitch again. "Good to see this doesn't involve me," I said, unable to keep the snark out of my voice.

He inhaled slowly through his nose, as if trying to maintain control. "I told you I wasn't good company right now," he said tightly. "I'm not going to say the right things, so please just—"

"Go. Yeah, I know," I said. "I heard you. I don't care." My phone went off again, but I ignored it.

He shot me a sideways look, but at least it was a look. "Whatever," he said, defeat in his tone.

"Look, I know this sucks, and I know it probably brings it all back—"

"You don't know what it does," he snapped.

"Then talk to me, damn it!" I yelled. "You said things made sense here. Then make sense of it. Tell me."

"I don't need to talk. I'm fine," he said through his teeth.

"Oh, yeah, this is model behavior for *fine*," I said. "Sitting out in the cold rain glaring at the river."

"And what's your excuse?" he shot back.

I love you.

The words drifted across my brain in neon purple and red letters before I could even register them and argue. *Oh, no. No, no, no.* My skin lit up with a million tiny fires. No, I couldn't go there, but I had. And he saw it.

The look he gave me hit me to the core, pinning me down. I couldn't move, couldn't look away, was stuck there helplessly with rain bouncing off my nose and my mouth working and no sound coming out. I tried to suck back the emotion, to do his glaze-over trick, but it wasn't working.

Then he did the miraculous. He blinked and looked away, releasing me from the spell, but also looking thrown and off balance. And slightly less robotic. Dear God, I'd found the switch. But at what cost?

His jaw muscles worked double time, and he probably wanted to snap my neck, but at least he looked more human as he did it. I realized that I was most likely far outside my element, but what the hell. Breaking rules and boundaries—wasn't that what everyone was always after me to do?

"My first instinct was to get on the next plane back to Italy," he said finally. My stomach burned at the words, but I kept my mouth shut. "Back to the life I know. Or to make some calls—I could have any government job I wanted. Anywhere." He rubbed at his eyes. "And anywhere would be easier than here."

My chest felt like a gorilla took residence there. "So, you're leaving?"

Noah shook his head minutely. "I don't know what I'm doing. All I know right now is that the last time I was and will ever be a father, I was sitting on this bench. All three of us were here."

Tears burned the backs of my eyes, but it didn't matter anymore. They'd just mix with the rain.

He looked at me. "That's why you painted it."

"At the time, it was just a way to preserve something my mother couldn't take away," I said. "She didn't know about this." My chin trembled. "This was ours."

"It's not meant to be for me," he said, more to himself than to me. "The only shot I had is a grown man now—"

I got up and knelt in front of him, raking my wet hair back and leaning on his knees. It was physical and a risky gamble, but one he'd taken when I was crumbling out behind a bar.

"And that grown man is still your son," I said. "You *are* his father. Maybe you don't ever get the child part of the deal, but you get to know *him*."

His eyes softened. "I know."

"That's a miracle."

He nodded. "I know that, too."

"And whether you want to hear it or not," I continued, "someone raised our son and loved him. You could do the same for this one."

"It's not the same situation."

"I know it's not," I said. "I know you feel betrayed, but—" I pictured the words like on a chalkboard. *Just read it, Jules.* "You have a woman who loves you, who's willing to follow you to the ends of the earth just to be with you. Crazy town, crazy father-in-law, secret children, and ex-girlfriends all lurking everywhere."

I finished with a smirk, trying to lighten things up, but the smolder in his eyes as he leaned forward only made my skin heat up. On the upside, he was looking at me. Fully looking at me.

On the downside, he was fully looking at me.

"Your ex is still in love with you, too," he said, his face only inches from mine. "That enough for *you*?"

As all my breath left me, I was wishing for that glaze-over to come back. Maybe it wasn't so bad. Definitely had a purpose. My phone buzzed for a third time. Someone really wanted me, something might be on fire somewhere, but I let it go.

Closing his eyes as if completely worn out, he leaned his forehead against mine. Every nerve ending in my body came to attention, and I could hear my breathing, feel my blood move.

"Feel that, Jules?" he said softly. "That rush? That draw? The electricity?"

What I felt was the breath from his words on my lips, and my extremities going numb as thunder rumbled in the distance. Protecting the heart again. Oh, if only something could.

"Electricity is dangerous," I whispered, even as my lips moved upward all on their own. I couldn't stop.

"Jules," he breathed against my mouth.

"I'm sorry," I said against his.

"I'm not."

Heat burned my eyes as his mouth claimed mine, hungry, taking, pulling all he could from me as fast as I could give it. My body flipped on switches everywhere as the taste of him filled my senses again. Rain pounded harder, soaking us to the skin, but all I could feel were his hands fisting in my hair and the feel of his neck and face and head under my fingers. His whiskers were rough and scraping, but I pulled him in closer, tighter, needing to give as much as he needed to take.

Lightning flashed and thunder rumbled louder, closer. Thoughts flashed with it. We couldn't do this. *We can't do this*. He wasn't free. And he might run again. And yet those words in my head had been real, and he'd seen it and they were there, reeling me in. My need for him balled up in my belly like a fireball, pushing its way up until I was trembling with it. Shaking as I held him and made love to his mouth, kissing him with all the passion I had, trying to give him the love I couldn't say out loud.

But it wasn't just me. As another round of thunder crashed around us, I realized he was shaky, too. He pulled away from me with hot angry tears in his eyes and a growl in his throat.

"Fuck, how do you do this to me, Jules?" he said, angry frustration making his voice husky. "I don't break like this. How do you always break me?"

I took his face in my hands again before I lost the ground I'd gained. "It doesn't make you less, Noah," I said, my voice trembling, my eyes burning. "It's okay to hurt, to feel, to be angry. At me, at Shayna, your dad, my mom—whatever."

"Getting mad doesn't solve anything."

"Sure it does!" I said. "It lets it out and makes you feel a hell of a lot better, and it's better than run—" I stopped myself, knowing it could go very south very quickly. "It's better than leaving."

Even the wind blowing the rain sideways into our faces didn't hide the deep-rooted stare he gave me.

"You were going to say *running*."

Damn special-ops people picked up on everything. "Whatever fits, babe," I whispered. "But you have to figure out what's right for you." Damn it, his mouth was right there and I had the overwhelming urge to kiss him again. Before I'd never get to again. I dragged my gaze to his eyes instead, which wasn't much better. "Just do me a favor," I added.

"What?"

I swallowed hard against the words I couldn't ignore. "Don't leave without saying good-bye this time."

He looked like I'd just punched his dog. My phone buzzed again, and I grabbed it for something to do so I could look away before I started to cry again. I hunched over it to protect it from the downpour, and saw it was Hayden. Great. At least he didn't have his own ringtone. The other missed calls were from him as well, which put my nerves on alert.

"Hang on," I said. "He doesn't call me unless—hello?"

"Where are you?" Hayden demanded through the phone.

I flinched as if he'd yelled in my face. "What the hell?"

Noah started to pull his hand away from mine, and I grabbed it, meeting his eyes. I didn't want to let go. To lose that contact. It was as if he'd teleport back to some other part of the world if I did.

"I'm at the bookstore, where are you?" Hayden said.

"I'm—nearby," I said. *Across the street in the park, in the rain, making out with Noah.* "Why are you at the store?"

"To find you because you wouldn't answer your phone," he said. "Is there a reason Becca's out of school today? Exam exemptions or something?"

Doom that reminded me of my real life settled into my skin. Real life that didn't include romance or man drama or old flames, but was more centered on homework and bad plumbing and utility bills. And Becca skipping school.

"Why?" I asked.

"Because I just saw her on the back of a motorcycle with some guy going down the highway."

CHAPTER 21

Shit.

In the few minutes it took Noah and me to make it to the store, Seth arrived there as well. He took one look at our faces as we jogged across the street to get under the awning, teeth chattering and my face probably raw, and raised an eyebrow.

Glorious.

I yanked open the door to blessed warmth and some rather unblessed looks from Hayden. Ruthie was mouthing an *I'm sorry* in the background, and his prepared words died on his lips when his eyes landed on Noah. They narrowed back on me. On us. And our disheveled, drowned-rat appearance.

"Really?" he said.

"Becca?" I said, refocusing him.

Hayden blinked that particular irritation free and picked the more relevant one.

"I was headed to Katyville, just before the sky opened up, and what should pass me but a motorcycle going ninety-to-nothing. My first thought was, well, they're trying to beat the rain. My second thought was, oh, hey, look, there's Becca's hair."

"No helmet," I said, like that was the biggest issue.

"No," he said.

"You're sure it was her?" I asked, although with her history I didn't really question it. I blew on my frozen fingers.

"I'm sure," he said. "I tried to follow, but they exited on Cayman Boulevard and I lost them. Been calling you ever since."

"Jules," Ruthie said, her face wary, her eyes darting to Hayden. "Cayman is—"

"I know what Cayman is," Hayden said, wheeling around. "Thanks."

"Hey, don't be a prick, Hayden," I said, my teeth chattering harder and my whole body shaking at that point. "She's trying to help."

He closed his eyes for a second to pull it together, and I knew it was hard. Noah's presence wasn't helping. Knowing that his daughter just went to an infamous part of town known locally as Sin Alley was enough. Cayman Boulevard was lined with seedy motels that generally charged by the hour. I was pretty nauseous over it myself.

"I'm sorry," he said. "I'm sorry," he echoed, turning to Ruthie. "I'm just—"

"I know," I said, peeling my soaked jacket off.

"Jesus, Jules," Hayden said, coming forward and rubbing my arms. "You're, like, gray."

"I'm good," I said, catching his hands, too aware of Noah standing there. Which was crazy since he had a woman at home waiting on him. Kind of. "What do we do? Drive up and down Cayman till we see the bike?"

"I don't think that's wise," Noah said, having miraculously controlled his own reaction to the cold. He wasn't even shaking anymore. I didn't know how, but then again, he *had* been trained to be Superman.

"I'm sorry, were you consulted?" Hayden asked.

"Hayden—"

"Don't *Hayden* me, Jules," he said, an edge curving his words up at the ends, a tell that meant he was at a breaking point.

"I'm just saying," Noah continued, his voice even and calm, "to think back." His eyes bored into me. "You were her age. *We* were. How would it have gone down if *your* mother had walked in?"

"Oh, I don't know," Hayden said. "Maybe she wouldn't have gotten pregnant at seventeen with a bastard child she'd mourn for the rest of her life."

"Hayden!" I yelled, my eyes going directly to Seth, who was trying to stop Noah.

Noah was quick, crossing the few feet to Hayden in seconds, backing him up to the counter. Seth had a hand on his shoulder, but he wasn't budging.

"I've had about enough of you," Noah said through his teeth. "We are trying to help here, and you really need to help yourself."

"Noah, it's all right, really," Seth was saying. Not that either of them heard him.

Hayden was too pissed off to be cowed down this time, however. He bowed up and shoved Noah's hands away, looking him eye to eye. My stomach plummeted, knowing that the timing was bad for both of them.

"You gonna put my head on a table again?" Hayden seethed. "Go ahead. Give it a shot." Every muscle in his face and body twitched. "You may very well succeed. You might kick my ass. But I'm stone-cold sober this time and I will take you down with me."

It was too much.

I could see the pain in Hayden's eyes, and it wasn't just about me or Noah or his pride this time. His baby girl was out there and he felt helpless.

"Please," I said. To the room. To either one of them that would hear me.

Noah was the one to finally back up, and Hayden followed suit. As Noah turned, his eyes met mine for that second, and I knew he'd given Hayden that. It was a gift to a man hurting over his kid.

Deep breaths went all around, and then Seth, who had been watching quietly, said, "I have her cell number."

Hayden turned to him and narrowed his eyes in question. "And who might you be?"

Seth offered a hand. "Bastard child. Nice to meet you."

Hayden stared at him as he slowly moved to shake his hand, and his face fell. He looked back at me and then to where Noah stood looking spring-loaded. Mortification draped over him like a blanket.

"Oh, fuck me," he said under his breath.

He sank into a nearby chair and leaned his elbows on his knees, all the hot air knocked from him. He looked defeated and deflated and sad, and it squeezed my heart. I knelt at his feet, and the irony of that being the second time within the hour was not lost on me.

"I'm sorry, Jules," he said softly, staring at the floor. "I didn't mean that."

I pulled his forehead to mine. "It's okay. We'll figure this out."

I looked up and saw Seth calling someone and Noah raking fingers through his wet hair to dry it. He had his own demons. Lord, they seemed to be running amok lately.

"Noah, you need to go home," I said softly.

He looked down at me comforting Hayden, with so many words spilling from his eyes. I couldn't read any of them, so I tried to give him some of my own. *Please don't leave town.*

"I just tracked the GPS on her phone," Seth said, walking back. "I can go straight to her."

"Wait, what?" I said. "I don't have that on her phone."

"You don't have to," he said with a wink. "I have magic powers."

Hayden stood up. "What?"

"He's a police detective," I said, pride oozing from my voice.

"Oh, thank God," Hayden said. He grabbed Seth's hand again. "Man, I'm sorry—I didn't—I shouldn't have said that."

"It's all good," Seth said. "Don't sweat it." He turned to me, all business again. "She's not a criminal here, and both being minors, neither is he." He paused and studied my eyes as if weighing his words. "They are two kids doing what . . . two kids do. You can go barging in there and scar yourself and her forever, or I can go make sure she's safe and just wait and bring her home."

Hayden turned and paced the room, but I knew Seth was right. I couldn't control this one.

"Thank you," I whispered, going to him with a hug that needed to fill twenty-six years.

◆ ◆ ◆

Ruthie sat across from me in the biggest chair we had, crossing her legs under her, which made her look dwarfed. For once, I was glad of a slow day and no customers. The quiet and simplicity of rain hitting the roof was soothing.

Hayden left to run work errands but was staying in town and told me four times to call him as soon as I heard something. Noah had left when Seth did, giving me a last look as he went through the door. A look I couldn't read and refused to agonize over. I had other things eating at me.

"Talk to me," she said.

"Pick a category," I said, rubbing my temples. "Never thought I'd long for a simple Johnny Mack drama."

"Yeah, that does seem like ages ago, doesn't it?" Ruthie said. She paused, and I knew where she was going. "Tell me about Noah."

I felt the stab to my heart and the strength ebb out of my bones. "I don't know."

"Well, last I heard—"

"Yeah, that was a mistake," I said, remembering the summary I'd given her and not wanting to revisit it. I didn't even want to revisit the last hour. That was torturing me enough.

"And so what was today?" she asked, eyebrows raised.

"Shayna—oh, crap, that's right," I said, leaning forward. "You don't know."

"Hell, no, I don't know!" she said. "I'm in the Land of the Lost over here."

I held up my hands in surrender. "The baby isn't Noah's."

She tilted her head. "Say what?"

I relayed the Shayna visit with all the details I could.

"Holy hell," she said when I was done, putting her hands over her face. "Even I feel sorry for him on that one."

"It's so messed up."

"And the romp in the rain?" she said, gesturing to the door. "That was—what?"

I paused. *Good intentions.* "Me finding him in the park," I said.

"Because that was your obligation?"

I huffed out a breath. "No, Nana Mae, that was me looking to help a friend who was hurting."

"By falling into his mouth."

I stared at her. "So—my daughter's having sex right now."

She paused and raised her eyebrows as she looked down. "Better subject?"

"Frighteningly so," I said, closing my eyes. "I just hate sitting here waiting. I need ice cream and a blanket."

"Wow, desperate measures," she said, then winked and shook her head. "Jules, she'll be fine. Seth will find her. He's amazing, by the way."

Warmth spread through me at the mention of his name. He *was* amazing. Not that I had anything to do with it. His adoptive mother deserved the credit for how she raised him. The child I raised was currently ditching school and shacking up in a hotel.

"Yes, he is," I said. "Funny, smart, introspective. He's so much like Noah, it's eerie."

Ruthie hung her head. "And all roads continue to lead back to him."

"Ruthie, quit," I said. "Please. This thing you have against Noah is—"

"Is completely justified," she said. "Or do you not remember that?"

"I've been just as badgered by his dad for a choice *I* made at seventeen, Ruthie," I said. "I chose to let my mom railroad me. He chose to leave. We both made mistakes."

Ruthie chewed her bottom lip. "I watched you go through twelve kinds of hell, Jules. And you were never the same again."

"That wasn't all on Noah."

"God, Jules, do you hear yourself?" she said, swinging her legs down. "You will defend him to the hilt."

"What has he done so wrong?" I asked.

She widened her eyes. "Uh, I don't know, ask Shayna?"

"The woman who lied to him." Which I realized was exactly the opposite tack I'd taken with Noah, but my fence was dissolving.

"Who he evidently almost cheated on if you *almost slept with him*," she said. "So he's no angel in this."

I covered my face with my hands, knowing there was some merit to her words and not wanting to hear any of it. "You don't understand."

"I do understand," she said. "Jules, you are one of the strongest women I know. No one gets through that wall you have. Except Noah Ryan. He is like fucking kryptonite. You completely lose all sense of yourself around him."

I took a deep breath and let it out slowly. "You're right."

Ruthie got up and knelt in front of me. "Sweetheart, you are my best friend and I love you."

"I love you, too," I whispered.

"I know what Noah means to you. What he has always meant," she said, squeezing my hands. "But he is dangerous when it comes to you. Neither of you have any control. And I don't want to see you get hurt again."

There were tears in her eyes, and that broke my heart. She was wrong.

I wasn't the strong one—she was. She might look like a waif, but she was a Viking in disguise.

"I know," I said, taking a slow breath in. "But Ruthie, you've got to trust me on this. And I know my history with him doesn't warrant that," I added when her expression changed. "But we're adults now, and we've both come to terms with how we got here. He's not the bad guy anymore."

"He *has* someone," she said without blinking.

I nodded. "Yes, he does, and I have no idea what he's going to do with that. He's messed up right now and conflicted. They were breaking up when she got pregnant, so—"

She scoffed. "He told you that?"

"She did."

Ruthie started. "That's twisted, her talking to you about him."

"I guess I'm all she has here," I said. "Which is getting exhausting." I squeezed her hands again to refocus. "Anyway—there are other things in the mix. He has job options that he might take, he doesn't know what's going down with Shayna yet—and I'm not part of the equation." Ruthie gave me a skeptical look. "Seriously," I said. "I told him to figure things out."

"Wow."

"Yeah," I said. "So quit with the kryptonite and trust me."

Ruthie chuckled. "And if he leaves again?"

My heart will shrivel into a prune. "Then he leaves again."

◆ ◆ ◆

Four hours later, I was useless.

I checked my phone for the sixty-seventh time, cursing myself for not getting Seth's number. No answer from Becca on my nine texts and thirteen unanswered calls. All I had was eight texts from Hayden, the one person I did not need to hear from.

It didn't escape me how much I wanted to see or hear from Noah. We'd never exchanged numbers, so there wouldn't be anything from him, but I was craving it. Crap, Ruthie was right. I was a hopeless twit when it came to him.

Unable to stand the menial tasks of the day any longer, I told Ruthie I was going for a walk—in the rain, which she knew was bunk but just nodded. And I went next door. Not that there would be anything soothing there, but I needed the distraction.

Wondering what went down with Becca had my stomach churning. Wondering what went down with Noah and Shayna—well, Ruthie was right in one respect. That wasn't my business.

I pulled open the door, oblivious to the delicious aroma of what the chalkboard specials said was gumbo, and wandered in slowly. What was I doing there? Linny spied me and headed my way with a wink.

"You meeting them?" she asked, gesturing with a tilt of her head. "They're over in the corner."

"Them?" I asked, confused.

"Becca and Seth," she said. "I'll bring you a menu if you want."

"Shit," I muttered, heading their way and waving a hand back at Linny to let her know I wasn't cursing at her.

There they were, lounging in the far corner booth, and my steps faltered as I watched them together. My kids. My beautiful babies, laughing at something, unaware I was watching. Looking like they'd grown up together. If I could have stopped time and taken a picture of the moment, I would have.

Seth looked up, however, and the moment passed. He nodded and I approached slowly, taking measured breaths as I slid into the seat next to Becca.

Her expression went from open to closed in a split second. Glorious.

"Hey, Bec," I said.

"Please, don't start," she said, making my hackles go up immediately.

Seth sat back and shook his head. "Dude, who was in the wrong here?" he said. "I told you, suck it up and own it. It goes better."

She closed her eyes and inhaled slowly. "I'm sorry," she said, eyes still shut as if she'd found some Zen place.

I glanced at Seth, who sat there like an instructor, arms crossed, waiting to see what she would do.

"For?" I said.

"Skipping school again," she said softly and took another breath. "To be with Mark."

I was going to throw up. Right there in the basket of chips. I grabbed a cardboard coaster and mangled it instead.

"Becca, you—went way beyond that today. Not to mention ignoring my texts and calls."

"I know, Mom," she said. "I'm sorry. I just—I had a lot on my mind."

"Oh, I can imagine you did," I said, grabbing a chip and breaking tiny pieces off. "Did Seth mention who saw you?"

She leaned forward on the table. "Yes."

"Do you want to know how fun that was?"

Seth rested his hands on the table and pushed back. "Ladies, I'm gonna let you two talk," he said. "I've got to get on the road home in about an hour, and I have some people to see first."

"Already?" Becca said, frowning.

He reached across and bumped fists with her. "I'll be back," he said. "We'll work something out. I'll come visit, you can come visit, whatever. We'll keep in touch." He smiled crookedly, sending me down the Noah Express again. Ruthie would slap me. "I've got a little sister now, with lopsided hair. I have to keep up with that."

Becca smiled and took out her phone. "Selfie before you go—come on," she said, nudging me out with her elbow.

I moved before I was pushed out on my ass, and she slid next to Seth so they could put their heads together for the picture. He nodded toward me as they stood. "Take one of us, Becca," he said, looping an arm around my shoulders. I knew quite well what I looked like after the rain escapade and my hair drying on its own, but I didn't care. I hugged his waist and smiled. I had a hundred pictures of him with other people. Now we'd have at least two that would mean something. And the one with him and Noah that I hadn't looked at yet. Didn't let myself the night before, and for sure I couldn't now. Not after—all that.

"You have my number, Bec," he said, hugging her tightly. "Send those to me before you get your phone taken away."

"I will," she said, hugging him hard.

"And use that number. I'm expecting it," he said.

"I will," she said, her voice a little wobbly. "Thank you."

Then he turned to me, reluctantly, as if he didn't know how to do this. I didn't, either. But when we locked eyes, I was shocked to see genuine emotion in his.

"Thank you," he said, grabbing my hand.

"Thank *me*?" I said, surprised. "I didn't do anything, baby. You were the brave one coming here. And doing this today? God, Seth, thank *you*."

"No, you made it easy," he said, shaking his head slightly. "I didn't know what I would find here, and you made it all—okay." His eyes misted. "I honestly feel like I have another family in my life now, and I didn't expect that."

Oh, holy hell, that did me in. Tears filled my eyes. "I'm so glad you feel that way," I said. I smiled up at him and laughed as they spilled over onto my cheeks. "I know, I know, I'm a walking waterfall."

He grinned and hugged me so tight, it was all I could do not to completely break down. I was holding my son. My son, the man. When we pulled back, he swiped at his own face.

"I don't want to sound condescending or go all parental on you," I said. "But, Seth, I am so proud of the man you've become." My voice choked on the new tears that wouldn't be denied. Especially when his face struggled to hold his in. "You tell your mom and dad—thank you for me," I said. "For being such fantastic parents."

My voice caught on the words. I heard Becca sniffle behind me, and Seth lost the fight. He blinked tears free from reddened eyes and nodded as he wiped them away quickly.

"Damn, you two can even make me cry," he said on a laugh, and Becca laughed with him, going to hug him again. "Not many people can break me like that."

The words sent goose bumps down my back, echoing Noah's from that very morning.

"Well, I have to go say some other good-byes and go by Nana Mae's and Noah's, still," he said, making another pass at his face. Crying was embarrassing him. I'd become accustomed to it.

"Oh—um—something to be aware of there," I said. I filled him in quickly on the whole Noah-Shayna-baby debacle so he didn't say anything awkward.

"Wow," he said, scrubbing hands through his hair. "That sucks."

"Yeah."

He narrowed his eyes and darted a glance toward Becca, then me. "So—I don't want to sound condescending and go all know-it-all on you," he began, making me laugh, "But you and Noah—"

"Oh, seriously?" Becca said, contorting her face.

"Go check your Facebook while you can," I said, giving her a way out of the ick factor. She took the out, dropping back into her seat.

Seth chuckled and then met my eyes again. "I've only known you and Noah for less than two days now, and I can see it."

I averted my gaze to the floor. "So I've heard," I said. "It's just complicated."

He nodded. "Well, I've been told that sometimes the harder, complicated relationships that you have to fight for are the ones worth something," he said, bringing my gaze back up. He had a small grin on his face as he held his palms up. "Or something to that effect. But hey, not my business. I can go check my Facebook, too."

I grinned through my tears. "Point taken. Can we talk about your love life now?"

"Leaving," he said, backing up.

I chuckled. "What I thought."

He stepped forward again quickly with a glance toward Becca, leaning over in my ear. "She didn't do the deed, by the way. Listen to her. Let her talk."

I widened my eyes as he backed up, smiled, said another good-bye to Becca, and headed for the kitchen to see Linny and Johnny Mack. Watching him walk away pulled at my insides, tearing at me as if he were an infant all over again. I clamped a hand over my mouth to hold it in, and then I felt an arm through mine. Turning, I met Becca's eyes, full of tears, too. I wrapped my arms around her and hugged her like there was no tomorrow.

CHAPTER 22

After texting Hayden that Becca was back safe and sound, and asking-slash-begging him not to come confront her just yet, she and I went back to the bookstore. Ruthie made hot chocolate—the real kind, not powder from a packet—and left us alone in a far corner couch.

She was softer, I noticed. More introspective. Seth was good for her.

"So is this store going to me one day?" Becca asked after a long moment when neither of us knew where to begin.

She'd never asked me that before, and honestly it had never crossed my mind. Odd, that.

"Do you want it to?" I asked. Becca looked at me uncomfortably and shrugged. "No, seriously," I said. "Be honest with me."

She took another sip and licked her lips. "Not really," she said. "I'm sorry, it just isn't something I can ever see myself doing. Sitting in a bookstore reading? Yes. Running one?" She shook her head.

Boy, I knew that feeling, and it gave me the willies all the way to my toes.

"Okay," I said simply.

"You're not upset?" she said.

Not about that. "Not at all," I said. "You should do what you want. I wasn't given that choice." Echoes, echoes, déjà vu.

She gave me a long look. "I don't want to be a teacher, either, Mom."

I took a slow swallow from my mug. "I kind of picked that up. So what *do* you want to be?"

"I don't know for sure," she said, looking down into her cup.

I let some moments pass. "Tell me about today."

Becca grimaced. "Can we just pretend I went shopping or something?" she asked.

I raised an eyebrow. "Sure. How was the shopping on Cayman Boulevard?"

She chuckled and looked away, probably surprised that I played. *I* was surprised that I played. Not my normal way. Maybe Seth was good for me, too.

"Not good," she said. "I didn't buy anything."

Goose bumps. I looked at her. "Why not?"

She shrugged. "Wasn't ready to, I guess. Decided to save my money for—something worth spending it on. Maybe wait for something I can't live without," she added softly.

I had no words to describe how that floored me. All I could do was stare at her in awe. She'd made her own choice. Made her own rule for herself. Her own rule.

Granted, she'd skipped school and snuck off to do it, but I had to recognize the hugeness of what she had done.

"I think that was a brilliant decision," I said when I found my tongue.

Becca met my gaze. "And if I'd went the other way?"

I cleared my throat. "Well, I guess I wouldn't be able to say much, would I?"

Memory clouded her expression. "I shouldn't have said that about Seth—about you—I'm sorry."

I touched her hair. "It's okay, babe. There was truth in it. It's a hard truth for a parent to justify, is all." She nodded and ran a finger around the rim of her half-empty mug. "I'm very proud of you, Bec," I said, feeling the burn behind my eyes. I swear I was going to dehydrate. "That was a very grown-up decision you made."

She looked up and misted over as she smiled. "Grown-up enough to not get punished?"

"Oh, no."

She laughed. "Yeah, it was worth a shot."

"It was, but the playing-hooky part of your day takes the grown-up part down."

"I know." She covered her face. "God, what does Dad know?"

"Enough," I said. "You need to talk to him like this. He deserves it."

"That's what Seth said."

I turned sideways to face her. "How *did* all this go down with Seth?"

Becca swept her hair back and it fell in its little choppy layers.

"He was sitting on the hood of his truck all badass right outside the door of the—" She stopped and gave me a sideways glance. "The mall."

It was all I could do not to spit hot chocolate. "Of course."

"Mark about pissed himself," she said. "Then Seth told him he could leave, that he'd take me home."

"And you just said, *Okay, see ya, Mark?*" I asked, incredulous.

If Hayden or I would have done that, there would have been sounds only dogs could hear. Seth was right.

She held up a hand. "I don't know, I guess I was so embarrassed that he was sitting there waiting on me, it didn't even cross my mind to argue."

"Wow."

She rubbed at her face. "Then he brought me to St. Vernon's."

I blinked. "What?"

She looked at me questioningly. "It's a place for teenage mothers that have nowhere to go."

"I—I know," I said, my voice cracking. "I've been there."

Becca's expression changed as her thoughts took off. "Did you— have to go there?" she asked.

"Briefly," I said, my stomach going sour at the memory. "My parents thought a weekend there would change my mind about keeping him."

Becca's eyes filled. "Did it?"

"Probably," I whispered.

"Seth volunteers there once a month," Becca said. "Talking to people who need it." She wiped away two tears. "Takes on a whole new meaning now, when you know him," she said. "I wish I could have grown up with him."

"You wouldn't have, baby," I said, swiping under my eyes. I'd come to terms with that. "If Noah and I had stayed together and got to keep Seth, I wouldn't have met your dad and wouldn't have you now." I took a deep breath. "Everything happens for a reason."

"That's messed up, Mom," she said, more tears falling.

"Life generally is, baby."

"I don't want messed-up crap like that," she said, hiccupping through her tears.

I laughed and hugged her head to me. My baby girl. "I don't want messed-up crap for you, either, baby. Let's hope for the best."

◆ ◆ ◆

The next week went by in a haze of the normal things most people take for granted. I used to. It was hard to remember that. Just weeks earlier I'd gotten up and gone to work every day, made sure Becca had what she needed, made sure our little world was in order, ate, slept, and did it all again the next day.

Things may not have been shiny, but they made sense.

Now, Becca and I were doing better, but it was taking large amounts of pretend patience on my part. Trying not to be my mother proved harder than I even wanted to acknowledge. And then there was that other thing.

That thing I kept trying to ignore or forget or at least not care about, when in reality some part of every hour seemed to ring a little Noah chime in my head.

Interestingly enough, where he'd been friggin' everywhere before, now he and Shayna had both disappeared off the grid. Which probably didn't help my chiming. I had no idea what their status was, where they were, and there was no way in hell I was going to ask anyone. The closest I'd come was chatting up Linny on the sidewalk one evening, and she talked about everything else *but* Noah. I know. I waited it out.

What I did have was photos. I'd printed out the ones of me and Seth and of him and Becca, and framed them for the living room tables. Finally, I had both my kids there, without hiding or secrets. I could look at him every day. Twice, I attempted to do something with some of his baby pictures, but I couldn't do it. I was glad to have them, but they represented pain and betrayal to me. Of a time where my mother got to know of him but kept it all from me. So I put them all back in the book box, put the whole thing in a plastic tub to protect it, and set that back on the shelf. I could go there if I chose to, but I would rather look at the photos taken now, where everything was out in the open. There would be more. I'd make sure of it.

There was another photo I still hadn't seen. But just knowing it was there was enough.

On Friday night, I decided to take Becca out for dinner before she headed off to spend the night with Lizzy and her family. They preferred that so that they could get an early start with the float the next morning. Good grief.

Of course, Becca picked the damn diner for our dinner out, which blew my mind. Of all the good places to go, she wanted the same crap we ate for lunch all the time. Or I did. And she did when she wasn't eating at school. Which was more frequent than she admitted.

I didn't want to go there at night—not that I was afraid of someone being there, but then again, maybe I was. I was accustomed to the lunch crowd. He didn't show much for that, and I could relax. I had no idea who to expect for the dinner crowd. Geez, I had to move on.

"You sure you don't want to go get Mexican or Italian or something?" I said as we pulled in front of the diner.

Little snowflakes frosted the glass, and red flyers were on a box outside the door. Red flyers were everywhere now. On every street post and every corner. On the far end of the park, the carnival rides were already set up, just waiting for the next day to kick things off. *Just two more days of this*, I told myself. Tomorrow would be chaos and crazy people on cheap floats, kids waiting for candy and carnival rides, and the chili battle would commence. The next day would be more of the same, but wrapping up at nightfall.

"We could even go to Katyville," I said. "We don't have to stay here."

"Nah, I want to go here," she said. "This is home."

True, and I loved that, but home was kind of beating me with a stick lately.

"Okay," I said on a sigh, getting out of the car.

A quick perusal of the other parked cars didn't produce any heart palpitations, and I mentally kicked myself for feeling disappointed by that. Good Lord, I was losing it.

Linny was getting off as we walked in, and she met Becca with a giant hug.

"You don't get enough of this place already?" she asked, laughing, her round face looking softer with her hair pulled down.

I realized I hardly ever saw her that way. Like her sole existence was in that diner. I gave a little shiver at that thought, hoping no one ever looked at me that way. Like I was a walking bookstore.

"Becca's choice," I said, shrugging.

"Well, at least you get a discount," she said, winking as she walked out the door.

I frowned, confused. "Discount?"

"Counter tonight?" Becca asked, her eyes all giddy.

Just kill me. "How about that booth right *by* the counter," I said, pointing. "Compromise."

"Deal," she said.

"What is with you tonight?" I asked, studying her as we sat. "You're all, like, sparkly and stuff."

"And what do you have against sparkly?" she asked.

"Nothing," I said. "Except I'm gonna check behind your ears for alien cloning when we get home. Somebody sucked the smart-ass out of you."

Becca laughed. "Nah, it's still there, I'm just learning to channel it."

"Oh, that's so much better," I said, sitting back in the seat. "Good to know you're still in there."

"Ha ha," she said with her customary eye flutter.

A waitress I didn't know walked up, which was weird enough. Her nudging Becca with a grin upped the oddness. Her tag said Chloe, and she was easily twenty-five, so not a friend from school. And then I reminded myself that I didn't need to know everything and to back off the crazy train.

In honor of the night, I ordered something completely different. Becca's favorite, the shrimp po'boy. With onion rings. And fried okra. And a Coke.

Her look of utter astonishment was so worth the saturated fat I was going to ingest.

"I'll have the same, with sweet potato fries," she said.

"Amen," I said.

"Cool, I'll put your discount in," Chloe said, walking away.

There was that word again. "What discount?" I asked.

Johnny Mack came out from the kitchen and pulled some plates from the hot tray, barking orders to Chloe and another girl I didn't know.

Becca bit back a grin, and then laughed. "I got a job."

Didn't see that one coming.

"You did what?" I asked.

"Got a job," she said, sitting up proudly. "I start next week, on the night shift, and when summer comes I'll maybe get moved to days."

"You—" My head tried to put the words together. Not the job part. The working at the diner part. "Here?" I said. "Like, *here* here?"

"This very shift," she said.

I felt my face grimace. "Needed a challenge, did you?" I glanced over at Johnny Mack, who did a double take on me, and then winked—*winked*—at Becca before griping about a plate that was wrong to someone behind him.

Becca snickered as I gasped.

"What the fuck was that?" I said, the sentence falling out of my mouth before I could remember who was sitting with me. I clapped a hand over my mouth.

"Mom!" she said, full-out laughing. "Such *language*."

"Explain," I mumbled behind my hand.

She shrugged, although her pleased expression was priceless. "We've been talking."

"You've been—talking," I repeated, before the crazy bubbled up. Tired laughter worked its way out and I leaned my face into my hands. "Wow." To be a fly on that wall.

"Is it okay? Me working here?" she said. "I didn't tell you because I wanted it to be a surprise."

Success. It was a surprise.

"Yes—yes, baby, it's fine," I said, chuckling and squeezing her hand. "I'm just—taken by surprise, is all." I looked over at Johnny Mack again with skepticism. "Especially on his end."

"He's all right," she said, rearranging the sweetener packets. "He's more noise than anything else."

I licked my lips, so many responses waiting to fly out, but I swallowed them back. My past with him didn't matter. She had her own path to make, and she didn't need my funk messing it up. Besides, maybe it was his way of moving forward, mending fences and all that. And if she could handle him—

"I'm proud of you, Bec," I said. "Of who you are—who you're becoming. The world's a crazy, mad place, and I think you're gonna be okay in it."

She smiled. "Thanks, Mom." Then lightbulbs went off in her eyes. "That can be my tattoo!"

I blinked. "Say what?"

"My tattoo!" she reiterated. "There's a line in *Alice in Wonderland* that the Mad Hatter says, 'We're all mad here . . .'" she said, holding up her wrist. "That would look awesome on my wrist."

Well, I had a few short seconds, anyway.

"So, have you thought any more about college?" I said, phrasing my words carefully. Didn't want to come across as controlling, or planning her life, or rule-enforcing, or any of the other various crimes I'd been labeled with.

Her eyebrows came together as she looked down at her silverware, studying them as if they held an answer to my question.

"Compromise?" she said, looking up.

Cute, I thought, *playing on my words*. But her eyes were serious for once, not defensive as they usually were on the subject. Steeling myself, I smiled.

"I'm listening."

She took a deep breath and let it out slowly, which did nothing to reassure me.

"What if I wait a year?" she said. "And then decide."

The old reflexes and irritability over disarray and laziness started boiling under my skin. *Wait for what, Becca? Why? So you can be a waitress? Ask Linny how much she enjoys a lifetime career of that.*

That was just the kick-start of the comebacks tickling my tongue. There were more. And as I looked around to see where my Coke was so I could drown them, I found myself looking up at Noah.

CHAPTER 23

Really, really, truly could have used that Coke just then, as my mouth turned into a sandbox. He was headed behind the counter and stopped cold when he saw me, shrugging out of his jacket and walking our way.

"Oh, crap," I muttered, not meaning it to be out loud, but that was my life.

"What?" Becca said. "Ohhhh . . ."

A very particular kind of stabbing, wrenching, piercing pain sliced through my middle as his eyes met mine. They were freakishly blue in that light, and warm, and I had to look someplace else. Like at Becca, who was clearly watching me to see if I'd disintegrate.

"Ladies," he said, his expression jovial with a side of longing.

Shit.

He looked positively friggin' edible in a long-sleeved button-down black dress shirt and black jeans. I didn't see his feet. I couldn't care less about his feet. I wondered if he was meeting Shayna for a night out. Maybe dancing. Maybe I'd throw up, later.

"Hey, Noah," I said.

"Mr. Ryan," Becca said.

"Oh, no, no," he said, rubbing his eyes. "See that ornery, crotchety old man over there? That's Mr. Ryan," he said. "Please—Noah or *hey, you* will work just fine."

Becca laughed. "Okay, *hey, you*, what's up?"

Noah laughed. "That's good. You're a joy, aren't you?"

"That's the rumor," she said, snickering at her own wittiness.

I wanted to be witty. All I was was sweaty. His hand landed on my shoulder then, nearly sending me into sweaty orbit.

"I wanted to see if you still had that picture you took of me and Seth—here at the diner?" he said.

The one I still couldn't look at? Sure. "Of course," I said, fumbling with my phone.

Photos—where were the photos? Nope, that wasn't it. Finally, I pulled them up and scrolled, hoping he didn't notice that my fingers were trembling. Jesus, this was ridiculous. A week without seeing him and I was right back to the blithering idiot I'd been when he arrived in town.

My thumb froze on the photo in question, and my heart did a jump around in my chest. Their heads together, looking at me, so alike. And Noah's eyes—shit.

"Here you go," I said, handing it up to him.

He didn't take the phone from me, he just put his hand over mine, holding it with me as he gazed upon the image and smiled.

Glaze over, I told myself. *Don't show weakness. Don't show anything. Glaze, damn it. Glaze over, glaze over—*

"Great picture," he said. "Mind if I send it to myself?"

I let go of the phone, letting him do his thing, fully aware that I'd now have his number. And he would have mine. And now I could completely officially obsess over him never calling me.

"Didn't Shayna take some, too?" I asked, bringing his eyes back to me like a wrecking ball.

"Yeah, but she left before I got them."

Everything in me went still.

"She left—like—on a trip?" I asked.

"One-way trip," he said, typing in his number. He met my eyes again. "She's back in Virginia with her family."

He handed my phone back to me, and as much as I wanted to look away, I couldn't. I was stuck. What the hell did that mean, Shayna leaving? And when did this happen?

"Are . . . you okay?" I asked, clearing my throat.

He nodded. "I'm fine. How are you?"

I smiled at Becca and patted her hand. "A night with my girl. Never better." When I looked back up, there was a look of something that made my breath catch in my throat.

"So!" Becca said, clasping her hands together. I jumped at the sound of her voice breaking the gravity his gaze held me with. "You look nice, all duded out. Big night?"

Bless you, Becca, for asking that.

"I hope so," Noah said. "Leaving to meet up with my old boss about a job."

That jerked my head around again, and this time I searched his face for answers. For something. No tells, no clues. When he looked my way again, his eyes were clear.

The two seconds of hope I'd felt at the news of Shayna's departure were stomped down and ground out. He was focused and clear and driven.

And ready to leave the place that always muddied that.

It wasn't meant to be. It never was. And that had to be okay. I nodded and smiled up at him.

"Good luck, Noah," I said.

There was a long pause and a look I couldn't read.

"Thanks," he said with a small smile. "You two have a good night."

He walked away, leaving a gaping hole in his wake. And it was everything I could do to hold it together. I turned to face Becca, not quite able to look her in the eye. I couldn't. My eyes were burning, my chest was tight, and I looked around the room for a focal point. I clamped my jaws together as tight as I could to push it back.

"Mom."

"Hmm?" I said as the blessed Coke finally arrived and I drank down half of it before even finding the straw. Anything to cool my jets.

"You still love him, don't you?"

◆　◆　◆

Her words, spoken soft and mature and knowing, as if she were twice her age, made me chuckle.

"Don't be silly," I said.

She gave me a look. "I thought we were being honest. I know what you look like when you're trying not to cry, Mom, so save it."

I smiled, though it wasn't real. Opened my straw and stirred my ice.

"Yeah, I guess you are more perceptive than I'm prepared to admit," I said.

Becca scoffed. "Not really," she said. "But after Seth said that about you and Mr.—Noah—the other day, well, now it just seems crazy *not* to see it."

"Well, it doesn't matter, Bec," I said. "People can see all they want, it doesn't mean it's gonna work out that way."

"But it makes you sad."

I smiled slowly. "Tell me about this year-off idea you have."

"Wow, subject change of the century," she said, taking a drink.

I widened my eyes at her. "Take the moment, baby."

She inhaled and let it go. "Okay. I'm not talking about blowing it off, I just—" She stopped and looked at her hands for a minute. "I'd like to concentrate on my writing for a while without having to do school stuff, too."

I sat back. I hadn't expected an actual reason. "Your writing."

"Yeah," she said, licking her lips and fidgeting with her napkin. "I don't even know if I'm any good at it, but I'd like to find out. Maybe submit a story to a magazine or something. I did some research online and I have a—list . . ." Her voice trailed off as she looked up at me. "I just don't want to settle for something else before giving it a shot, Mom."

The tears I'd managed to put away came back for a second attempt. It was like sitting across the table from my mother years earlier, having a very similar conversation.

I'd been accepted at a state school for the arts. It was four hours away and a chance to find my sanity again. But that wasn't practical or logical, and so the dream I'd manufactured for years was shredded in a matter of seconds. I took business courses instead, to ready me for running the store.

I looked at my daughter's hopeful expression, my skin buzzing from head to toe.

"Take the year," I said, my voice gone husky and foreign to me.

Becca blinked. "What?"

I nodded, a rush of warmth spreading over me, making me stop and take a deep breath. "Take the year, and do it seriously," I said. "If at that time you decide you want to go into creative writing or journalism or whatever, or something else entirely, then at least you can make an educated decision."

Becca's face was priceless. "Are you serious?" she whispered.

The absolute relief and joy and hope in her tone made my heart heal a little, right there on the spot. For one second, I felt I'd done something right.

"Never settle, baby," I said, quickly whisking a rogue tear away. "Never, ever settle."

Her eyes misted up, and the smile that grew as her mind started working on her newfound possibilities was refreshing.

"Thank you, Mom."

"So, do I get to read any of this stuff?" I said.

Her smile grew even bigger although a little anxious. I recognized that anxiety. Once upon a time, no one saw my work until my signature was at the bottom and I'd deemed it done. Even then, I'd panic a little.

"Yeah, but I have to work on some things first."

"Whenever you're ready," I said.

Becca looked at me, leaning forward, a new energy in her eyes. "You know, there are some noncredit summer writing classes I heard about, that are just like a few weeks long."

"And your job?"

"I can work around that," she said, shrugging off what had been the biggest news of the night just thirty minutes before. "What if you take some art classes, too?"

I nearly spewed a mouthful of Coke.

"Oh, wow."

"I'm serious!" she said. "We could be part-time students together."

I laughed, tickled at her sudden gusto. But would that just tease me back into something I didn't have time for? Then again, why the hell not.

"Get me the info," I said. "I might just take you up on that."

"Deal."

Our food came and I took that fried food down like it was my last meal. I looked at it as only the beginning of a heartburn-filled weekend. The chili cook-off guaranteed the rest.

Sitting back, fat and happy, I studied Becca's demeanor. It was like the weight of the world had been lifted. How is it that I never saw how simple that would be?

"I want to be with you when you get your tattoo," I said.

Another look of astonishment. I was really learning to love that shock value.

"Who *are* you?" she said, looking at me like I'd sprouted horns.

I opened my mouth to respond something cute, and then paused and closed it. "Maybe someone I wished my mom could have been," I said. "And seriously, I want to be sure you're at a safe place—it'll be my graduation present. Start researching it."

Her jaw dropped. "Seriously, you're trusting me? With all of this? School and everything?"

Burn. Again.

"Yeah," I said. "I am."

And that, dear Mother, is how it's done.

◆　◆　◆

There was a letter stuck in my door when we got home, like I'd closed it in the jamb a couple of times. Must have missed it. Wasn't hard to figure out the pretty handwriting on the envelope, but it made my stomach hurt just the same.

I waited till Becca left to open it.

Hey, Jules,

Short and sweet, but if you don't know already, I'm going back home. I need family around to do this thing alone, and it's not Noah's fault about that. I'm actually glad it all came out, because I don't think I would have had the stamina to hold that secret forever. And that would have been even more wrong.

I just wanted to tell you good-bye. You have been a really good friend to me. One I would have never expected to have, and I was blessed to know you.

He loves you, Jules. That's a hard thing for me to write . . . it took me a few minutes to do it. But it's true, and impossible to miss. And it's okay, because I feel in my gut that it's probably meant to be that way. I think you still love him, too, although you don't admit it, maybe not even to yourself. You two have that thing that we all hope to find. Cherish that. Take care of him.

Love always,
Your friend, Shayna

I was trembling as I read it again, and folded it up. Yeah, I was a great friend, all right.

I lay in bed awake a long time that night after Becca left, watching the shadows on the walls move with the sway of the tree outside. Listening to the many settling noises of an old house, that only seem noticeable when the life inside goes quiet.

Somehow, I'd found the secret key with my daughter. Ironically, it was the same one I'd always needed myself, and my mother refused it time after time. All the way to her grave. I was so grateful that I learned this lesson now, so that Becca hopefully had a chance at the life she wanted. Or at least the opportunity to try. And maybe she wouldn't be lying awake at forty-three, lamenting her life and cursing me.

I grabbed my phone from my bedside table and pulled up my photos. One in particular. Seth and Noah looking at me, making my heart hurt again. *You still love him, don't you?* Becca had said. And the letter from Shayna: *He loves you, Jules.*

I'd spent a week of nights just like this, falling asleep to the memory of being in his arms. Remembering every touch and every kiss and every inflection of each word we'd said since he hit town. And every look. God, those looks of his—they were worth more than a million words. Did he go to sleep every night remembering those things? Could he close his eyes and smell me the way I could him?

My heart, that I'd kept protected and sealed off for so many years, even in some ways from Hayden, was now open and exposed and battered. Over a man that was taken, or so I thought. Now, all my wonderings over whether they were going to work things out—if he decided to take on another man's child—that was all null and void. And meant nothing if he was leaving.

If he was leaving.

A very selfish and immature imp inside me kept asking how he could leave. When a second chance was right there for the taking. When he could look at me like he did—how in holy hell could he walk away again?

But that wasn't the reality of the world. We weren't independently wealthy people who didn't need incomes. And Copper Falls held only grief and pain and bad memories for him. So, the logical thing to do would be to go.

I'd survived it before. I'd do it again.

And there was something else. Something that kept circling around after my talk with Becca. Something that made my heart race every time I considered it, and reminded me of the exhilaration on her face.

It was going to be a long night.

CHAPTER 24

It was freezing out. Not really, but colder than my thin robe and bare feet like to dance with for long. Luckily, my newspaper was just a few feet off the porch, and Mrs. Mercer couldn't frown too much about my attire.

Not that I cared. Mrs. Mercer was likely the only one to ever see me that undressed again.

But it was okay. Just not being depressed on this day was a first. For the first time in so many years, I could face January 29 with joy, because I knew the person it belonged to.

"You should teach Harley to come pick that up for you," said a voice to my left as I stooped to pick it up; it sent my skin to a whole new level of goose bumps.

I dropped the paper as I whirled around, leaned over to pick it up again, and stood up feeling like a jumping bean. How the hell did he always manage to catch me naked? And then that thought dissolved as the expression on Noah's face warmed me from my very core on out.

Gone were the tortured, troubled, conflicted expressions that I'd become used to seeing on his face. In its place was a calm, a contentment. Dare I say he even looked happy? Had that been there last night?

They offered him his dream job.

He was leaving. This was my good-bye.

Everything in me died.

"I—um—well, if I did that, what exercise would I get?" I said.

Jesus, what drivel was that? I wrapped my arms around myself and wished for an ankle-length robe. One that wasn't sending frigid air and too-close-to-Noah vibes up into my girlie parts. No, it wasn't just being so close. It was the look. Not the death glare. Something entirely different, and damn it to hell, I was just getting used to the other one.

"Today is Seth's birthday," Noah said, not blinking.

"Yes, it is," I said, a small smile pulling at my lips. "First time I can actually put a name to it."

"Do you have to work today?"

What the hell was this? "Yes, it's the first day of the carnival, it'll be crazy down there." I licked my lips and adjusted my robe. "What's up, Noah?"

His expression grew real. Too real. "Wanted to talk to you."

I nodded, feeling my heart go numb. "Okay."

"But what's Mrs. Mercer gonna say when I follow you into your house now, with you just wearing that?" Noah said, gesturing toward me and then waving toward her window.

Was he playing with me? I couldn't tell. He was different, but if he was jacking with my head, it wasn't funny. I tilted my head to study his eyes and clenched the paper tighter in my hand.

"Follow me in?" My knees started to shake for reasons that had little to do with the cold. "That's okay, we can talk out here."

"You aren't quite dressed for it," he said, his voice smooth.

"If you came to tell me good-bye, Noah, I'd rather it not be in my house," I said. I was pretty impressed that the words made it out of my mouth without pause or stutter.

His eyes narrowed just slightly. "And if I came to tell you I love you?" he said, taking a step closer. "Do I get to come in then?"

All my breath whooshed out of me like a hippopotamus sat on my chest, hope dancing around on top, and the newspaper landed on my foot with a thud.

"Not fair," I whispered.

Noah's eyes smiled as he picked up the paper at my feet and rose again only inches away. "Never claimed to play fair," he said.

His smell enveloped me, subtle and oh so sexy, making my senses take off like a tornado. I wanted to climb inside his jacket and live there forever. But that wasn't an option. For days I'd waited. Waited for this moment. For him to leave again. To tell him good-bye. And now—what the hell did he just say?

My mouth worked with rapid-fire questions pinging my brain, but it wouldn't form the words.

"Shayna's gone," he said.

"You said that last night," I said. "I'm sorry. I know you wanted that."

"We weren't going to make it, Jules," he said. "We both knew it. It was a last-ditch effort we were making for the baby." His jaw tightened. "But now—"

"You could have been—"

"I'm taken, Jules." Noah's hands landed on my upper arms, and the heat branded me through the thin fabric. "I always have been, I was just too bullheaded to face it."

"So what are you saying?" I asked, my head swimming.

"Clearly not enough," he said, laughing. "Did you miss the part earlier when I said—"

"No, I heard you," I said, my fingers landing on his lips to keep him from saying it again. "That's back where my heart stopped, I'm pretty clear on it." His eyes darkened with desire at my touch, and that along with the feel of his mouth under my fingertips sent heat to every inch of my body. Was it possible to sweat in forty-degree weather with nothing on but a piece of faux silk? I dropped my hand but he caught it, holding it against his chest. Yeah, not better. "I just—it's not that simple, Noah."

"Oh, yes, it is," he said, using my hand to pull me closer. "It's what I should have depended on back then, and I didn't." His gaze bored into mine. "I won't make that mistake again."

"But your job interview," I began. "It—you got what you wanted, didn't you? I can see it on your face."

"Really? I'm that eaten up that my *job* is what's on my face right now?" he said. "Because that is very much *not* what I'm trying to say."

"So you did get it?"

"I did," he said, so close that I could feel the heat from his body.

My breathing quickened. "And?"

"And it's a job, not a life," he said. "I've had it the other way around. This time's different. Part of the deal was that I live wherever I want," he finished. "With the woman I love." His hands slid upward into my hair, holding my head as he leaned his face toward mine. "I . . . am . . . taken," he said softly, not blinking. "Do you understand?"

My heart was thundering in my ears. "Starting to catch on."

His lips brushed my forehead and then moved down my cheek. "Thank God."

"Hmm," I whispered, my hands moving upward to his face all on their own. "No more obstacles?"

"Nothing."

"No girlfriends—"

"Maybe one girlfriend, if she'll have me," he said, his lips touching mine lightly and making my bare toes curl on the sidewalk.

"No 'Love Shack'?" I said against his mouth.

"I'll throw my phone in the toilet," he said, claiming my lips with his. "I'm yours." It was the friggin' sexiest thing anyone had ever said to me.

His mouth was warm and electric and on fire. And mine. He was mine. Hot emotion burned my eyes at that realization as I wound my arms around his neck and pulled his head in tighter to me. The ground left me as he lifted me off my feet, kissing me like a man starved.

"We should probably go in," he said finally on a breath, then kissing me again. "Mrs. Mercer's going to have cardiac arrest."

"So might I," I breathed.

"You don't have a man upstairs again, do you?"

"Not today, it's been a slow week."

He chuckled and drew my bottom lip between his teeth, running his tongue along it and making my fingers tingle. "For me, too."

"We should remedy that."

Noah groaned against my lips, and I felt his fingers flex in my hair and around my waist where he held me up. "Is that an invitation?"

It was everything in my power not to wrap my legs around him right there in the front yard and hump him like a dog. God, I'd never wanted or needed anyone more than I wanted him. *Right there.*

"I love you, Noah," I said with every ounce of everything I had in me, relishing the rush of emotion that passed across his face.

"Those are good words," he said, his voice a whisper.

"Yeah," I whispered back.

Gently, he set me on my feet and took my hand, and we walked up the porch steps and through the front door. Harley was back asleep on the couch, guard dog that she was, but I was grateful. I didn't want the distraction. I didn't want him to have to stop for anything.

I didn't even pause to turn around as he closed the door behind us. I walked steadily up the stairs, letting the robe slip off me as I went.

"Jesus," I heard him mutter under his breath before the sounds of footsteps followed me.

By the time I reached my bedroom, my need was cranked so high he could have made me orgasm from the stairway. And the look on his face when he reached the doorway and I turned to face him just about did it.

His eyes did a slow drag of my body, stopping at my face with a look of so much—everything—I had to grip the bedpost behind me. Not in twenty-six years had I seen intensity like that. Desire, lust, love, happiness, and—raw energy. He approached me slowly, never taking his eyes off mine, and when he simply pushed a strand of hair from my eyes, my knees nearly buckled.

"Say it again," I whispered raggedly.

"I love you, Jules," he said, his eyes dark with heat and love and something primal. Shit, that took my breath away. "And you're lucky I didn't know you were naked under that robe or we'd have never made it to the porch."

Oh, holy crap. I started unbuttoning his shirt with trembling fingers, trying to keep from just ripping it apart.

"Are you saying that you want me?" I asked, smiling up at him, attempting cute through my haze of lust.

Electricity emanated off him, like we'd spark if we rubbed together too much. Oh, I was all about finding that out. I almost had those damn buttons undone, and I needed him. I needed skin.

"I'm saying I really planned on making love to you slow and sexy, but—"

The last button gave way and I went for his chest with my mouth, cutting off his words as he sucked in a breath. He tasted as amazing as he smelled. I couldn't do slow. I was about to derail.

"Oh, God, Noah, please," I said against his chest, my nails raking down his abdomen as I set to work on his jeans.

"Holy fuck," he growled, his fingers tangling in my hair as he grabbed my head and tugged it back. "I need you, Jules."

"I need you *now*," I said, my voice sounding odd and animalistic to my ears. "Please, let's do slow later."

Noah's mouth came down on mine with a smile. "God, I love you," he breathed, ridding himself of his jeans in two seconds flat.

Skin to skin, his kisses diving deeper, his hands roaming my body, I lit on fire. I couldn't get close enough. One lift and I was up and wrapped around him, hard body in front of me and hard bedpost at my back.

His shoulder muscles rippled as he held me in place and his expression was all fire as he looked into my eyes.

"Say it again," he said through his teeth, playing on my words in a much hotter way.

I moved against him, his hair in my hands. "I love you."

Growling desire, his fingers found me, and as I moaned and bucked with arousal at his touch, he thrust into me.

Oh, God, finally. We both cried out, the sounds foreign and primal as we finally got what we wanted. His fingers dug into my thighs as he slammed into me again and again. The post punished my back, but all I could feel was the exquisite torture of riding a building wave. And all I could see was my Noah. My Noah. His face contorted with exertion and ecstasy as he rode that wave with me. It didn't take me long. My body started to shake uncontrollably as I reached the top and digging into his shoulders wasn't enough. I arched into it, reaching over my head to the bedpost behind me as it twisted me out of control.

Crazy noises came from my throat, from somewhere I'd never visited before. Noises of losing control. Screaming his name. It was taking me over. Through it all, I heard him rumbling and cursing and then it was hitting him. His whole body shook as he pounded me harder and let out his own roar of release.

We came down together, slowing down, my arms wrapped around his head, our bodies slick with sweat. Both still trembling and gasping for air, whispering each other's names. And I was hit with something very exposed. We were one again. After twenty-six years, we were one. I leaned back to take his face in my hands and was touched to the core by the look in his eyes.

"Say it again," he breathed.

Laughter bubbled up from my chest, and I kissed him, saying the words against his lips.

"I love you."

"I love you back."

I would never, ever get tired of that.

"Well, that didn't take long. So much for foreplay, huh?" he said, a sheepish grin pulling at his lips.

"My living room floor was foreplay, baby," I said. "I've been ready for you ever since."

He chuckled silently. "Me too."

"That was hot," I said.

He leaned his head back to look in my eyes. "Like that, did you?"

"Oh, my God."

"Well, I'm glad, because I can't feel my legs anymore," he said.

"They're probably off visiting my spine wherever it went to live," I said, now feeling the bedpost a little more now that the monkey sex wasn't distracting me.

Laughing, he let go of one leg at a time as we tried to disentangle ourselves and flop onto the bed.

"Think we're too old for crazy like that?" he asked, threading his fingers through mine.

I looked at his body, and my God, he was glorious. There was nothing old there.

"Hell, no," I said. "In fact, that's how I want to go out."

Noah grinned, rolling onto his side. "Banged against a bedpost?"

"When I'm eighty," I said. "No, eighty-nine. Ninety-five."

"Damn, we'd better get a gym membership," he said.

Laughing, I leaned in to kiss him, enjoying the soft slowness of it. His fingers played in my hair as we languished in the moment. God, he was delicious.

"I've missed you," I said softly, kissing him again.

"So have I," he said, looking into my eyes. "Never have to again."

It was surreal. "I almost can't believe we're here."

"I can't believe I finally had sex in this house," he said, and then grimaced. "Probably a little late to ask if Becca is here, huh?"

I snickered and thumped him in the chest. "Yeah, I wouldn't be dropping my robe for you on the steps if she were."

"God, that was hot," he said, running a hand over my hip as if remembering where his eyes had traveled.

"Way outside my box," I said on a chuckle. "Never done that before."

"I'll let you do it again," he said, nuzzling my neck.

"Oh, you will, will you?" I said, closing my eyes to enjoy it.

"I'm generous like that," he said. "Anytime you want is fine."

I laughed with him and our eyes met for a quiet moment. The feeling was so overwhelming, my whole body tingled with goose bumps.

He noticed and ran a hand over my arm. "You okay?"

"I really thought you were leaving," I said.

He shook his head. "Never again."

"I love you," I said, touching his face, and watching his expression change with the words. He inhaled quickly and blinked, and I knew I always wanted to do that. Keep him surprised and take his breath away.

"I've always loved you, Jules," he said. "I'm sorry for leaving that behind."

I shook my head. "No more sorries. We move on from here." I kissed his lips and relished the rush of being able to do that at will. "You've had my heart from the first time you ever kissed me till now. Even when I took your ring off, I just closed up everything inside so no one else could go where you'd been."

"Lord, that tiny ring," he said, lifting my hand and threading his fingers through mine. "I saved forever to get that tiny little chip." Noah smiled and kissed my fingers.

"I still have it," I said.

He looked at me in surprise. "Seriously?"

"Of course," I said. "What did you think, that I'd throw it away?"

He widened his eyes. "Basically."

I frowned and shook my head, rolling away. "Hang on a second.

Let me show you something." I got up and strolled naked to my hope chest, which sat under a window and held everything special to me since I was twelve. Inside, under two quilts, multiple boxes of cards and mementos, and all of Becca's baby stuff, was a small wooden box. I pulled it out and went back to join him, where he still lay propped up on one hand, watching me.

"You're beautiful, Jules," he breathed.

I warmed from my scalp on down and smiled at him. "I'm yours."

I took a little preparatory breath before opening the box that had remained closed for over two decades. The little hinges squeaked as I lifted the lid.

Yellowed paper notes, folded and stacked, were inside. Along with a small black fuzzy box, some Polaroid photos of us being silly and one of me about six months pregnant, a piece of string, my hospital bracelet, and a foil-covered roll of Life Savers without the label.

Noah picked up the Life Savers and looked at me in question.

"You bought them for me on the way to the hospital," I said, causing his eyes to water. "Hey." I touched his cheek.

"I can't believe you saved that," he said, his voice thick with emotion.

"It mattered," I said. I picked up the string and held it to my lips. "So did this."

Noah grinned and wiped quickly at his eyes. "The real first ring."

I smiled. "Yep." I reached for the black box, but he covered my hand.

"I don't want to see that, baby."

"Um—okay."

He blinked and another tear fell out that he whisked away with annoyance. "I made you take that off and bury it away. It's tainted—it was from an *us* that didn't get to finish."

My eyes filled at the emotional words from him. Especially when he picked up the little piece of string and sat up.

Taking my left hand, he started tying it onto my finger, as I watched, unable to speak.

"One day I'm gonna put another ring on this finger. When we're ready," he said, clearing his throat of the emotion that was taking over. "That may sound fast, but it isn't really. We've just been on hold for a long time. This time I don't let go."

My chin trembled and I tried unsuccessfully to blink back tears as I looked at the little string on my finger again and nervous laughter bubbled up from my chest.

"Is that a proposal?"

"Well, this *is* the proposal string, isn't it?" he asked.

I laughed and pulled him back down to me, kissing him until it got serious again and he rolled over, pulling me on top of him.

"Mmm," I said against his chest, loving the feel of his body responding under me. "You know all that noise you made earlier? I'm gonna make you do that again."

His eyes darkened. "Well, that's a coincidence. I was thinking the same thing about you."

"I like the sound of that," I purred.

"Very slowly," he said. "Starting with my mouth."

Holy crap, I was halfway there.

CHAPTER 25

Thank God I didn't have to be at the store till nine o'clock. Which I was late for, rolling in around nine forty-five.

"I'm so sorry," I said, rushing in the door fifteen minutes before the parade started.

Ruthie was finishing sales and directing people to the hot chocolate on their way out. She gave me an exasperated look as I ran behind the counter to relieve her. I was better there. She was better out on the floor, doing the actual mingling thing.

I got a once-over and a raised eyebrow as she took note of my jeans and white lace sweater.

"Liking this casual thing once you crossed over to the dark side?"

I smiled at a customer as I bagged up her books and thanked her. "A bit tight for time this morning."

"Doing what?"

When I rang up the next customer without answering, she leaned over in my face.

"Is Patrick back?" she whispered, mischievously.

I scoffed. "No!" Laughing, I said, "Don't you have people out there to be all festive with?"

After fifteen minutes and a lull in the activity, she hit me up again.

"Okay, chica," she began, her voice low for the three people still in the store. "You are all glowing and crap, you need to spill—"

Her words stopped abruptly as her eyes fell on my left hand. Grabbing it, she held it up to me as if I needed to be made aware of the violation.

"No," she said, shaking her head. "What the living hell is this?"

"It's me," said a voice behind us. We turned to see Noah strolling in, hands in his jacket pockets and a lazy smile on his face.

My bones melted inside me, and it was sheer force of will to stay on my feet. I instantly wanted to curl up all over him and do naughty things.

"Hey," I said with a smile, my skin tingling all over when he placed a soft kiss on my lips. I think I was trembling. I looked at my hand. Most definitely wiggling a little.

Ruthie's eyes went back and forth between us, widening progressively. "This is new."

"Actually, it's pretty old," Noah said, patting her shoulder. "Which makes you old, as well. You gonna have a problem with me?"

She frowned like she'd woken up in the wrong movie and twisted her hair up in a messy clip, as if that would clear the fog. "Possibly. You plan on being a dick again?"

Noah grinned. "See, it's that charm that makes you special."

"I'm not joking," she said, smiling for the minimal public but shooting ice daggers from her eyes. "I don't know what happened between yesterday and today, and I'm pretty sure I've missed something key, but if you're coming in here with PDAs and doing this again"—Ruthie lifted my hand with the string still around my finger—"you'd better damn well not be messing around."

My personal mama tigress. I loved Ruthie.

Noah's face got serious. "Do I look like I'm messing around?"

"Found that I'm not a great judge of character when it comes to you," she said, her eyes narrowed. "So I don't know."

"I'll have to prove my intentions, then," he said.

"We'll see."

"Wow," I said. "Y'all realize I'm right here, right?"

A smile entered his eyes as he looked at her, oblivious to what I'd said. "Hmm, a challenge, Ruth Ann."

She gave him a sarcastic smile. "Lots of heavy books in here to pummel you with. Don't test me."

"I'll restrain myself," he said.

"Just don't be a dick," she said.

"I won't," he said.

"Then we're good." She picked up some bestsellers from a display and started to walk up front with them, displaying them for effect before the parade started. "You're sure?" she asked me, pausing as she passed.

I smiled and hugged her with her arms full of books. "I'm positive. And hey, I need to talk to you later. Before we leave tonight."

"That sounds ominous."

I shrugged. "Not ominous. Just a thought."

Outside, the parade was beginning, and thanks to a pretty day, we could prop the doors open a bit so people could mill.

"Snowflakes," Noah said on a laugh. "Never understood that."

"Oh, don't even get me started," I said.

"Still a skeptic?" he said. "I remember it snowing the day Seth was born."

The pang to my gut was still there, but followed by a face. A happy face.

"Yes, and today it's now over fifty degrees and sunny. So I don't see snow in our future. It's not like Groundhog Day." I scoffed. "I see a lot of melted soap later."

"Supposed to get cold tonight, though," Ruthie said. "Saw it on the forecast. Big blast coming through."

Georgette Pruitt drifted by, all plump and happy on her trailer of white flowers, followed by a giant snowflake-encrusted castle, manned by none other than Becca and Lizzy's family.

We hooted and hollered and generally did everything we could to embarrass her, but I didn't miss her questioning glance at Noah's arm resting on my shoulders.

I texted her: *Yep.*

She texted back *OMG* with a smiley face.

The communication generation.

"So, what are you doing tonight?" Noah asked in my ear as another truck went by with fluttery white things that were intended to be snow but really looked like aliens.

Hopefully, a repeat of the morning. If he kept talking that close to my ear, however, things could very well take care of themselves. My nerve endings were so hyperaware of him, it wasn't taking much.

"No plans, why?"

"Come to the carnival with me?"

Oh, blech. I gave him a beseeching look. "Really?"

"I haven't been in decades," he said.

"I assure you, you were bored then, and we always found other things to do," I said. "It hasn't changed."

"Humor me," he said, his voice a whisper, his eyes dancing. "I want to walk around town with you tonight. Eat chili and fried everything. Celebrate this day."

I watched his lips as he spoke, and I wanted to lick them. Okay, so he'd brought out my more carnal urges.

"You play dirty," I said. "Not fair bringing Seth into it."

"I wasn't just talking about Seth's birthday."

Oh, he was good. "You're an evil man."

"Told you I don't play fair," he said, staring at my mouth. "Is Becca home tonight?"

"No, she's staying another night at Lizzy's," I said.

"Then I promise I'll make it worth your while after the carnival," he said, pulling me close to him.

◆ ◆ ◆

Ruthie and I were cleaning up after a very chaotic, productive day. "I'm proud of you," she said while she ran the sales tape for the close of the day. "You actually watched the parade for once. Can't remember the last time you even bothered to go outside for that."

"When Bec was little," I said, collapsing into a chair. My muscles were stiffening up a little from the morning's acrobatics. I smiled as I thought about that.

"Bullshit," she said. "I'd take her out there and you've always had something else to do."

"Customers," I said, gesturing around me as if there were hoards to prove it.

"Oh, whatever," she said. "So, was it Noah's influence that got you out there?"

"No," I said, scoffing. "Maybe it was just a good mood? I do have those. And Becca was in it, so I had to watch for her."

"Maybe it was a sex high," Ruthie said, giving me a cockeyed questioning look.

"I vote for that," I said, raising my hand.

"I knew it!" she said. "I knew you had that just-laid look about you." She laughed and threw a stale cookie at me.

I took a bite. I wasn't proud. I didn't have time to go get lunch.

"I'm hoping I have that look again tonight," I said. "But I have to go to this stupid carnival first."

Ruthie sighed. "Annnnnd . . . the Grinch is back."

"Please, you don't get tired of it?" I asked. "We hear that damn music all day, smell the grease all day. You want to go back at night?"

"Sure!"

"Well, you're demented."

"No, you're just tainted," she said. "This year's different."

"Oh, my God, so different," I said, laying a hand on my chest. "I need to call Seth again, speaking of that. He didn't answer earlier."

"Listen to you," Ruthie said, stopping. "Did you ever think you'd be able to say those words?"

I smiled. "I know."

"So, what did you want to talk to me about that wasn't *ominous*?" she asked.

I looked at her for a couple of beats, taking a deep breath before making the jump. *Hope you're okay with this, Mom. And if you're not, I really don't care.*

"Settling."

She frowned. "Settling on what?"

I shook my head. "I don't know what I'd do here without you, Ruthie. Especially the last few weeks while I lost my mind."

Ruthie laughed softly and came to flop in the chair across from me. "No big deal, that's what we do," she said.

"No, that's what *you* do," I said. "You take care of me. You always have. But you also took over the store." I gestured around us. "You ran the place. And let's be honest, you were doing most of that already anyway."

Ruthie shrugged. "I enjoy it, Jules. I love this store. We grew up in here."

"I know," I said. "But I never fell in love with it like you did."

"That's just because you mom shoved it down your throat," she said, chuckling.

"No—I mean, yeah, that's part of it," I said. "But also I'm just not wired for this. Running a business."

"What are you saying?" Ruthie said, leaning forward, looking concerned. "That you want out?"

I looked around me, at all that my mother had created and handed over to me. *Never settle, baby.*

"I settled on my whole life because my mother told me to," I said. "Gave up my son, my dreams, and my guy because she said to. Took this store—even moved into her house because she designed it that way."

"Jules," she said, pulling my attention back. "Where are you going with this?"

I took a deep breath. "I want to sell the store."

Ruthie sat back, looking conflicted.

"To you," I continued.

Her jaw dropped. "Holy shit," she whispered.

I grimaced. "Is that good?"

She waved her hands around in lieu of the words that eluded her. "I—I don't know. I'm kind of—wow."

"Well, you said you wanted to start a business, and I know this one's not new, but no one I know has the passion and drive to take this place on like you do," I said. "And I wouldn't just leave. I'd stay to help you with anything you need. I just have other things I want to dive into."

"I'm—blown away," she said, getting up and sitting on the arm of my chair to hug me. "Oh, my God, Jules, this is surreal, my head is spinning."

"So is that a yes?" I asked.

"Well, let me talk to Frank about it, but let's whisper yes right now and yell it on Monday," she said.

I laughed and hugged her again. I had thought that would be difficult, but once I started it was like the store was jumping to get away from me. I couldn't really blame it.

"Oh, my God, and I got a rocking chair!" she said, pulling back. "I forgot to tell you."

"That one I failed you on?"

"Nope. A better one at Old Tin Barnes," she said. "I saw Savanna Barnes at the bank and she hooked me up. She had one much more rustic, and cheaper, and Frank is making it awesome." Ruthie stopped and hugged her arms to herself. "Oh, wow, and it might be the first thing I put in my store," she whispered.

It was contagious, her giddiness. Like watching Becca see everything ahead of her.

Ruthie shook her head free and smiled, her eyes shining. "So, what are these things you want to do?"

"No concrete plans, but—Becca suggested some art classes, and—"

"Yes!" she exclaimed, jumping up and making me laugh. "It's about time you got reacquainted with your freaky self! I used to love your artwork."

"Well, I'll have some time and money, now that Becca is putting off college a year—"

"Wait, what?"

I laughed. "Yeah, that's another story. She's going to work on her writing."

Ruthie backed up and studied me. "Who *are* you?"

"That's the exact thing Becca said," I said, smiling, feeling the weight of old crotchety me lifting by the minute.

"Well, you are stepping outside your box, that's for sure," she said.

"It was time."

"Just think of that tonight at the carnival," she said, to which I groaned. "More box-stepping," she said. "You can do it."

CHAPTER 26

The temperature dropped thirty degrees since our sunny day at noon. Even Harley gave me a look when I told her to go outside and do her business. I'm sure she was thinking the hall bathroom would do just fine.

Becca came and went, restocking for her second sleepover night, and then texting me a few hours later with a line of smiley faces. She was in a great mood. I was, too, in spite of the carnival plans in freezing temps. I was going on a date with Noah Ryan for the first time in twenty-six years.

With the possibility of a sleepover of my own.

I was so easy.

And when Noah arrived an hour early, with a delicious look of desire in his eyes, I was eager to explore that. Which we did. All over my kitchen. And I didn't even obsess about sanitization. I figured I could worry about that later, and he was worth every bit of it. If I could have kept him naked 24/7, I would have.

Lord, who *was* I?

Evidently I was a woman held down by rules and boundaries for far too long.

There was also something to be said for Noah in clothes, too. In faded jeans, boots, a dark-blue button-down shirt and that do-me-on-the-table leather jacket of his, I was salivating.

"You taste like cupcakes," he said later, licking and kissing my neck as I attempted to get ready. We'd already gone two rounds.

"Vanilla and coconut lime body splash," I said.

"Mmm, it makes me want to—"

"Again?" I said, laughing.

"I was gonna say go buy some cake," he said on a grin. "But I'll be game again in a couple of hours."

"Have you talked to Seth today?" I asked. "I've tried calling him, but he hasn't answered."

"Yeah, right after I left here, before the parade," he said.

"Hmm, guess I just keep missing him," I said. "Does he have big plans for the day?"

"He said he was spending the day with family," he said.

I felt a prick of pain to my heart on the word, but then let it go. It was right that he do that. It was right.

Icy air hit me like a wall when we parked in front of the bookstore and got out.

"Déjà vu," I said. "Sure seems like I was just here. Oh, geez," I muttered, pulling my coat tighter around me. "What is wrong with these people?"

Food aromas assaulted our senses. Either it had gotten stronger with the thicker, denser air or we had some serious post-sex munchies going on. I wanted it all.

"Don't suppose there's like a sampler platter," Noah said as we approached the various chili booths.

"Uh, no," came a familiar voice behind us. Linny stood behind a table with a patio cover overhead, a giant red apron announcing "1st Place Winner" emblazoned across the front. A matching banner hung overhead. "There's only one bowl of chili you need to get."

I sucked in a breath and ran to hug her. "Oh, my God, Linny!" I said. "You won! Holy shit!"

"I know, isn't it crazy?" she said, her face pink with pride and the cold.

"Crazy?" I said, laughing. "It's awesome! It's about time."

"You've entered before?" Noah asked behind me.

"Every year," she said.

"Georgette Pruitt has won every single year for—I don't know, fifteen years?" I said under my breath in case she was lurking.

"At least," Linny said.

"Way to go," Noah said, hugging her. "Serve us up some. I'm starving."

"I'm so proud of you," I said. "And I want extra. I'm even hungrier than he is."

"You don't know that," he said, looking down at me with mischief in his eyes.

"Oh, yeah, I do," I said. "You're saving room for cake, remember?"

"I can have both."

"I'm sorry," Linny said, raising her hand. "Have I missed an announcement or something?" She pointed to us in turn. "When did this happen?"

"This morning," I said, unable to keep the ridiculous smile off my face.

"Oh, thank God!" she said, coming around the table to maul us at the same time. "Oh, man, I prayed this would happen. Not that Shayna wasn't nice, but—you're just family. Oh, Lord, I'm so excited."

When I laughed, she clamped a hand down on each of our arms and looked up in Noah's face with amusement in her eyes. "Dad's gonna shit a brick."

"He'll get over it," Noah said.

"Hey, he actually hired Becca," I said. "So maybe he's mellowing in his old age."

"True," she said, pointing at me. "And—I haven't seen the cane in action for a while."

"Nope, the music has evidently stopped," I said.

"It's the day the music died," she said, nodding to keep a straight face while I snickered.

"So can we have some chili now?" Noah asked.

"Oh, men," Linny scolded. "We're talking drama, and all they can think about is food."

Not all, but I wasn't going there with Noah's sister. She ladled up two helpings of steaming chili and a generous handful of shredded cheese into two plastic bowls.

"Fritos?" she asked.

"Of course," I said, while Noah declined. I shook my head at him. "Italy ruined you."

He turned to me before he took his first bite. "Well, then you have the rest of our lives to get me back in line."

The cold almost disappeared there for a second as those words warmed me down to my toes. The day couldn't get any better, and I was afraid to keep thinking that. Afraid I'd jinx it. Only downside was that I hadn't gotten to talk to Seth.

"Your Nana was here just a little bit ago," Linny said.

"Really?" I said. "How'd she get here?"

Linny shrugged. "Don't know, but she's eating like a wild boar on a tear."

I laughed. "Probably bribing people for their recipes, too."

"Oh, she tried," Linny said with a wink. "But I don't cave easily. Did you hear that it might actually snow?" she said, grinning like a kid. "Wouldn't that be something?"

Yeah, it would be something. Especially today, but the odds of that were nearly zero. "I wouldn't hold my breath," I said. "We'll just get sleet or something."

The chili thawed me completely. Only thing better was if I could have soaked my hands in it. But it left my mouth warm and tingling with Texas spice, the way chili ought to be.

"Mmm, Linny, this is amazing," Noah said. "I never knew you could cook like this."

"Always thought it was the best," I said. "Has Hayden been out yet to get some? You know he goes loopy for your chili."

She pinked up again. "He did, actually. Came by a couple of hours ago—with a date."

"Really?" I said, warmth flooding me again. "Good for him. He needs someone."

Heavy music started up nearby, rumbling the very sidewalk under my feet.

"Go check out the band," Linny said. "I heard they're supposed to be good."

Okay, so far the carnival wasn't a complete bust. I had to admit it. Even with the silly snowflakes hanging—wilted and floppy in some cases, spiky wooden weapons in others—it wasn't so bad. Maybe it was the company.

Walking around hand in hand with Noah made the very air around us feel full of magic and promise. It was like being a teenager again in an old body.

We bought a slice of cake, and the look in Noah's eyes as I fed it to him was priceless. I was pretty sure my fingers and toes had frostbite, but I no longer cared.

We reached the makeshift bandstand, which was really an oversized tractor trailer in front of the gazebo, and the band was pretty good. And when Noah grabbed my numb gloved hand and pulled me into his arms for a slow dance, I decided it was the best band ever. I'd even buy their CD. Yep, I was a teenager again.

Noah's arms wrapped inside my coat, and his face came down to mine as I pulled him closer.

"Don't let go," I mumbled against his mouth.

"Never," he said, smiling at the words, shutting me up with a slow warm kiss that moved my blood all the way to my fingertips and back again.

The whole town disappeared as the music vibrated the air and I was enveloped in everything Noah. His scent, his taste, and the feel of his body. And I wasn't stealing a forbidden moment or taking what wasn't mine. Noah Ryan was mine. Had been since that long-ago day with the Dr Pepper. We'd just been on hold for a while.

I chuckled as the song ended and he glanced at his watch.

"Somewhere you have to be?"

"Kind of," he said, winking at me. "Come with me."

He led me around more food booths, where I found Nana Mae and another lady loading up on funnel cake.

"What are you doing out here in the frozen tundra?" I asked, giving her a hug.

"Getting my sugar high on, sweetheart," she said, nudging the other woman who had just stuffed a large doughy piece in her mouth and proceeded to laugh around it. "Trolling for old men. You know Clara Sullivan?"

"Hi, I'm Julianna White," I said, holding out a hand and chuckling at my grandmother.

"So nice to meet you, sweetie," she said. "Mae talks about you all the time." And then both women looked at my date.

"This is Noah," I said, looping my arm with his. "Noah Ryan." I looked Nana Mae in the eyes. I didn't know what to call him, but it didn't matter. She knew my heart.

"Nice to see you again, Noah Ryan," she said, a knowing smile warming her face.

Noah hugged her, making her widen her eyes at me like a schoolgirl. "Nice to be back."

"How did you get here?" I asked, touching her arm. "Mrs. Sullivan drive?"

317

"We got a ride," she said with a wink. "Now, you two go do what you were headed to do," she said. "I've got fried crap to indulge in."

I laughed and eyed that funnel cake, making a note to revisit it. It had been many years since I'd indulged in that. Lord, how I'd fallen. We twisted and turned through the rides until we emerged on the other side, looking at the park.

"I think we have a date with a bench," he said.

Warm tears touched the backs of my eyes, but they were happy ones. And that in itself was a miracle for this day. Happiness instead of hollow, empty regret. Having a face and a personality to put with the memory of what we'd created.

It being Seth's birthday, instead of the day we lost everything.

"I think you're right," I said, linking an arm in his and hugging him to me as we walked the winding path.

It was odd and somewhat surreal to walk it with him instead of alone. But that was nothing compared to the view that awaited me when we rounded the last bend.

Standing in front of our bench was Seth.

◆　◆　◆

I blinked in the low light glowing from the solar lamps and my whole body buzzed with energy.

"Oh, my God!" I exclaimed, letting go of Noah and running to him.

Seth laughed as I tackled him, hugging him tight. "Surprise," he said.

I let go and backed up, holding his beautiful face in my gloved hands. "Oh, holy crap, you aren't kidding," I said. "Happy birthday, baby."

I knew I was crying and didn't care. He'd seen me weepy more than not, and one day I might not cry every time I saw him, but I wasn't there yet.

"I figured this birthday warranted something a little different," he said, smiling down at me with Noah's young face. "And when Noah told me about this place and how it all went down—well, I remembered the painting in your living room. Thought it was fitting."

My chin trembled and I nodded. There were no words. I turned to gaze at Noah as he strolled up, hands in his pockets, always the casual-yet-spring-loaded pose.

"Happy birthday, bud," Noah said, pulling Seth to him in that backslapping man-hug thing that guys do. "Good to see you again."

"You knew about this," I said.

He widened his eyes at me. "I'll never tell."

I shoved at him and turned back to Seth. "Have you had a good day?" I asked. "Did you get cake? There's about fifty pounds of it back there," I said, pointing behind us.

He smiled guiltily. "Actually, I did. Earlier," he said. "I met Becca and her friend and hung out with them for a bit. She made me have cake. Two pieces."

My jaw dropped. "Seriously?" That explained the random smiley faces. That girl.

"I made her promise not to tell you," he said.

I loved it. He hung out with his sister. Oh, holy hell, I loved it so much I was going to cry again.

"And Linny?"

"Yeah, her too," he said.

I wiped at my face and reached for them both. "I love y'all," I said, overcome, hugging them tightly to me. Then I turned to face Noah, trying to convey with my eyes everything I was too emotional to say. He dropped a sweet kiss on my lips, telling me he got it all.

"This is new," Seth said.

"Took your advice," Noah said with a small grin.

"Glad to hear it," Seth said, chuckling.

"Enough with the man code," I said, linking arms with both of them and walking to the bench. Our bench. "What advice?"

"None," Noah said. "You don't need to know everything."

Used to think I did, but I had to say, I was learning.

"Suffice it to say," Seth said as we sat, "that all appears to have worked out." He glanced sideways at me. "Kinda cool that y'all are back together," he said. "Like it's all come full circle."

Noah was quiet, and I looked at his profile as he gazed off at where the river glistened black and sparkling.

"What are you thinking?" I asked softly, nudging him.

"Full circle," he echoed. "The music back there," he said. "Sitting here on this particular day, the three of us." His voice grew husky and I knew what he was going to say. "The last time we were all here together was the day he was born." Noah looked at both of us. "Now, here we are. Together again." He blew out a breath and shook his head, facing forward again. "I never thought I'd see this day."

I wiped the tears that were streaming down my face too quickly to freeze there, and I noticed Seth discreetly rub his eyes as well.

"Seth, I've come out here every year," I said. "And this is the best birthday of yours I've ever had." He laughed and I laid my head against his shoulder. "Thank you so much for coming."

"Wouldn't have wanted it any other way," he said.

As I looked out at the river, my two guys on either side of me, I realized my chance had finally come.

"That painting in my living room," I said, lifting my head to look at him. "It's yours."

"What?"

"I did it for you, a couple of weeks after you were born," I said. "In my mind, it was a gift to you. Something to save the moment. Something my mother couldn't steal."

Noah's other hand came over mine.

"It was all I had of you, but now it's not," I said. "I have more than a memory on a canvas now. I have the real thing."

"You're giving it to me?" he asked.

"If you want it," I said. "I've been holding it for you for a long time."

"I'd love it," he said, blinking away. "Thank you."

I was wrong before, thinking I'd had the perfect January 29. Now I had. Nothing could ever top this. Not ever.

Then Noah started laughing.

"What?" I said. Then I saw it. "Oh, holy—"

"Yeah," Noah said.

Two snowflakes drifted down between us. Then three more. It wasn't possible. Zero odds.

I met Noah's eyes and remembered that other day—as snow began to fall, with his Life Savers clutched in my hand and his words about miracles.

Our son was right. We really had come full circle.

EPILOGUE

How quickly a year can pass.

They say that children make time speed up, and that's true enough, but I had something else causing my time warp. Happiness. A whole year of it.

Peace.

"Mom!" Becca yelled from upstairs. "Where's my dark-blue sweater? The one with the buttons?"

Peace was a relative term.

"I don't wear your clothes, Bec," I called back, pulling Noah's old plaid flannel jacket from the hall closet and climbing into it like a blanket.

"But you wash them," she yelled in a singsong voice.

"More reason to end that trend," I answered, mimicking her cadence. "Closet, laundry room, or black hole. Those are your options."

"Ugh," I heard her utter.

I snickered as I rolled the too-long sleeves up over my hands and headed toward the kitchen, where Ruthie was wrapping her discarded scarf back around her neck.

"Every time I regret not having kids, I just listen to the two of you," she said.

"Nah, this is the fun part," I said, grinning.

Ruthie chuckled and did a fist pump with widened eyes. "Yee-hah. Now let's get outside with those weenies."

She opened the door and the sensation hit me all over again. Seeing Seth standing out there by the fire pit, laughing and looking completely at home, never failed to steal the breath from my chest. How I had been so lucky for that amazing boy-man to come back into my life, I had no idea. And today, on yet another birthday of his, I felt nothing but pure joy. I had missed so many. But not anymore.

Seth shoved a hand in his pocket as he pulled the woman standing next to him closer. He kissed the side of her head, her blonde locks framing an adorable face that kept gazing up at him like he were a god. I knew the feeling. I was still doing the same thing with his dad.

Sigh. Speaking of his dad . . .

"What do we think of the new love?" Ruthie mumbled behind a gloved hand, interrupting my thoughts. I set the bowl of weenies on the table with the wire hangers Becca had deconstructed into make-shift skewers.

"Branson? I think she's perfect," I said under my breath so that Seth couldn't hear. "But it's what *he* thinks that counts."

"He does look happy," she whispered.

I watched him, smiling down at something Branson was saying. Looking so damn much like Noah it was scary. Not venturing too far from her, as if rubber bands kept pulling him back. Yep, I recognized the signs.

I smiled and crossed my arms, hugging myself and Noah's jacket at the same time.

"Yes, he does."

Nana and her date—yes, her date, a quiet man who most likely had no idea what he'd signed up for—sidled up to inspect the weenie skewers. "Becca did well," she said. "See, I told you there was no need to go buy the fancy kind. These do just fine."

"I can't believe this is all you wanted for your birthday, Seth," I said as he wandered over to the table as well. "I could have cooked you anything you wanted."

"And you are," he said, pointing at the fire. "I'll let you cook my hot dog for me."

I rolled my eyes. "You're hopeless."

He grinned. "I love this."

Harley's big nose landed on the table, smelling the meat.

"Hey, that's not yours," I said. "Don't be rude."

"Come here, girl," Seth said, making Harley turn and go into a fit of giant wiggles on her way to Seth. "You know I'll save you one, don't you?" he whispered loudly as he squatted to attack her with scratches and love.

"You've turned her into a hopeless beggar, you know that?" I said.

"It's my birthday," Seth replied, holding up his hands. "Anything goes."

Becca came sashaying out in new boots and a bright-red sweater with a jean jacket over it. "Heyyy," she drawled.

"Hey, baby girl," Nana said, wagging a skewer at her.

"Give up on the blue sweater?" I asked.

"It's moved on to the dark side," she said. "So I moved on, too."

I laughed, enjoying the easy contentment in her eyes. The last year had been so much easier. Graduating high school, working on her writing, and getting two short works accepted in an online webzine had done wonders for her self-esteem. She moved with a grown-up confidence and air I never expected to see in her. I'd given her a year from graduation to figure things out about college, and while originally I was still secretly worried about the outcome, I wasn't so much anymore. Turns out, she had a good head on her shoulders when I'd finally cut the puppet strings to see it. She would be okay.

"Hey, wild child," Seth said, moving around the fire pit to give her a hug. "Nice of you to finally join us."

"Hey, old man," she said, rocking back and forth with him before she jabbed him playfully in the ribs. "Happy birthday. How does it feel to be ancient?"

"Hey," Nana said, pointing. "Don't be knocking ancient."

"This is Branson," he said, reaching for his woman. "Branson, this is my sister, Becca."

His sister. Oh my God, I couldn't even express how much I loved hearing that.

"Branson—cool name," Becca said approvingly.

"Thanks," Branson said on a laugh. "Wasn't cool when I was little and nothing came pre-printed with it, though."

Everything was good. It was solid. It had come full circle. Except for one thing.

"So, Noah's late," Ruthie said.

"Yeah," I responded, watching the flames lick at the wood. "Think it needs more lighter fluid?"

"You want to roast the weenies or the roof?" Nana said.

"Y'all okay?" Ruthie asked, narrowing her eyes at me.

"What?" I asked, looking at her. "Who?"

"You and Noah."

I scoffed. "Of course," I said. "Why?"

She raised an eyebrow and smirked at Nana. "Because you're being evasive and worrying about things like lighter fluid."

"I was just making an observation," I said.

"So where is Superman?" Ruthie asked, turning her attention to Nana with her hands on her hips. "Isn't he, like, never late?"

"Not usually," Nana said. "And doesn't he live here, now, anyway?"

I gave them both pointed looks. "Yes, he lives here now," I said, the subject being a round-and-round one. As forward thinking as Nana was—much more than my mother had been—I knew that still gave her a twitch. "He had errands to run. We were out of milk and stuff," I added, hearing how lame that sounded.

"During my party?" Seth said. "Rude."

I gave him a look, too, but he just winked at me. I knew he wasn't really bothered by it; he was messing with me. But the truth was, *I* was a little bothered. Noah should have been back by then. He should be there, rounding out the family. Working on the fire and being all alpha male.

Lord, I was hormonal.

"Y'all quit getting me all flustered," I said. "He'll be back any minute."

"Yeah, well, you know what they say about milk," Nana said in a mumble that was intentionally loud enough for me to hear. "Oops, did I say that out loud?"

"Pardon?" I said with a smile.

"Just sayin'," she said with a shrug and a wink. "Milk and cows and all that."

Ruthie snorted.

"Well, I tend to do things backward," I said. "What can I say?"

Still. She was saying it to play with me, but she knew it had been weighing on my mind. One year ago, Noah and I had officially found our way back to each other. An obstacle course of monstrous proportions might have jumped into every pathway, but we found each other anyway. It was meant to be. *We* were meant to be.

One year ago, he tied our old proposal string around my finger, and told me that we would be together forever. That he would propose to me again for real when we were ready.

Well, I'd been ready for some time.

I was ready on Valentine's, on St. Patrick's Day, on Mother's Day, my birthday, *his* birthday, and on Christmas. Clearly he wasn't. Milk and cows and all that, indeed.

But it was okay. We were together, we were in love, we were happy. He had a job he loved, I got a job teaching advanced drawing at the community college, we had an amazing relationship with our son, Becca was doing well—everything felt good. And I needed to not let semantics get me all discombobulated.

"I have news," Becca said, an energy bouncing off her I hadn't noticed before.

"Please don't say you're pregnant," Nana said.

She scrunched up her face again. "Really?"

"Really?" I echoed, looking at Nana, who smiled giddily.

"Hey, it can only go up from there, right?" she said, holding her hands out to the warmth of the fire.

"You know that online magazine I sold those two stories to?" Becca said, ignoring Nana's bait.

"Yeah," I said.

"They've offered me a regular position," she said, going up on her toes as her tone traveled upward in excitement. "On staff!"

My jaw dropped. "What?"

"A paying job," Becca said, her eyes dancing. "They loved my writing, and really liked that I wrote the second one on spec so quickly. They've offered me my own monthly section, with a new story each month. Possibly even doing a serial one later if it takes off."

"Bec!" I yelled. My whole body broke out in goose bumps. Was it what I really wanted for her, long term? Probably not. It probably paid pennies. But it was her dream. It was her validation that she was good at what she did. I understood that all too well.

"I know!" she squealed, running to me on her tiptoes.

"Oh my God, baby, I'm so proud of you!" I said, squeezing her to death.

"Thanks, Mom," she said, laughing. "Loves."

"Loves, baby girl."

"You're gonna be famous!" Nana said, coming up and hugging us both.

"And we knew you when!" Ruthie added, hugging us all.

"Ha ha, not quite!" Becca said, yelping as Seth put her in a choke hold from behind. "But thanks for thinking so," she said in a mock choking voice.

"Proud of you," he said against her head. "I knew you could do it."

"I know you did," she said, turning to beam up at him. "I think that's why I knew I could."

"Oh, y'all are killing me tonight," I said, fanning my eyes. "Damn, I wish Noah would have been here."

"He—" Becca began, then clamped her mouth shut. "He'll be here." She twirled out of Seth's arms. "Why don't I go get the other food ready?"

"I'll help you," Branson said.

The two—God, dare I say, *women*—went into the house. How scary to think of Becca like that, but it was frighteningly true.

Seth picked up a smaller piece of wood and used it to stoke the fire, while Nana went back to chatting up her man.

Seth's phone buzzed and he glanced down at it. "Excuse me a second, I need to go make a call."

He gave my shoulder a squeeze as he passed, and his eyes looked—I don't know. Distracted? Mischievous? Maybe he was meeting Branson in the bathroom to cop a feel. He *was* a grown man, twenty-seven years old, I wasn't born yesterday.

"I'll take over the fire," I said, taking the stick from him.

I poked at the fire and pulled out my own phone to check for messages. None.

"Seriously, Noah?" I muttered.

"I'm gonna go show Marvin where the bathroom is," Nana said. "We'll be back."

They walked into the house. Well, maybe Nana and Marvin would be the ones hitting up the bathroom. Hopefully they picked a different one.

"My gosh, everyone's dropping like flies," Ruthie said. "Maybe you, me, and Harley will get all the hot dogs."

Harley's tail thumped against the table.

"I think she likes that plan," I said.

"Or we could go in and give the girls a hand," Ruthie said.

"Well, I really don't want to get started till Noah gets here," I said. "I mean, this was supposed to be a family thing."

I knew the snippiness was starting to leak out. I could feel it sitting on my skin.

"Oh, come on," she said, looping an arm in mine. "He'll be here soon enough."

"Fine," I muttered, setting the stick in the fire pit, sending it to its doom. "Let's go."

We walked in, holding the door open for Harley, and the first thing that struck me funny was the lack of sound. Becca and Branson weren't in the kitchen getting anything ready.

"What the heck?" I said. "Becca?" Nothing. No Seth on the phone anywhere, either, unless he was upstairs. "Seth?" I turned around in place. "Nana? Ruthie?"

"I'm here," Ruthie said, holding up a hand.

"Just checking," I said. "It's like a Stephen King novel. My house ate all my people. Where did everybody go?"

"Well, they can't just disappear," Ruthie said, frowning. "Let's look out front."

She gestured for me to open the front door, and as I reached for the knob I caught a glimpse of something through the window. Something bright.

"What is—" I began, leaning over to move the curtain.

"Door," Ruthie said sharply, opening it quickly and shoving me through it.

"What? Door—what—" I stuttered, looking back at her. And then back at—that. "Oh, holy crap," I breathed.

My feet took root on the porch as I laid eyes on the vision before me. Little white Christmas lights were strung around the porch, leading the way in a swoop toward an equally sparkling lit archway that had been resurrected in my front yard. Bathed in the soft light around it, was everyone who was supposed to be in my backyard. Their smiling faces glowed as they all looked from me—to Noah.

He was standing under the arch in that damn leather jacket and looking good enough to lick off my lawn. A tiny smile pulling at his lips made my knees forget how to be knees. Seth walked up to the bottom step and held out a hand.

"What the heck?" I asked, laughing. "What are you doing?" I whispered then, just to him.

"Helping you down before you fall."

"No, I mean—"

"Shhh," he said, chuckling as I reached the sidewalk. "Go over there."

Over there. That entailed passing a smiling Nana and a beaming Becca, and then Ruthie as she jogged to stand next to Seth and Branson with a cheesy grin.

"What are you up to?" I said without moving my lips, to which she just tilted her head.

"Hey," Noah said as I reached him.

I took a deep breath, his voice making me go all wiggly inside. Not sure why. I had lived with this man for the past year. Heard him talk all the time. Heard him snore, belch, and other less pleasant things. The newness had calmed down. So, why was he giving me the school-dance shakes right now?

"You're—" I began.

"Creative?" he finished. "Sneaky?"

"I was going to say late," I said with a grin.

"Yeah, well," he said. "Lights."

I nodded, looking around, feeling like every single one of those little bulbs was on me. "I noticed. Quite the décor you have going on here. You know Seth's party is in the *back*yard, right?"

"This isn't for Seth," he said, the face and the unblinking eyes and the voice all clicking again to send my internal parts rolling on a Dr. Seuss highway.

I chuckled and glanced around at all the smiling faces. *O—kay.* "Well then, I think you got your nights mixed up, big guy, because—" I stopped and blinked in the low light at the man standing on the other side of Nana. "Johnny Mack?"

Noah's dad raised a hand awkwardly as Linny then came tiptoeing across the yard from her car to join him.

"Hey," she whispered, dabbing at her eyes.

"Close your mouth, babe," he said, touching my chin and laughing.

"What the heck are you—"

And then one of my hands was in his and he started to sink.

To one knee.

"Oh—" I breathed, the cold air puffing out in front of me. His face lowered slowly while his eyes never left mine. "Oh my God. Oh my God."

I heard whispers and *oohs* and muffled squeals but I was too transfixed by the look of absolute love on that man's face.

"Jules," he said finally, his thumb working back and forth across my palm.

I cleared my throat. "Noah."

"I did this once before—you might remember," he said.

I laughed nervously and heard snickers around us, but I couldn't look away. It was as if those eyes held me captive. And that was so okay. I could stay right there on the front lawn looking at him for the duration. His knee might give, and Mrs. Mercer might get nosy, but I didn't care. He was doing it. For real. *For real.*

"I have a vague recollection," I said.

"Well, we aren't seventeen this time," he said.

"Or knocked up," I said.

"Or at the park," he said.

I touched his face, unable to keep my free hand away. At my touch, his eyes closed, and he kissed my palm.

"I love you, Jules," he said softly, opening his eyes to claim me again. "It wasn't our time then, love. But it is, now."

I nodded as my eyes filled with tears.

"Here in front of our family," he said, pausing. "Our kids." His voice cracked on the words, and I felt everything in me turn to pudding. From out of nowhere he was suddenly holding a ring.

A beautiful ring. The most uniquely cut square stone I'd ever seen surrounded by—surrounded by other sparkly things I could barely see through my tears. It could have been another string for all that mattered. That had won my heart the first time.

"It took us a hell of a long time to get here, babe," Noah said, one tear escaping down his cheek. "But we did it. And I want to spend the rest of our lives celebrating that."

I nodded vigorously, hiccups starting to accompany my tears. "Me too," I squeaked.

"Will you be my wife, Jules?" he said, the words rushing from his chest just above a whisper. "And spend forever letting me be your husband?"

I went to my knees. I knew it was supposed to just be him down in front of me and all that, but I wanted to say it to his face, his eyes, up close. I held his face in my hands, feeling the tremble and not caring.

"I would marry you a million times over, Noah Ryan," I said.

"I only need once," he said pulling me to him, his arms coming around me.

I wrapped mine around his neck and pressed my forehead against his, relishing the feel of being all wrapped up in Noah.

"Then that would be a yes," I said against his mouth.

"Yeah?" he said, smiling.

"Yeah."

"Hot damn."

I giggled and his mouth covered mine, as hoots and hollers and catcalls abounded behind us. I laughed at Becca's groan of protest when he pulled my head in for a deeper kiss.

"Okay, okay, save something for later," she said.

"Mmm," he said against my mouth, backing up a little. "Definitely later."

"Definitely," I whispered back. "Fiancé sex."

"Well—about that," he said, letting go of me long enough to take my hand and pull me up with him. "There's one more little thing."

"One more little thing?" I asked, and then had the epiphany. "Oh! Yes! Ring please!" I said, laughing, wondering why everyone still stood off to the sides, surrounding us. I expected Becca to be tackling us.

He slipped the ring on my finger and I looked at my hand. My God, it had been a long—*long* time since I saw a ring there. And nothing that made me feel like this.

"Wow," I breathed. I looked back up at him, overwhelmed with happiness. "You are amazing, you know that? This was phenomenal. This was so romantic. It was—what?"

He was listening to me with an increasingly growing look of amusement. He was placating me, his smile going a little mischievous.

"It's not over," he whispered.

I raised my eyebrows. "There's more? Dancing monkeys? Clowns?" I mock-frowned. "Oh, no clowns. They're kinda creepy."

"No clowns," he said. "Monkeys are optional."

Seth walked up next to Noah, carrying that very similar expression on his face as he grinned at his dad and then down at me. Then Becca was suddenly next to me, trying her damnedest to look innocent but she had no poker face.

"Um," I said, looking at each of them in turn.

"Tonight," Noah said.

"Tonight, what?" I asked.

"Marry me tonight."

I felt my eyebrows go all the way back into my hairline. "Say what?"

"I didn't stutter."

I laughed but his eyes were serious. And Seth and Becca stood there completely unfazed.

"You're not joking," I said.

He smiled. "I'm not joking."

"But—"

"Noah has a best man," Seth said.

"And you have a maid of honor," Becca said, looping her arm through mine.

I couldn't pull in a full breath, I was so overwhelmed with the hugeness of it. Our family. Joining. Tonight. An hour ago, I was ticked off that Noah wasn't thinking about this, and—well, he'd evidently had a thought or two.

"Holy crap, y'all," I said, swiping under my eyes.

"And you have a witness," Ruthie said, moving to stand next to Becca.

I laughed. "Well, do any of you happen to have a preacher in your pocket?"

"Done!" Nana said, raising her hand and taking Marvin by the hand with the other.

"Reverend Marvin Michaels, at your service," he said, smiling like he was so proud to have kept the secret.

All I could do was stare and blink. "Are you serious?" I asked.

"Always serious about God, dear," he said.

I knew my mouth was gaping open again. I was dumbfounded and bewildered and in absolute awe. I turned in a circle, looking into the eyes of all the sneaky little liars that I loved so damn much.

"Well?" Noah said, turning me around. "We can wait and plan it up." He pulled me close and let his gaze burn down to my toes. "Or we can be husband and wife right now."

"But—"

"But what?"

"I'm wearing flannel," I said.

"You look stunning."

"And it's Seth's birthday," I said, knowing it was lame. Feeling like I needed to find reasons to be responsible and structured about this.

"What better present than having my parents finally get married?" Seth said.

"Oh, you're good," I said.

Seth did a mock bow. "I officially allow my birthday to be something amazing for you now."

"It already is amazing," I breathed.

"But it was something sad for a long time," he said.

"It's not now."

"And you can make it even better," he said. "Why are you fighting it?"

"I don't know!" I said. "I—guess it just feels—"

"Impulsive?" Becca said, one eyebrow cocked.

"Unplanned?" Ruthie added.

"Too spontaneous?" Linny chimed in.

"Against the rules?" Nana said slowly.

Against the rules.

I looked at her and her wisdom peeked out under all her sarcasm. *Let that crazy run a little, sweetheart.*

"Whoa, you just got goose bumps," Noah said, chuckling, running a finger along my cheek. "You cold?"

I met his eyes and felt so immediately warmed I knew I could never be cold. I would never want for love again, and neither would he. Noah Ryan was my soul mate, my everything, and he wanted to marry me in my—in *our* front yard. What the hell was I waiting for?

"Not even a little bit," I said. "Let's do it."

His head moved back in shock as his smile broadened.

"Right now?"

"Marvin?" I said. "I'm sorry, I mean, Reverend Michaels?"

"Yes, ma'am?" he said, scooting over closer.

"Got your Bible and all your—marrying-people stuff?"

He smiled huge. "I sure do."

I looked back at my two babies who weren't babies anymore, who were willing to stand up with us and make a family out of our little band of misfits. And then I looked at the man I could never get enough of.

"Ready to make an honest woman out of me?" I said.

"I've been ready, babe," he said.

"Wait!" I said. "I don't have a ring for you!"

"Yeah, you do," Johnny Mack said, pulling his from his finger. He walked slowly over to me, not breaking eye contact, and lifted my hand, folding my fingers over it. "Until y'all find one he likes better."

Jesus Christ, I was going to disintegrate right into the grass. My eyes filled again as my chest burned.

"Don't get mushy," he said, blinking fast and turning away to walk back to Linny.

Noah swiped a finger and thumb over his eyes on that one, and slapped his dad on the shoulder as he walked by.

"God, let's do this thing," I said, chuckling. "Before we both melt into a puddle of goo."

He laughed and pulled me to him.

"Okay, Reverend," he said. "It's your show, now." Noah took a deep breath and moved a piece of hair out of my eyes. "You really want to marry this old man?"

"I do," I said. "You want to hitch yourself to *this* forever?"

"I do, too," he said, grinning.

"Wow, you two should write greeting cards," Ruthie said.

"Not time for the *I dos* just yet, folks," Reverend Michaels said, opening a Bible that truly must have been divinely beamed down. It wasn't there before. "All right," he said, smiling at both of us. "Dearly beloved . . . "

NANA MAE'S MISSISSIPPI MUD

Cream together:

2 cups sugar

1 cup unsalted butter (the real thing)

⅓ cup cocoa

Add:

¼ teaspoon salt

1 cup vegetable oil

4 eggs (one at a time)

1½ cups self-rising flour

1½ cups chopped nuts

2 teaspoons vanilla extract

Bake in a 9-by-13-inch pan at 350 degrees F for 30 minutes. While hot, spread one 7-ounce jar of marshmallow creme on top of the cake and let it cool (10 minutes).

Then mix this together separately:
½ cup unsalted butter (or 2 sticks margarine), melted
1 cup chopped pecans
1 teaspoon vanilla extract
1 box (16 ounces) powdered sugar
⅓ cup cocoa
⅓ cup Eagle Brand condensed milk

Spread on top of the cooled cake.
Enjoy!

ACKNOWLEDGMENTS

Love forever and always to my wonderful readers, who have waited a long time for this book to come out in print. I hope it was worth the wait! Jules and Noah are two of my all-time favorite characters, and I love the quirky, fictional little town of Copper Falls, Texas. Love happens here. Life happens here. I hope you laugh and cry and feel these people like I do. And for so many of you who wrote me wanting to know what happened with them, I heard you! I hope you enjoy the new epilogue, and get the happy ending you've been waiting for!

Don't Let Go wouldn't be out in the world without my Wonder Woman agent/cheerleader/hand-holder/champion, Jessica Faust, of BookEnds Literary Agency, and my awesome editor at Montlake, Maria Gomez. My happy dance is dedicated to you both! You rock.

My everlasting love, appreciation, and deepest thanks go out to my family, with huge hugs. My kids may be grown and gone, but believe me, they still hear about my journey way more than they probably want. And my husband—let's just say he gets the brunt. He not only listens to me rant but listens to me do it about fictitious people who aren't following directions, and then reads the finished product even though he would most likely rather jump in front of a bus at that point. He's my hero.

I love hearing from my readers, so please shoot me a line on Facebook or Twitter (@sharlalovelace) or from the contact page at www.sharlalovelace.com.

Enjoy!

ABOUT THE AUTHOR

Photo © 2011 Leo Weeks Photographers

Sharla Lovelace is the bestselling, award-winning author of small-town love stories. Being a Texas girl through and through, she's proud to say she lives in Southeast Texas with her retired husband, a souped-up golf cart, and two crazy mutts. She is the author of *The Reason Is You, Before and Ever Since, Just One Day, Don't Let Go*, and *Stay with Me*.

Sharla is available by Skype for book-club meetings and chats, and loves connecting with her readers! See her website at www.sharlalovelace.com for a complete book listing, events, and book-club discussion questions, and to sign up for her monthly newsletter.

You can find her on Twitter (@sharlalovelace), Facebook (facebook.com/sharlalovelace), and Goodreads.

D1524156

OPEN
THE DOOR

OPEN
THE DOOR

Rosemary Manning

JONATHAN CAPE
THIRTY BEDFORD SQUARE LONDON

For permission to quote material appearing in the book the author and publishers are grateful to the following: Robert Graves for 'The Song of Blodeuwedd' on p. 73, which appeared in *The White Goddess*, published by Faber & Faber Ltd; Gwyn Jones and Thomas Jones for the extracts on pp. 7, 68, 75, 76, 174, 175, 176, all of which were taken from their translation of the *Mabinogion*, published by J. M. Dent & Sons; New American Library for the lines on p. 112, which were taken from a poem by Giacomo Leopardi, 'Le ricordanze', in *Selected Poems and Prose of Giacomo Leopardi* edited and translated by Iris Origo and John Heath-Stubbs.

First published 1983
Copyright © 1983 by Rosemary Manning
Jonathan Cape Ltd, 30 Bedford Square, London WC1

British Library Cataloguing in Publication Data

Manning, Rosemary
  Open the door.
  I. Title
  823'.914[F]   PR6073.A/
  ISBN 0-224-02112-5

Printed in Great Britain by
Butler & Tanner Ltd, Frome and London

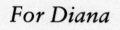

For Diana

He opened the door and looked on
Cornwall and Aber Henfelen. And when
he looked, they were as conscious of every
loss they had ever sustained, and of every
friend and kinsman they had missed, and
of every ill that had come upon them, as if
it were even then it had befallen them . . .
And that is what the tale says.

Mabinogion

1

From our Archaeological Correspondent:

Interest has been aroused in archaeological circles by the find of a bronze bracelet and other artefacts of possibly Iron Age provenance in a remote peat bog some ten miles west of Welshpool in Powys. The objects were found by Mr Evan Evans, a farm labourer in the employment of a local land-owner, Mr John Harrison. He and another man were erecting a fence on the boundary of Mr Harrison's property. They had to take the fence across an area of peat bog known as Gors Ddu, 'the black bog'. Mr Evans showed the finds to friends and his accounts reached the police and, through them, Professor Davidson of Deeside University.

Mr Evans was persuaded to show Professor Davidson the bracelet, which he had given to his wife. This was of the twisted cable type and Professor Davidson dated it, in the absence of other associated artefacts, as belonging to the second or third century BC. In fact, Mr Evans, persuaded to regale himself at a local inn one evening, admitted to me that as well as the bracelet, he had found in the fence post-hole he was digging a pebble-like object with human features carved on one side of it. This he had given to his small son as a toy. It was produced with some reluctance and proved to be c.160 mm in diameter, with simple and clearly cut human features. It is now in the hands of Professor Davidson and is arousing much interest as possibly a votive offering.

It appears – the story took some time in the telling – that Mr Evans and his fellow-labourer had also found a few broken and rusted pieces of thin metal. These they had thrown back into the bog as worthless, with the exception of a ring-headed pin, which Mr Evans had given to his companion. This was lost almost immediately. 'It was worthless, anyway,' said Mr Evans with a shrug. Your correspondent sent an account of the conversation to Professor Davidson. We understand that the Professor has now obtained permission from the landowner to make an exploratory excavation of the Gors Ddu area in July.

From a national newspaper, June 15th, 1979.

The train came to a standstill in the drab fields of Bedfordshire. The guard hurried down the track. About half-way down, an outer door was swinging gently. A smell of wet earth from the furrows beyond the railway embankment drifted through the door. Professor Hubert Loders and his team had left their compartment when the train halted and were standing not far from the open door. Hubert still held his bridge cards in his hand. He glanced down at them. 'Bloody good hand, too,' he thought to himself ruefully. He brought the cards together with a sharp click. In his mind's ear, it had the abrupt reality of a revolver being cocked. Inspired, he held the cards in the palm of his hand, raised his arm and extended his forefinger as though he were shooting someone down the corridor.

Meg had seen his action and almost looked beyond him to see his target. She shivered slightly and let her gaze return to the swinging door, and then to her husband's face. Irrelevantly, her mind admitted the word 'handsome'. Yes, now that his hair was grizzled he was more handsome than ever. She was trapped behind him in the corridor. She saw the open door to the fields as the way to freedom, blocked by Hubert's substantial and attractive tweed-clad shoulders. They were now not far from London. They would change stations and within an hour and a half they would be back in Kent. Nearly home. The three young people would be at the station to meet them. The three who were left. And she was not intending to be there. All the way down from Shrewsbury, as they played bridge or read or talked, her mind was working over her decision, examining every detail. She would leave Hubert when they reached Euston. He would travel home to the three children by himself. She called them 'children' but Barbara was nearly twenty and the twin boys were seventeen. She would give Hubert an excuse to tide him over the awkwardness of the first few days, before she had written personally to the three children. 'Your mother', he could say, 'stopped off in London to visit Gran.'

Meg looked past Hubert's shoulder. The open door was still now. There was no wind, no motion. The fields beyond were a brown and sombre background. The corridors were crowded with questioning passengers. The guard had found the point where the communication cord had been pulled and where it now hung loosely, like a necklace. He noted the group of passengers standing near it and when he asked: 'Who pulled the cord?' one of them came forward. Before she could speak, Hubert was answering for her.

'This lady is one of my archaeological team, Dr Gwyneth Morris. She was in the corridor – we were playing bridge in our compartment. She saw someone – '

'Perhaps the lady could answer for herself,' suggested the guard drily. After writing down her name, he asked her a few brief questions. Had she been in the corridor? Yes, she had. Did she see anyone open this door? Or lean against it, perhaps, and fall? Yes, she had seen someone at the far end of the corridor as she was coming back from the buffet. She could tell that the figure was that of a woman. She saw her walk along, swaying from side to side, for the train was travelling fairly fast. No, she could not see from that distance whether the door opened when the woman pressed or fell against it, or

11

whether she had opened it herself. The window could well have been down, for though it was a wet day it was a warm one. No, there was no one with the woman. She, Gwyneth Morris, had at once pulled the cord above her in the corridor. She was near her own compartment and she had gone in and told the others what she had seen.

The guard urged all who could hear him to return to their compartments. He himself had certain procedures to follow to ensure the safety of the train and passengers, and to locate the woman and ascertain her condition. They would be moving on as soon as possible, and he would be returning to ask some routine questions as to the woman's identity, if anyone knew it. He would be obliged if passengers resumed their seats at once. He was speaking now in tones of authority. He examined the open door at the end of the corridor, closed it and hurried back along the track.

Professor Loders and his team returned to their compartment. They did not resume their bridge. After a brief outburst of questioning and conjecture, they fell silent, occupied with their private thoughts.

Meg noticed that Alan's face was beaded with sweat, that he had watched Gwyneth intently as she spoke to the guard. Being the youngest member of the team, he was more likely to change, she thought, than the rest of them and certainly he *had* altered, especially in the last two or three weeks of the excavation, when he seemed to have adopted deliberately and somewhat brashly the role of ambitious young archaeologist. Had he been trying to free himself from his passion for Gwyneth? From the expression of his face as he watched her closely now, it looked as if he had not been entirely successful. All the painful awareness that they were soon to part was in his strained, youthful face.

Meg had not seen as much of Alan as she would have liked. There had not arisen opportunities when she might have been able to help him in what she sensed was a despair that in his tormented ignorance he did not know how to deal with. There

12

had been only that one occasion when he had asked her to go for a walk with him one evening. Then he had told her of his feelings for Gwyneth and his recognition of their hopelessness. He spoke with some difficulty. It was not merely his own youth, so many years younger than she was. It was Gwyneth herself. Gwyneth being . . . as she was. He could not say more. He was wrestling not only with a personal experience new to him, but with a situation he had never met before. He was ignorant. He had not acquired the habit of noticing people and their relationships. He wasn't really interested in them. He had just got on with his work, in a narrow groove.

At last they had sat down on a wall in the growing darkness, and with his face shadowed by the trees, he found words to speak more openly to her. Meg had felt herself a mother figure, that comforting person, the elderly confidante. For she would appear elderly to Alan, she supposed. To herself she seemed, if anything, especially in the light of her recent resolution, younger than her forty-three years. On this she reflected now. Alan's confidences and problems receded under the pressure of her own approaching crisis. Standing close beside her in the corridor was the fifth member of the team, Ralph Shroton. Older than Hubert, and working in the same Institute. Glancing at him, Meg saw that although he had taken her arm, he was detached, his eyes guarded, looking out of the window at the lifeless fields, abstracted into some inner train of thought.

And what did I do at this interesting point in our affairs? Perhaps I should have been more forthcoming with the guard and confirmed Hubert's statement that we were playing bridge – did he think one of us had pushed the woman out of the train, for God's sake? But I didn't want to get involved. I took Meg's arm on a sudden impulse. She was upset. Her arm was tense. Why, exactly? I wondered. She was restlessly looking about her. She who had always seemed the still centre of our ill-assorted team. And she made no response to my hand under her arm. It remained braced as if ready to ward off something.

I still had my bridge cards in my hand, like that oaf Hubert. He was playing about with his. Acting out some game. Looked quite murderous. Extraordinary fellow in some ways. I slipped my cards in my pocket and pressed Meg's arm in a conspiratorial way to reassure her that I was on her side. I couldn't believe that she had much love for that husband of hers, especially when he appeared to be imagining himself James Bond, cocking his cards like a revolver. God knows what he was up to. 'Ralph,' Meg murmured in my ear. 'Someone's killed herself, hasn't she?' 'We don't know,' I replied. I had made a profession of not knowing things. It paid off. Just for a few minutes, however, I was prepared to involve myself in the situation to the extent of loaning my years (fifty-eight) and my sympathy to Meg. Typically, her husband had not noticed that the incident had upset her. You must understand that this was only my own impression. I did not question Meg. In whom I was more interested, after seeing her for several weeks at close quarters, than in any of the other members of the expedition. I had known her, though only slightly, for years. She wasn't interested in me – why should she be? She had nothing but Hubert's disparagement of me to go upon. And seeing me recently, living in the same hotel for over two months, how would I have struck her? I thought of the salient points about me that *I* should notice, were I a woman: the scruffy, balding head, the paunch, the soft-living cheeks, the mean mouth – I always disliked my mouth and my father for handing it on to me, the Shroton mouth. I think I am to be commended for admitting my deficiencies. What else? My shirts were often far from clean. I wore Hush Puppies, rather down-at-heel. If anyone looked that far, if their eyes travelled from my ill-knotted tie to my shoes, there were other things they would notice: food stains on my trousers, frayed turn-ups. I didn't usually care what people thought and was amazed that I was moved that Meg

14

should have almost made a friend of me in Wales. But there's nothing in it for the future. She and Hubert will go back to their precious converted oasthouse outside Canterbury. In any case, I am not interested in a future that involves another woman in my life. Not even Meg. I shall return to my small terrace house and my work in the Institute under that bounder Hubert – a typical example of 'our man at the top' if ever there was one, arrogant, pompous, insensitive. But at least my home is a place where I need not care what I look like or how much I drink. A place where I shall forget that Welsh valley which carried me back so mercilessly to my earlier self, the self I have spent thirty years in keeping at bay.

God, to think that Ralph Shroton will still be with me in the Institute when we get back, thought Hubert, watching his colleague's tall, shambling figure as he returned to the compartment. Why the hell is he clutching Meg's arm? For a solid two months and more I've lived with this oaf. Site Assistant, my God! And for some reason, he facetiously refers to himself as 'liaison officer'. Some obscure joke of his. I wish to heaven we could get rid of him altogether. Boot him out of the Institute. The trouble is it's so bloody difficult to sack people these days. You get into trouble with the unions. Even in the professions. The fact that Ralph doesn't pull his weight and never has, isn't sufficient excuse to sack him, apparently. He keeps the rules. He gets by. I'd like to know why he dreamed up this ludicrous term 'liaison officer'. Liaising with whom? God damn it, at this moment with my wife, it seems.

He's not without his good points. He's kind. He took my arm because he'd seen that I'm upset. I don't know why it's so comforting. He's such an unattractive man to look at, though I've become rather fond of him on this expedition and he doesn't seem so scruffy in appearance now I know him better. I think I understand why he is as he is. Which has helped me to understand why we are all as we are.

15

Hubert is trying to get Ralph made redundant, but why shouldn't he stay on at the Institute until he retires? Surely the place is big enough to carry a few failures like Ralph, even if he does drink too much and wash too little? Hubert's contempt for him springs from his passion for perfection, for moral perfection in Ralph's case. That's an irony, when I think of Hubert's easy way with women, but there it is again, isn't it? This urge for perfection. He thinks of his mistresses not in moral terms which might apply to himself, not as each one an infidelity to me. To Hubert they provide examples of his perfect technique of seduction. God in heaven, I should know this. Does he not seduce me? It is now the only strong link in the chain that binds me to him and I am about to summon all my strength to break it. To me it's a weakness in my nature that I so easily succumb to him. Now that I recognise this, I feel an added strength in my determination to leave him, to be freed from my own sensuality as well as his. Free also from the anger and cruelty that rise so readily to the surface in him. They spring from his refusal to accept Patrick's death. It is a thorn in his side, that goads him. He likes to think me heartless. I could not live and nourish my family if I laboured under such a debilitating open wound, deliberately kept open as his is, displayed so that he can contemplate it perpetually. But the wound is there in me, too, under my heart, though I do not touch it with probing fingers. I wonder sometimes – would life, would our marriage, have been different – I mean happier, more enduring – if Patrick had not died. Probably not, for it would never have reached Hubertian perfection.

Here in the compartment he sits opposite me, deep in thought. What is he brooding on so darkly? On this presumed suicide of an unknown person? We readily believe that she is dead, for death and loss encompass us all. Nothing comes up to our expectations. I should like to say aloud in this dismal compartment where the five of us sit silent among our ruined thoughts, I should like to say: 'There is no perfection on earth.

16

Cease to grieve over what you imagine you have lost or never found. Rejoice in the freedom you have gained – freedom from the bondage of love and loss. Forster said *'Only connect ...'* If I could write, I would make a book around the words: *'Only accept.'* Ralph has accepted his pain. Despite appearances, he has made a passably good job of his life. And I? My flight from Hubert is an acceptance of myself as a free-standing individual. No family. No obligations. No 'marital duties' as they used to be called. No longer a mistress among mistresses. That humiliating position rejected in favour of a reality that I shall create for myself.

I saw her. I am certain that she opened the door herself, but I will not say so. If she wanted to die, I hope to God that she has died. As I thought to die, but have lived and feel such a painful awareness of this unknown woman that I cannot forget her image. Disappearing through that open door, like a bird taking flight to freedom from the bars of who knows what grief?

Christ, thought Alan, back in the compartment. Why did she do it? Why did she want to die? If of course that's what it was, not just an accident. I'm so ignorant about things like this – there's awful gaps in my experience of, well, of life, I suppose. But then ... when I think of what I ... I, Alan Veltham, discovered on this excavation. A fabulous find – that sword. The others don't like you saying things like that. Where I come from, you have to shout about your achievements or no one takes any notice of you, but of course we're a team. Ever so Public School that sounds. How'll I say it: 'As a team, we've done pretty well' – God, they won't stand for that back home. Better keep it to myself. What does it all mean to them, anyway? The wooden figurine, the harness, the chariot pieces, and – the sword – and it's more than these things to me. I ... I'm changed ... curious about things I never thought I'd be interested in. Gwyneth, for instance. Gwyneth. Her

17

unhappiness. That took me by surprise. She's so damned successful at her work. Well-known in her field. That ought to chuff her, I'd have thought. I don't want to let personal things get in my way. They nearly did on this excavation. And yet . . . I can't quite stop being fascinated by Gwyneth. And I've got to stop. I've discovered in myself something more important than Gwyneth, an ambition I didn't know I had. My passion for this woman . . . was it really just an infatuation? It's so changed me. It's done something for me. That's for certain. If it hadn't been for all that happened during the last few weeks and all it's aroused in me . . . well, it was like being cracked open. I saw deep into myself. My ambition came up to the surface, into the light. I found that sword. I can't forget that. I can't say it, but I feel almost that it's mine. That I'll carve my way with it. All the same, I've made another find. People are interesting, too. You can use your trowel on them and come up with some surprising stuff hidden in the deposits. This unknown woman who's fallen from the train. It's not just a newspaper story to me. I'd like to find out what happened. Why she did it. I got carried away a bit. My stammer's been so much better these last few weeks. Bloody stammer – it all came back talking to that guard. But most of all, I go back to Gwyneth and want to find out more. I suppose it's useless. We're about to separate. I've discovered all I'm ever likely to know. The team'll break up in a few days. Once I don't see her, I'll forget her. There's so much ahead of me.

'Oh, God! Alan's stammer!' muttered Hubert. 'I swear it's put on.'

Meg remembered how, some two months ago, Hubert had commented to her when they were pegging out the site: 'If Alan says p-p-p-peg again I'll hit him with the mallet.'

'He can't help it,' Meg had said and thought the conversation over. She was surprised when Hubert exclaimed, hours later, while they were undressing in their room: 'Alan *can* help it, you know. He puts it on. Some people find a stammer

18

attractive, at least some women do. Alan's probably a bit taken with Gwyneth and stammers when he thinks Gwyneth will hear him. Or even you.'

Even me, thought Meg.

2

From our Archaeological Correspondent:

Readers who follow these occasional reports will remember that a site near Welshpool, known as Gors Ddu, has featured in this column more than once since Professor Davidson of Deeside University first learned in June last year that objects of possible Iron Age provenance were found there. Preliminary excavation of part of the 'black bog' undertaken by Professor Davidson and some students last August revealed sufficient of interest to consider mounting a full-scale excavation. There has been some difficulty in raising the necessary funds and this, added to Professor Davidson's unfortunate illness this spring, has compelled him to hand the work over to an old friend and colleague, Professor Hubert Loders of the Institute of Archaeology at Canterbury. An expedition to Gors Ddu will be mounted in July this year. It is hoped that the site will yield Iron Age artefacts of at least comparable interest with those of other Powys sites such as Fridd Faldwyn and the hill-fort at Breiddin.

We shall be given full information of the progress on site when the excavation begins. We understand that one member of Professor Loders' team will be Dr Gwyneth Morris, well-known for her work on Iron Age weapons. She will be an additional asset to the team in that she is Welsh-speaking.

From a national newspaper, May 13th, 1980.

For all five of those who had set out over two months before on the journey to an archaeological site in North Wales, the return, interrupted by this unexpected wait in the gloom of a wet Bedfordshire landscape, was an expedition in itself. For none of them was it a simple return home.

Ralph's small terrace house in Canterbury would receive him without comment. He had let it to a friend while he was away, but Terence had already left. He thought of it lovingly as the train resumed its journey to London. Good to see his books again, his record player, most of all his cellar. He had locked the door of this when he left and put the key in his pocket. He liked Terence and trusted him in most ways or he would not have let him rent the house when he wrote and told him he needed a peaceful and solitary spell to allow him to finish a novel. Writers, Ralph surmised, are apt to seek inspiration in the bottle, so he locked up the cellar. Remembering this fact, and pondering upon the sudden loneliness that would engulf him when he returned, it grew in importance for him. It became the thing he most looked forward to, for to enjoy drinking demands no effort, but the anodyne bestowed by books and music can come only through a certain discipline. A Montrachet, he thought, would give him the warmth and sense of welcome that he desired and could only contrive himself. The bottle would be a personal libation to his lares and penates. He was going to miss Meg, he realised, of whom he had seen a good deal. In a different way, he would miss Gwyneth. She would become a valuable but mercifully silent picture on the walls of his mind, for she was the most beautiful creature he had seen for thirty years. Her beauty had not faded for him during the months in Wales but grown to be something he actively savoured and delighted in. He placed her on the same plane as his Montrachet, his record of Schubert's C Major Quintet, his volumes of Proust. He was relieved that his heart had suffered no disturbance from Gwyneth, proof of the potency of his cellar and other indulgences over the years, a long ritual he had practised over

21

the grave of memory. Now he could say easily: 'What was Gwyneth to him or he to Gwyneth?' recalling, with his usual pleasure in dredging up quotations, Hamlet's 'What's Hecuba to him ...?' Precisely. No more pains of love. No more tears. He had shed enough to last a lifetime.

Ralph thought of his cellar and planned his evening. First of all he would go down the stairs, unlock the door and select a bottle. Then he would light the sitting-room fire. The room would be cold and damp after this foul weather. While the wine gently rose in temperature with the growing warmth of the room, the curtains drawn and his chair pulled up to the hearth to welcome him later, he would unpack and hang up his clothes and make his bed. Get those disagreeable domestic chores out of the way. At last, he would select a book to hold his attention. Then he would sit and read and drink himself gently to sleep, into an oblivion reaching back over the years, over thirty years, a dark cloak trailing behind his shoulders, obliterating even his own shadow.

Hubert Loders, Professor of Archaeology, fifty-five years old, leader of this expedition now returning from North Wales, sat back in the carriage and closed his eyes. He did not wish to look at his team, yet even with his eyes closed he was very aware of them, breathing in the silence of the carriage air while the wheels pounded an accompaniment to their thoughts. And his. Professionally, this excavation would be important to him but not overly so. Personally, it had been crucial.

It could have been called a season in hell, he thought, but he had come through it. He had returned sane. Yes, I've come through, he said to himself, opening his eyes for a moment to watch the familiar fields and woods of the Home Counties rush past his vision. I believe that at last I have come to terms with Patrick's death. At first Alan seemed almost a reincarnation of my dearly loved son. His youthful and brilliant mind, his enthusiasm, his quick grasp of essentials. I could

22

have rejoiced in the fact that it was he who made the most important find, as if he had indeed been Patrick. But no ... not Patrick. He was utterly different. I had not thoroughly understood Alan in the first weeks. Perhaps this important find was a catalyst that released Alan's true nature. He should certainly go far, for it seems that he's consumed by ambition. Is this the road that Patrick would have taken? I cannot think so. Ambition is not bad in itself, but in Alan it appeared so raw, so *graceless*. He seemed incapable of grasping that we were a team. It wasn't a matter of one member's finds being more valuable than another's. The change in him has alienated me and in a curious way it has ... no ... not alienated me from Patrick – how would that be possible? But it has forced me to accept that ... he is dead. At last I find that I can use the word 'dead'. I think I understand fully now the meaning of the words: *requiescat in pace*.

Patrick, wherever you are, my beloved son, you will rest in peace. I've no beliefs. For me, you are ... no more. Except in my heart. There you will live on, but could not live while my grief was like a bloody flux. Now *requiescat in pace*, my grief, my pain.

This is a time of partings as well as returnings. I shall be genuinely sorry to say goodbye to Gwyneth Morris. Gwyneth ... a most attractive woman, a really beautiful woman. But of course I could hardly have precipitated an affair with a member of my small team. God knows, it would have been easy enough. I've never found it difficult to make women fall for me. Oddly enough, Gwyneth seemed to have a somewhat guarded attitude towards me. Perhaps she was afraid at first that she would fall in love with me. I greatly respected her, of course. She was damned competent, a real expert in her field, but I felt sometimes that she was a misfit. Socially. Perhaps her Welshness. Anyway, I had other preoccupations.

Hubert opened his eyes and looked across at his wife. She turned away from his gaze but he felt no resentment. He was not looking for a response. It was his own reaction he sought.

23

Meg, sitting opposite to him, familiar, reassuring simply by her permanent status in his life, compelled words to enter his mind with such plangency that he found his lips were framing their syllables, and put his handkerchief to his mouth. The words that trembled on his lips were: 'For over two months I have been under a sentence of madness.'

And as he expressed them, he felt himself sweating. It suddenly became urgent to catch Meg's eye, to assert the reality of his marriage, but Meg's face was still turned away. Desperately Hubert conjured up his home, his children, the coming reunion with the twins and Barbara. As he relaxed, his stiff mouth began to smile.

Now Meg turns and sees me, sees me smiling but makes no response. She looks puzzled as though she does not recognise me. Fool that I am, how can she know my thoughts? She gazes out of the window. I've lost the moment of intimacy that I needed so urgently and I cannot call across the compartment to her: 'Meg!' I can't appeal to her to help me in this new life. When we get home ... it will be easier when we get home. The three children. Young people now. But not Patrick, who would be nearly as old as Alan. Never Patrick. Never, never again. The words come as readily as usual. I have lived with them for five years, but now they have a less compelling resonance in my skull. The bonds of pain begin mercifully to loosen. The 'never, never again' that has paralysed my inner self can be accepted and put aside. The frightening end to which those words were leading me, as though I were a paralysed prisoner in a wheelchair, unable to control my course, has not been reached. That secret lake in Wales where I took Meg, where we so nearly went sailing, where I had planned ... But there were no boats available. Do I accept this as a miracle? What am I saying? I am no Christian. No believer in miracles. Yet ... something like a miracle happened there. There was no boat. Are all miracles so simple?

Meg felt in her pockets for a handkerchief and brought out a

24

crumpled leaflet. Someone on Shrewsbury station had handed one to Hubert who brushed it aside with deliberate ill-humour, not even looking to see what it said. Ralph evaded it by stepping away from the proffering hand. Alan took it, read it and handed it back with a candid and laborious, stammered explanation that he did not believe in God or Jesus so it meant nothing to him. Gwyneth took it, held it in her hand, did not look at it until they reached the carriage, then stared at it, not seeing the words. Finally, she folded it carefully, opened her book and used it as a marker.

Meg, having retrieved her leaflet from her pocket, smoothed it out on her knee. It was printed in black letters on cheap, soft yellow paper. It read as follows:

JESUS CHRIST
THE SAME
YESTERDAY TODAY
AND FOR EVER

It made her think of Hubert. The same yesterday, today and for ever. That was a good enough reason for leaving him, apart from anything else.

I am not going home with Hubert, she repeated to herself several times. Then she relaxed and concentrated her thoughts upon practical considerations. When we reach London, I shall tell him: I am not coming home to Canterbury with you, Hubert.

As the train began to weave its way through the northern suburbs of London, Meg finalised her plans. At Euston, as soon as Hubert led the way out of the compartment, she would catch his arm and say: 'I've decided I ought to go up to Highgate and see mother. She's not been well. It's such an opportunity. I'll come down by a later train. Or tomorrow. I'll ring you.' He would have no time to protest or argue.

But, no. It wouldn't do. He was too powerful. She would write him a note and slip it into his coat pocket. At Euston,

25

she would leave the luggage to him and murmur: 'Must run along to the Ladies'.' Then . . . a taxi . . . where to? Liverpool Street? Liverpool Street would do. There would be trains to the north-east and the north. She would telephone Hubert in the evening, to reinforce her note, her decision not to return home. All the problems: the children (surely old enough to take care of themselves), money, the whole structure of their married state which she was intending to dismantle, must be dealt with later. It was a brutal decision and she knew it, but she had come to believe that her very life depended upon it. Any argument about details at this stage would weaken her determination. The prime thing was to leave Hubert. To leave Hubert at last, after twenty-two years with him. It would bring obloquy upon her head. She must bear it. She must refuse to listen to special pleading. 'For the children's sake' was an obvious argument that would be used, and not only by Hubert. Blackmail from relatives. Disapproval from friends, condemnation from Hubert's colleagues. She must resist their weight. The children were young people now and could look after themselves. The first step had to be taken no matter what was said or thought of her. Her way forward was to leave Hubert.

Gwyneth's book was open in her hand, but she had ceased to read its words. Once this week at the Institute is over, her thoughts ran, there will be the rest of the long vac, and I've nothing planned. There is always work. I have to write a paper on the tools and weapons found on the site. But there were very few weapons except that superb sword. It will be a thin paper. I feel no enthusiasm for it. Durham unfortunately will expect a substantial paper. Well, then: compare the Iron Age finds with others on a similar site. Or sites. I suppose I can think up something to satisfy them. The train's moving again. Someone travelling in it opened a door and found an escape . . . from sorrow? It's only my surmise. I'm being very subjective. Except that my own sorrow hasn't led me to take that way out. It has brought me to anger, to a determination that I will not waste my mid-thirties in flight. *'Lover and friend hast thou put far from me'* – how readily the psalmist's words come back to me. All my youth of chapel-going. But I believe in nothing now except my own pain with which I must wrestle. My childhood's religion is dead. My old, deep-rooted passion for my country of mountain and river is alive ... but will not save me. I have to survive in my own bones and sinews and brain. Hubert is speaking to me: 'Where are you going after the Canterbury week is over, Gwyneth?'

This useful question sends my mind darting hither and thither and without conscious consideration it comes up with the words: 'I'm going to Ireland. I want to see two or three sites there. I've a paper to write.' God bless the healing inventions of the inner mind.

'Ah, yes,' agrees Hubert, sagely. 'Comparisons are meat and drink when one's battling with a learned paper for which the material's a bit thin. Except for the sword, the site wasn't all that productive in your special field, was it?' I answer him pedantically: 'Yes, provided the comparisons are fruitful.' How priggish I sound. No wonder Hubert smiles and returns to his newspaper.

I don't know him any better than I did two months ago. He doesn't know me. He is not curious about me, or if he is, it makes him uneasy because I have not behaved as women usually do with him. He would never understand that the writing of this paper is unimportant to me except as a useful, prosaic bridge between those summer hopes and the realities of life without Deborah. Life with no one. Those hopes that dissolved into ashes on a grey July evening in Deborah's Aberystwyth flat. If only I had myself burnt the letter I wrote. Oh, God, if only *I* had had the burning of it, I should not now remember it so clearly.

I told her I'd been taken on as a member of the Gors Ddu team by Professor Loders. I'd be able to get to Aberystwyth to see her. And I told her what hell Durham had been all these

27

months without her. I knew she'd been pretty hectic at Aber in the new job but I'd felt horribly out of reach. It was good to hear her voice when she phoned but somehow the telephone only made me feel more isolated. I brought up the Easter vac that we'd not been able to spend together because of her demanding parents. We hadn't seen each other since February and that was a foul wet weekend and we hadn't been all that happy. It had frightened me. Wasn't it going to be more difficult to pick up the threads the longer we were apart? Would we ever be able to live together again as we did at Durham? It was all I wanted – to live with her again.

Deborah. I love you more than anyone else I've ever loved in my life. Sometimes I wish you'd never taken that admin job at Aberystwyth. Then the practicalities. I told her we started at Gors Ddu on June 24; that I couldn't get away the very next weekend, but I'd hope to the one after. Presumably the admin staff would be staying on when the term ended, and that would overlap with my work in Wales. I'd ask the Prof if I could come to Aber on July 8. I'd ask for the Saturday off instead of the Friday. I'd get to her on Friday night.

That was the bare bones of the letter. There was so much else. And it lies heavy on my memory because I did not destroy it myself. Because I sent it and Deborah destroyed it and with it our life together.

3

Disappointment for Wales

ENGLISH ARCHAEOLOGIST HEADS DIG

Excavations started this week in an area of old peat bog where some artefacts dating from the Iron Age were found in the summer of 1979. The site is on the south flank of Moel Llafn. The public are asked to keep away from the area. Discussions about the possibility of carrying out excavations here have dragged on for some months. The delay has been caused partly for financial reasons, but latterly the unfortunate illness of Professor Davidson of Deeside University forced him to withdraw from leading the excavations. It was hoped that one of his colleagues might have taken over. However, Welsh institutions have not been able to raise sufficient funds to mount the operation. It is now to take place under the leadership of Professor Hubert Loders of the Institute of Archaeology at Canterbury. It appears that even this well-endowed Institute required further financial support and this has now been offered by a Midlands businessman, who wishes to remain anonymous.

It is a sad thing, in our opinion, that this generosity was not bestowed upon our own Deeside University, to enable the excavation to be made jointly, at least, between a Welsh and an English Institution. We are, however, pleased to learn that one of Professor Loders' team is a distinguished native of Wales, Dr Gwyneth Morris BA, PhD, and we shall be profiling Dr Morris in this newspaper next week.

Leading article in the *Powys Echo*, June 26th, 1980.

29

'Site Assistant!' Professor Loders had exploded. Meg was sitting opposite him at the dining-table. Supper was over. Hubert continued angrily: 'Did I tell you that that fool Ralph Shroton has been appointed Site Assistant? My God! I'm heading an important excavation in Wales and I'm lumbered with Ralph Shroton.'

He had fulminated on among the remains of supper, moving plates and cutlery from place to place as though he were demolishing a model town, even knocking over a glass as though it were a factory chimney. Meg got up and started to pile the debris of the meal. The children had gone to their rooms.

'For God's sake, sit down and listen,' he shouted suddenly.

'I'm sorry,' said Meg and at once hated herself for saying it. This propensity for apologising, for saying 'sorry', angling for a forgiveness she neither wanted, nor thought she required.

'Well, go on,' she said, propping herself on the edge of the table. 'What exactly will Ralph have to do? I thought he would be coming anyway to do the photography and drawings.'

'Yes, he'll do them, of course. About all he's fit for. But they must give him this status of Site Assistant – they sent him down a couple of weeks ago, to deal with the accommodation and hire a few natives to do the preliminary digging. We'll be having a few students – '

'Why do you call them natives, Hubert?' she interrupted.

'Because I have an exact mind, a liking for precise words. They *are* the natives, damn it. What am I supposed to call them? And they need a forceful – er – kind of bailiff over them, not a lazy, incompetent – ' Hubert pushed his chair away and stood up. 'I can see you're itching to get on with your domestic duties,' he observed, more calmly. 'I've work to do myself, plenty of it.'

How like him to call them 'duties' rather than 'chores'. He was hesitating and Meg knew that he was waiting for her to ask him: 'Will you need me?' But she turned away with her hands full of plates. 'I'll clear this up,' she said, 'and then I think I'll go through the clothes and sort out what we need.'

'You do that. You do that, my dear,' and Hubert went out, leaving the kitchen door open. The raucous sound of the twins' radio playing pop music came across the passage. 'Turn that down!' shouted Hubert.

Meg switched on the dishwasher and wondered whether the twins had turned their radio up to mute their father's angry tones in the kitchen drama over Ralph Shroton.

In mid-June, the team had assembled at the Institute at Canterbury to be briefed by Hubert about the excavation. He was taking his wife, Meg, with him. Though she was not on the staff of the Institute, she was a trained archaeologist. She was to look after day-to-day administration and act as Finds Assistant, booking the objects discovered on the site. Apart from Ralph Shroton there were two other professional members of the team, both of them coming from elsewhere. Alan Veltham was a young man of 24, who had just acquired a 2/1 degree in Archaeology at Preston University. When he heard about the Welsh excavation, he immediately applied to join it and was accepted as a Trustee, in charge of two or three students who would be joining them. The other member of the team was Doctor Gwyneth Morris, lecturer at Durham University. She was an expert in the field of Bronze and Iron Age weapons, and a recent paper she had written had interested Hubert and led him to invite her to join him. There was, of course, the additional advantage that she was Welsh and spoke the language.

The team met at Canterbury with only Ralph missing. Although bookings had been made by post at a small local hotel some weeks earlier, Ralph made a visit to Wales to inspect the hotel and assure himself that arrangements were satisfactory. It also fell to him to hire a Land-Rover and finalise arrangements with some local labourers. The site was on a small plateau on the shoulder of a mountain, where a peat bog had formed, though it was now mostly dried out.

31

Ralph had overstayed his term at the site, and came back to the Institute to find Hubert deep in discussion about the project with Alan and Gwyneth, who had already been at the Institute for three days. Hubert had not been pleased and Ralph had to spend some time not merely reporting on the arrangements he had made, but explaining the reason (a purely fictitious one) for his prolonged absence in Wales.

'You're better, are you?' asked Hubert, eyeing Ralph with a look that spoke plainly of his disbelief in the malaise which had allegedly caused Ralph to return four days late.

'An attack of migraine.'

'Oh. If that was all, I suppose – '

'There's no need to beat about the bush,' interrupted Ralph, quite at his ease, which Hubert was not. 'You think I went on a drinking binge.'

'I didn't say that.'

'Then don't suspect it, Professor. Take the doctor's certificate for gospel.'

'I haven't seen it.'

'No, of course. It went to Personnel. It just stated that I'd had a migraine and needed a few days off. Could we now leave the subject?'

'You've got everything done? The Land-Rover?'

'Almost new and a reasonable hiring charge. I've given the bursar the details. I suppose some of the team will bring their cars.'

'I'm not taking mine and I've told them not to take theirs. I don't believe Gwyneth or Alan have got cars anyway. I saw last year when I went to the site that it's impossible to use an ordinary car in that terrain, and the Institute doesn't want any responsibility for accidents or broken axles or whatever. What's the hotel like?'

'The Powys Arms? Very pleasant. Victorian. Not beautiful, you know, but decent-sized bedrooms, and they've arranged to put a desk or table in each of them.'

'Are we going to have a private lounge, a place to ourselves?'

'Yes, I saw to that.'

'What else was there I wanted to speak to you about? Damn nuisance your not being here for our meetings. Ah, yes, there'll be two or three students joining us. Alan is Trustee but you'll be expected to teach them something about technical drawings and so forth.'

'I *have* done this before,' said Ralph drily.

'Yes, yes, of course. Before my time, I suppose.'

'I'm sure I shall enjoy working with you on site, Professor,' observed Ralph with a genial smile which was not returned.

Hubert Loders tapped his fingers on the edge of his desk, ill-humouredly. 'Was there anything else?' asked Ralph.

'Yes – the labourers for the preliminary work before the students arrive. If they *do* arrive – always an uncertainty about these young fellows in my experience. That's why I thought we needed a few native labourers. You engaged them?'

'Natives somewhat hostile, I felt, but I engaged four and they seemed better-tempered when I mentioned the wages.'

'Right,' said Hubert. 'Thank you, Ralph. That all seems very satisfactory. You haven't met the two others on the team yet, Dr Gwyneth Morris and Alan Veltham. We're meeting again shortly, in about half an hour. Here in my study.'

Ralph agreed to be there and left Hubert's room. Back in his own room with half an hour to spare, Ralph felt bored. There was little for him to do but pack up his photographic equipment and drawing materials. The six days he had spent in North Wales had contained a curious and painful personal experience which he found it difficult to put out of his mind. It was a strange twist of fate that he should have gone for a long walk and come upon that particular scene, in remote Welsh country, so evocative of a past that he had buried, he thought, most effectively. He got up and walked about his room restlessly. When exactly was it? He took out his pocket diary and thumbed back the pages. The date was June 12th, 1980. But he could not bring himself to bring back the details

33

of the scene here in this official monkish cell in the Institute, a cell which formed part of Father Hubert's monastic order, as Ralph put it to himself, with a touch of humour that relieved the pressure of memory and the pain of memory. Uncertain that he could withstand what he could feel mounting within him, he pulled out from a filing cabinet the half-bottle of whisky he always kept there. A half-bottle because this gave him the illusion of restraint. He drank from it and before long the urge to bury the experience he had had in the Welsh valley under something in a totally different mood led him to recall his interview with Hubert earlier that afternoon.

I have just had neat, precise, correct, affable and utterly hostile interview with H.L. He is, of course, convinced that I went on a blind at the end of my trip to Wales and that this is the reason I returned to this bloody monastery four days late. Against his will, he is forced to concede that I did all that was expected of me. His passion for getting everyone slotted into his particular plan as uniformly as possible extends even to a virtual embargo against anyone bringing their own car. True, a car would be useless for the track to the dig, but people might have wanted to keep a car at the hotel, so that they could escape in their free time into the country around. Perhaps there won't be any free time. It would certainly save the Institute money in hotel bills and hiring charges for the Land-Rover if we worked solidly through every weekend. It's probably what he plans. I couldn't care less about the car business. I live very well without one.

Ralph's pen had been doodling on the back of a letter and a neat drawing of a veteran car with a begoggled driver at its wheel emerged in the centre of a network of curlicues. The last loop ended in the words 'the combustion engine', and after another pull at the whisky he continued writing: 'has been responsible for far more than the lead poison in the air we breathe, the perpetual noise that dulls our hearing and obliterates the song of the lark equally with the wail of a

34

pop-star on the radio, and the reduction of our towns and villages to traffic slums. Like an autocratic grandmother still resident with the family, whose stick rattles against the banisters, whose deafness promotes shouting, whose white hair commands respect while her continual presence inspires hatred, the motor car grows old along with us, and like grandmother, stinks with its own peculiar and characteristic odour. Both car and grandmother are more than ready for the grave, and those who cling to either are merely expectant children, hoping for a mention in her will or a car more powerful than their neighbour's. They are as passionate in their love for this lethal toy as they were once greedy for grandmother's diverting stories and tooth-decaying sweets, secretly dealt out from a black pocket in defiance of parental rebuke.'

Ralph sat back, immensely pleased with this Proustian paragraph. But his pleasure did not last long. Proust, he could never forget, was the author to whom he clung when his life was at its nadir. At that time, Proust, by the very length of his novel, had carried him over and past the desire to commit suicide. His twelve blue volumes were faded and worn, for he had often carried one in his pocket to read in a bus or a train. The pages of some were stained where he had dropped food or drink on them. For Ralph, in a sorrow he found beyond his capacity to deal with, Proust had many virtues. *Remembrance of Things Past* is very long. Weeks, months pass and still the work does not draw to its end. And when Ralph did eventually finish it, being uncured of his pain, he started again at the beginning and found no tedium in doing so, for passages that he had read without much understanding, chapters that could not compete with his bitterness, were now read as though for the first time, and yielded a solace, even a pleasure, unsuspected at a first reading. Above all, Proust transported him into another world, a complete milieu in which he not only came to know a wide variety of characters in all walks of life, but which also provided music, art, literature, architecture;

35

which introduced him to city, village and seaside town, every house with detailed interiors, furnished recognisably in the style one would expect of their owners. In his determined and single-minded devotion to Combray, the hawthorn walk, the Guermantes Way, the Faubourg Saint-Germain and Balbec, Ralph felt himself rooted in Proust's scenes as though he had always known them long before he had lived with Phyllis. Gradually he was able to return to the reality of life without her, to rooms she had never shared with him, places they had never explored, and work – in the Institute of Archaeology near Canterbury – of which she would have known nothing. He was not well-off, but he was reasonably rewarded for his work, and had no one to spend his money on but himself. He became agreeably lazy, easy-going, a mildly enthusiastic collector of furniture, prints and wine chosen for his own pleasure, mercifully divorced from the painful desire to share them with someone who was no longer there, or with anyone else selected in the futile hope of finding a substitute for Phyllis. Ralph had chosen well, yet there were moments when the whole carefully constructed fabric of his world collapsed around him and nothing could save him then but a bout of drinking. He could not, however, drink seriously, drink for oblivion, here in his office. He concealed the whisky bottle in its usual cache. The meeting would have started. He looked at his watch and found that he was five minutes late. He hurried to Hubert's study, greeted the newcomers, explained who he was, apologised to the Professor, and having disrupted the meeting, sat down and took no further part in it. Forty minutes later he left the Institute for home and oblivion.

'*We are a small team. This will make the work harder. Everyone will have to pull his and her weight. But it has its advan-
tages. I see us as a – as a family. We are very disparate in ages,
as of course members of a family must be. For these two or
three months we are going to live at very close quarters, also
like a family. But enough of that.*

'*This site promises to be of great interest, perhaps of great
importance. We are fortunate in having a Welsh-speaking
member of the team and one eminent in her knowledge of
Iron Age weapons, Gwyneth. Every one of us has his or her
own expertise to contribute. Your photography, Ralph, your
– er – your drawings. We shall be joined by two or three
students and I hope they will learn much from you, Ralph, in
those two fields. As for Alan, he has his youth and enthusiasm.
He has much to contribute ...*'

> *Extract from Professor Loders' talk to his team on
> their first evening at the Powys Arms.*

*The Professor concluded his remarks with these words:
'Now I'm going to buy you all drinks. We'll celebrate the
beginning of our work as a team.'*

*Comment by Ralph Shroton, scribbled on the back of his
photography record book: 'Bloody crap.'*

'I hope to God that fellow Ralph won't go pub-crawling while
we're here. I've made it plain to the team that there's to be

no attempt to "mix with the natives". They don't like the English, to start with, and a dig is always a sensitive area. If the team want drinks in the evening, they must have them in the hotel where we're all staying. My dear Meg, I'm sorry you think that I'm treating them like children. I am making a rule that I think is necessary and they must all be treated alike, the mature with the immature.'

'I think you misjudge Ralph, but of course, you know him better than I do, Hubert. I must get some letters written. Anything you need?'

'No, no.'

Certainly I know Ralph. I know him all too well, having had him on my staff at the Institute for some eight years. He is not, to be fair, an habitual drunkard. He would not have survived had he been so. His drinking bouts take place roughly three times a year. Usually they start at his own house and he is capable of phoning us at the Institute to say he's not coming in, making the excuse that he's not well. In fact, although rumours have reached us, I don't think that many people at the Institute know that he has this failing. I certainly didn't realise how serious it was until the morning he opened the door of the library where I was consulting some book, took a few steps forward and fell flat on his face. A couple of students and I hauled him on to an old couch between the french windows, and I saw at once what the trouble was. There's a sickroom at the Institute, of course, and a nurse. We managed to get him along there, after he'd been violently sick over the library floor. God, it was a squalid scene. I was revolted and angry and refused to let him stay in the sickroom. I was fairly certain that he'd been drinking for several days, for he'd been absent for almost a week. I overruled the nurse, rang the local hospital and arranged for an ambulance to come for him. I know one of the consultants there – a man called Harvey. I had a few words with him on the phone and he said he'd arrange with the houseman that Ralph should be admitted to the emergency ward and 'dried out'.

I then reported what had happened to Childs, our Principal. We do not see eye to eye on a number of matters. We disagree about Ralph Shroton. Childs' view is that Shroton is a first-class photographer and a competent draughtsman (which I don't deny) and that his work is worth a few days' drunkenness now and then.

'I've known about this for some time,' Childs said, and I remember feeling extremely angry that he had not informed me, his senior professor, about it.

'I should have thought it was a serious enough matter to justify getting rid of him. There are plenty of other photographers and draughtsmen about. We could appoint one certainly as good, possibly better. And younger, I may add.'

'I should have thought it was a serious enough matter to justify getting rid of him. There are plenty of other photographers and draughtsmen about. We could appoint one certainly as good, possibly better. And younger, I may add.'

'His age has nothing to do with it,' retorted Childs. 'Or rather, I suppose it has, in a sense.'

And I knew at once that his sympathy for Ralph largely sprang from the fact that the two of them were much the same age and due to retire in the not so distant future.

'If he were incompetent, I'd feel justified in sacking him,' Childs went on. 'But he is not. Neither is he *habitually* drunk. Not habitually, you know, Hubert. He has only five or six years to go till he retires, till he gets his pension, that is, of course, and I feel very strongly that we have room to carry a few – one or two – what shall I call them?'

'Drunkards?'

'No, no,' expostulated Childs. 'Misfits. Difficult chaps. His drinking is a symptom, you know, a symptom of something deeper.' He spoke like a damned shrink. 'Even misfits is the wrong word. Ralph is not a *happy* man, Hubert. Not *au fond* a happy man, as I am, as I imagine you are. With a stable marriage and home. I don't think he's ever disclosed to any one of us here what his actual trouble is – his – his grief – or

39

trauma, if you like – '

He maundered on, more like a psychiatrist with every word, adding: 'Whatever it is, it causes him to break out occasionally into drinking. There must be some reason.'

'Perhaps he'll disclose it to the house physician at the hospital,' I suggested, with a sarcasm that was lost on Childs.

'Well, Hubert, I must say that I'm sorry you sent him off to the hospital. It was somewhat highhanded of you.'

I said nothing.

'I think it would have been better to call a taxi and send him home.'

'He couldn't stand up.'

'All right. *Take* him home.'

'*I* take him home?'

'I don't see why not, but in fact, I'd have sent Nurse Maynard with him. I think it's unfortunate that the whole story will now get about, perhaps outside the Institute.'

'It would have done that anyway. There were students in the library, not to mention the assistant librarian.'

The Principal pursed his lips and I could see that there was no point in arguing. I turned to go but he called me back and said: 'Hubert, there is something I must say to you, have been meaning to say for some time. I think you are, shall we say, a trifle intolerant. I think you should regard the staff here as a *team*. We are responsible, one for another, you know. I really do believe that we have a joint responsibility. Members one of another, as it says.'

At that point I strode out of the room. I couldn't stand any more of his crap. Responsible for Ralph Shroton, God help me!

A letter from Deborah by second post. I found it when we came back from the dig. I couldn't trust myself to open it in front of the others. I slipped out by the hotel side door and walked down the road till I came to a farm track. Holding the letter in my hand unopened. A valley farm with two or three

40

cottages. The fields very green and lush. Two women, perhaps mother and daughter, working in a corner of a field cutting broad beans from tall untidy plants, trailing over their stakes, heavy with pods. They called out 'Good evening' in Welsh as I passed. It is sweet to me to hear the Welsh tongue again; to pass under the shadow of a mountain peak and out again into the western sun. Deborah's letter. 'I hope you'll find this letter waiting for you, my darling. I can't find your last just at this moment, but I know you said you'd come to Aberystwyth your second weekend. The date July 8th is stuck in my mind. Is that right? I see I've pencilled it into my diary, anyway. I'm longing like hell to see you. The parents were the absolute end. I felt I'd utterly wasted Easter and much of April, being with them. A time you and I might have had together, but I can at least say that I've done my duty. For another year. I'm not intending to spend Christmas with them.'

With me, then? She doesn't say so. I'm under a double shadow – from a mass of cloud that's hiding the sun and from this letter. Do I read too much into her words – or her lack of words? I suppose I expect too much. Always have. Deborah hated planning things ahead, being definite about dates. I know her so well. I'm sitting on a stone wall. Brown boulders, bright with yellow lichen. I watch the women leaving the field with the slow lumbering gait of people carrying heavy baskets. A man in a small van has come along the track and loaded their beans. I can hear their voices faintly, contained in the walls of this valley. Contained . . . as I long to be contained in your love, Deborah. Oh, but I am, I am! Rereading your letter, I know I have misjudged you. It's all so clear: the new job . . . your parents . . . I've been demanding, though you're generous enough not to say so. Anyway, what does it all matter now? In ten days I'll be with you in Aberystwyth. My heart leaps. I'm lyrical with happiness. I must go back. I'll find out the train times this evening and write to you. Oh, God, it's nearly seven. I'll have to hurry. Must be back for dinner. The hotel will have a train timetable. I'll take it upstairs and write

41

her a short letter about possible trains.

There's Hubert and Meg coming out of the lounge, to go up and change.

'You've been out? My God, what energy, after a day at the dig.'

'You forget. I belong here, Professor. I had to go out and look at it all. Greet it at last.'

'D'you mean this is actually your part of Wales?'

'Yes, it is. Not the actual place here – this village. But the shapes of the mountains are familiar. I was brought up not so far from here. Went to school locally.'

'You must feel as though you've come home,' suggests Meg.

'Oh, I do. It's marvellous to be here.'

I run up the stairs after them. I've put it into words. I've convinced myself – I'm home. And Deborah is only sixty miles away. I've been unhappy, suspicious even. But I've convinced myself about this, too. I think it's the distance that's between us that has created my doubts. We might have been living at opposite ends of the world – impossible to meet for a weekend when she was at Aberystwyth and I at Durham. I don't know ... I think if I'd had the car, I'd have made it, even if ... but she has a lot of admin work to do at weekends, it seems. Oh, I hate the way, the insidious way suspicions weave in and out of one's thoughts. Yet perhaps it's better to pull them out into the light of day. Letters, for instance. I've judged her by my own inclination for letter-writing. She did write marvellous letters – when she got down to writing them, but she's not like me, ready to pick up a pen at the slightest opportunity. Look at me now – I could phone the train times to her, couldn't I? But I hate the telephone. It doesn't really connect. It emphasises separation. A disembodied voice in a plastic speaker. Lord, I must change. I'll write to her after supper.

Gwyneth came down from her room later that evening and found Alan and Ralph reading newspapers in the lounge.

'I suppose one of you hasn't got a stamp? I want this to go tomorrow first thing, and the Post Office won't be open.'

'I've got one,' said Ralph. 'No, don't get your purse out. I can afford to give you a stamp even on the pittance the Institute pays me.'

'I'm sure you're not paid a pittance, but thank you, all the same.'

'Will you have a drink?' suggested Ralph.

Gwyneth hesitated, then answered: 'Yes, I'd love one. I feel celebratory.'

'If we're celebrating something,' said Alan, 'will you tell us what it is?' He stammered badly over the words and Ralph cut him short with: 'Let's get the drinks first. What's yours, Gwyneth?'

'I can't think of anything that exactly fits my mood, except something awfully extravagant, and I won't have you buying that on your pittance.'

'When in doubt, have a Pimm's Number One,' said Ralph.

'But that was exactly what I wanted! That'd be marvellous.'

'What's yours, Alan?'

'Oh, look here, don't buy me one. I'll come to the bar with you.'

The men disappeared to the bar on the other side of the passage and returned, Alan clasping two glasses of Pimm's.

'He's bought us each one,' he said, with a hint of surprise in his voice, for he had not yet been able to see an amiable side of Ralph.

'For a celebration, I thought we should all drink the same liquor,' Ralph announced. 'It's important for the ritual. Now, before we raise our glasses, let's hear why and who and what?'

Gwyneth was now disconcerted. She regretted her words about a celebration and looked at her glass without speaking.

'Let's guess,' cried the genial Ralph. 'You've written a letter. That we know. I suggest you've written to accept some poor chap who's been begging you to marry him for years. His last letter mentioned a broken heart, a possible jump off a pier, or a prolonged sojourn in foreign parts. You've capitulated at last.'

He raised his glass.

'Don't be absurd,' said Gwyneth, colouring.

Alan scowled. He was partly angry, partly embarrassed.

'I'm sorry I said that about a celebration,' said Gwyneth. 'It was stupid of me. Let's just drink to Gors Ddu, to the Black Bog. It's good to be with such a nice team. I'm really enjoying it.'

'Splendid!' cried Ralph. 'Here's to our dig!' But after they had begun to drink their Pimm's, conversation flagged. Each had their private thoughts. Ralph, anxious at the silence, asked with heavily assumed interest: 'Where did you get your degree, Gwyneth?'

'Cambridge. You could have looked that up,' she replied. 'And then I went on to Bangor.'

'For your PhD?'

'That's right. What about you, Ralph?'

'You could have looked me up too, and then you'd have discovered that I'm not really an archaeologist at all. Just a fraud. I've got a History MA which got me into the archives department of a provincial museum. And then I graduated – some might say I declined – to the recording side of the Institute at Canterbury. I'd become quite a good photographer and polished up my capacity for drawing. Perhaps I ought to have been an architect.'

Alan looked at him with slightly more respect and said: 'To work under Hubert – under Professor Loders – you're bloody lucky.'

Ralph swallowed most of his Pimm's at a gulp. 'Yes,' he said solemnly. 'Oh, yes, I am. I thank God for it on my knees, fasting. Every day.'

Gwyneth burst out laughing. 'You're incorrigible, Ralph.'

'I never know what people mean by that,' mused Ralph. 'Literally it means uncorrectible, but in what have I erred? Why do I have to be corrected?'

44

'For not telling the truth,' said Gwyneth, a reply which disconcerted Ralph for a moment. Then he said: 'We all need another drink,' and strode off to the bar. This time Alan did not accompany him.

'What made you say that?' he asked Gwyneth.

'Well, I'll put it another way. Perhaps he was being ironical, but from what I've observed, I don't think he likes Hubert much, nor does Hubert care much for Ralph.' She regretted the words as soon as she had said them. Alan picked them up quickly.

'You can't blame the Prof for that,' he said. 'Ralph is hardly pulling his weight, is he? He's forever sitting about doing – no, I'd better not say that – I just don't care for him much myself. He's – he's not my type.'

'Don't let's discuss each other. It's generous of him to buy us the Pimm's, and a second round at that.'

'Meaning I ought to have bought the second round?'

'Well, perhaps you might have offered, but please don't get het up about it. It's a beautiful evening and I'm extremely happy. I don't want to spoil it.'

Alan began another question, stammered badly, and became silent as Ralph returned with three glasses on a small tray. The atmosphere relaxed.

5

Turn to private life
And social neighbourhood; look we to ourselves.

Wordsworth: *The Excursion*

The day was oppressively hot. The Welsh labourers leaned on their shovels and talked to each other in lilting voices while they waited for their next instructions. The shovels were wooden grain shovels of an old pattern, produced by a local farmer who had kept them as a curiosity. Metal tools were inappropriate for digging in peat, where the finds were likely to be fragile. Excavation in the three trenches now exposed was a matter of working almost entirely with the hands. Only one of these trenches had so far yielded any significant finds, trench A in which Gwyneth was working: fragmentary portions of iron harness-fittings. Later in the day, however, a more substantial find was an almost complete bridle-bit of bronze-coated iron. At this point in the late afternoon, the others were discussing with Professor Loders the feasibility of pursuing the excavation of the existent trenches any further for the present, or shifting to a section of the site nearer trench A. The decisions were taken and marked on the plan of the site and then Hubert, sweating in the heat, looked at his watch.

'We'll knock off early,' he said. 'It's been a long day.'

'I'd like to go on a bit longer,' said Gwyneth. 'Would that be OK?'

Hubert had made his pronouncement and Meg expected him to check Gwyneth. If she stayed on, all of them would have to stay with her, because of going back together in the Land-Rover. But Hubert, to her surprise, sat down among the coarse grass just above the site, and said lazily, lighting a cigarette: 'You go ahead, Gwyneth, if you want to. I'll send the men home, I think.'

'You'd like me to tell them to go?' asked Alan and at Hubert's nod, he walked down to the edge of the site to the Welshmen, who fell silent at his approach.

'The Professor says there'll be no more work today,' said Alan, saying the words slowly as if the men were little acquainted with English speech, and controlling his stammer except when he came to the word 'today' which one of the Welshmen kindly supplied for him. With the obstinacy of a stammerer, Alan insisted on adding quite unnecessarily, as though the labourers were slow of understanding as well as foreigners: 'You can g-g-g ... you ... can g-g-g – ' 'Go,' suggested the Welshmen together. 'Home early,' added Alan loudly, but they had already turned their backs on him and were walking towards their hut, their stream of talk starting up again immediately. They put away their tools and disappeared down the rough track in an ancient jeep.

As he walked back, Alan went over to trench A and looked down at Gwyneth, kneeling in the trench.

'Can I g-g-give you a ... a ... a ... hand, if you're ... going on?' He stood hesitating by the trench, observing Gwyneth without speaking. He felt that a new element had entered the expedition now the preliminary work was over. He was seeing beyond the team to its individual members and Gwyneth was the one with whom he most wanted to be at ease, after Hubert. Looking down at her now, he realised that since they first met at Canterbury he had been obscurely aware of feelings insistent but unrecognised. Once they were working on site, he had found himself watching her more and more often and with a growing wonder at her strikingly beautiful appearance. He had attempted with shy persistence to approach her, to engage her in conversation. His present observation of her in the soft light of late afternoon, as she knelt in the trench below him, flowered into the discovery that her beauty had a special meaning for himself. He experienced with heightened perception the presence of Gwyneth in this strange and powerful country of which she seemed to be a part. He looked up at the mountain on whose lower slope the site lay, the mountain called Moel Llafn, which she had explained meant the 'hill of the blade', its summit being a long stretch of razor-like rock. The sun was on it now and such beauty was unknown to Alan. Looking down again at Gwyneth he was sharply aware both of her Welshness, her kinship with the strange place in which he found himself, and also of her unusual loveliness, as alien to him as the surrounding hills, but as compelling and fascinating. His heart began to race. He took a few steps towards the trench where she knelt and knelt down himself, leaning on a rough post at the corner of the site.

'My God, it's stifling,' he heard his voice say in matter-of-fact tones, while his eyes rested with intense pleasure on her. Her hair was a dark chestnut with reddish lights, worn loosely over the nape of her neck in untidy curls. Her face was now flushed and her eyes glowed with the intensity of her work. The sun began to disappear behind a massive shoulder of mountain, but to Alan it seemed as though another sun was rising from the mound heaped at the side of the trench. He felt himself in a new world, along with Gwyneth. Then she turned away from him, bent over her hands as they sifted the small pile of loose peat where she had made the finds. Alan rose to his feet and walked slowly, bemused, back to his leader, and sat down beside him. Meg was sitting a few yards away from her husband, writing in a notebook. She looked up as Alan came near, about to speak to him. She saw a look

48

in his face that made her remain silent. Ralph was sitting in the open back of the Land-Rover finishing a drawing and talking to the three students who had been fetched from Welshpool that afternoon and whose tents were now up. For them, serious work would begin next day. They were looking at Ralph's map of the site and his first drawings.

'The Prof's talking,' he said, laying aside his drawing suddenly. 'Perhaps you'd better go over and listen to him.' He thought but refrained from remarking that he recognised the tone of Hubert's voice as that of a sermon. He returned to his own drawing work, thankful that he was out of earshot of the actual words.

Hubert had opened his eyes when he realised that Alan was sitting down beside him. 'Have a cigarette, Alan,' he said lazily, tossing them. 'Are you sorry you weren't the one to make the first find of some interest? Disappointed?'

'N-n-no,' stammered Alan, taken aback at a question so out of key with his thoughts and feelings. 'We're a team, aren't we? In a way,' he went on slowly, pulling hard at his cigarette between the words, obscuring in smoke the colour that he felt rising in his face: 'In a way ... I'm rather ... glad that ... that ... Gwyneth ... she being Welsh ... it was somehow right.'

'Ah, yes,' agreed Hubert, smiling. 'The romantic view of archaeology. But you said yourself – we're a team. Gwyneth's a professional among professionals, and Welshness has nothing to do with it, my lad.' Alan would have liked to riposte with: 'Then why did you ask me such a question?' but he had not the courage. He floundered into a half sentence: 'I just feel somehow – ' but Hubert brushed his words aside. He had a speech prepared for Alan, a speech carried over from a solitary walk he had taken the evening before. Now seemed the moment to make it, though with Meg near him, his thoughts took a less deeply personal turn. He shifted his ground, modified the speech into a fatherly interest in Alan's youthful eagerness and dedicated love of the work he was doing. Leave

Patrick out of it. Alan was in any case no substitute for Patrick, but at least Hubert allowed himself to recapture pleasures denied him since Patrick's death, the relish of being a mentor, of guiding a youthful enthusiasm, rewards of teaching that he too seldom experienced now in his eminent position at the Institute. Here the scene was just right: the piles of turf and peat, shovels resting against the bank, the first trenches. And now the students squatting on their heels near him. Hubert leaned back against the long grass, relaxed, and spoke directly to Alan, but loud enough for the students to hear.

'You know, Alan,' he began, 'I've never lost the initial excitement of marking out an area and lifting the first sods, and then of course the real work begins – digging down further, supervising the workmen and so on, but even then, the excitement, the thrill remains with me, as we peel away the layers patiently. To use an onion as a simile is too crass. No, it's more like some work I saw done in an old church near Canterbury. I watched an expert lifting the flakes of whitewash delicately from the damp walls and revealing little by little a most beautiful wall painting.'

He paused and lit another cigarette. Leaned back, looking up at the sky.

'For me, this is the poetry of the whole process, the revelation, as one sifts through layers of soil. Of course it's scientific work, but the poetry of it is never far away, for me at any rate. It's those moments of discovery that remain with one. Like the memory of a love affair.'

Meg had stopped writing to listen to Hubert. About to reject Hubert's words, to cry out in her mind: 'How phoney, how sentimental!' She found herself thinking of him as he was when she had first known him. For a moment she was overwhelmed with the tenderest love for him. His words called up all the romance of their early days together. If it could have lasted between them, she thought, and created a fusion of strength, they might have been able to bear the years that

50

followed. Tragedy could have been caught up in the narrative of their lives together. As his words died away into silence under the shadowed hillside, she felt that a door had been opened, and that she had suddenly been made aware of all the suffering she had endured and all the loss she had sustained.

He did not turn towards her. He put his arm on Alan's shoulder and heaved himself up. 'Come on,' he said. 'It's getting cold out of the sun. Time to go back. We must tear Gwyneth away from her work by force, if necessary, or we'll be late for dinner.'

'The food here,' observed Hubert that evening, 'is a damn sight better than I'd thought it would be – at the back of beyond like this.'

'We *are* on the edge of Snowdonia,' remarked Gwyneth with a touch of asperity.

'That needn't have any influence on the food,' retorted Hubert. 'Tourists are often enough expected to put up with frightful meals in the midst of stunning scenery, as though the natives assumed that the scenic beauties should be food enough.

'These natives, as you call them, don't think anything of the kind, I assure you,' said Gwyneth, now angry.

'Hubert, do stop talking rubbish,' put in Meg, by which she meant 'stop being so offensive'.

'OK, OK,' said Hubert, irritably. 'I apologise for treading on your Welsh corns, Gwyneth. I suppose I put things badly, but I'm paying a tribute to this place. The food and the service generally are extremely good. I hope that'll satisfy your nationalist feelings.' Hubert smiled as he said this, but his eyes were troubled and his manner withdrawn. He was not exerting his charm upon Gwyneth, and Meg was surprised.

'It's one up to Ralph,' she said, 'for choosing this hotel.'

'I didn't choose it. It chose me. I simply looked on the one-inch map, found the nearest hotel to the site and spun them a yarn about the importance of our excavation, the eminence of our Professor Loders, not to mention Dr Gwyneth Morris, sole prop and stay of archaeology in north-east England, not to mention Alan Veltham, adornment of Preston University, and, let me see, what else – '

Meg prompted him, good-humouredly: 'There's yourself and me, Ralph. What about us, or didn't we figure in your eulogy?'

'Yes, oh, yes. I gave them to understand that your gourmet cooking was celebrated from Canterbury to – to Cornwall, so they'd better engage a first-class cook if they hadn't got one already. As for myself, I said I wouldn't dream of booking us in until I'd perused their wine list. By this time the management was grovelling. In fact, a wad of bank notes was pressed into my hand to persuade me to make the booking.'

'What did you do with them?' asked Gwyneth, her good humour restored by Ralph's ludicrous tale.

'My dear, what could I do with them?' answered Ralph. 'I couldn't keep them. It would have been most improper. I gave them to Plaid Cymru.'

Even Hubert joined in the general laughter at this and the evening might have ended well but for Alan's next remark. He looked round the table at the team, and said cheerfully, with hardly a trace of a stammer: 'You know, this is how I've always imagined an ideal family. Meals at home with my family were absolute hell, always in dead silence with Dad firmly reading the newspaper, and – but, no, I'm not going to sit here describing my family to you. It's just that this is so different: Ralph's a kind of clown of an elder brother, if he doesn't think me offensive calling him that – I mean he's a nice clown – there wasn't much humour in my family. Gwyneth – well, I'm *going* to say it: Gwyneth's the beauty of the family, and myself, well, I'm not sure what my role is, except to be the tailpiece, only it's odd that I don't feel diminished by this. I don't feel the odd man out as I was always made to feel at home.'

There was an uneasy silence at this frank and, for Alan,

52

lengthy speech. It was at last broken by Hubert saying icily: 'Alan, you've been drinking too much. I'll go up to my room if you'll all excuse me. I don't want any dessert.'

He got up and left the dining-room. They heard his footsteps going upstairs and the door of his bedroom shutting with a heavy slam.

'Oh, my God!' exclaimed Alan. 'What have I said? What – what – *am* I a bit drunk?'

Meg made no answer to Alan's words. The family picture at home was too clear in her mind. The others were equally silent, Gwyneth puzzled and Ralph dismayed by Alan's words. The waiter came in at this point, bringing the sweet.

'Ought I to apologise about something?' asked Alan, anxiously. 'I'd do anything rather than offend the Prof.'

'Look here,' said Ralph, 'never mind your curious description of me as a clown. I've been called worse things. But your speech was remarkably unfortunate. You don't know why and it's not really for me to tell you. Perhaps Meg will explain.'

But Meg said nothing. She slowly spooned out the caramel custard and handed the plates along the table.

'Well, then, *I*'d better say something,' said Ralph. 'I'll have a shot at explaining it briefly. Hubert and Meg once suffered a – a tragic loss. Something you said – in perfect innocence – touched Hubert on a raw nerve. Will that do for the moment, Meg? I haven't said anything about *your* feelings.'

'It will do. Thank you, Ralph. Leave me out of it.'

'And I'll just add this rider,' went on Ralph. 'Don't apologise, Alan, or make some damn fool speech about being sorry. Just forget it. Hubert knows you were entirely in the dark. He won't hold it against you. Some time, I think I should tell you and Gwyneth the facts, but not just at the minute. Would you agree, Meg?'

'I'd agree.'

They ate their caramel custard, with Ralph jollying them along, in the clownish elder brother's role. Somewhat to his surprise, he found himself assisted by Gwyneth. At last they retired to the lounge for coffee.

There was little for the team to do in the evenings at the Powys Arms. There were walks, of course, in the light evenings, and Alan and Gwyneth, and sometimes Meg, went out for an hour or so, but the work was tiring and they more usually spent the evening in. Gwyneth would read, or talk lightheartedly, seeming to enjoy drawing out the others into talking about themselves, offering as her own contribution few facts, but an aura of happiness and expectancy. If the others proved unresponsive, she was prepared to entertain them, playing upon her Welshness as if it were a joke, telling stories of her upbringing and family, delighted to be back in Wales after what she regarded as an exile in Durham.

Hubert seldom allowed himself to be drawn into these conversations, but he was very willing to play bridge, and had brought cards and bridge-markers with him. It had been the last chance, thought Meg one evening, watching her husband trump Alan's king and gather the tricks together with bored triumph. She observed the long black hairs on his fingers with a sudden wave of loathing. He shuffled the pack expertly and she watched his movements, hating his hands which she knew too well. He cut the pack and said: 'You deal, my dear.'

She dealt the cards, picked up her hand and saw that she held the king of spades. How like the king Hubert was: handsome, his moustache rising a little at each end (though not with such an arrogant upturned curl as the king's upon the card), most like him in the heaviness of jowl which had grown with middle age. The same large eyes that so captivated women. Eyes that could melt into sympathy or admiration for a pretty girl, and as he gazed into her face, seemed to brim as though a soft wind lifted the water's edge of a lake. She called: 'Two spades.'

'Come on, Meg. It's our last chance,' said her partner, Alan.

Why had she ever conceived that this Welsh expedition was the last chance? It was only one after so many last chances. To spend a few months away from Canterbury gave it a special power, certainly: a period engaged on a common professional task which had originally brought them together, when she was a student and Hubert a young don of some brilliance, entrusted with an important excavation in Somerset. After her marriage she had given up archaeological work to look after the four children she bore him and the home he provided, a converted oasthouse, much admired by their friends. But the children grew older and the charm of improving the oasthouse began to pall. Hubert was often away, lecturing at other institutes or universities. Meg had become Hubert's amanuensis. She filed his notes, made extracts for him from learned journals, answered letters, dealt with money matters. If he made a careless or inaccurate statement in an article, which he sometimes did, she corrected it and put up with the ill-temper this caused, a rancorous half-hour nearly always brought to an end by a bout of maudlin gratitude and a demand to make love.

Hubert had centred his hopes of a partner in his archaeological work not upon Meg, but upon their eldest child, Patrick, whom he loved with the deepest passion he had ever known, a passion quite distinct in quality and power from that which inspired his sexual affairs. Hubert and Patrick had searched together for flint arrow-heads and other artefacts; they had built a small museum in the garden, made slides, written labels for the objects on display. It was shown off to friends, always with the inference that Patrick was a budding genius. The other three children were excluded from his interest and pride. He appeared to care little what they did and it fell to Meg to devise opportunities for them to develop interests, to find their own talents outside archaeology. Barbara, the next eldest to Patrick, was musical and Meg did all she could to encourage her. Edward and Michael, the twins, were not bright, but stolid, loving and dependable children.

Once, an unforgettable climax to a horrible day, Hubert had said bitterly in the privacy of their bedroom: 'They've only one brain between them, those twins. Always so predictable, too. They never surprise one.'

Yet she gave him another chance. The river ran near the house and she bought a small boat, taught the twins to row, and finally induced Hubert to recall his youthful sailing days at Bosham with his own family. The twins were practical and proved apt pupils, soon becoming reasonably expert with the boat, whereupon Hubert became bored with the whole business and refused to give up time to it. 'There's nothing on-going about it,' he complained. 'On-going' was a cant word of his at the time. There was too little to teach them when they had so quickly become proficient; nothing he himself could do on this placid river to surprise *them*.

It was therefore a bitter stroke of irony that Patrick should have gone sailing with his young brothers on a rough day in March, when Hubert was away lecturing in Cambridge. The boat overturned in a gust of sudden driving rain and wind, and it was Patrick who was drowned. The twins clung to the upturned hull and lived.

After the funeral, the family sat round the dining-room table, Meg, Barbara and the twins, pale and silent, but no Hubert. Barbara reached out a hand to her mother. 'Where's Daddy?' she asked.

'Can't we start?' demanded Edward sullenly.

'He's in his study,' answered Meg. 'We can wait for a few more minutes. I – I wanted us to be all together for the meal.'

'It's awful for Dad,' remarked Michael, simply and without bitterness. 'He always liked Patrick much better than us.'

For Meg, this major crisis suddenly illuminated the slow accumulation of small trivial episodes which had corroded her marriage. The death of Patrick, she had briefly hoped, might arrest the process, might draw herself and Hubert together, until, like enemies upon a raft, they would be forced to help each other to survive. But Hubert locked himself into a grief which he refused to share. It fell to Meg to live through the loss of Patrick as best she might, and the largeness of her own love gave her a broad foundation on which she tried to rebuild the cracked and shaken fabric of her family, and with a certain success, at least as far as the other three children were concerned. It was as if Hubert inhabited some outside structure – perhaps the museum he had built for Patrick – and he refused to take shelter under the family roof. It was painful to her to see the widening gulf between herself and Hubert. They had slept in separate beds for some time before Patrick's death. Now Hubert removed his personal possessions to his son's room and insisted on sleeping there. He returned to the joint bedroom only to make love. He settled down into a surface relationship with Barbara and the twin boys. Outsiders who visited the family thought them united, admired the way they had drawn together after the death of the eldest son. Hubert allowed himself on these occasions to appear an integral part of the family group, as though they were standing with frozen smiles, waiting for a photographer to take his shots. Only occasionally, within the family circle itself, did he allow his inner suppurating misery to surface and discharge itself over them like a caustic spray. Meg could not forget these occasions, though to be just they were not, in their worst form, very frequent.

The worst, the most indelibly imprinted upon her mind, was a supper when they all waited for him and he came in nearly an hour late. From the museum in the garden. He surveyed his family sitting round the table, and, still standing at the head of it, he said deliberately: 'It's always the best one who is taken.' He then sat down. What did he expect, thought Meg, anger rising within her. Applause? Sympathy? She almost flung the supper dish of curry and rice on to the table, but checked her pain and fury, and served it to the silent children whom she was powerless to help. Hubert, bitterness and cruelty like the forked tongue of a snake, withdrawn within himself again, now gave one of his performances to the

57

family: the much-travelled man. This time, the meal of curry gave him the opportunity to regale them with an account of a fairly recent trek he had taken across India. His voice only stopped for him to take another mouthful. The children stolidly ate their way through their helpings, but Barbara didn't finish hers. 'I don't feel like eating,' she said. 'I'll go, if you don't mind.' 'I'll pop up and see you later,' murmured Meg. 'Don't bother, mother,' answered Barbara. 'I'd rather be alone.' That night was a turning point for Hubert. He had heard his own voice pronounce the terrible words: 'It's always the best one who is taken.' This thought possessed him. It summed up the totality of his grief, drawing together every strand of circumstance that had encompassed Patrick's death: Meg's responsibility, the twins' incompetence, Barbara's indifferent self-centredness, and her later intrusive sorrow which he resented as an impertinence. She had no lien on Patrick. Not one of them had. Suffering was his alone, and Barbara's grief an offence to it. She retreated before his hostility into silence. At the actual time, he had been for a moment appalled to hear his words fanning out over the dining-table like a clutch of bombs over a village. Then his intelligence took over. 'Raid performed successfully,' it might have reported. He felt relief that his family was now clearly apprised of his verdict. However faithfully he performed his duties as head of the family, they would have no excuse for thinking that he absolved them from their joint culpability, no easeful hope that he was 'getting over' Patrick's death.

Alone in his study, he refused to admit any flaw in his treatment of Meg or the children. To the latter he had conversed agreeably over the curry and rice, he thought, and he would continue to give them his fatherly attention, without forgiveness but also without unkindness or resentment. His verdict was given. Did a judge feel resentment or guilt? As the meal ended, his mind concentrated upon Meg. A plan was forming in his mind, and to reinforce it he went out after supper into the garden and unlocked the little museum. With deliberate concentration he stared closely at the shelves, at the labels written in Patrick's already mature hand, the maps he had drawn, the photographs he had mounted. He gripped the back rail of the only chair, a brown kitchen chair. His newly-formed plan was swept away for the moment by a flood of pure grief. He let his sorrow embrace him, force him on to his knees beside the chair, bury his head in his arms and weep without restraint.

At last he stood up, wiped his face with his handkerchief and searched for immediate relief, as a man might reach for alcohol or a drug. Hubert stood in the small dusty room reaching out his arms for a moment and as he let them fall, he knew beyond doubt that the only anodyne was Meg's guilt. The thought of it swelled like a roaring in his ears and in the calm that followed, he heard his own voice saying aloud: *If I could, I would kill her for this*. He went into the garden and locked the museum behind him. He walked slowly up and down the lawn in the growing darkness. His mind played almost tenderly around the theme of Meg's guilt, as if he were working out the details of a seduction.

When he finally entered the house, he met Meg coming down the stairs. He put his arms round her and held her fiercely against his cold body. 'I want you,' he whispered into her hair. 'Let's go to bed.' As he pulled her behind him up the stairs, he turned at one point and looked intently into her face. The madness in his eyes told Meg only that he desired her, and she responded helplessly to the demand, her blood roused by his sensuality, as it almost invariably was.

POKER ... *An American card game, a variety of* BRAG, *played by two or more persons, each of whom, if not bluffed into declaring his hand, bets on the value of it.*

O.E.D.

They are all so Anglo-Saxon. Gwyneth felt her Welshness rising to a pitch of anger. Their noses to the ground like beagles – not such a mixed metaphor as it sounds. I mean they're only interested in objects. We might as well be excavating a drain in Oxford Street. If this is what archaeology makes you, I'll drop it and find a new career.

And in a sense it's rather like being marooned on an island, this dig. One quickly becomes aware of sharp differences in our personalities. I would find this absorbingly interesting if I weren't preoccupied with my own thoughts. The Prof, for instance. He can be inspiring, even exciting to work with, yet at times there's an aggressiveness that shows itself. It's as if he had within him something poisonous that he must eject or it will sicken him. He's never attacked me or Alan. He takes it out on Ralph and his own wife. And Meg's such a lovely person. Why is *she* his target? He acts suddenly like an adder that strikes when it's startled and afraid. Of what is Hubert afraid, I wonder?

When I get out of this stifling hotel and walk alone, my thoughts rest on Deborah. Then I no longer have to conceal anything. I can laugh or run or leap over a gate from the sheer joy of my feelings and there's no one who asks for an explanation. Only three days and I'll be with her in Aberystwyth.

As we finished dinner tonight, I looked round the table and said to myself: I'll go out alone this evening. I'll plan this weekend with Deborah. We'll walk on the hills and spend a day at Strata Florida. Only I can show it to her. Only with her am I prepared to share it, a place where I feel the full impact of ancient Wales, a place where I'm more conscious of my roots than anywhere else. I conjure it up to my inward eye – I've not been there for years: the wide valley within a range of brown hills, and at its heart the grey ragged stones of the abbey. A few scattered cottages. A farm. That's how I remember it. I could see it clearly even in that stuffy dining-room, with the others eating their dessert course.

When I chided them because they wouldn't come out in the evenings, they mumbled excuses, so I suggested that one weekend we should climb Moel Llafn – they call it a mountain but it's really a high hill, and Ralph, poor fat Ralph, groaned and said: 'Gwyneth, you alarm me with your enthusiasm for the open air. Don't you get more than enough of it on the site, especially these last few days when it's been drizzling most of the time as well?'

I said that it wasn't drizzling now, and went on: 'The light's wonderfully clear after the rain over the mountains. They look as if they'd been washed down and groomed like thoroughbreds.' Rather a silly remark on my part, and it raised an even louder, theatrical groan from Ralph and the quip: 'You'll have us all on horseback, pony-trekking, before you've finished with us, whatever.'

He thinks 'whatever' sounds very Welsh, but I'll forgive him. He's so good-humoured. In fact, I wouldn't mind taking him with me on a walk. I could chaff him and he wouldn't mind. He'd chaff me back, and we're a bit low on humour in this hotel. But I'm afraid he's too lazy to come. Meg? Yes, I'd like to know her better. I don't see much of her for she hardly ever comes up to the site. Hubert? He could be dangerous. He could demand my thoughts, or he might savage me if he were in one of his strange, dark moods. Oddly enough, he's the only one who feels at all Welsh to me, variable, devious, as cruel as the razor edge that gives its name to this mountain: Moel Llafn – the hill of the sharp blade. Dinner's over. What will it be tonight? The inevitable cards, I suppose.

Gwyneth was not interested in card games. Perhaps she had never played any and was not now inclined to learn, as Alan was. He'd become almost fanatically keen on bridge.

I've watched them playing and it bores me and makes me rather ill-at-ease, said Gwyneth to herself, having observed the deadly seriousness with which Hubert played, and the ambitious determination of Alan. This evening she felt exasperated when Hubert once again suggested cards, this time poker.

'Oh, really!' she expostulated. 'Here we are – five people who are virtually strangers, except for you, Meg, and Hubert, of course, and – and – '

'Do count me in,' Ralph interrupted amiably.

Gwyneth looked at him amused, her annoyance quickly subsiding, and said: 'I'm not sure that I *will* count you in, Ralph. You may be more of a dark horse than we think.' Then she went on quickly, for she sensed a curious change in atmosphere, as when a sudden gust of cold wind ruffles a still, sunny patch of water: 'I mean simply that we are going to be here for several months and there's plenty to talk about, isn't there, when you're getting to know people. For heaven's sake, we're not just archaeologists on a job. You four look like our Iron Age ancestors, with your fistfuls of cards held up like shields in front of your faces. I ought to shout in Welsh: "Who goes there?" or "No surrender!" or something suitable to your military appearance.'

She leaned her flushed, animated face over their shoulders, and looked at the four of them, frozen in defensive postures.

'OK,' she said, in response to their obvious discomfiture. 'OK, it's a lovely evening. I'll go for a walk.'

'Wish I could come with you,' exclaimed Alan, but Meg leaned quickly across the table before Hubert could explode with anger, and said: 'No, you can't do that, Alan. Another time, perhaps, but not when Hubert – when we've all settled down to play.'

Alan blushed with embarrassment. Ralph called out as Gwyneth disappeared: 'Have a good walk! Maybe I might have accompanied you myself, if you'd have put up with me, but not this evening. Not with this marvellous hand.'

'Oh, God, Ralph!' shouted Hubert furiously, throwing down his cards. 'We'll have to have a redeal. You can't begin a game in this disorderly way, and commenting on your hand. For heaven's sake, play seriously or we won't play at all.'

'Now Gwyneth's gone,' said Meg, as Hubert shuffled the pack, 'may I say that I think we might consider her more. It's rather . . . excluding, to play cards too often, when she doesn't care for them.'

'She can go out or read,' said Hubert.

'Perhaps – ' began Alan, nervously. 'Perhaps we d-d-don't – '

'I'll say it for you, old chap,' cried Ralph, genially. 'Perhaps we're not *all* so damned enthusiastic about cards as our chief. Speaking for myself, I enjoy them. You might say that for me duty is combined with pleasure. It's just a pity that we've one extra person. But I don't think Gwyneth feels excluded, you know.'

'Are we going to play or aren't we?' enquired Hubert in glacial tones. The game began after the redeal. At the end of the second, or third game, Hubert tossed his cards into the centre of the table, saying: 'I haven't time to play any more. There's some work I want to do. I'll say goodnight to you,' and he left the room.

'I think I *will* go out,' muttered Alan, and also left the lounge.

'No doubt he hopes to find our Welsh lady – she might be a witch, who knows?' remarked Ralph. 'Perhaps she's out gathering herbs and berries for her potions. We must ask her.'

'You'll do nothing of the sort, Ralph,' said Meg. 'I wouldn't mind going out for a stroll with you now, but I know you won't come, and anyway, I don't want – '

'To be a spoilsport?' interrupted Ralph quickly.

'Well, don't you think that Alan – '

'Oho! I'm not going to make any forecasts, but when have you seen a more beautiful and tempting woman, Meg?'

Meg gave him a rather wry smile and he seized her hand and gave it a mock-gallant kiss. 'Hardly a tactful remark on my part, I realise, Meg, but I'm not a ladies' man. I'll take this chance, though, to say that although you and I have known each other distantly for years, I'm glad that being here for a few months, I may get to know you better. I'm *enjoying* getting to know you better. Does that make amends?'

'It more than makes amends, and I'll reward you with a game of piquet, if you know it.'

'Know it? I certainly do, though it's years since I played it. Not since I was a boy, except for – anyway, not for years. I hope you remember the scoring because I don't.'

'I play it with the children.'

'I played it once with an aunt. A wonderful woman. Perhaps I'll tell you about her some day. But just before we leave the subject of Gwyneth for tierces and quints, she *is* beautiful, isn't she? She doesn't flutter my mummified heart but I like looking at her as I like looking at a superb rose. With early dew upon it.'

'Really, Ralph. I didn't know you could be so poetical.'

'Words, words, words,' said Ralph and began to deal the cards. 'It's twelve each, isn't it?'

They played two sets. Then Meg said: 'Ralph, I think I'll go up to Hubert. He may want me to help him with some work.'

'I hope you're being paid for this curious position you

occupy in the team. And it *is* the evening. Surely you're permitted to spend your evenings at leisure?'

'Goodnight, Ralph. I'm Hubert's wife, you know. I don't have to think in terms of a nine-to-five job, like a secretary. I work for – or rather, with him when he needs me.'

She left the lounge. Ralph pushed the cards slowly over the baize table, mixing them up mechanically. Then he rose, leaving them ungathered together, and went out to the bar.

'A double whisky,' he said morosely and stood drinking it, listening to the news. But found he could not pay any attention to it.

Hubert was not in his room. He had gone out.

It's impossible to work. I was a fool to insist that no one need bring a car. It's not my business how they spend their free time. We're penned up here. Even walking like this I may run into Gwyneth and Alan. I hope to God the boy isn't falling in love with her. She's far too old for him. And I want him to prove himself on this excavation. Slater of Lancaster wrote me an excellent letter about him, and I know Slater well. He wouldn't recommend a chap if he wasn't sure of his worth. Actually, Alan didn't get a brilliant degree and has done little practical work till now, but Slater insists that he has immense potential, that his failure to get a first was due to troubles at home. He's a working-class lad – not that I care. He's come on this trip and if I do nothing else, I'll make an archaeologist out of him.

Hubert paused to lean over a field gate. Through the deepening dusk he could see a pair of horses grazing. In the silence, he could hear the rough tearing of the grass.

Patrick was more than my son. He was a gift to the world. I saw from the first his brilliant intelligence, his intuitive ability to pinpoint a find, his prodigious memory and above all the breadth of his vision, remarkable for a boy only in his teens. He would have been a Flinders Petrie, a Schliemann.

Hubert left the gate and walked slowly on.

65

There's a lake about sixty miles away. I heard some fellows talking about it in the bar the other night. They were planning to go over there and sail. They'd been told they could hire a small sailing-boat from a local man – Griffiths, his name was. Lives in a village on the edge of the lake. I'll have to look it up on a map. I couldn't catch the name. The barman might know. Sixty miles away. I could hire a car, I suppose, without too much difficulty. Meg and I could take a Sunday off. Take a picnic with us.

God, how dark it's getting. No moon. I suppose Alan and Gwyneth must be back by now. Meg will wonder where I am. And it's not too warm. Damned cold, in fact. I should have put on a coat. I'll walk back. I feel ... not ill, exactly, but a bit dizzy. It's my thoughts. It's Meg. Up here in Wales, out of my ordinary routine at the Institute, I feel the pressures weigh upon me far more heavily. What I kept in the back of my mind seems released here and intrudes upon my thoughts with incessant importuning. Suddenly here it all seems so feasible. It only remains to plan it. We could go to the lake one weekend. The ... poetic justice, as they say. Justice ... for the woman who drowned my son Patrick. She will come sailing with me. I can't plan it further. The words won't formulate themselves. I'm choking on them. God, the loneliness of these hills and valleys. Frightening. Thoughts spin like mist among them. I can't see them, I can't grasp them. They press about my skull yet won't come within reach ... only emerge as single words, like trees from a mist: sailing ... wind ... lake ... accident ... Is this madness? Am I going insane? Ah, thank God, there are some lights. That must be the hotel down there.

'Hullo! You alone in the bar, Ralph? Yes, thanks ... I'll ... I'll have a brandy. In fact, make it a double, if you will. I'm bloody cold. Alan and Gwyneth back? Good. You look as if you need your bed, Ralph. OK, have a last whisky on me, then. There's something about this damned Welsh air. You were ill yourself, weren't you, when you came up here to book the hotel and so on? I was feeling dizzy just now. That's what I felt. Dizzy. You'd think we were living at a high altitude but of course we're not. OK, Ralph, but I'm bound to point out that you're very drunk. I ought not to have bought you that last one. For God's sake, go to bed before you make an exhibition of yourself.'

But he did not wait to see Ralph leave the bar.

7

'Why', said Pryderi, 'gladly would we have a tale from some of the young men yonder.' 'Lord,' said Gwydion, 'it is a custom with us that the first night after one comes to a great man, the chief bard shall have the say. I will tell a tale gladly.' Gwydion was the best teller of tales in the world. And that night he entertained the court with pleasant tales and storytelling till he was praised by everyone in the court.

From Math Son of Mathonwy in the Mabinogion, translated by Gwyn Jones and Thomas Jones.

The evenings could be so perfect here. Of course, most of us are tired. At the site one's crouching or kneeling most of the time, and it's often wet and dirty. In the cool of the evening it's good to walk up these farm tracks, with the mountains around one's head. No one with me tonight, thank God. It's drizzling a bit. Fine soft rain. A strange day it's been. I made another find in my trench: a beautiful little bone ornament, a brooch finely carved with the body of a leaping deer. I was tempted almost beyond bearing to slip it into my pocket. To give it to Deborah. Only two days now. Oh, God, no – not Alan. He's stopped about fifty yards away. I shan't move.

She's standing quite still on that outcrop of rock, outlined against the grey light of the sky. Perfect – like a tree growing from the stone. She's half-turned away from me, looking down on the swirling mists in the valley. The sun's gone down behind the mountain. Darkness is striding upon us, and she, this extraordinary woman, Gwyneth, seems to hold the light of the absent sun in her hair and her face.

I walk towards her. She doesn't move. I take her hand and tell her she is a witch, summoning up her spirits from the mists below. Hopelessly inadequate, foolish words. Oh, God, why do I have to use words at all? I'm holding her hand and she swings it to and fro as if it meant nothing to her. It might be a branch, a piece of wood. She is remote. She's far away, perhaps in her Celtic dream. It's dark now and she looks up at the sky behind Moel Llafn (she's taught me to pronounce the name after a fashion) where the moon is rising, a new moon, a thin blade of silver, and she says strange words about the new moon, with the old moon in her arms. I can't follow her thoughts or her words.

'It's like that for me, anyway,' she says. 'I'm renewed. I'm immensely happy, Alan. I'm holding my old love in my arms and my heart is rising like the new moon.'

But it's nothing to her that I still hold her hand. All this romantic talk. I'm no good at words. It seems as if she's thinking of someone else, she's so remote. At last she begins walking again on the springy turf.

She says: 'It's the in-between time, the true twilight, double light. One light in the sky and another down here in the valley. That's what twilight means – double light. We might meet Lleu Llaw Gyffes striding down the mountain in search of his flowery bride.'

I don't know what she means. I wish I could understand her, share these strange thoughts with her. She swings her hand loose from mine and as we turn back towards the hotel, she says: 'I'll have to read you the Welsh story one evening.' Then she adds: 'You're cold! Come on, Alan! Back to the hotel!'

But I would rather stay here, I want to say that I'd like the darkness to come down over the mountain and enclose us. I'd like to see the twilight deepen into night and see it with her.

But I can't find the words. The enchantment of which she is a part still holds me but means nothing to her. She is pulling me towards the hotel. In a way I am afraid of this enchantment as I am of all things irrational. It's strange to me, perhaps dangerous. I'd like to tell her this, but already I've said things that I regret. I've called her a witch, summoning her spirits from the elements. Stupid, romantic ideas. And it's not really as a witch that I see her but as a goddess. I can't say this. I'm cursed not only with a stammering tongue but a stammering mind. My thoughts begin on one course and then turn off into another path. They lead me into places where I don't really want to go. I've been incapable of telling her how beautiful she is. All I've said is: 'You're a witch, Gwyneth.' In the end, she ran back across the field to the stile and I ran, too, overtaking her, so that I sat astride the stile, waiting as she came up to me, flushed with running. I could have seized her then and kissed her, but I hesitated and lost the moment.

She suddenly changed her mood. 'Oh, that was fun!' she cried, like a schoolgirl. 'Thank heaven I prised you out of your bridge and your slavery to work.'

We walked down the darkening track. The lights of the hotel came into view.

'I ought to make Hubert come out here some time,' she said. 'He needs shaking out of *his* work addiction. Is he always going to disappear half-way through the evening to write notes or whatever?' I could not answer her. The spell had been broken. The enchantment was swallowed up in the mist we had left behind us.

I ought to tell Alan it's impossible for me to care for him. I'm not being honest. I should tell him the truth – that I love someone else. That I'm committed. Quite apart of course from the barrier of my age, but he won't wear that. Moel Llafn is still in the light of the dying sun but the valley below is thick with mist. And Alan is holding my hand.

'This is how I love it,' I find myself saying to him, for I must say something. 'The clear sky above the mountains and the mists below, a kind of sea on which you might discover the boats of the Blessed Bran and his companions, setting forth for Ireland, or Tristan's steersman guiding the ship that carries Isolde down the Irish Sea to Cornwall and King Mark.'

Alan tells me I am a witch: 'a witch beckoning up your familiars, as you stand on that rock, looking down into the swirling depths.'

'I'm not a witch at all. Just a "native", as Hubert calls the Welsh, and a "native" who's been away far too long.'

I swing his hand lightly forward and back, wondering what to say to him. Aware that I am giving him so little. Nothing. How can I ignore the hand and let it go, destroying for him the enchantment of the moment? I am feeling the spell of these mountains, interwoven with my love. No matter that my hand longs for the touch of Deborah's. Alan has the right to his enchantment.

The fine soft rain has caught up with us. 'I'll go and dry my hair. Don't wait for me, Alan,' I say. I run down the passage and up the stairs to my bedroom. I meet Ralph on his way down.

'What's the hurry?'

'I – I must dry my hair.'

'Coming down to the lounge?'

'Well, I wasn't going to. I wanted to look something up in a book.'

'Gwyneth, you look a fair treat. I wish I were a dirty old man. I'd follow you to your room and seduce you. No reading of books, God help us. However, I'll kiss your hand chastely instead.'

'Oh, Ralph! You're a dear. I do like you.'

'Well, don't leave me to languish in that beastly lounge without you. What were you looking up, anyway?'

'Something in the *Mabinogion*. I wanted to find a story in it.'

71

'Oh, Gawd! That Welsh thing.'

'Ralph, don't you dare be scornful about it. It's lovely and I bet you've never read it, anyway. A bit of it came into my head this evening, while I was out in the rain. A bit about a girl who was made of flowers.'

'Damn it, you look as if you were made of flowers yourself. Come down soon.'

She goes up to her room and I know that I am a fat old fool, and that I don't even want to seduce Gwyneth as most old lechers would. But the look of her eyes and the feel of her hand against my mouth gave my heart a jolt. I'll not let it happen again. That way madness lies.

As I rub my wet hair with a towel in this drab little room, I am transported. I feel Deborah's hands caressing it. I see her beside me with the clarity of a vision. Not as tall as I am. When I hold her, her mouth kisses my neck. Her nut-brown hair with its reddish lights, the rich colour of her skin which gives off a faint, intoxicating scent, her warm, sensuous mouth. Her skin is as soft as rose-petals – she's Blodeuedd, the girl made from flowers. I can't remember the whole story but it doesn't matter. She was the bride conjured up from meadowsweet and the flowers of the broom for Lleu Llaw Gyffes.

8

Not of father nor mother
Was my blood, was my body.
I was spellbound by Gwydion,
Prime enchanter of the Britons,
When he formed me from nine blossoms,
  Nine buds of various kind:
From primrose of the mountain,
Broom, meadowsweet and cockle,
  Together intertwined,
From the bean in its shade bearing
A white spectral army
  Of earth, of earthly kind,
From blossoms of the nettle,
Oak, thorn and bashful chestnut –
  Nine powers in me combined,
  Nine buds of plant and tree.
Long and white are my fingers
  As the ninth wave of the sea.

Quoted by Robert Graves in *The White Goddess*

Here it is ... Blodeuedd. Where's the bit I want? Ah, here's Gwydion taking his son Lleu Llaw Gyffes to his fellow-magician, Math, to ask him to find a wife for his son, who's destined never to have a wife of the race of earth-dwellers. And Math says:

Let us seek, thou and I, by our magic and enchantment to conjure a wife for him out of flowers,' and he was then a man of stature and the handsomest youth that ever mortal saw. And they took the flowers of the oak, and the flowers of the broom, and the flowers of the meadowsweet, and from those they called forth the very fairest and best endowed maiden that mortal ever saw, and named her Blodeuedd.

'Hi!' Ralph's voice came up the stairs. 'It's nearly time for dinner. There's a drink waiting for you.'

'All right! Coming!' She laid the book open on her bed and went down to the lounge. It was as she went in to dinner that she remembered and felt a chill at her heart. The end of the story came back to her. Blodeuedd is the unfaithful wife. She loves another and through her cunning deception her husband is tricked and finally slain by her lover, Gronw.

'Did you find your story in the – the whatever it's called?' asked Ralph.

'The *Mabinogion*. Yes, I found it.'

'What's it about, this book?'

'It's a collection of Welsh folk tales. Tales of revenge and magic and . . . love.'

'And your girl made of flowers, where does she fit in?'

'Blodeuedd. Well, she was unfaithful. Her father turned her into an owl as a punishment.'

'There could be worse things. I wouldn't mind being an owl.'

'She was nicer when she was made of flowers.'

Ralph looked round the table. 'Why don't we appoint Gwyneth our lector,' he suggested. 'To read to us while we eat?'

'Wouldn't she need to eat herself?' queried Alan.

'Ah, dear boy, how practical you are.'

Hubert got up to leave. 'At least, we might persuade you to read us something from the *Mabinogion*, one evening,' said Meg. 'You go on, Hubert. I'm going to read for a while.'

Mutual goodnights. Upstairs to the separate bedrooms, except for Meg and Hubert who share one. And this weekend *I* shall be sharing one. With Deborah. Not Blodeuedd – how was it that I'd forgotten how she nearly killed her husband? One remembers what one wants to remember, I suppose. Her skin as soft as flower petals.

The telephone rang in the hall and I hear the barman calling my name up the stairs. Would I come down to the telephone, please?

The phone's very public here, love . . . No, I do understand. I just wish that your job wasn't so demanding, but if this weekend's impossible, then it'll have to be the next . . . Of course I've looked them up. I know them by heart. There's one getting in at 9.25 on Friday evening. That was the one I was coming by . . . Well, I did actually tell you in my letter . . . Saturday morning? Darling, it's been so long, we must have a whole weekend. On a site you generally get the Friday off – one works differently, but the Prof's said I can work Friday and have Saturday and Sunday which is decent of him. Then Friday night's OK? . . . July 15 . . . Of course I'll understand if you've got some work to finish, as long as I can come on the Friday. If you can't meet the train I can make my way to your place. Is it far from the station? . . . OK. I can remember that but I hope you'll be able to meet me . . . Goodnight, Deb. Goodnight. You know all I can't say.

I think of Deborah. Of Blodeuedd. As I walk upstairs – for I don't want to go back into the lounge – I find I'm still holding the *Mabinogion*. I pause on the stairs and am compelled to open it. Yes, here it is. Blodeuedd's lover, Gronw, strikes Lleu Llaw Gyffes with a poisoned spear and Blodeuedd uses her magic to turn her wounded husband into an eagle:

Then Gronw rose up from the hill which is called Bryn Cyfergyr, and he rose up on one knee and aimed the poisoned spear at him and smote him in the side, so that

75

the shaft started out of him and the head stayed in him. And the wounded Lleu flew up in the form of an eagle and was seen no more.

His father, Gwydion, turned him back into his human form, emaciated and near to death. Then Gwydion sets out to seek revenge and makes for Mur Castle, where Blodeuedd lives.

I will not slay thee, I will do to thee that which is worse ... Because of the dishonour thou hast done to Lleu Llaw Gyffes ...

He turns her into an owl. She will never show her face by day for the fear of the other birds, for it is their nature to mob and molest her ... for ever called Blodeuwedd. For ever fair of name but shunned by the birds of day.

I can't forget that story of Blodeuedd that Gwyneth told us tonight. Why that particular story? A savage tale of revenge. I remember the story. I ought to be doing some work but I haven't drawn the curtains. I can't settle down. Outside, the mountains heave their shoulders into the sky, closing us in. Mist creeps up from the valleys. We're living in a country of cruelty and enchantment, of magic and betrayal and sudden bloody death. I am strongly aware of it, here by the open window. It's alien and it's powerful. It draws me under its spell. What of the others? Meg is still down in the lounge, talking to Gwyneth. Ralph's gone for a stroll by himself. Extraordinary fellow. I'd have thought he was too lazy, but he's been gone for at least an hour. I look out over the entrance and I haven't seen him come back. I left Alan pretending to read but his eyes were on Gwyneth most of the time. Poor young sod. As long as it doesn't affect his work. How like Patrick he is in the way he tackles things. He'll go far. As Patrick would have gone far. Oh, God, the waste of it. The bloody waste of it. And it was Meg's fault. I'll never believe otherwise. She let them all go sailing that March day. She let them go on the river in what was little less than a gale. The eldest son lost. They'd call it murder in the *Mabinogion*. And they'd be right. So it was. Bloody, bloody murder. That story ... Blodeuedd betrayed her husband, the bitch. And so Meg betrayed me, betrayed our marriage and family. She betrayed Patrick. Did she *want* Patrick to die? Was she jealous of my love for him, for God's sake? Christ, how can I work? I think of nothing but her sending those boys out on the river. Blodeuedd's husband was speared by the lover, Gronw, as he stood on the bank of a river. And Blodeuedd was turned into an owl, a bird that must never show its face by day. All these enchantments, these spells, these revenges. They're not ancient folk tales to me. I have lived through them in part. And now I stand over Meg's bed. *Meg ... I curse your bed. I curse you.* Her pillow is soft against my face. Soft as her deceiving flower-face. Meg, you killed Patrick. You killed my eldest son. It was your enchantment that drowned him. And so ... over your bed ... I pronounce my curse: *May you drown, Meg. May the waters swallow you up. May you drown as my son Patrick drowned.* A handkerchief, for God's sake ... I'm sweating. Oh, God, I can't go down to the bar like this. My face looks ... possessed. I *am* possessed. If I ring ... a brandy ... no, I'll wash my face. Comb my damp hair. Go down and get a brandy in the bar. Then get drinks for all of them. For all the happy family. Myself the ... the *paternal* professor.

9

It can be seen that Julien had no experience of life; he had not even read any novels.

Stendhal: Scarlet and Black

'You can't put me and the mountains together like this, Alan. I wish you didn't think me beautiful. What's beautiful anyway? I'm nothing special.'

'You are to me.'

'Well, I *can't* be special to you. I'm sorry. I can't. No, don't start protesting. These mountains and valleys are special to me, but I can't be ... whatever that is ... to you. Of course I'm glad that you find it so lovely here. I'd want you to discover something in Wales that other places haven't got. I feel not only that I belong here but it all *belongs* to me. Have you got a feeling about any place, it needn't be particularly beautiful, but a place that you feel is a – a kind of personal possession? D'you understand what I mean? Can you say of anywhere: this belongs to me and I belong to it? As I feel about Wales –'

'No, I don't belong anywhere, or if I do, it's not somewhere I want to belong to. Everything round me has always been so ugly, so mean and dirty and dreary, and the kind of people I come from – they're ugly and mean too.'

'Oh, come off it, Alan, people aren't generally ugly and mean. What about your own family? Let's start with them.'

'Well, I've a father and mother living. Dad was a meat porter. I don't know why my mother married him. She's a cut or two above him.'

'Don't be stupid, Alan. She didn't marry a meat porter. She married a man. There must have been something about him that attracted her.'

'It's difficult for me to see what. I guess she wanted to get married, like most women. We've never got on, my Dad and me. He drinks too much and he's a bit of a bully. At least, he is now, whatever he was when she married him. He likes my brother Tim better than me. Tim's big and burly and has a head as thick as an ox's.'

'OK. You were different, and you've gone to university. But I'm working-class, too, as a matter of fact. I just don't think much about it. Perhaps class doesn't count so much in a Welsh town. In fact, I know it doesn't. Most people were working-class and they didn't think me a freak because I wanted to go to college. They set a lot of store by learning.'

'They did me – think me a freak, I mean. Worse than that. They were hostile. They thought I ought to stay at home and work. The old man had an accident, you see. Got knocked down by a lorry so he couldn't do portering any more. Of course, I became important to him then. I could go out to work, couldn't I? My brother was already a porter, like Dad. Mother got together with my headmaster and between them they hatched a plot, with the help of mother's sister, Aunt Gracie. The plot wouldn't have worked if it hadn't been for her. Oh, I can't go on. I know I'm boring you. All this bloody family stuff. What does it all matter anyway? I want to talk to you about something quite different. I want to tell you what I feel about you.'

'But *I* want to say something, Alan. I don't want you to be under any illusions. Don't like me too much. It'll . . . well, it'll complicate things. I think I ought – '

'You mean, you've got someone else.'

'Yes, I mean just that.'

79

'I don't care. I'm going to kiss you. Let me kiss you, Gwyneth. No – please – don't turn away. I don't care about whoever it is. It's me that's with you at this moment. Gwyneth ... please.'

'It's not just a matter of a kiss,' said Gwyneth, but she tried still to evade his rather clumsy embrace. He managed to get one arm round her and kissed her cheek. She turned her mouth away and said: 'Alan, I'm sorry. Look, I will tell you some time, but not now. Just go on talking. Tell me about ... about your home.'

'You've not been listening. I *have* tried to tell you. My life's been lived in such bloody hideous surroundings. No one in their senses could have any feeling for them except relief at getting away. And I had to work so hard. My degree was just a long grind. I *had* to do well. I was the first one in my family to go to the university. Mother and Aunt Gracie were behind me all the way. They're the only good things in my life till now. Till I met you. Aunt Gracie gave me every penny of her savings so that I could go on an excavation in Egypt in my second-year long vac.'

'Well, wasn't that beautiful and exciting?'

'No. As a matter of fact I didn't like Egypt much. And I didn't like the people I was with. All terribly public school. Of course it was interesting, but that's rather different. You don't seem to understand what I'm trying to say. I'm ... ignorant ... inexperienced. I've been out with girls – of course I have, and I've not lived in a filthy old city all the time. I've got away from it at holiday times, though only to boring places with the parents. I didn't learn much about people. D'you understand? I suppose I loved my mother, but the love was mostly gratitude. I never really saw her as a person in her own right. And I've never seen anybody or any place that excited or thrilled me. Made me feel different. Now suddenly I come to this marvellous, ancient country, and I begin to understand, a little anyway, why you go on about being Welsh. And for me you're a part of it. Part of its loveliness. You say that you feel that you possess it and that it possesses you. But nothing owns me. I'm not part of anything, anywhere. I'm on the run, away from everything that belongs to my past and that wants to hang on to me. I want to belong – to belong to somewhere like this – ' He swept his arm out and as he dropped it, grasped Gwyneth's hand. 'I think,' he went on diffidently with a return of the stammer that had almost disappeared, 'that I want to be owned by you. I want to be yours almost more than I want to possess you myself.'

Gwyneth said nothing. She let her hand rest in Alan's and they walked on in silence.

'What have I said wrong?' asked Alan, at last. 'Did what I say offend you?'

'Nothing. Nothing like that,' answered Gwyneth. 'It's difficult, Alan. You're offering me something I can't ever accept. You're going to get hurt, and I'm sorry.' She paused and then added: 'We ought to be turning back.'

'All right then.' Alan gave a deep sigh. She still held his hand but when he raised it to his mouth and began to kiss it, she drew it away gently but firmly, and said: 'Let's sit on the bridge for a moment. I'm a bit tired. Tell me something I don't understand at all – why you went in for archaeology.'

'I don't know why you want all this stuff about my past, when I don't mean anything to you.'

'Tell me all the same.'

'OK. Well, the history chap at school liked me. I suppose because I was keen on the subject and quite good at it actually. One day he showed me a stone battle-axe. It was incredibly beautiful. Heavy, smooth. He said it must have been a ceremonial axe. It didn't look as if it had ever been used. He let me hold it in my hands, me and two or three of the other boys. I'd never seen anything like it except in a museum. I was suddenly aware that I was holding the axe a man had carried hundreds of years ago. My hands trembled. It was an extraordinary sensation. It . . . well . . . it almost made me a different person.'

81

'Yes ... yes. I can understand that. How had he come by it?'

'His grandfather had given it to him. An old countryman who could hardly read. He'd been out walking, apparently. I forget exactly where, some place in the south of England, and he'd thrust his stick into the bank beside him every now and again. Suddenly it struck something hard. He thought it was just a stone, of course, but the earth fell away and he saw something gleaming a bit as if it were polished. He put his hand into the earth bank and pulled it out. And he kept it. I suppose he ought to have given it to a museum but he didn't, and before he died, he gave it to his grandson, my teacher. Later on, he let me have it for a weekend. I took it home but I didn't show it to anybody. I just ... gloated over it. And then I made up my mind – I'd be an archaeologist. It was the feel of the axe in my hand. I kind of fell in love with it.'

He paused, staring down at the ground, and then went on: 'And I'm in love with you, Gwyneth. Give me your hand again. It's like the ... it's far more than the axe to me.'

'Listen, Alan. It's impossible. It's not just the difference in our ages. There's something else. Since you've told me so much about yourself, I think I ought to tell you something about me. I'm not attracted to you. I'm in love, too, but it's with a woman. Can you understand this?'

Alan let her hand go and said nothing for a moment. He was attempting to push away from his mind the associations that her words had brought into his mind – the sniggers, the contempt, the dirty words that were his sole knowledge of her way of life. So that he could only mutter: 'I don't know. Let's walk on for a bit.'

'Perhaps you haven't met anyone like me, yet, not to talk to as we're talking.'

'Oh, yes I have. Of course I have. At least I've known several men. But I can't think about you being like them. In love with another woman?'

'But I am. Accept it. It doesn't make me an outcast, you

82

know. We're quite ordinary women.'

'Accepting it won't make any difference. I find it so hard to believe. You're so beautiful.'

'Some of us are.' Gwyneth smiled at his discomfiture.

'I shall still love you.'

'Please think about it and perhaps it will help you to get over it.'

'To get over loving you?'

'Yes.'

'It wouldn't be as easy as that. Just thinking about something won't change my feelings. And I don't see why *you* couldn't change. Love is love, surely, whoever it is? I don't see why you couldn't come to love me. In time. Why couldn't you get over your feelings for this woman? Why ... why...?'

'It's no use, Alan. I'm not going to change.'

'I can't talk any more. Let's get back to the hotel.'

It was two nights later. They had finished playing cards and were talking desultorily among themselves. Only Alan stood alone and silent by the window. Suddenly he turned to Meg, with whom he seldom spoke, and said: 'Meg, let me buy you a drink.'

'That's sweet of you, Alan, but I was just going out to get a breath of fresh air, now the bridge is over. To tell the truth, I'm glad it didn't last too long tonight.'

'I was glad too. It's awfully stuffy in that lounge. I wouldn't mind stretching my legs if you'd let me come with you, Meg. Would you mind? We've been playing bridge for three solid evenings now. I feel a bit ... shut in.'

'OK, Alan.'

'Are you ready to go as you are?'

'I'll pick up my jacket. It's only in the hall.'

'Thank you for letting me come. I wanted to talk to you. Let's go towards the farm. It's away from cars and there's a lane going up to the barn on the side of Moel Llafn.'

'How good we're all getting at pronouncing that, aren't

we, Alan? It's a lovely evening. What did you want to talk to me about?'

'I'd just as soon not talk at the moment. I want to get away. Really away.'

They reached the farm and when they had left its lighted windows well behind them, Alan took Meg's arm and said: 'Could we sit on the stile over there?'

'OK,' answered Meg. 'The stone's still warm from the sun. There's a marvellous milky smell coming up from the farm. Must be from the little dairy they've got. It's all like a toy farm, so small and tidy, and they don't seem to have more than a dozen cows.'

'Gwyneth talked to the wife. They're gentry. English. Doing it for fun.'

'Well, there are worse things to do. Gwyneth probably thinks they ought to be Welsh.'

'Meg, please listen. It's about Gwyneth I wanted to talk to you. You must know ... you can't help seeing ... that I'm pretty well hooked on her. Meg, I'm terribly in love with her.' He got it out with difficulty and fell silent. Meg prompted him gently and he went on: 'I've never known anyone like her. She's a kind of ... a kind of spirit of these Welsh mountains, in my eyes. That sounds bloody daft. I don't know how to explain. Of course she's flesh and blood to me too. Very much so.'

'Alan, she's a great deal older than you are. You have to face that obstacle first.'

'I have faced it. I don't think age matters. Not if she could love me.'

'And she doesn't?'

'Meg, it's far worse than that. She says she can't. I don't think I can spell it all out. It's something I've never met, at close quarters, so to speak, before. I've never thought about it seriously, just picked up what other people said. D'you understand?'

'You mean she's attracted to women, not men?'

84

'Yes, I mean that.'

'And she told you herself?'

'Yes. She made it all sound so final. As if she could never alter.'

'Why should she? I don't think you can expect her to alter. She's made her choice, presumably some time ago.'

'I can't believe it's a matter of choice. I find it all hard to take.'

'D'you find yourself shocked?'

'Yes, I believe I am. I was brought up in a very narrow way. I know I must sound appallingly square, but even in the university I never met women like this. Or perhaps I never recognised them. I didn't meet all that many women anyway, and they were mostly girlfriends of other students. I want to know what you think. D'you believe, as I do, that if I love her well enough, long enough, she could care for me? Couldn't she change?'

'Let's walk on, Alan. I'm a bit cold.'

'Yes, all right. But listen, Meg. Couldn't she change?'

'Well, I suppose she could. But by her age, I should think she's made her choice, she's found herself. She *wants* to be a lesbian. Try and get over the shock first, Alan. Then accept her as she is. And accept too that *you* might easily be attracted to someone of your own sex. All right. I know you think that's impossible. Let's leave that point, and stick to what I said about Gwyneth.'

'She's so unutterably lovely, Meg. She makes my heart turn over when I suddenly look up and see her. I feel that everything I'm doing at the site, is for her. Only for her. To win her. That's what I've set myself to do: to win her love away from this woman. You don't say anything, Meg. Are you warmer now we're walking?'

'Yes, thanks. I am. I've been thinking. Your feelings ... romantic feelings, but I don't mean anything derogatory by that ... this love for Gwyneth. Alan, do you realise at all the idealism with which you've surrounded her?'

85

'D'you mean my feelings aren't real?'

'No, not that at all. They *are* real, but they're limited, limited by the idealism. You don't love the whole woman. Suppose you had told me of feelings that had no foundation beyond physical desire. They would be just as real and just as limited.'

'Because I haven't talked about my physical longings for her, it doesn't mean I'm not ... tormented by them.'

'*Are* you tormented by them? How strong are they? How much are *they* wrapped up in a romantic, idealistic vision? You don't answer. Perhaps you think that I, a middle-aged woman, am not likely to understand these things?'

'I don't think that.'

'You well might. The young generally do, if you don't mind me saying so. But you'd be wrong in my case, at any rate. I'm a very physical person. People are still inclined – at least *men* are all too inclined – to think women aren't given to such strong sexual longings as they are, not until they have kindly come along and aroused them – but perhaps I'm talking to myself. This is really another subject, isn't it?'

'No, I don't think so. I'm glad you're talking about it to me. I suppose I'm very ignorant about women. Ignorant about myself as well. I've never discussed these things on a serious level. Chaps at college hadn't much to contribute except dirty stories. And I don't read – '

'Ah, that's a pity, Alan. You should read. In books, you sometimes find keys to your inner self, to the unknown areas inside you.'

'I don't think *I* could. Books, especially novels, seem to me unreal, unless they're books connected with archaeology, that kind of thing. The classics ... well, the ones I was made to read, were worse than unreal. They were dead boring.'

'Well, I won't try to persuade you, only – examine your feelings about Gwyneth. I could be downright unkind and say that I think your feelings for her are a bit unreal.'

'Unreal?'

'Like the romantic novels you don't read.'

'Oh, hell – I couldn't suffer as I do if my feelings weren't real.'

'Aren't there different aspects of reality? But we're getting almost metaphysical. Let's turn back, shall we? I'll try to explain. As I see it, you have to grasp the hard fact that Gwyneth loves someone else, never mind that the other person's a woman.'

'I don't want my life to be frittered away loving someone who can never be mine.'

'That's a grudging admission, but it's a start.'

'A start? It seems to me it's the end of everything.'

'Not necessarily. Gwyneth – that is, your feelings for her – could remain a part of you even if you never see her again after this summer. Life has to be lived, Alan. You'll fall in love with some girl – I'm sure of it – some girl who will want you and accept you and make you happy.'

'You're really saying that I shall grow out of Gwyneth.'

'I'm not saying that. I'm saying that you probably won't ever have her love but you'll carry a small piece of your love for her with you, built into you, a kind of touchstone when you come to love for real – '

'But my love *is* real.'

'I'm sorry. Let me go on. It'll get caught up, this love for Gwyneth, caught up into your love for some girl who will become your wife or your lover. It'll enrich it and in the end disappear into a more lasting down-to-earth relationship.'

'I can't believe this, Meg.'

'You will. You will.'

'I'm in such pain. I didn't know how much loving someone could hurt. I imagined that being in love would make me happy. And I *did* enjoy it at first. I've seen college friends with their girls and envied them their happiness. Now I've been in love with Gwyneth for weeks and I'm tortured by it. It's a pain that invades every part of me. Everything I'm doing. It's she, she herself who gives me the worst pain, because when I'm

87

apart from her I can gain some happiness from the feeling of being in love. I suppose I enjoy my fantasies, you'd say. And yet . . . I can't wish this love away. I'd almost rather she hurt me than didn't respond at all.'

'But if she loves someone else, can't you see that she has to hurt you to make you let go?'

'I suppose so. But no, I don't see why she has to be so indifferent. Why can't she give me a chance? She often doesn't respond at all to what I say. Just remains silent. I don't even know what she's thinking. She doesn't respond to my hand when I touch her. I've even written to her twice. It's no good. I feel I'm cursed by this love, yet I go on loving her and I can't see any end to it.'

'The hotel's in sight. We've got to go back. I'm touched – flattered I suppose, that you've told me this, Alan. I'll keep it to myself, of course. I hope it's helped a bit, just to talk about your feelings.'

'Thank you. I can't say . . . no, it hasn't really helped. I'm still left with them.'

'I'm sorry. Don't expect me just to agree with you. I've tried to make you stand aside and look at yourself, and I – '

'I do look at myself. And I don't like what I see. A fool, who's wasting his life – '

'Well, that sounds more realistic – '

'You're being pretty unkind.'

'That isn't what I meant to be. You've got to be tough with yourself, Alan. There aren't any quick answers and there certainly isn't any salvation from outside oneself.'

Alan said nothing. He was almost wishing that he had never spoken to Meg. Wishing that he'd kept everything to himself. Kept the dream.

Alan, thought Meg, is too young to know that pain has a term, that we do not have to live with it for ever. He does not know either how little the instruments of pain matter. Even the physically tortured lose their fear of the rack, and enter some-

88

times into a kind of alliance with their torturers, almost a dependency upon them. Yet once the torture is over, the instruments no longer seen, the torturer no longer present, all these gradually recede into oblivion and it becomes incredible that we were once under their dominion. When I think how unspeakably I suffered the first time Hubert was unfaithful to me, I am amazed at the familiarity that has grown up over the years between his infidelities, his personal injustice and unkindness, and my acceptance of it all. It is as though pain was a river on whose bank I stand; a wide river but one that has shrunk now to a mere winter bourne. Hubert and his mistresses, who once hovered like shades on the far bank of my suffering, can now touch hands with me across the narrow river bed. Familiarity with those once menacing figures has brought indifference and forgetting, and left me immune to their threats and Hubert's hostility. Now I can walk on along the river bank and leave them and Hubert behind me. Why, then, have I come to this decision to leave Hubert, if he no longer has the power to hurt me? I think it is the falsity of our marriage that now makes me so unwilling to continue in it. I do not wish to lend myself to such a deception, to occupy a house built upon such unreliable foundations. When I leave Hubert, I shall, I hope, be sure where my feet are treading. Certainty is something we all search for, and when the dusty answers have been given, we have to go alone into a silence where we can hear our own thoughts, choose our own direction, and establish some measure of personal assurance.

Alan cries out against his pain: 'I waited for Gwyneth. She never came. I gave her a letter three days ago and she has not mentioned it.' He swears that his wounds will never heal. But they will. They will. The pain itself may last for a time, even a long time, but he will forget the provocations that caused it, the disappointments, the breaking of promises, the letters unanswered, the apparent indifference to himself. Life has to be lived, and though we burden ourselves with a load of hurtful luggage, we shed it as we go on, for life as I've said must be lived, and often it is time, and often it is preoccupation with work, or with pleasure, that subtly filches a piece from the pack we carry and drops it aside on the road, and we shall never see it again.

10

I feel here no restraint, and none is wished to be inspired ...
We rise at whatever hour we choose; breakfast at half after
nine, take about an hour to satisfy the sentiment *not the*
appetite, *for talk, for we talk – good heavens! how we talk!*
and enjoy ourselves most wonderfully.

> Samuel Rose in a letter to his sister when staying
> with Cowper at Mrs Unwin's house.

Meg opened the door of the lounge. They had all returned
from the site in time for a late tea, all, that is, but Gwyneth,
who had not yet returned from Aberystwyth. The tea-things
were still on the table. Ralph was alone, stretched out on the
couch. He looked up at Meg warily, his eyes watchful to see
if Hubert was following her. 'Have I woken you up?'

'Only from boredom. I'm delighted to see you. I now realise
why we read Sunday papers – to dispel the gloom of an
English Sunday. A Welsh Sunday is worse but there are no
papers. The bar is shut of course at this hour. Perhaps at any
hour. As a matter of fact, I willed you to walk in and see me.'

'You've been successful.' Meg sat down on the arm of the
sofa near his feet. 'What substitute can I offer you for the
missing Sunday newspapers?'

'Conversation, dear Meg. Let's consider this interesting
question: why don't we read more books now we have the
chance to, being deprived of our Sunday reading fodder? Or

perhaps I ought to say, why don't *I*?'

'D'you really want me to think up an answer?'

'No, I'll give it to you. It's the general malaise produced by this terrible hotel lounge. Lounge – what a word! I sink into a kind of lethargy that prevents me from going upstairs and getting a book.'

'As a matter of fact, I came down here myself to read. In a comfortable chair.'

'Read what?'

Meg held out her book.

'Ah, catching up with culture, Meg.'

'Not quite. I've read *Dombey* before. I find Dickens ideal reading when I'm away from home.'

'Well now, why didn't *I* bring a Dickens? Determined to improve my mind, I brought Stendhal and find I can't read him. Good God! What's that row? Not the Land-Rover going off?'

'Yes it is. Hubert and Alan are going back to the site.'

Ralph groaned and closed his eyes.

'Would you like to play piquet?' suggested Meg.

'What a splendid idea! I'd love to. I'll get the cards.'

The time passed, punctuated by such arcane phrases as: 'A tierce major,' and 'No go. I've a quint to the queen.' 'You're the elder hand. Lead away.'

At last Meg sat back and said: 'Ralph, I've played enough. D'you remember saying you'd tell me how you came to learn piquet? So few people know it.'

'It's old-fashioned, that's why. You need to have had a father or an uncle or aunt who could teach you the delights of the game. In my case, it was an aunt.'

'Tell me, then.'

'In a minute. After I've consumed this rather nasty scone.' He smothered the scone in a pippy, dark-red jam. 'Actually, this scene takes me back to childhood, quite apart from the piquet. My mother was an execrable cook. Her scones were just like this. Tasting strongly of soda, and thick as a bootsole

92

on the outside. I can't think how scones like this are produced. It must be quite an art to make them so horrible.'

'Try the cake.'

'No, that I will not do. Don't you either, Meg. It's lethal.'

'Have some more tea then, and tell me about your aunt.'

'My mother first. I had to have a mother or I wouldn't be here. Are you sitting comfortably? It may take some time. Did you hear me in the bar the other night, Meg, when everybody was talking about their pasts and their childhoods?'

'I heard the beginning of it, but Hubert and I went upstairs before you started on your past. I'm sorry I missed it.'

'Well, I'm afraid I lied flagrantly. Why should I part with the truth to a bunch of strangers, "natives" as Hubert will persist in calling them? I'm sorry. Perhaps I shouldn't have said that.'

'Let's leave Hubert out of it. You invented a past for yourself?'

'Well, yes, I did. I invented a spacious, well-conducted life, a pure fantasy, and felt a bit guilty afterwards for telling so many lies that were taken so seriously. I thought someone would blow the gaffe on me, but no one did. However, I spent most of my early life feeling guilty about something or other, so it wasn't unfamiliar. You know, according to these ancient Welsh tales that our dear Gwyneth is always talking about – '

'Not always.'

'Well, a lot, and as a matter of fact I had a session with her a few days ago, all by myself. Anyway, it seems that the bards very often strung their stories together in threes. It was a kind of mnemonic. There were the Three Unkind Blows and the Three Dark Riddles – I can't remember them exactly. Guilt has plagued me, especially in my youth, like the Three Unkind Blows, under the guise of Mother, God and Conscience. These three, and the greatest of these is Mother. In fact, I dismissed God fairly early on and learned to evade

Conscience, though never with total success, as witness my present guilt about my spurious account of my life. But in my first twenty-five years, my mother never released the tentacles that she wound – *octopae maternae tentacula* as you might say – around my spirit. I was freed from them only when I courted and married Phyllis. I didn't intend that her name should enter this conversation – '

'D'you want to talk about her?'

'No. Not now, anyway, when I'm wearing my facetious hat. I'll concentrate on those tentacula. To keep the octopal metaphor, those rubbery appendages held themselves firm upon the frail bark of my youth by a glutinous substance called Guilt. In the first place there was my name, Ralph. It was my mother's wish that I should have the same name as my father, and no second name either, which often led to confusion, but that was the least of it. Every time I heard that name Ralph I was reminded that not only was I my father's son, but that I was intended to model myself upon him. Mother put this into a formula: "I hoped you'd be worthy of your father's name," with the strong implication that I wasn't. If you ask me why I didn't change my name as soon as possible, you don't appreciate that Guilt is not to be evaded by such ruses.

'My mother's formula might have worn thin but for an unfortunate incident. My father fell off a horse, cracked his skull and died. I was about ten at the time. Father's flesh and blood presence having been removed and my memories being still only those of a child, my mother grabbed the chance of building him up into a paragon of virtue, whose strength was as the strength of ten. I've no idea what he was really like. I knew no way of stripping off the palimpsest created by my mother's artistry, to find out what was underneath. Only once was I given a clue, when I was staying with my Aunt Beatrice. Perhaps if I'd questioned her she might have told me more.

'Mother had been whisked into hospital with a burst appendix. Someone had to feed and minister to my thirteen-year-old self and Aunt Beatrice stepped in while mother was still under the anaesthetic – the operation was a long one fortunately – and I was taken off to Frinton-on-Sea before mother came round from it. A kindly neighbour had alerted Aunt B. Aunt Beatrice was my father's only sister. I was braced by the Frinton winds and emboldened by the rather jolly way Aunt Beatrice had of saying things like: "Do what you like, dear boy. It's Liberty Hall here," and "Talk away, Ralph. I'm just your elder sister, in spirit anyway, even if I *am* old enough to be your mother, which thank God I'm not."

'I think it was that last sentence – "Thank God I'm not" – that struck such a strong response in my heart. Here was an elderly woman who actually did not relish motherhood, who was not trying to stand *in loco parentis*, and even if I found it difficult to regard her as a sister, she was at least outside the family circle, in the sense that I'd hardly ever seen her and she appeared to be without tentacula. Not an octopus, in fact, but a friendly, flat, sand-loving soul, if you'll forgive the pun.

' "Do I *have* to go for a swim, Aunt Beatrice?" I asked timidly, the second or third day of my stay.

' "Call me B, dear, I never could abide that appellation of aunt. No, of course, you needn't bathe. I never do. Far too cold at Frinton for any sensible person to bathe."

' "Why d'you live here, then, if it's so cold?" I asked her, my curiosity about another person aroused for probably the first time in my life. She stared at me.

' "That's a very good question," she said. "Let me see. How shall I answer it?" There was a long silence, and it dawned upon my mind – also for the first time, probably – that there are many different ways of answering a question and obviously some of them must be false. I wondered if she would tell the truth, something which I doubted from my youthful experience of mothers, teachers, clergymen and grown-ups in general.

' "I think I shall be honest," she said, having weighed the problem judiciously and turning upon me an eye that was both candid and affectionate. "This is the reason. Or one of the reasons. I came here to be married when I was 23. My future husband had just obtained a post in a bank. Barclays' Bank, it was."

'"But you're not married, are you? I mean, you don't wear a ring?" I said, not quite liking to call her B but at least bold enough to question her on this delicate subject.

'"No, I'm not," she answered. "Very observant of you to notice I don't wear a ring. It's rather tight for me now, because I *was* married and did wear one. But he died. Fifteen years ago. Just before he was going to be made manager, which was unfortunate for my pension."

'I did not properly understand the last part of this speech, but I felt that I must say something, so I murmured in what I hoped was a tenderly sympathetic tone – unfortunately it emerged as a croak because my voice was breaking at this time: "I'm terribly sorry." I added in an even more gravelly voice: "Dear Aunt B."

'"Just B, if you don't mind," she corrected me. "And you needn't try and sound sorry. I don't know, looking back on it, that I think very highly of the married state. I've enjoyed myself a lot more in the last few years than I ever have before. Though I'd have liked more money." She laughed suddenly, a harsh, raucous laugh, saying: "Wouldn't we all?"

'If I am to pursue the figure three with which I began this story, I would say that Aunt B taught me three things in the short time that I stayed with her. The first was that I need not slavishly do what was expected of me (in the immediate case, swimming), that marriage was not necessarily a desirable state – a novel idea to me, I must say, and one that I subsequently came to disbelieve. The third thing she gave me was a passion for cards which has remained with me all my life. B found that I couldn't even play patience. She immediately taught me two very interesting games of patience. Each required a double pack of cards. "Patiences that only need one pack are not worth playing," she pronounced.'

'I wish you'd teach them to me,' interposed Meg. 'I'd like

to have a couple of patiences I could play when I'm ... when I'm by myself.'

'Certainly I'll teach them to you. They are Les Huits, very intellectual, and Senior Wrangler, mildly mathematical but well within my limited scope in this field. B then pressed on with my education. On the third night of my stay she taught me Bezique. It was discarded after one evening as too easy, and we went on to cribbage. "I love it!" she exclaimed. "One for his heels! Two for his nob! It's delightful, but the cribbage board is badly cracked and besides, you're such an apt pupil, my dear boy, that I'm going to promote you to piquet. Now that's the aristocrat of two-person card games." It certainly is, as I'm sure you'd agree, Meg. We played it for five blissful evenings, after the initial period of instruction, and on the second evening we went on to play it for money stakes, which gave me a delicious sense of being wicked and quite unlike my noble father, who, I was certain, would never have gambled. In fact, on the fifth evening, I asked B why *she* didn't think gambling was wrong. She opened her eyes very wide. They were, despite her somewhat raddled appearance, very fine, rich brown eyes that shone like her mahogany dining-table. "Why ever should it be wrong?" she asked. "It's the spice of life. While you are here, I've had to give up my bridge evenings, but I can't give up playing for money altogether. It seems unnatural. So we must play for stakes if I'm to have any satisfaction out of it. Small stakes, of course, suitable to your age."

' "Do you generally play for very high ones?" I asked boldly.

' "When I can," she answered. "One has to choose one's company," she added with a giggle. I felt out of my depth. I realise now that she must have been imbibing sherry too liberally. She had given me a small glass of it, to keep her company, and I was so overcome at this enormity, as I was certain that my mother would think it, that I never counted up how many glasses she had to my one.

'On that fifth evening, I had to confess that I hardly had any money left. "Then I'll give you some," said B at once. "Here's a pound. In small change." She counted it out carefully from her purse, stacking it on the green baize table. That evening, she won most of the pound back from me, but I didn't mind. On about the twelfth day of my stay, my mother arrived in Frinton, unannounced in a hired car, looking very pale and still weak after her operation.

'"I have come to take Ralph home," she said. She then went into the drawing-room with B and shut the door.

'After only a few minutes, she came out again and said: "Run down to the sea, Ralph. You don't look at all well. Your cheeks are pasty. Get some colour in them, please, before I take you home."

'"When can I come back?" I asked.

'"When the promenade clock says 1.30," she replied.

'"What about lunch?"

'"Never mind about lunch," she retorted and shut the drawing-room door firmly.

'When I came back, dragging my feet, she was waiting for me at the front door, with her outdoor clothes on. Perhaps she had never taken them off. My suitcase was packed and ready, standing beside her sensibly-clad feet. Aunt B wore sensible clothes and shoes, too, but of a quite different quality. Somehow more likable.

'"We shall eat sandwiches in the train," said my mother. "Say goodbye to your Aunt Beatrice and thank her for having you."

'I looked miserably at B, unable to speak for the lump in my throat.

'"Goodbye, dear boy," she said, clasping my hand. "We won't kiss, but we won't forget each other. Memories are stronger than kisses." My mother tossed her head and started to walk down the front steps, past the heavily flowering fuchsias. B suddenly bent her mouth to my ear. "Your father," she hissed, "was an inveterate gambler. Don't forget. You might find that fact the key to many puzzling things."

'"Come along, Ralph. Hurry!" cried my mother, and I stumbled down the steps, hardly able to see where I put my feet.

'"Good heavens!" exclaimed my mother, as she observed the signs of tears in my eyes. "What on earth would your father think if he could see you blubbing, just because you're going home?"

'I wanted to cry out: "Leave me here! I want to stay with B," but I hadn't the courage. I was only thirteen.

'B died two years later in circumstances that I was not permitted to know. I was not allowed to go to the funeral. It was as though she had never been.

'Well, there you are, Meg. I suppose it's not time for a drink? I could do with one.'

'It's after five. I think you deserve one after telling me that long story. It was fascinating. Rather sad, too. Why is it that so many good things are broken off before they've reached a real ending? I'm not explaining what I mean very well. I'm trying to say that most kinds of love seldom seem to reach a point of stability. They end abruptly. D'you see what I mean?'

'I see it exactly. It's as though one was climbing a mountain with a companion and before reaching the summit, the one who was with you fell down a precipice and you were left alone.'

'I think a drink would be very nice,' said Meg. 'Will you get me one, Ralph? I'd like a gin, I think.'

Ralph disappeared and Meg heard him knocking on the hotel proprietor's office door, for no barman was on duty on a Sunday. He came back at last with two gins and they sat and drank them slowly, in companionable silence, a silence broken at last by the return of Hubert and Alan.

99

11

'Cut for partners!'

The soft hills of Aberystwyth are behind me. Ahead, the mountains come into view. The weekend is over and with it five years of my life. On Friday much was left unsaid. Silences fell between us and fed my certainty that Deborah had found someone else. She was loving, almost desperately so at times, as though she was trying to prove – to herself or to me? – how strong her love was. And then the silences: thoughts hanging in the air between us like clouds of vapour, obscuring the hard truth. Next day, when I suggested that we took the car to Strata Florida, she was evasive, and in the end we drove along the coast and walked for most of the day. And little was said between us. In the evening I found myself talking more and more at random. Perhaps, I thought, the test of the truth lies in the future, to which there had so far been no reference. I deliberately filled this gap by reminding her that just before I was accepted on this expedition we were planning to go to the States for a year. We had been thinking about it for ages. Her letters last autumn were full of it, I reminded her. And there were other more far-reaching plans; that after a year or so in America, I should try to get an academic post in Wales. Deborah would get a job in the same university, as she did when I first went to Durham. We had agreed that I ought to stay there for three years, even after Deborah left to come to Aberystwyth nearly a year ago. 'You have to consider your career,' she had said. 'Mine doesn't matter as yours does.'

My mention of the States now acted almost immediately upon her. She got up and walked to the window, with her back to me. Then said at last: 'There *is* no future. I ought to have told you this before, but I couldn't bear to write it in a letter. I wanted to tell you myself. I am . . . I've found someone else. I want to live with her.'

'You mean you want to share a house, a flat with her? Presumably you *are* living with her in the sense of sleeping with her?'

'We're in love. Yes.'

I stare out of the window. The mountains come closer in their massive certainty. I think about the future. But my certainties have been left behind at Aberystwyth and I can never now go back to recover them. With no certainties except a future without Deborah, how do I realign my life? Why realign it at all? It's such a fearful effort to push grief aside and think soberly, and anyway, where does feeling end and thought begin? At the moment, all I want is to opt out, and my brain is so well-trained, faithful dog that it is. At once it asks: Why don't I? It would be simple to end things. No more decisions to be taken. No empty career to pursue. We're travelling fast. The track runs along the side of a steep slaty mountain. Go out in the corridor, find a door out of sight of the few passengers in this carriage. Open it . . . would the gods of these Welsh hills be merciful and break my neck?

'Would you like a caramel?' The elderly lady opposite me holds out a bag. Automatically I take one and thank her. It's excessively glutinous. It gets wrapped round my teeth. No, Dr Gwyneth Morris, you are not going to be found with a broken neck among the shale, your jaw cemented with Aberystwyth caramel, made of brown sugar and the best Welsh butter. I find myself smiling at the lady opposite, who smiles back and offers me another. She doesn't know from what she has saved

101

me. She doesn't know that her caramel has worked my salvation like the blessed Host. I feel very clear-headed. Now is the moment to write that definitive letter of farewell to Deborah. I rest a pad on my knee, and begin. A letter that will tie up the loose ends neatly. The last letter I shall write to Deborah.

I am not so naïve as you think me. I am also far more intuitive than you have allowed for. I suspected before this weekend that there was someone else. I refused to let myself believe it. I deceived myself very successfully. Where your deception was equally successful was in making me think briefly that you were merely indulging in a casual affair. This is what you hinted in a letter months ago and said no more of it. And I held my tongue because my trust in your love has been so total. I knew when we lived together that you occasionally had it off with someone else, but I never thought I had the right to monitor your life. The position now is wholly different. The deception is different. You are not concealing something you might later confess wryly, and that we might laugh over together, as we did over your brief and disastrous affair with the awful Beryl Beamish. This, alas, is no laughing matter.

Deborah, just before we parted yesterday, you talked to me about my 'academic gifts'. You waxed enthusiastic about this particular dig. I think you were inferring that I had little to complain of in life, since I was blest in having an intellect that would carry me far beyond human relationships or any need of them. Please disabuse your mind of the comforting thought that I shall find consolation for losing you in making love to a thesis, and adopting as my closest companions the learned periodicals that lie stacked on my desk. I have another, to me more important gift: the gift for loving. I loved and still love you. This will take time to remedy, if remedy is the word. You have now found your happiness elsewhere. The breach is absolute. I ask

102

you to be honest in your new life. You have not been honest
with me and this increases my pain.

I finish writing and look out of the window again. The train
is running through the hills now. We have only about twenty
miles to go. I contemplate this long, ill-written letter, hurriedly
scribbled as though I was trying to catch her before she took
the final step, as though I could then bring her back to me. I
cannot. I shall not send her the letter. It had to be written.
Now it has to be destroyed. Out in the corridor several
windows are open. It is a hot afternoon. I tear the letter up
into small pieces and drop them out of the window. They
flutter down the railway embankment: snow in July. I return
to my seat and pretend to read a Sunday paper which I cannot
see.

'It's rather breezy in here,' observes the lady opposite me.
'D'you mind closing the door of the compartment. I think you
left it open.'

'Of course. I'm sorry.' I shut it for her because she is old
and I am still young. Young enough at thirty-six to have much
time to fill. And miles to go before I sleep. And miles to go
before I sleep.

'Gwyneth not back?'

'No. She'll probably be on the last train. Hope she catches
the little bus.'

'Ought I to take the Land-Rover and fetch her from the
station?'

'Oh, I shouldn't think so, Hubert, especially as we're not
certain which train. She may have ordered a taxi, anyway.'

'Yes, of course. She probably has. Anyone else want any
cheese? OK. Let's go to the lounge. I must say, Sunday night
supper here hardly invites one to linger. It reminds one of
Sunday night at school, eh, Alan?'

'I didn't go to boarding school.'

'No, nor you did. Never mind. You didn't miss much.

103

Damned prison of a place. Now, what about a game of bridge?'

This eternal bridge that he's taught me to play. In fact, I often enjoy it, I admit. I like the competitive thing. I've had to be competitive all my life. But I wish I'd thought of meeting Gwyneth at the station. It's too late now. They've dismissed the idea of the Land-Rover. I may as well play bridge as try to make conversation. I can't make conversation. And that goes for conversation with Gwyneth, too. Oh, hell. A whole weekend away. I don't even know where she's been. I know so little about her. We're thrown together in this bloody hotel, miles from anywhere. The five of us – like goldfish in a bowl. Revolving round each other. Our mouths opening and shutting. I want to break out of it. I want to establish myself in Gwyneth's life. I want my own life, a good job, responsibility. Maybe if I could get to know her well now, I could go on seeing her after this work's over. Maybe I could get a job at Durham ... I'd see her every day. Oh, Christ, I love her. I can't face the thought that this is all I'll ever see of her. There's so little time. It's nearly half over now. Tonight's been wasted, this bloody bridge. Oh, God, the Prof's going on at Ralph. He's rounding us up. The table's set out. The cards.

'Ralph, I insist. I've been working all day. I want to relax. *You*'ll play, won't you, Meg? And you, Alan? You need an evening off after working all through Sunday.'

What a damn good brain that young man has! It was a rewarding afternoon. He responded so readily to everything I suggested, picked up the thread of my thoughts so deftly. So like Patrick. So like Patrick, God help me. And now to come back to this. To that soak, Ralph. God knows why I had to be burdened with him. And Meg. The afternoon with Alan only sharpened my decision. Patrick should have been with me on site, should have been with me all day. She – Meg – let Patrick go sailing when any fool could have seen that it was

104

dangerous. If she didn't think of Patrick, she might have thought of the twins. God, how stupid women can be over a thing like judging the wind. They can look after babies, take major decisions about *them* and so on. Yet Meg couldn't judge the strength of the wind, couldn't assess the obvious danger of taking out the boat that March afternoon. Sometimes I've asked myself: why didn't *Patrick* see the danger? But why should he, a boy of fifteen? And a boy with a love of adventure. Natural that he should want to go. There was nothing he didn't know about sailing a boat anyway.

There was a moment this afternoon. Alan was down in the trench. His back thin and bony through his shirt. His hair tow-coloured, his neck and arms brown with sun. I looked down on him as he worked for some minutes. I put aside professional expertise. I forgot where we were. All I knew was that the figure below me could have been Patrick. That I could have jumped down beside him and put my arm round his shoulders. The pain that gripped my heart at that moment was so acute that I had to press my hand against my ribs. I could have cried out. Patrick lies in a trench, too. The memory of that lowering of his body into brown earth overcame me. Tears sprang to my eyes. Alan asked me something. I just couldn't answer him. I turned away, then called back to him, with a constricted throat: 'Back in a minute. I want my cigarettes. In my coat pocket.' And as I stumbled over the long coarse grass ... Patrick ... Patrick ... Patrick.

Meg sits there, sipping her coffee, chatting to that oaf, Ralph. My thoughts are crystallising. There is such a thing as just retribution. Well now: get the cards out. Stack them on the table. Set the chairs. The bridge-markers. I have suffered long enough. Christ, I have suffered. I will repay. Come on, all of you. Sit down. Cut for partners. My inner mind works at the theme of revenge like a terrier down a foxhole, even while I'm acting the dedicated leader of the team. It won't be long. Even while I'm playing bridge with them, my mind is drawing up the blue-print.

'Right, let's start playing. Ralph, I hope you're in good form, seeing that we're drawn to play together. I warn you – I'm in an aggressive mood. I'm out to win and I expect you to respond.'

12

> *When they join battle they generally promise the spoils of war to the war god. After the victory captured animals are sacrificed to him and the rest of the booty is gathered up in one place. In many towns heaps of such things are to be seen piled up in sacred places. It is very rarely that anyone has so little respect for religion as to risk either the concealment of booty at home, or the removal of anything that has once been deposited as an offering. For this offence a terrible death is decreed.*
>
> Caesar: *De Bello Gallico*

A week's gone by. When will memory cease to stamp the phrases on my mind? This time last week – this time last month – this time last year? Oh, God, why is there no satisfactory ritual for parting? After a funeral, relatives and friends meet together over sandwiches and sherry, at least. We stand round chatting to people we've not seen for years. It takes the edge off grief. The Irish and country people elsewhere still make more of a true ritual of death. Let's be thankful we still retain the sherry and sandwiches. A poor survival but at least it gives time for grief to sink a little deeper into the heart, where it can come to rest. But there's no ritual for separation. The pain is raw at the edges – no healing balm of sherry even.

The sun shines hotly. We've had hardly any rain here since we came. Hubert and Alan are working in their trenches, stripped to the waist. I work my way relentlessly along my trench, sifting carefully, putting aside what may be, I suspect, the parts of a scabbard. I have to force myself to finger them with professional interest and curiosity. So it goes on. The mind awash with tears, idle tears, like the brown bog-water seeping into the trench this end. Routine work and a constant inner battle against the memory of travelling to Aberystwyth last Friday. Lunchtime. Perhaps the mental battalions will consent to bivouac, too. Will warm sandwiches and the professional talk of my colleagues provide any ritual barrier against my pain?

The others were speculating about the possibility of finding any human or animal bones. 'Wrong sort of peat-bog,' said Hubert, dismissively, but it was enough of a lead to make Ralph turn to Gwyneth as she sat down and ask genially: 'Any corpses found today?' And she was surprised at the sudden comfort this foolish question gave her. She asked him what he'd been doing and he said he'd spent most of the morning taking photographs. He went on: 'My God, it's dry work eating sandwiches up here in this heat. I must say when Meg and I are sometimes down at the hotel during the day, we fare a bit better. There's a sameness about their lunch, mind, but not so much bread. We've persuaded them to give us fruit-juice instead of the everlasting minestrone soup, but the main course does tend to consist rather often of cold meat and salad and they just don't know how to make a salad.'

'What's it like?' I ask, since no one else speaks. 'The usual lettuce, with three slices of cucumber and half a tomato?'

'That's about it,' says Ralph.

'I think the food's pretty good at the hotel,' says Hubert heavily.

'It's bloody better than I've ever had,' says Alan and stammers out: 'B-b-ut then, I was b-b-brought up in a . . . slum and had d-d-dinners at school that . . . cost thirty pence and t-t-tasted like it.'

'Oh, God!' expostulates Ralph. 'You lay out the chips on

your shoulder like artefacts on a tray, Alan. Shall I photograph them for you?'

'Leave Alan alone,' says Hubert.

'He asked for it,' retorts Ralph, unperturbed.

And then Alan turns to me and is so clearly appealing to me to rescue him that I feel I have to get up and ask him to show me what he's been doing. He gets up quickly. He leads me to his trench and shows me, lying on a tray covered with polythene, a few fragments of wood and, more interesting, some pieces of metal that he's slipping into small cases and labelling. A comparison with my own finds begins to form. Are we discovering fragments of weapons which might, since Alan's trench B is close to mine, be part of a hoard? But I'm not certain yet that the fragments come from weapons. From horses' bits? It's too early to tell yet and Alan's attention is not really on what he's showing me.

'God, I hate that fellow Ralph,' he mutters with venom. 'I suppose he went to some bloody public school and then Oxford or Cambridge. OK, say he did – I can knock spots off him where archaeology's concerned.'

'Look,' I explain patiently (Alan's got such an outsized chip on his shoulder that I don't like to be too hard on him), 'Ralph hasn't got a degree in archaeology. He's not in competition with you. Don't let yourself get so rattled, Alan.'

I find myself taking his hand. Better to be sorry for Alan than for myself. He looks up quickly. His face clears. 'No one can see,' he mutters as he kisses my hand over and over again. 'Come out this evening,' he urges. 'Please come out with me. It'll be a beautiful evening.'

'I'll see.'

'Thank God you'll be here this weekend. Last Saturday and Sunday were hell without you.'

I can't comment. I disengage my hand.

'Please promise you'll come out tonight,' he pleads again.

'I've told you. I'll see what I feel like. I can't promise. No, Alan, leave me alone. You can't kiss me here. I must get back

109

to work anyway.' He's hurt. I suppose he works as I do, his thoughts engaged on the surface with what he's doing while his heart is full of love and the pain that seems inseparable from love.

Half-way through the afternoon, the wooden spatula I'm working with reveals the edge of something larger than anything I've so far found. I'm deep in the trench and there's no evidence of disturbance by peat-cutters. Whatever it is has lain there for two thousand years. I use my hands and work gently through the soft peat. Before I get it completely out I know what it is: the upper part of an iron scabbard about 30 cm long. It still has its loop intact, the vertical loop for the strap that fastened sword and scabbard to the warrior's belt.

When I've got it out completely I don't immediately tell Hubert. I crouch in the hot trench and turn it over and over in my hands. It's in beautiful condition, and there may be more of it further into the peat. What was it? Or rather whose was it? Part of a warrior's weaponry? Insignia of a chieftain? And why here? As a votive offering to the gods of the place? Or possibly was its sword used in sacrificial rites? It raises a host of questions. And here's where the mind plays a malicious trick, for I am totally absorbed in this discovery, and happy in my absorption, when suddenly the words come into my mind: 'God, I wish I could show this to Deborah!' All right. If that is the deception I can play upon myself, it's more than time I showed the scabbard to Hubert. Oh, why could not my churlish mind be gracious enough to suggest that the recovery of this, the most important find so far, has been granted to me by the gods, perhaps by the ancient spirits of the place who dwell under Moel Llafn, as some sort of compensation, inadequate but well-intended?

I climb out of the trench and am about to call to Hubert when I see that he is in trench B quite near me and the students are there too, and Ralph, taking photographs.

Hubert calls out to me: 'Come over, Gwyneth. There's no

110

doubt about it. Can't be anything else, though it's badly corroded. A wrought-iron sickle. A socketed sickle, its blade eaten into by the acid peat but none the less we've a right to feel elated by this.'

They are all so absorbed in this find that I hold back. I give them time to record it, the ordinary routine work of photography and so on to be done. Then at last I pull Hubert aside, and take him into trench A and show him the part of the scabbard that I've found, with its vertical loop beautifully preserved, and the fragments that belong to the rest of it. Then photography again, students crowding round, recording and packing up the precious pieces. At last the routine work is done and we sit back as the sun begins to sink lower in the sky and much of the site is in shadow. The trenches are covered with sheeting, our tools are put away, but Hubert doesn't make for the Land-Rover. He lights a cigarette and draws us all round him. 'I'm not going to make forecasts, it's too early,' he said, 'but these finds set up a train of thought that I'm going to pass on to you. That sickle's not local work. I doubt if the scabbard is either, and if there's a scabbard, shall we find a sword? I'm going to stick my neck out a bit, all the same, and say that here we may well be on to a hoard of loot. When that figurine was handed in by the Welsh labourer last year, and the pebble with its human features, it was tempting, even then, to think of votive offerings. These finds today bring us a lot closer to this idea. A votive offering to whom? God knows! This peat was once the edge of a larger mountain tarn. There are standing stones beside it. They hold their secret. Are we presumptuous in thinking that a local goddess presided over this secret lake? That here was flung part of some loot, a ritual offering to her after a successful raid by these upland warriors on the richer lands of the south?'

There was a long silence and then one of the students started to speak, but Hubert cut him short with: 'Time to go home, all of you. We're late. Can't keep the hotel waiting.' And he lumbered to his feet and went over to the Land-Rover.

13

But O Nerina, does not this place speak
Of you, and can it be that you indeed
Are faded from my thoughts? Where are you gone?
For memories, O sweetness of my life,
Are all I find of you.

> From Leopardi: *Le ricordanze*, translated by John
> Heath-Stubbs.

'Ralph! You're still up. It's awfully late.'

'Never mind. Late or early, it doesn't matter. Both equally horrible.'

'Sleep isn't horrible. I suggest you go to bed.'

'Shan't be able to sleep, Meg. Not until I've finished this bottle. Anyway, what are you doing down here at whatever time it is?'

'I couldn't sleep, as a matter of fact. I came down to fetch a book I'd left here that I've nearly finished.'

'Books useful certainly ... but at this time of night ... drink better. Share what's left of my bottle?'

'Thank you, Ralph. I won't.'

'Don't go away. Don't leave me.'

'D'you want me to help you upstairs?'

'I do not. I wouldn't accept your help in the first place, and in the second, I've no intention of going to bed. I just want you to stay with me. Nice Meg. I'm very fond of you. Listen to me.'

112

'All right, Ralph, but I can't stay long.'

'Why? Hubert?'

'He's asleep.'

'Good. No reason why you shouldn't stay then.'

'Except my own reason. I happen to be tired, Ralph, and ... I won't be used.'

'Oh. Won't be used. Won't even listen? Call that being used?'

'Depends what I've got to listen to. Frankly, it would be better for you if you went to bed rather than tell me your life story.'

'It is not my life story. My death story. Quite different. Why should Gwyneth have the right to bore us all with her Mabin-thingummy? I can tell stories, too. Anyway, it's all her fault.'

'I don't follow. Whose fault?'

'Gwyneth's.'

'What's she done, for heaven's sake?'

'Found that blasted sickle.'

'She didn't find it, Ralph. You're getting confused. Alan found it. What does it matter anyway?'

'You're right. I am confused. Of course it was Alan. It matters a lot. It's a symbol of death.'

'Ralph, you must be very drunk. What *are* you talking about?'

'I'm talking about that sickle. The finding of it brought something home to me a bit too forcibly.'

'I see. D'you want to tell me about it? Will it clear your mind? Will it help? What is it about?'

'My marriage. I told you I'd been married, didn't I, Meg?'

'I'll have a small drink, Ralph. No, sit still. I'll pour it out. I don't want to appear unsympathetic, but I'd really rather not stay too long. I *am* tired.'

'And nothing more boring, is there, than the maunderings of a drunk.'

'I didn't say so.'

113

'Well, they are. I'll try not to maunder ... if you'll stay ... just a little while. That glass is clean, Meg. Have some of this bottle. Stop me drinking all of it.'

'Here we are, Ralph.'

'Will you drink it neat?'

'Yes, I'll drink it neat, thanks.'

'Meg, d'you remember, I had to come here before the work started in my capacity – my phoney official status – as site-something-or-other, to rope in some of the locals to do the heavy digging, and to make arrangements for our team at a nearby hotel, and so on?'

'Well, I do remember something about it, yes. I heard from Hubert that you'd gone, I suppose, but I wasn't actually part of the team then.'

'I was up here for over a week. There's a place near here, a soft, enfolding valley, almost welcoming among these hostile mountains. I'm thankful that I was alone when I found it. It unmanned me. It broke down the defences of years. And yet ... I believe it was necessary for me. I'm trying to keep my mind clear ... won't have another whisky ... you have another, Meg. It must have been the fourth or fifth evening that I was here. I'd done most of the work I'd been sent to do. I ought to have gone back to the Institute, of course, and put in some work there and travelled up with the rest of the team. I phoned and said I wasn't well. I invented some reason – I'd eaten something that disagreed with me ... could I have a few days' sick-leave? It was granted and I persuaded a local doctor to give me a chit on the grounds that I needed rest. He was not a Welshman but a Scot, practising in a nearby town, an old man, tired himself and sympathetic to my feeling of alienation among the Welsh churls I'd been dealing with.

' "Lovely country," he observed, as he handed me the certificate. "Get out and take some long walks. Ye'll be a new mon, I assure ye. Walking'll get ye to terms wi' the mountains, poor southerner that ye are."

'So I did what he said. And on the third evening, I walked

114

over the flank of a mountain and down into a valley with a stream running through it. Suddenly I was out of the rough mountain scenery. It was more like the West Country – soft, green turf, a flock of sheep, fat and white. Even the farm looked as if it might have been transported from Wiltshire. Built of grey stone. But it was the formation of the hills that was most familiar, and the placing of a wood at the head of the valley, a triangle of wood, broad at the top, tapering down to a point in the cleft of the valley head. It could have been Dunshay where we lived when we married, Phyllis and I, a village not far from Marlborough. I had a post in the archives office of a local museum. We used to walk across the fields at the base of the valley, up to the top of the hill opposite the house, along to the wood, and then we'd take a footpath that ran along behind it. Sometimes deer sprang up almost at our feet. Then we'd walk down into the valley bottom when the wood ended, and back to the house. It took less than an hour, a pleasant breather after I arrived home from the office, before we settled down to a drink and a meal. That soft, June evening in Wales, there was a man walking across the fields. I hailed him, climbed over a stile and walked towards him. He didn't look pleased, a surly fellow, but I wanted to know something. Urgently I wanted to know the name of this cleft in the hills, thinking – no, more than that: I was *convinced* – that hidden within its name there might be some message for me, some explanation as to why chance had set me walking there and conjured from the distant past that fold in the Wiltshire downland at Dunshay, where Phyllis and I had walked so often. "What's this valley called?" I asked. The Welshman spat and uttered some unintelligible words. No matter, I thought. I would look it up on a map. But the map of course would also only give the Welsh name. I wanted to know the meaning of the words. I almost pleaded with him. He looked me up and down disparagingly, then repeated the Welsh words: Ergyd y Fwyell.

'"The English for the words is what I want," I said slowly,

in case he had not understood what I'd said. He looked up towards the head of the valley where the triangular wood lay.

' "Your home's here," I went on, trying to be personally interested in him, "your farm?"

' "It is," he answered. He gazed in silence up the valley and then said, deliberately drawing out his words, making me wait: "The name of it means, as you might say, the Blow of the Axe." He made a chopping motion with his hand. "Like it was an axe that split the head of the valley, so deep it is, the cleft," and from the way he spoke and the intensity of his eyes, I knew that he had always belonged here and that he loved it. I thanked him and he suddenly smiled.

' "You're welcome," he said and went on: "You're the first man ever asked me that in all my fifty-five years. But it is better in the Welsh: Ergyd y Fwyell." And then, unwilling to be drawn into further conversation with a questioning foreigner, he put two fingers in his mouth and gave a shrill whistle. Out of nowhere appeared a Welsh collie and the pair of them crossed my path and went on their way.

'I walked over the fields, up the steep escarpment of the hill opposite, and towards the wood, remembering as only places can make one remember – as if we were transported not merely in place but time. And there is no need for it to be the actual place itself where we once loved, perhaps, or suffered. Even a smell of woodsmoke among cottages, or wild garlic in a lane, can be painfully or joyfully evocative. So it was now.

'They were all a long time ago, our walks up the valley near Dunshay ... just a few more minutes, dear Meg ... I was 28 then. We had been married for just over two years and we were enormously happy. Our life in Wiltshire was everything we wanted from each other, everything that we desired to give each other. A perfect framework. And then in August, the beginning of our third year together, Phyllis had to fly to Canada, after an urgent telephone call saying that her mother was seriously ill. I didn't want her to go. But she insisted. She said she had a presentiment that her mother was going to die.

116

I drove her up to the airport and when we said goodbye to each other, my heart felt painfully enlarged in my chest. I could hardly speak. Was it I who had a presentiment? "Darling Ralph," she said – she loved my name, loved saying it. "It'll only be for a few days. I'll be back – oh, within a week or ten days. Don't look so unhappy. You know I must go and you're making it harder for me."

'Driving home, I switched on the car radio. The Third Programme was giving the Monteverdi Vespers, and at first I experienced a mounting joy as the music began to absorb me and allay the irrational fears I had had at the airport. The Vespers seemed to make those fears irrelevant. We both knew it well and I re-lived the occasion when we'd heard it for the first time in Bath Abbey. I recalled the Christmas before last when I bought records of the work in Germany. But the music ended and as I approached home in the darkness, I felt a sudden stab of pain, so unbearable that I had to slow down and pull in at the side of the road. Something terrible was happening – somewhere. I felt a certainty of disaster. I found myself sweating heavily. The pain was clouding my thought like a pall of smoke. I could see nothing clearly in my mind. I could only feel. Then after a few minutes, my head cleared. The pain became less acute. I felt intensely cold. Words emerged from the mists of my brain. They repeated over and over: something has happened to Phyllis. I slept the sleep of exhaustion when I reached home. The air crash was announced on the early news the next morning. But I had had a phone call from Canada during the night. Phyllis had not arrived: the airport admitted trouble but refused to be explicit. The early news announced that the plane had come down into the sea off the coast of Newfoundland. There were no survivors. Relatives were being informed. The telephone rang. I did not answer it. I took my stick and walked across the fields. The sun was coming up, already the air was warm. That Welsh valley brought it all back to me, Meg.'

'D'you want to tell me about it?'

117

'I'm not sure. Perhaps I shouldn't have embarked on this confession, this soul-baring. Very stupid of me. Very boring for you.'

'If you'd rather not say any more about it, I'll understand. Don't feel you have to go on, Ralph. I'm touched that you should have told me as much as you have.'

'I think I'd like to tell you the rest of it if you can bear it. I stood at the threshold of a small valley. To my left lay the triangle of woodland between two rounded spurs of hill, like thighs enclosing ... enclosing my beloved Phyllis's ...'

Ralph said nothing for a few moments. He seemed hardly aware that Meg was beside him. He stared into his empty whisky glass. At last he went on: 'I remember that I picked up a black feather and took it home with me, stroking it obsessively. It was silky. Like her skin.' He paused again. 'D'you really want all this?'

Meg laid her hand on his arm and said: 'I think you need to spell it out and why not to me? It will never go any further. I'll never refer to it again if you don't want me to.'

'OK, Meg. Just leave your hand there. It's reassuring. I walked along one side of the valley and I thought of our love and I knew that I could not live life again as I had lived it with Phyllis. My only hope of survival was to live somewhere else, away from those Wiltshire downs and the valley with its reminders of her. I didn't see any deer in the wood as I passed along its upper boundary. But I've never forgotten the butterfly, a tortoiseshell butterfly darting in front of me as I walked down the field towards the empty house. It kept coming down on a stone or a leaf in the early sun, flying just ahead of me whenever I caught it up, until at last another joined it, they danced along the hedge together and I left them behind. I suppose they were happy. Whatever butterflies are. That's what the Welsh valley brought back again to me.'

There was a silence. Then Meg said: 'Words are not much good. I simply don't know what to say.'

'Don't say anything. The whisky's almost finished. I'll have

118

a last tot. You go to bed, Meg. You've heard it all. Thank you for listening. Somehow it's set those memories at liberty. And think of this, as I so often have: think of the illusion of lasting love. At least Phyllis and I didn't see our love go into decline. We didn't have to suffer because one of us became attracted to someone else. It was exactly what the name of the Welsh valley offered me: the clean blow of an axe.'

'D'you want to go on talking?'

'Not really.'

'Then come on to bed.'

'No, Meg. You go on up.'

Meg hesitated, began to speak, but saw that Ralph was not listening. Quietly she left the room, seeing as she turned at the door that he was draining his glass slowly.

Ralph sat staring at the empty glass for some minutes. Then he put it down and began to tear the pages out of his 1980 diary. He rose unsteadily to his feet and walked over to the fireplace. Carefully he moved aside the jar of greenery that stood in front of it, stumbled and spilt most of the water. Cursed and gripped the mantelpiece for a moment. 'That's better,' he muttered and knelt down in front of the grate. He tore the pages into pieces, dropped them into the fire-basket and felt for his matches. The small sheets of paper burned away quickly. He shuffled the charred pieces to make sure that no writing remained, then made his way to the door, leaving the jar of leaves where it stood, in a pool of water at the side of the fireplace.

He climbed the stairs slowly. The lights were still on. He saw Meg cross the passage from the bathroom to the bedroom she shared with Hubert. They looked at each other for a moment. 'Goodnight, Ralph,' Meg murmured. He didn't answer. He looked at her as if he didn't recognise her and went into his room.

119

14

I fling my question at your iron sky
Where clouds evasive race down azure rides
And cerulean horsemen as they pass
Wind their shrill horns above the secret wood.

Peopled with phantoms and dark heraldry,
Raucous with raven thoughts, the wood abides
And weaves its black destruction on the grass
Which once sprang green in glades where lovers stood.

Now the embossed and dripping trunks reply
Only in echoes, whispering asides.
Reflected from your silent sky of brass,
My question gabbles through the solitudes.

Anon.

Alan and Gwyneth worked alone on the site. Ralph stayed down at the hotel finishing off some drawings. It was Thursday. Hubert and Meg had returned to Canterbury that afternoon to see the twins off on a Continental holiday with friends the following day. The students had gone off to Deeside University for a few days to study the collections of Iron Age finds made in North Wales.

Alan and Gwyneth worked in adjoining trenches, though not parallel to each other but at either end, so that conversation was impossible. It was not until they sat in the sun-

120

drenched bracken to one side of the site to drink coffee from a Thermos that they began to talk to each other. It was some minutes before Alan realised that he was conducting almost a monologue to which Gwyneth was contributing only a few random remarks. He suddenly turned and looked into her face.

'I don't believe you're listening.'

'I'm sorry, Alan. No, I wasn't. I was thinking.'

'Have you found anything interesting?'

'Nothing. Nothing in the trench, that is.' But in my mind, yes. I've found enough there to occupy me all day and beyond. Let him go on talking to me so that I can withdraw into my own thoughts.

'I'm very deep in trench B now,' said Alan. 'Over five feet. It's been badly disturbed by old peat-cutting. In fact, at the moment, I'm working my way back through the trench but I'm not hoping to find anything much. The Prof's right, of course. After finding the sickle and the pieces of the scabbard, we've got to cover the whole area round them. I suppose his thinking is that we can gradually move in towards the centre of the workings and there we'll find the main items of the hoard – if it *was* a hoard. Your section hasn't been disturbed much, has it, Gwyneth? It might turn out to hold something more interesting than mine.'

'Sorry yours is boring,' murmured Gwyneth.

'Well, when you get level with where I am now, you'll meet the disturbance. The later peat-cutting has gone diagonally across four of the trenches.'

'Oh, has it?'

'More coffee? No? I'll have it then. I need something. I'm browned off. I'm sifting through the stuff, of course, but I doubt if anything of interest remains. Anything worthwhile has probably been filched years ago. Maybe centuries ago.'

'Yes, I suppose so.' Do I feel Bronwen has filched Deborah from me? 'Filch?' – it's such an expressive word. But no, I can't look at it that way. Deborah fell in love with her, and

121

that's the sum of it. That's the unprofitable situation I've got to deal with. I need to work out my future. Let that god-like attribute, reason, provide me with a blue-print. Let the damned beast work for me. I'll harness it, drive it, lash it as though it were an unwilling horse. Which it is, when it's an emotional matter it has to deal with. It likes dry details to sort and put in order. Artefacts dug up from a trench. They suit it exactly. Bloody, bloody reason, that cannot dry my tears.

'Alan, let's get back to work.'

'OK. Curse this peat and sand that gets into my boots and through my socks, even under my shirt. I'm so deep in the trench.' I suppose I miss Hubert. His inspiration and encouragement. He's taught me so much. That's stupid of me. It all rests with myself. I've got this bloody awful hang-up about having to prove myself. The parents ... the neighbours. My old Prof at Preston. They've all invested in me, curse them. I don't want their investment. I've got to invest in myself. In my own brain. It's got to pull me to the top.

Gwyneth's working so deep in her trench that I can't see her. I'm smoking a cigarette, leaning against the bank, with my boots soaking in the ooze. I can hear her every now and again. I can almost hear her breathing, the silence is so absolute. Nothing but the birds and a faint wind in the birches and alders. Something's up with her. She's been so withdrawn since she came back on Sunday night from her weekend away. Silent and preoccupied. If I made a really important find, would it just be for myself, for my own satisfaction? I admit I'm ambitious. I've found that out here on this Welsh site. I don't think I knew it before. But it's all tied up with Gwyneth too. It's partly for her that I want to make my find. What's the matter with me? Here we are alone on the site all day and going to be so for several days. Why can't I take my opportunity? Why can't I bring myself to the pitch of seizing her in my arms and kissing her? Making love to her up here in the bracken, under the birches. I've no experience. I'm an ignorant fool. As far as love goes, I'm worse than any amateur. I can be OK in discussion in spite of my stammer, as long as I know what I'm talking about. Better than that, if I'm confident that I'm the expert, confidence carries me over the stammer. But I've not got the nerve to embrace Gwyneth, to kiss her mouth. Oh, Christ, the hours I'm wasting ...

So much was left unsaid last weekend. In the silences between us grew my certainty that Deborah had found someone else. I endured our long separation, never doubting that she longed to end it as much as I did. I have lived this last year as if I were a traveller waiting for a boat due into harbour at a certain hour. I have kept my eyes on the rim of the sea, over which the moving ship would rise like a tiny insect. I should first discern its mast and funnel, the details of its superstructure, then the name, and finally among the passengers leaning over the gunwale, the radiant figure of Deborah herself. Then the hours, the days I had waited would be nothing to me. Not once had I looked around me or opened the door of the harbour offices behind me, to enquire whether the ship would arrive on time. Yet the truth was there. Others who had been waiting had discovered it and had long ago melted away. Only I remained, my eyes resting on that distant horizon, while on a notice-board behind me were chalked words telling me that the ship was not coming into this port at all. She had been diverted to another harbour in a quite different part of the country. If only I had turned round and considered what I saw, I should then have known the fruitlessness of my hopes and recognised the hard truth sooner, and had time to re-order my life in accordance with it.

One thing I know, to leave off this fantasising metaphor: had I discovered that Deborah was living with someone else in Aberystwyth, I would not have come to North Wales. Exile in Durham would have been preferable. Now I am forced to begin the long and bitter acceptance of her loss, while I am actually nearer to her than I have been for over a year. I am working only sixty miles away, but that's not it. No, it's not just this matter of having come on this Welsh expedition. It is the agonising knowledge that for months she has deceived me. She has allowed me to write of plans we had before I took this job, plans to go to the States. Her letters supported this idea, and there were other, more far-reaching plans: that I need only stay at Durham for one more year, and – yes, Deborah agreed with enthusiasm that I ought to stay that one more year so that I should have completed three years in the Durham post. 'You have to consider your career,' she had written in one letter. A year of my life lost in the fog of untruth and false hopes. A year when we have not met as often as I had thought we should, but there have been long weekends, a couple of weeks at Christmas and she was as always with me. Every kiss, every caress, every word whispered in the intimacy of love-making has been as corrupt with deceit as if it had been suffused with poison.

And what difference is there between Alan and myself in the *quality* of our idiotic and unfruitful passions? A difference of age which only serves to underline how far more unforgivable it is in myself, so many years older than Alan, not to be able to come to terms with reality, with the hopelessness of my love. Both of us, Alan and I, are people of good serviceable intellect. We are, in common parlance, 'clever' and our academic careers will each probably reach at least reasonable heights. Both of us come from working-class homes where we learned to expect little, to work hard, to 'do well'. Our accidental gift of intelligence was welcomed and acclaimed, not for itself, but for its potential to shift us up the social ladder – all this perhaps more emphasised for Alan than for me, because in Wales such social aspirations are not so seriously held, and intellect is more important in itself and admired.

And so? Our high-prized faculty of reason that gave us learning and a foot in the groves of Academe, is powerless to help us live our lives reasonably. For Alan there is hope. He is getting through the journey of his fantasy world, and he will emerge from that dark wood with no more than a wry memory of the 'belle dame sans merci' that he thinks I am. But I have entered the wood late. I am thirty-six and am still lost in its maze and look where I will, I see no light. Much-vaunted reason is a spent torch. Deborah has ceased to love me. She has emptied her heart of me and filled it with the image of another. There is no altering the situation, no turning back and, it seems, no going forward. Yet I continue to carry on in my mind long conversations with her. I tell her truths to which she will not listen. I ask her questions which will never be answered.

Good heavens! Is being happy, is being loved no more than that? were Julien's first thoughts when he got back to his room ... like a soldier returning from parade Julien had been absorbed in reviewing every detail of his conduct. Have I been wanting in anything I owe myself? Have I played my part well?

And what a part! That of a man accustomed to success in his dealings with women.

Stendhal: *Scarlet and Black*

They ate their sandwiches at lunchtime, washed down with a couple of bottles of lukewarm beer. Alan had insisted on bringing them and then forgotten to cover them in the shade. It was very hot at the site. The breeze idled along the flank of Moel Llafn, now hurrying a little, now dropping almost to nothing. He and Gwyneth lay back among the bracken fronds, hoping to cool down before starting work again. Gwyneth closed her eyes, turned a little away. Alan chain-smoked. Suddenly he rolled over towards Gwyneth, first stubbing his cigarette into the ground.

There had been a long silence between them, during which Alan had shaped his feelings deliberately, fitting them into a neat pattern. He had seen this pattern as though on a screen in his mind: young man (himself) parts the bracken, raises his shoulders on one supportive arm, while the other reaches out across the woman's breasts to grasp her shoulder. His head lowered, he would place his mouth over hers. During the long kiss, his body would follow the path of his arm in a precise arc, ending up on top of her.

He smoked his way through three cigarettes while he scanned these mental images, refining upon their design. He never doubted that his passion for Gwyneth would take fire once he was on top of her. He never doubted that she would respond. She's been friendly this morning, he thought. I don't believe all this lesbian crap. It's not natural. She's probably lacked opportunity, teaching in a stuffy northern university among a lot of dreary dons. Now opportunity's here. She's alone with me.

A pause in his thoughts. Hardly framed in words came the awareness of his own ignorance and inexperience. But it won't matter, he told himself. Having sex must be like riding the crest of a wave. You can't check its power. It lifts you up, takes charge of you, carries you away. She'll come with me OK.

The time had arrived. He stubbed out the last cigarette and rolled over towards her. At this moment, Gwyneth sat up. 'Back to work,' she said briskly.

Confused, his body already embarked on its sideways journey, Alan reached out clumsily towards her and ended up lying across her lap, his arms scrabbling behind her back and his face buried in bracken. He tried to retrieve the situation by pulling her shoulders and head roughly towards his. She resisted and he raised himself into a sitting position, close to her, face to face. Easy to clasp, easy to kiss, if he could prevent her from getting up. Though his original design had not worked, things had ended up pretty well, he felt, as he pulled her face towards his. But something quite outside his fevered, solipsistic schemes confused and embarrassed him, presenting him with a situation he had no idea how to deal with: Gwyneth's eyes were opaque with tears which had brimmed over and were streaking her warm cheeks.

127

She pushed him away abruptly with: 'Don't be a fool, Alan.' She drew her hand across her face and started to scramble to her feet. Alan stammered out a few words but she ignored them, leapt down the bank into her trench and strode along it to her working position at the far end.

Alan worked in gloomy silence, sifting through the loose peat, moving along his trench with indifference, his mind mulling over what he might have said, what he might have done, to take advantage of her apparent unhappiness, for surely even unhappiness offered him some kind of opportunity? He escaped from his discomfiture by diverting his thoughts to a new direction, as he noticed a marked difference becoming apparent in the texture of the wall of the trench. It was no longer disturbed by peat cutting. He sat back on his heels and scanned the solid, packed texture of the peat. His ambition, closer perhaps to his feeling of desire for Gwyneth than he divined, was immediately engaged and induced him to work with the utmost care. The trench was still deep and narrow. He took off his shirt and with methodical pertinacity sifted every inch of the peat on either side of him. His shoulders and back ached with concentration. At last he stood up, his head clear of the trench. He saw Gwyneth, now much nearer him, stand erect and straighten her back as he was doing.

'How are things?' she called out.

'Just reached an undisturbed part of the trench,' he answered, his heart lifting in response to her glowing face and smiling mouth. He found it hard to believe that he had witnessed her tears.

'Isn't it a glorious day?' she commented. 'I'm tired and I'm hot. Wish there was a place to swim round here.'

He hesitated for a moment, his heart racing. Then called back: 'There is, I think. In a river about twenty miles away. I noticed it on the large-scale map they've got in the hall of the hotel. We could drive there in the Land-Rover.'

Gwyneth reached out towards the bank where she'd left her

watch with her jacket. 'It's just half-four,' she said. 'I'd like to tidy up this section, even though it's been so damned unproductive.'

'OK,' he answered. 'I'll do a bit more, then.'

But as he sifted the peat through his hands, it was automatic. His mind was again occupied with the strategies of his passion for Gwyneth. Images flashed through his brain, throwing off a few words like sparks: the Land-Rover ... Gwyneth driving ... the river. Let there be trees there. Trees and seclusion, a quiet bank away from the road. Plan nothing. Wait for the event. I've planned too much. Oh, God, she's got to let me make love to her. I ought to be driving. Wish I had my brother's motor bike here. Why couldn't the swine have lent it to me for this dig? Gwyneth on the back of it, streaking down the lanes to the riverside, her arms clasping me round the ribs.

God, I'm filthy, covered with bits of peat and earth, sticking to my sweaty body. But I'm brown. I'm tanned, thank God, in the wind and sun up here under the mountainside. The hair on my arms is bleached almost white. Haven't got much on my chest, worse luck. If only I could drive that damned Land-Rover, I'd feel more ... in command. Bumping down the track to the metalled road ... get up a real speed in the valley ... then turn up left to the river. I worked it out on the map but didn't think we'd actually ... the river looks widish there. Hope it's deep enough to swim in. The one and only sport I was any good at. I can never forget the bloody games field and that gym. Always behind the others. Laughed at. But swimming ... Saturday mornings at the public baths. The smell in the sour, dirty cubicles. I didn't care. I practised for competitions. Actually won two or three awards. Never anything spectacular, but I didn't mind. It was pretty well the only thing I enjoyed and I had the university ahead of me, not just the other end of the sodding baths.

Wish to God I was driving her in my own car. A powerful sports – that's what I'd like. I'm in the wrong profession to

129

make money, aren't I, stupid bloody ass? I suppose the Prof doesn't do too badly with his converted oasthouse, whatever that is. I must have a car. I've nothing. Not even an electric razor. I'm not going to teach. Look at this group. Where will they end up? Gwyneth will write some book that sells a couple of thousand copies and end her days Dean of the Faculty in some grotty provincial city. It's in some excavation, some important discovery that I'll get fame. Then one gets money too, if one's clever enough ... television shows ... that sort of thing. My accent ... my bloody stammer ... but I could get them cured if I had the money.

The way the Prof speaks to his staff, to workmen – and they take it all right. His air of authority doesn't come from his learning. He's small beer really. Does he think to make his name by excavating an obscure Welsh peat-bog fifty yards square? No, his authority is a *class* authority. I can't ever get that, but I can get authority by my brains, by my ambitious drive if I let rip.

Here's the river. She's been driving pretty fast, my arm round her shoulders. She never tried to shake it off. I was damned uncomfortable, in fact, half-sitting on the brake. Well, here it is at last, and there *are* trees and it looks wide and deep. Got to undress now. And she's beaten me to it. There she stands at the edge and I'm still trying to get my shoes off – bloody laces knotted – oh, hell, one's broken. She's wearing her bra and pants. Flowery ones. Very pretty, I suppose. She pushes her hair back. Now she's in, calling out to me: 'Alan! Buck up! It's cold but lovely!' She turns on to her back, swims a few yards, rolls over and breast-strokes her way further out from the bank into the middle of the river. My flesh has come up in goose-pimples. My body's so skinny. One day I'll do something about it. Go to evening classes or something. I'll bet Hubert looks marvellous when he's naked. Well, he had all the chances, didn't he? Public school and before that one of those places where they beat the boys and teach them Latin and cricket. But it seems to produce the goods. How typical of Hubert to assume the other day that I went to boarding-school. I suppose I'm a bit of a freak to him. Working-class boy makes good. Well, I *have* made good and I'll make out even better before I've finished. But I look – I look like a rat. Might be better if it weren't for these grubby briefs. Don't like to take them off. Not yet. Will it matter my not having brought anything with me – these sheaths the boys were always talking about and sniggering over? I've never bought anything like that. Never needed to. French letters – for God's sake why are they called that? She's calling me again. I must get into the water quickly. Here goes.

It's good once you get used to it. Not as warm as the sea. Lying on my back staring at the sky, not a cloud in sight. A fast crawl up the river against the current. Wonder if she's impressed. Lovely now to float slowly down with the stream. The banks mostly wooded here and dark in shadow. The water sparkling in the sun and I never knew how good it could be, to swim in a river. I'll never go to a swimming-bath again. I roll over and swim lazily towards her. Her hair is floating in the water. God, how beautiful she looks.

'I'm swimming over to the other side,' she calls.

'OK, race you!' I shout.

Of course she wins but then we didn't start even. Unfair. No, the fates are being kind to me. I can see her, all of her, as she sits on the banks dangling her feet in the river. A river nymph, that's what she is.

'Coming out?' she calls.

'You bet! I'm getting cold.'

It was so predictable. How much of this did he plan consciously? Probably no more than the drive itself. The map pored over. The anxious listening to weather forecasts. I found him yesterday with his transistor, as absorbed as if he were picking up the racing results. For him, the first time. Very inept, poor Alan. And for me? Not the first time. Did he mind this? His stammer would have taken over if he'd tried

131

to explain his feelings. He silently accepted. I've no idea if he was disappointed. Probably. Men get such a kick out of knowing that it's *your* first time. And Alan's ego needed that boost. What a fine fellow – I've deflowered a virgin. But of course he wouldn't use that literary phrase. He'd use some cant term he learnt off other boys at school. He's still a schoolboy in some ways.

No, not the first time for me. There was Michael when I first started as a lecturer in Bristol. And thought myself desperately in love. Then the long emptiness. The pain when Michael left me, but relief too. Yes, a strange sense of relief which I didn't really understand. I kept telling myself it ought to hurt more, it ought to make me unhappier. How slow knowledge of myself came. Came at last through E.D. But she would not stay for me, like the girl in Housman's poem, and for the same reason. Death took her on the road in a bloody, stupid accident, and then I really knew what grief was. From E.D. I learned the grammar of two things: love and death. I thought I should never get over her loss. I thought that I should never be able to love again. And then Deborah came, who carried me into a realm of love beyond anything I'd ever dreamed of. E.D., I do not forget you. Without our brief affair I should not have grown to be the woman I was when Deborah met and loved me.

This *al fresco* coupling with Alan means nothing to me, nothing but the discomfort of grass and thistle and a lump of stone bruising my ribs. Nature declaring her contempt for our brief joyless copulation.

I was able to let Alan make love to me because my heart wasn't in it. My heart was numb. It was a physical sensation not unlike swimming, not unlike the plunge into the cold river. I suppose I ought to feel guilty. I'm letting Alan imagine that I'm giving him more than I am. But I don't feel guilty. I am simply a staging post on his progress, and his progress I suspect is fundamentally heartless, inspired – again I'm guessing – by cold ambition. Making love like this – no, it's not making love. That's just it. It's a brief physical arousal. Suddenly now, watching the river below me that could be so beautiful, that might have been a murmured accompaniment to love, I am overwhelmed with grief. Deborah, Deborah, why was this necessary? This stupid, cruel attempt to cash in on Alan's romantic passion, an attempt that has finally left me ashamed. I wish we'd been anywhere else. Wish almost that he'd come to my room one night. An impersonal hotel bedroom – that would have been better, more acceptable to me than this lovely river. Its shallows on the far side, with water pirouetting over the stones in the late sunshine. The broad channel across which I swam. Not really deep. I could touch the bottom. Despite the sun, the water still cold with the intense cold of mountain snow. And everything so full of Deborah's presence that once I turned my head as I was swimming and imagined her beside me, and I cursed my vision, my wounding illusion that carries these fantasies into my head and so … I gave my already abandoned, indifferent body to Alan.

'We'll have to swim over again for our clothes. God, I'm cold now. You don't say anything. What are you thinking about, Gwyneth, as you stare across the river? I'm swimming back now, anyway.' He sounds angry and his teeth are chattering. Oh, poor Alan. At this moment, I believe I could take him into my arms and give him a little of the warmth he lacks and needs. He's escaping from me. He's half-way across, looks back, but doesn't smile.

Christ, I was cold. I *am* cold. I need a drink. She's driving fast. Probably she wants one too. Why was it so unsatisfactory? I wish there wasn't this silence between us. It seems there's a barrier between us now. Can't make it out when we've been physically so close. And I don't find myself wanting to put my arm round her shoulders, as I did when we were driving over to the river, with my hand caressing her neck. No, I don't

133

want to do that now. I just want to get back to the hotel and put on a pullover and have a drink. Funny ... right in the middle of making love to her, I found myself thinking about the site, wishing I'd found something really interesting today. We could have talked about it.

God, don't drive so fast, Gwyneth. Gwyneth! I can't use endearments. I never heard any at home. It's only middle-class people who say 'darling'. Best to keep silent. It can't be far now. I wonder, would she come again tomorrow? I might do a bit better. I thought at first I wasn't going to make it today. But tomorrow ... yes, I think she'll come. She enjoyed it. All that talk about being a lesbian was a blind. Driving over to this river was a bloody clever idea on my part.

16

Yet they were made of earth and fire as we,
The selfsame forces set us in our mould:
To life we woke from all that makes the past.
We grow on Death's tree as ephemeral flowers.

Translated from Thøger Larsen.

But there was no more swimming. They worked on site all Saturday and much of Sunday. After lunch Alan, restive and disagreeable at his failure to persuade Gwyneth to come to the river again, took himself off without a word to her. She hardly noticed his departure and Ralph put his drawings on one side and suggested that they went out for a picnic. The hotel packed them up some tea and they walked off into the fields and did not return till after six.

Once they were away from the hotel, Gwyneth suggested a field path and when they came to a small group of trees, she flung herself down in the shade. Ralph was at his most easy-going and relaxed and sat down beside her, his arms clasped behind his head. They had hardly spoken while they walked. Now Gwyneth murmured: 'It's good to get away from the hotel, isn't it? Sorry I'm not entertaining you with sparkling conversation. You OK, Ralph?'

'Very happy, thanks. Happy in particular, if you want to know, not to have Hubert hanging round my neck for a few days. A very disloyal remark.'

'We're not school prefects.'

'Aren't we? Something very like it, I sometimes think.'

'Why d'you stay on at the Institute at Canterbury, Ralph?'

'Well, primarily for the money. I'm on the wrong side of fifty, my dear, and I'll need my pension. I'd not find it easy to get another job anyway. It's not too bad. At times – here, for instance – I'm enjoying it. And I have a very agreeable house in Canterbury. Plenty of books and records.'

'D'you mind me asking – are you married, or have you been?'

'Yes. I was married once. To save you asking embarrassing questions, embarrassing to you, I mean. She died. A long time ago.'

'I'm sorry, Ralph.'

'That's all right. I make out. Now it's my turn. Something's happened to you, recently. Would I be right?'

'Yes, you're right. Things come to an end, not always through death.'

'God, who'd be fool enough to pass you up?'

'That's a rhetorical question. And it doesn't deserve an answer. These things happen. To speak plainly, love doesn't always last. Perhaps doesn't ever last.'

'That's rather bleak.'

'Perhaps, but – forgive a pretty crass remark – your wife's dead.'

'OK. Point taken. I'll be crass now. It's my turn. Who have you lost?'

Gwyneth said nothing. Then she turned to face Ralph, and said slowly: 'If I told you about myself, you might be sorry for me and regard it as your duty to comfort me.'

'You mean, make love to you?'

'Well, could be.'

'Is that your only experience of male comfort?'

'I suppose it is. To be honest, I'm not interested in men. I mean, sexually '

'No? Well, I won't press you. Whatever it is, it's just hap-

136

pened, hasn't it?'

'Yes. Ralph, I'm hellishly miserable.'

'Have a shoulder. Have a handkerchief. Both very practical and quite non-sexual.'

'You're a dear, Ralph. I'll be OK in a minute.'

'Let's walk on. Alan might come along and think I've got designs on you. Which actually might be rather good for him. He's getting more than cocky. Come on.'

The warm air cooled as they strolled slowly along a rising path that wound through a forestry plantation.

'How much of a nuisance *is* Alan?' asked Ralph.

'Poor old Alan. The knocks most of us have to take in our teens have come to him rather late.'

'It varies, you know. I may have had a few childhood knocks, but I found life at the university plain sailing. Then I met Phyllis and married her.'

'How soon after that did she – '

'We'd only been married just over two years. She was killed in an air accident.'

'Oh, God, how awful.'

'That was my first and only serious blow from Fate. I'm not asking it to pull the rug from under my feet again. Beautiful though you are, Gwyneth, and easy though it would be to fall for you, I'll just enjoy your appearance and your company with chaste restraint.'

'It's as well, Ralph. I'm a lesbian.'

'Well, so I gathered, but not, I imagine, above a little flattering male interest. And how about Alan in that case?'

'He can't take it.'

She was going on to say: 'I even let him – ' but broke off her thoughts before they formed into words. One can be too confiding. There was a short silence between them.

'Suppose we eat our tea?' suggested Ralph.

That evening the three of them sat in the TV lounge, a different room from their own. They watched programmes in

137

the company of three or four visitors staying in the hotel on holiday. Alan was quite ready to talk to them. They came mostly from the north Midlands and he felt at home with them. Gwyneth endured TV trivialities until she saw that Alan was well away with his group of listeners, talking across the TV programme. The young archaeologist was explaining the technicalities of an excavation and making a gratifying impression upon his listeners. They respected brains, especially when the owner of them came from north of the Humber. They would go home and lay claim to him. One of our lads ... happen you'll hear of him one of these days. He'll maybe give programmes on telly like Michael Wood. Gwyneth and Ralph slipped away to the other lounge, collecting whiskies at the bar as they went, and talking. The conversation of the afternoon was not referred to. They told each other stories – about colleagues, about their childhoods, about holidays they'd taken ... commonplaces, but they roused each other to laughter and felt a comfortable affection growing between them.

On Tuesday, Meg and Hubert came back in the late afternoon. Gwyneth went to the station in the Land-Rover to fetch them, and on the drive back, she reported on the finds she and Alan had made, which were disappointing.

'We haven't that much longer,' said Hubert gloomily. 'About another month. The funds won't stretch further than that.'

Back at the hotel, dinner was eaten almost in silence. They drank coffee. No card games were suggested. Instead Hubert addressed his team, standing in front of the empty fireplace.

'As you know, once some substantial finds were made fairly close together by Alan and Gwyneth, I had to think rapidly about strategy. And before Meg and I went back to Canterbury for these few days I suggested that we fanned out, as it were, and then worked inwards towards the specific area of the finds. I'll call it the "sickle area". I left you, Gwyneth, and Alan, with the students to make a start on this strategy. We've

138

got to find out whether artefacts in the bog are scattered or concentrated, and we've got to work bloody hard.'

At least one member of the team felt that in this case, it was unfortunate that Hubert had found it necessary to spend five days on going back to Canterbury. But no comment was made and an uneasy silence settled over the company, until Ralph broke it with a conventional question:

'How did you find the twins?' he asked.

'Quite well, thank you, Ralph. Barbara's on vacation now, of course. She was at home working and holding the domestic fort.'

'What's she reading?' asked Gwyneth, backing up Ralph.

'Physics and music. I understand the two go together. Extraordinary,' added Hubert, somehow contriving to convey that he despised both. He then looked round at his team, his brows heavily knotted, his eyes hard and his mouth set as though daring anyone else to ask after his family. Ralph ignored the warning signs and began: 'The twins – Edward and Michael – they must be leaving school shortly, I suppose, if I remember – '

'We need some more coffee,' interrupted Hubert and rang the bell for the waiter.

'Would you like a hand of bridge?' asked Alan. 'Or poker? Yes, why don't we teach Gwyneth poker, then she wouldn't be left out of our card games. You'd like it, Gwyneth. You would, really.'

There was a short silence, a registered surprise. Alan blew cigarette smoke through his nostrils, stretching out his thin legs in front of him. He went on: 'You'd find poker – and bridge – useful games, really you would.'

Gwyneth reacted to this by getting up and moving towards the door. Ralph exclaimed: 'I don't think I ever learnt a card game because it was *useful*. My God, Alan, what an attitude! The reason I enjoy cards is mainly because they are useless.'

'You can make money at them,' said Alan, pontifically.

'I would have thought Gwyneth had an adequate salary –

139

don't you Gwyneth?'

She had paused at the door. Her face now showed amusement at the situation. Meg on the other hand was withdrawn, staring at her empty coffee-cup, while Hubert was glaring at Alan in amazement. Ralph had not finished. He could see that Alan was searching for a riposte and went on, with a wave of his plump hand: 'Or are you, dear boy, thinking that you might as well take up a career in the sunny casinos of Monte Carlo, since this dig is proving so unproductive? After all, you're young. You have time on your side.'

Gwyneth half turned back towards the room, saying: 'I don't consider the work's been unproductive at all. A number of small artefacts and that sickle make it reasonably successful. I've been on far worse excavations.'

'This is a very odd conversation,' observed Hubert.

'Don't leave us, Gwyneth,' exclaimed Meg, looking up at last. 'The coffee's coming. Let's get down to planning tomorrow's work.'

Hubert rose from his chair quickly and announced: 'What we'll do is this. We'll drive up to the site now. It's not too late. There's still plenty of light. I want to discuss my ... my strategy with you all.'

'Who d'you want to come?' asked Alan, rather sulkily.

'Everyone,' answered Hubert in a clipped, military voice. 'We're a team, are we not?'

'The generals make the strategy, not the junior officers,' Ralph observed.

'I can do without that sort of remark, Ralph,' said Hubert angrily. 'I am thinking ahead. I have ideas to put before you, and they demand discussion. On the site, Ralph. In fact, I'll give you some conception of the way my mind is working now, though it's not to be taken in any way as more than a purely intuitive idea. What I'm thinking is that if we can narrow the area of important finds down to what I've called the "sickle area", and if *there*, we excavate finds of the same importance as the scabbard fragment and the sickle itself, then we might conceivably be on to a hoard of loot, or possibly even a group of objects cast into the ancient lake as votive offerings. We all – all of us – need to look at this site with fresh vision. We'll go up there now. No time like the present.'

'You don't mind if we finish the coffee? We did order a second round,' said Ralph.

'I don't require any more coffee,' said Hubert abruptly. 'The site is more important. I should have thought that was obvious from what I've just said. Leave the coffee, for God's sake.'

The track looked different in the last light of day. It led through a forestry plantation of neat conifers that threw a gloomy shadow over the rough stony road. Emerging from this plantation, the track deteriorated, ran steeply up the side of Moel Llafn past a ruined farmhouse, and then branched off, becoming a rutted lane leading up to the pocket of marshy ground, Gors Ddu, the 'Black Bog'. Just beyond it was a group of standing stones. Lichened and hoary, their silent presence had watched over the team's activities. At first, the stones had provoked interest, and everyone except Ralph had walked round them, discussed them, compared them with other standing stones they knew.

Now Gwyneth, for one, saw them with new eyes. The standing stones ... they're bright gold. I suppose we've never been here when the sun's so low in the west. It's laying a long golden hand over them. Oh, God, how I love this country. I feel as rooted as the stones, but no sun warms me. I listen to Hubert telling us all what to do, like a general disposing his troops. He can't spare even a minute for the stones, and already the golden arm of the sun begins to withdraw its regal warmth. His voice is an intruder on this ancient, secret place.

'I'd like you to have another look at the bore-holes and shallow trenches we made during the first week, in the north-east corner. We abandoned them, you remember?'

141

Yes, Hubert, we abandoned them for what seemed good reasons at the time. Now I am appointed to re-examine them. No stone to be left unturned. Something *must* be found. It's an order. Idiotic to bring us up here so late. The sun will set soon. Christ's blood already streams across the firmament and Deborah will watch it from her Aberystwyth window, and her lover will watch it beside her. Just over a week ago. Oh, God, to end this repetitive pain. Last week . . . last month. To forget anniversaries. They are like a chain and ball at one's ankles. As for Wales, as for all this before and around me and under my feet, it will not save me. I shall desert it. Deborah has taken it over. With a lover who even – the irony of it – speaks Welsh. I'll go abroad, perhaps. I don't know. These trenches and holes are utterly unpromising and anyway I can hardly see them. But at least it's an occupation. Better than sitting in that bloody lounge.

Hubert's talking to Alan about the trench he's been working in. Alan . . . I suppose I sold him short, poor boy, refusing to let him make love to me again. In fact, he was not all that eager. It was almost as if he were apologising for selling *me* short. Leave him to his illusions, though I hope that the reality of sex will have cured him of some of his romanticism. But who will cure me of mine?

Hubert walked slowly along the trench where Alan had been working. 'Yes, yes. I see what you mean. Badly disturbed in parts. You say you and Gwyneth both worked at the far ends, that is the south-west and north-west ends of trenches A and B and so far there's been virtually nothing? Yet it was in the area of those trenches that the scabbard and sickle were found, and I think that we must work from the edges of the site inwards now. You know, Alan, I have a hunch. I have a – well, of course, we're scientists and I don't want you to misunderstand me. But it's very odd how what seems almost irrational sometimes comes up with the answer.

'Intuitions, hunches, dreams – you'll know all about Poincaré's famous lecture ... Jacques Hadamard ... von Kekule who pronounced those extraordinary words, after a revolutionary discovery in the field of organic chemistry: "Gentlemen, let us learn to dream." I'm deeply interested in such things.'

The others had gathered round the trench and were listening, but no one said anything. Hubert appeared not to notice. He went on in a musing way: 'My hunch may not be so far wrong. I feel it more strongly now I am standing on this site again. These two trenches, possibly the centre of C as well, are the most promising places. I'd like you to continue working along that trench, Alan. With a couple of students. Gwyneth, you continue with your work in trench A and the surrounding area. Make that chap – what's his name – Colin, yes, Colin, work with you but don't give him too much responsibility. Ralph, you'll be recording of course. I intend to work with Meg from the south-east corner that we've not so far excavated in depth. We'll make some sample trenches across the area. The sun's getting low – we must go back. Good God, what's that fellow Ralph doing? Ralph, what on earth are you taking photographs of? There can't be enough light for anything, surely?'

'Enough for this particular film. I wanted to record the standing stones.'

'What's the point?'

'I might ask, what was the point of my being here at all this evening?'

'I thought I'd explained. I wanted to keep the team together this evening.'

'But I'm not an archaeologist, I think you said recently. Quite rightly, of course.'

'My dear Ralph, I wasn't being offensive. Surely even a photographer might have a flash of that – intuition – call it what you like – which could illuminate the ... er ...'

'I rather doubt it, but I've enjoyed being up here this evening. I've got a stunning shot of the standing stones in the late light of the sun. Several, in fact. Let's call them my "art" photographs. And I've been taking some of the team on the site. After all, we're not often here all together. "Personal" photographs, we'll call them. Like this, for instance.' He lifted his camera and took a shot of Hubert, standing by the open trench. 'Suitable for the Institute walls, I thought. Professor Loders and his team at the dig that made archaeological history.'

'I see. Very interesting. I shall look forward to seeing them.'

Ah, but I don't know that you will, thought Ralph. Personal mementoes. I got a particularly good one of Meg. Means a lot to me but not necessarily to Hubert, I fancy. Dear Meg. She's the very – can't think of any word but 'nicest' – well, then, the very nicest person I know. And the kindest. And she thinks. Yes, Meg's a thinking person. I wish I could hope to know her better but I don't think that's possible. Anyway, I'll be glad to have the photograph. Trusty old camera. A man's best friend. I remember when Phyllis went, I bought a cheap camera and went away, to Lincolnshire of all places. But it turned out to be a good area. So flat. So unspectacular. I could concentrate on details. Wherever I went, I took photographs and it absorbed me. Shots of reed-beds and wild flowers, even one or two birds – not very successful, those – masses of churches and bits of church carvings that I've never looked at since. The capturing of them in my little black box was all. I nearly got to the pitch of talking to it. It developed a powerful persona. And of course it's stood me in good stead as far as a job goes. Ah, Meg, what are you thinking about, as you stand there? While Hubert positively flirts with Alan, the hand on the shoulder ... dear boy ... have my trench ... be my son ... claim your inheritance. God, he nauseates me!

Well, it's nearly over. Here among these ancient stones they probably sacrificed to their gods. I suppose we all at some time have to make a sacrifice to the powers of the underworld. They demanded my grief and I refused to give it to them. Till now, they've watched, like these stones, and waited, silent

144

and malevolent, while I buried my grief in the pursuit of hedonism. It's served me well enough and I shall go back to it.

I'm thankful to be back here at the site, to become again part of the plan I intend to carry out. Barbara and the twins will understand, especially Barbara. They saw and heard enough this weekend. Barbara said when we were washing up and alone on Sunday evening: 'This Alan ... Dad talks about him as if he were his son. Is he a substitute for Patrick, d'you think?' 'Well, yes,' I said. 'I think he is, in a way.' And then she asked me directly: 'What did *you* feel, Mother, when Patrick was drowned?'

What did I feel? The loss of a part of myself. Hubert feels it as the loss of something outside himself, an object he created and possessed. We felt so differently about it that we were unable to live through our grief together. We diverged and have never met again. Patrick was really taken from me when he was a small boy. Hubert made him his property almost as soon as he could talk and so I still, in a way, mourn him as a little boy. His actual death added only intensity to my already formed sense of loss. I had lost him years before. How much of this did I convey to Barbara? Certainly some of it, enough for her to say: 'I understand, Mother,' and then – extraordinary – she added: 'I can't think why you stay with Dad now we're old enough to look after ourselves.' It was the opportunity, wasn't it? The time to tell her my plans. Yet I did not take it. I fell silent and Barbara hugged me and said: 'Consider *yourself* for once, Mother. You've done enough for the three of us. After all, I've left home, more or less, and the boys will go soon. We can manage. Whatever you do we'll always love you.'

Barbara, I'll write. Sooner than you think. I want you as a friend now.

With a host of furious fancies,
Whereof I am commander,
With a burning spear, and a horse of air,
To the wilderness I wander.
By a knight of ghosts and shadows
I summoned am to journey,
Ten leagues beyond the wide world's end.
Me thinks it is no journey.

Anon., from *Tom of Bedlam's Song*

Back at the hotel the cold coffee had been cleared away. Alan went to bed. His feelings were in a turmoil – jealous of what he fancied was Hubert's interest in Gwyneth, having seen him watching her in the evening light, up at the site, and himself finding her more beautiful than ever, but bitter at his failure to make love to her again. Meg said goodnight shortly after, and went upstairs. Ralph went to the bar. Gwyneth found herself alone with Hubert and was about to say goodnight and go when he put out a restraining hand and said: 'I'll get you a drink,' and without waiting for a denial, went and got her one, saying as he put it into her hand: 'We've not had much conversation, Gwyneth. I feel I hardly know you.'

Gwyneth felt at a loss. She was tired and preoccupied. Hubert took a sip of his whisky and went on: 'Tell me what you think of Alan.'

146

'This site's important for him,' replied Gwyneth non-committally.

'That doesn't answer my question. What d'you think of his potential, to put it another way?'

'He's very competent. I've not seen enough of his work to give a more definite opinion.' She wondered what this was leading up to. Hubert had been in a strange mood since he returned from Canterbury. He made it clear in what he went on to say.

'I thought at first ... that is, I was led to believe by his professor – he's an old friend of mine – that he was very promising. I found it difficult ... forgive me for becoming personal ... but, you know, I had a son. Patrick. He would be about Alan's age now. I thought Alan very like him at first.'

'But you've changed your opinion?'

'I was fooling myself. It wasn't a matter of reasoned opinion. No one can ever replace Patrick. He was drowned. Did you know?'

'Yes, I knew. I'm very sorry, Hubert.'

'It's the worst blow I've ever had in my life.'

'I can't say anything helpful except that I do understand what this loss means to you, perhaps better than you think. I'm glad you see that Alan can't be a substitute. I must be frank – to have singled him out would have been damaging to us as a team and at first, I felt that you were doing just that.'

She drank the last of her whisky. Tired and increasingly longing to be alone and give vent to her own grief, what did it matter what she said to Hubert? But his hurt silence prompted her to add: 'I'm afraid you think this is very impertinent of me, that I'm criticising you.'

'No, no. Not impertinent,' muttered Hubert.

'I don't think we're cohering very well as a team, anyway.'

'A team is as good as its members,' said Hubert, showing anger in the mounting colour of his face. The conversation was not going as he had wanted.

'OK, OK,' said Gwyneth, wearily. 'I don't feel I want to

147

pursue this any further. I want to go to bed. But I would like to add one thing. I am really sorry that I've never found an opportunity to express my sympathy to you over the loss of your son, and I want to do so now. I imagine that going home for this long weekend has not been easy for you. I want to tell you that I know something of loss and therefore something perhaps of your feelings over Patrick's death, and how ... how places can bring back a grief.'

There was a long silence.

I shouldn't have spoken about it at all, thought Gwyneth. Certainly I should never have said that I knew something of loss. How stupid I am. He is utterly absorbed in himself. God preserve me from prolonging my own grief. If I still had any religious faith, I would pray for this.

Hubert was speaking again. She could not escape. 'You're not married, Gwyneth. You've never had children. You can't know what it is to lose a son.'

'Is it entirely a matter of *who* you lose? Doesn't the quality, the intensity of the loss matter more?'

'No. I can't agree. To lose a son – bone of one's bone, flesh of one's flesh – is a terrible thing.'

'Not only for you, surely,' I am bold enough to say. 'What about Meg?' But he sweeps my words on one side. He is not going to relinquish his hold upon the loss of Patrick.

'The loss of a son is unique. Impossible for even the mother to understand the grief of the father. My eldest son and a brilliant boy. Patrick would have gone far. I am grateful for your sympathy, Gwyneth, but I don't think you can begin to understand my feelings.'

'You imagine that I can't understand them because I'm an unmarried woman in my thirties who, in your masculine eyes, can have had no deep attachments.'

'I'm sorry. Of course I know nothing of your private life. I shouldn't have spoken of such personal matters in the first place. Well, it's getting late. Perhaps we'd better be off to bed. Goodnight.'

148

'Goodnight, and thank you for the drink.'

Patrick ... Patrick ... Patrick. This woman Gwyneth could dare to speak to me of Patrick. Could touch my grief with her feminine, probing fingers. Have these Welsh women second sight? How could she know that the half-term weekend brought it all home to me so cruelly? The empty garden. The silent, locked museum, the windows thick with dust and cobwebs, labels on the shelves curling in the heat. And his bedroom. I always sleep in his room. I chose to do so after ... but this weekend, after being away for several weeks, it was a desolation. I couldn't sleep. I went down at last and lay on the sitting-room sofa and slept a little. The family never knew. I crept up to his room in the early light. I was almost thankful to leave and come back here. It was as if Patrick's spirit haunted the place, the garden especially where we walked so often and so often in the little museum worked late into the evening. His spirit cried out upon me as if I had somehow failed him. I feel like Hamlet, who could not screw himself to the sticking-point. And yes, I *have* failed him. I have not done what I swore I would do. Patrick cried out from the dark summer foliage that has nearly overgrown the museum, his museum; cried out upon me as I stood in the dawn at the window of his bedroom, to avenge his gross, swollen body that was at last retrieved from the reed-beds so many miles from home, carried down on the force of the weir.

There is a link. I am conscious of a link. My thoughts flood down from my brain into my throat, into my chest, until I choke. Just so did the water flood into his throat, into his lungs, to suffocate him. For a moment – I had no sense of time, it may have been hours that I stood at that window – we embraced each other in some dark place beneath the water, but he – was this a dream? – he, Patrick, lay back at last in my arms, inert, and when I rose to the surface, I could not take him with me, but looked down through the turbulent water to see his beloved body swaying among the tangled weeds on

149

the river bed.

If this is madness, then I embrace it, I welcome it and call upon it to aid me in encompassing my purpose . . . my purpose . . . Meg's death, for by no other way can I satisfy Patrick's restless spirit or exorcise my own grief and guilt.

How? How? The plan was made weeks ago. I know it by heart. It is the opportunity only that is waiting in the wings, that hangs back and refuses to take me by the hand to the front of the stage. I open the bedroom door. Meg is in bed. I undress in silence, for what have we to say to each other? In our separate beds we lie side by side, parted by a river of non-understanding.

Then Meg's voice comes to me from her bed: 'Hubert, are you awake?'

'Mmm.'

'I'm glad you took us all up to the site tonight. I can't sleep and I was thinking about it. I know I didn't have much to do, nor did Ralph – '

'Oh, well, Ralph!'

'Never mind that. It wasn't the site I wanted to talk about. It was just that I hoped you had time to see the loveliness of the evening up there.'

'Yes, of course.'

'I wondered. It's so easy to become earthbound at a dig, if you see what I mean.'

'What are you trying to say?'

'I'm not sure. I was just moved by the evening light on the standing stones, by the distant mountains in the last rays of the sun. I think it's what I shall remember from this site when I have forgotten all else. I wanted to tell you that.'

'Perhaps you feel that we've all been too bound to the site, that we've not paid enough attention to the country here in Wales. It is of course astonishingly beautiful, I will admit.'

'I wonder about the others. They may have felt they were missing a chance to see this part of Wales, not having their cars with them.'

'We're not on holiday. Ralph has no car. Neither has Gwyneth, I believe. I doubt very much if Alan owns a car. I've certainly got too much to do to play at explorers. Even if we had the car, I can't see you driving round these appalling mountain roads by yourself. You've never been a confident driver.'

I've never been allowed to *become* a confident driver, thought Meg. In the short silence after this, Hubert became aware of the importance this conversation might have for him, and while he drove his thoughts towards the plan he had conceived, he allowed his words to follow well-used tracks, opening the conversation again with: 'It's pointless going on about that car decision of mine. As I've said, I doubt if anyone would have benefited except Gwyneth. You know well enough that Ralph, who's got the most time, has never even bothered to learn to drive, having discovered early in his parasitic life how willing people were to "run you home", "give you a lift" and perform other useful errands for you.'

Hubert turned over and closed his eyes. Underneath this long speech, words lay waiting. Meg said: 'You're hard on Ralph, as always. I believe he did in fact drive in his younger days. And Alan's said more than once he wishes he had his brother's motor bike here. He'd like to explore the district – I gather with Gwyneth riding pillion.'

'Good God!' snorted Hubert. 'She's not the girl for that, if I know anything about her. But to go back to what you were saying earlier, about the standing stones – all that. I'm not entirely insensitive to the beauties of this Welsh landscape, you know. I was having a talk with some chaps in the bar the other day, about a lake that's not too far away – a matter of forty or fifty miles – I actually looked it up on the map. I thought then – but going back to Canterbury interrupted my plans – that we might hire a car and drive down there on one of our Fridays off work, if there's time. Might be nice to get away from the site and from everyone else. What d'you think?'

'Of course. If you'd like to do that.'

'Well, wouldn't you? Or perhaps you'd rather come back here some other time and spend a holiday in Wales.'

'No, I wasn't thinking that. Hubert, I'm getting sleepy. Don't let's talk any more.'

'OK, but I won't forget. I'll find out about car hire. In a way, I really feel we *ought* to make an expedition somewhere. Seems rather extraordinary to have been working here in Wales for three months nearly, and go home with no more knowledge of it than the boundaries of a peat bog. Goodnight, Meg. I'll work something out.'

18

See how love and murder will out.

William Congreve: *The Double Dealer*

In the event, Hubert saw no reason to hire a car. He took the Land-Rover, announcing that he would give the same licence to other members of the team to use the vehicle if they wished to explore the local countryside before they left it at the end of the next month. This belated offer was received without enthusiasm. Gwyneth was the only one who could have availed herself of it, in any case. He set out with Meg fairly soon after breakfast. He made a mystery of the destination. He was jovial. He was almost uxorious, taking her hand, or laying his on her thigh possessively. They had an early lunch at an expensive hotel. Hubert drank liberally, while Meg watched him, disturbed and puzzled at his mood. She refused a schooner of sherry before lunch, simply asking for a long iced fruit-juice. This provoked Hubert to an almost tender regard for her well-being and her enjoyment of the day. She pleaded that she was hot with the drive, but drank some wine with the meal. While they were choosing their menu at the bar – though the choice was really Hubert's – his geniality expanded to the barman, to whom he chatted in a man-to-man way.

The barman didn't bother to look at him but continued wiping glasses. He was used to confidences and took no notice of them. Sodding English. He was not required to take any interest in them beyond serving their drinks. He did, however, accept a drink from Hubert. Guilt, he thought, contemptuously. Guilt for their treatment of the Welsh. They longed for the Welsh to love them, and the Irish and the Scots and the Indians, and all those peoples whom they had oppressed for hundreds of years. The barman had read some history. He knew all about the English. When he had saved enough money, he intended to emigrate to South Africa where he could lord it over his inferiors. Another whisky? Certainly, sir, though you've had more than enough already, and presumably you do the driving. That wife looks proper subdued. Beat down. The English had lost their colonies now, except for the Welsh, the Ulstermen and the Scots, so they colonised their wives. He'd seen it often enough.

They sat down to lunch and Hubert was domineering and extravagant, insisting on one of the most expensive wines on the list, and sending back the bottle he had previously ordered. However, he grew restive when the food was a little slow to appear and pushed away his plate before he had finished, saying impatiently: 'Come on, Meg. Don't let's bother with a sweet. I want to get there.'

'Where exactly?'

'Well, I'll let you into the secret now. Quite near here is that lake I spoke of recently. It's a large one. You can hire boats. I thought we might go for a sail. There's a fair breeze up here among the mountains. You don't say anything.'

'I'm ... a bit ... stunned. At the idea of sailing. Why sailing?'

'Well, you know I've always loved it. Brought up on it. Haven't done any for ages.'

'Yes, but – '

'I know what you're trying to say, my dear. There comes a time when one's got to get over these things. All right. Patrick died in a – in a sailing accident.' His voice faltered. He cleared his throat and went on more firmly: 'I don't think we can

154

allow that to turn into a general prohibition against sailing. There comes a time ... you must know what I mean.'

'It seems very sudden.'

'It has to be sudden. I've let myself become – I admit it – obsessed by Patrick's death ... his death by water. Meg, help me. I appeal to you. I want to break this obsession. I want to sail with you this afternoon. Of course it will be painful. But I'm determined and I'm certain we'll get caught up in the pleasure of sailing again, you and I.'

'But, Hubert, why court pain?'

'I don't look at it that way. I want to exorcise it. To *exorcise* it. Ah, here's the turning. Five miles to the lake.'

He swung the car round so violently that Meg was thrown against the side window. He didn't apologise. His eyes stared ahead. She rubbed her arm and thought: I feel an extraordinary sense of unreality. What am I doing, spending the day with Hubert as though we were a young married couple? And going sailing? We haven't sailed together since the very early days of our marriage before the children were born. I should have thought Hubert could never bear to sail again after what happened to Patrick, but it's I who cannot bear it. And see no reason why I should help him to exorcise his pain. It's all too late. I must make my protest.

'Hubert, it's a very hot, still day. Are you sure there'll be enough wind for sailing?'

'Of course. Of course. Plenty of breeze on these mountain lakes.'

I feel trapped. Trapped by Hubert as I was so many years ago. As I have been since all too often. I don't want to sail. I don't want this strange afternoon with a man who is also strange to me. This seems a moment out of ordinary time, a moment I could have entered with someone I loved but not with Hubert. Shall I be stubborn and refuse to go?

But it was not necessary. The boat-hire man had already let out the only boats that were fit for sailing. He could let them have a rowing-boat. They didn't want that? OK. Take it or leave it.

'I don't mind, Hubert. I really don't mind. Let's walk along the edge of the lake.'

'I'm sorry if you're disappointed, my dear.'

From old custom, I take his hand to comfort him because I sense that he is unhappy. There is some conflict within him that he cannot resolve. So we walk, Hubert and I, along a quiet path. We meet no one.

Her hand in mine – what shall I do with it? My plan has collapsed. The man had a malevolent look. He read my thoughts. I fear these Welsh people. Perhaps like Gwyneth he has second sight. He won't hire to me because he knows. He offers an ancient rowing-boat – Charon's ferry-boat – with undisguised malice, daring me to use it, for my purpose. I shall confound him. I put my arm round Meg. 'We'll stroll along by the lake,' I agree, as though we were young lovers.

And the hirer of boats says: 'You do that, sir,' and his mouth is sardonic. He could not care less what I do with my wife, perhaps guesses that my plan is collapsing, that Charon's ferry-boat is too much for me. Then he adds: 'If you walk far enough there's a tea place.'

We find a path among low-growing alders. The water reflects their images. After a while the path peters out. Never mind. We push on, force our way through undergrowth, and always there are glimpses of the lightly ruffled waters of the lake. Two or three sailing-boats. Two or three rowing-boats. Very few for such a lovely afternoon, but this is off the beaten track for tourists.

The heat is oppressive now. The sun's at its zenith. Meg ... Meg ... how long since we made love? No one's about. Say nothing more to her. Overwhelm her with sensual passion that so easily crosses the hairline that divides love from hate. What do words mean? In this context, nothing. It is her body I want to persuade, not her mind. And as always, she responds. For me there is a curiously impersonal quality about

156

making love. Meg never understood this. Women don't. As she never understood my infidelities. She knew of them but did not recognise their triviality. Indeed, what we are doing now in the lush soft undergrowth is essentially trivial. I make love to her with a kind of sleight of hand, an expertise that I happen to possess and enjoy exploiting. At the height of my own orgasm, intoxicated, I suddenly open my eyes and look down on her. This is Meg, my wife, whom I planned to drown this afternoon in the lake that I can glimpse through the trees. I find myself trembling, and then, overwhelmed at the realisation that I have escaped from a hideous danger, I burst into the laughter of relief, and she, in the extreme pleasure of her coming, laughs too. We lie here, united physically and ten thousand miles apart, my dear. Yet though it were ten thousand miles apart, as the old song says, divided in our hearts, we are none the less able to enjoy this brief illusion of unity provided by our willing bodies. God bless them, I feel inclined to add.

Hubert rolled over on to his back and closed his eyes. Meg felt as cold as though she had plunged into a deep mountain tarn. She stared up at the cloudless sky and wondered at it. No warmth from the sun reached her through the canopy of leaves and branches that broke the deep blue into fragments above her head. At my heart, she thought, is a cold region so solid as to be almost sharp under my skin. Ice beneath my ribs. I am surprised at myself, surprised at a sensual response so automatic, so untouched by creaturely feelings in giver and taker. Lying beside Hubert with the smell of some aromatic plant strong in my nostrils, I almost forgot his presence and my thoughts gather speed and carry me forward to the plan which must so soon be put into practice. Perhaps it is accommodating of my heart to chill its temperature so that my mind can function without disturbance from the heart's demands or comments. But one comment cracks the ice. I love my children, my heart reminds me, yet I am planning to leave them. Planning coolly, dispassionately. No, that's not true. My numbed heart comes to life for them, throbs painfully for Barbara and Michael and Edward, and I see them vividly in my mind's eye against this background of green. I am thankful that I saw them recently, that Barbara is already half-prepared for what I am about to do. When I have gone, it may be possible – it must be possible – to build up a new relationship with them, for they are more than children now. Allow myself no special pleading, all the same. What I am doing could be damaging, especially to the twins. But . . . these considerations cannot be allowed to stop me. It is essential that I leave Hubert. Only from a position of independence can I hold out my hands to the children and ask them to accept me in my new role. A mother should grow as the children grow if a fruitful relationship is to come about in a family. How I argue with myself while Hubert sleeps beside me. No tenderness that can be the wonder of the aftermath of love-making. He denies me that. The sweetest thing here, the scent of this herb, enfolds me as if it were conscious of my need for some pleasant fragrance to overpower the sour pungency of loveless sex.

Hubert opens his eye and yawns. He then sits up briskly.

'You know, Meg, what I'd like now is a really good country tea. There's that place the chap with the boats talked about. But I don't know where it is. Let's walk back to the boathouse and ask him. You'd like some tea?'

'I suppose it would be nice. Yes, a pot of tea – '

'Oh, God, I want more than that! Scones and butter. Cake, sandwiches. I'm as hungry as a hunter. Come on, Meg, we're having a marvellous day. Enjoy it.'

They walked back to the boathouse. Yes, they could get a very good tea at the far end of the lake just off the road, at a stone cottage. It belonged to his cousin, Mrs Pugh. She would cook them poached eggs on toast or anything else they fancied. She was a real cook and her bread and cakes were a wonder.

158

They found the cottage after nearly an hour's walk and sat down to varied and plentiful fare. Hubert wolfed scones and honey and went on to fruitcake, munching it with manifest enjoyment.

'I cannot understand why you are so ready to condemn poor Ralph for indulgence,' she heard herself say, 'when you can put away a huge tea like this, Hubert.' (But really, he was behaving like a pig.)

'Now, now, my dear Meg. How often do I get a tea like this? For one thing, one doesn't usually make love in the afternoon. You know it always makes me hungry but I never heard you say that I was self-indulgent, when I went down to the kitchen for some bread and cheese after we'd been going strong.'

'No. No, you never heard me make any comment. I really don't know why I make one now.'

'Besides, look at me. I've a pretty good figure for a man well on in his fifties. No spare fat anywhere, eh?' He thumped his belly and diaphragm. 'But Ralph – well, really, Meg, it's a bit much to compare me with a fellow who's let himself go to pieces like Ralph, physically and mentally. Well, never mind Ralph. I enjoyed that. In fact, my dear, I've enjoyed the whole day.'

A cloud passed over his face. He stared out of the window in silence and Meg wondered what he was thinking. Wondered still more when he stood up and held out his hand to her, helping her to rise. 'We must get back now,' he said, and kissed her lightly on the forehead.

She says nothing to me as we drive home. Her silence is extraordinary, after what we ... but how can she know how utterly different for me that love-making was? Today has been a watershed for me. The last five years have been leading up to it. Now it is over. Now we shall begin life anew. That is the meaning of today, the meaning of my failure to find a boat to take her out sailing. Fate intervened and we are set on a

159

different course, thank God. Extraordinary. I would not believe it if I read it in a book. But I know something that the events of today have shown me: that these five years have been a journey into the dark interior of myself and that during these weeks in Wales, especially these last few days, I reached the climax of a mounting madness.

His foot on the accelerator slackened for a moment, then pressed harder. The car went erratically along the narrow road as he repeated to himself the words: a mounting madness. Was I driving myself insane? Suppose one is pouring liquid through a funnel into a bottle or a jar. The hand must keep steady, absolutely steady. It lifts and the liquid pours faster, the funnel suddenly overflows. That was what it was like in my brain. I feel cleansed by this frightening, near-overwhelming flood that has risen within me and mercifully receded – by whose mercy? No God. No outside agent. No, my own watchful mind was keeping a close eye upon that funnel, and knew that once my murderous desires overflowed into action, madness would engulf me. So . . . I have cast away the opportunity, or Fate, if you like, has cast it away for me and now . . . life must be lived.

19

Heureux qui, comme Ulysse, a fait un beau voyage.

From du Bellay: *Les Regrets*

'Thanks, Ralph. Yes, I will have another. A double? OK. I must confess, I feel damned played out.'

'I thought you and Meg had taken the day off – in the mountains. You ought to be feeling splendid.'

'My dear Ralph, I don't wish to be offensive, especially when you are buying me a drink, but I rather doubt whether you can appreciate the point that when you're used to a routine of work, work to which you are devoted, moreover, the interruption of a holiday, or even a day's break like today, can be disruptive, and exhausting.'

'I see. Not being one of your workaholics, as you might say, I wouldn't know. As you point out. However, I have been exhausted in my time, you know. Drink up, Prof. No heel taps, as old-fashioned books say.'

The two men drank in silence, broken at last by Hubert. 'I thought a day off right away from everything was due to Meg. She seemed a bit off-colour. Were you ever married, Ralph? I've often wondered.'

'Yes. Yes, I was married.'

'You seem a very contented man, without – even if, that is – you have no wife. You're quite a sybarite, with your appreciation of good food and wine and your own version of

161

gracious living. Or so I hear.'

'One can enjoy food and wine even without a wife, Hubert.'

'Yes, I suppose so. Yes, of course. You were happy, were you, when you were married?'

'Very happy.'

'And what happened? She left you ... you – er – '

'In a manner of speaking, she left me.'

'Ralph, I want to ask you a question. D'you think it's possible to go back and start again? Can one return and pick up threads that've been lost?'

'No. There's no return.'

'What, then? A new beginning? An altogether new and different direction?'

'No. I don't really go along with new beginnings, either. So tiresome, all this New Testament stuff about being born new. Really rather awful, in fact, to have to start again. A kind of moral Snakes and Ladders.'

'Be serious, Ralph. What is there, if one's made a mistake, suffered loss, gone astray somewhere along the line? Surely that's when one *has* to make a new beginning?'

'Depends on how you look at it, Prof. I think I'd opt just for going on doggedly, taking the blow or whatever in your stride, even if it's knocked you sideways. You can go on growing. You can grow out of one person into another. Perhaps you think this *is* a kind of new beginning, but it's not. It's part of natural growth like a snake shedding its skin. The skin's dead matter. The snake leaves it behind without a thought – that's where it has the edge over us, of course, it doesn't think, it doesn't remember – and then it grows a new one. It may even change its life-style by finding a new habitat, but at least it doesn't go about weeping over its lost skin. It doesn't embalm it, or put it in a glass case or anything. Sensible creature. No return. No fresh start, really, in my view. You're the same person fundamentally. You grow a new skin, move off to another district, build a new burrow or whatever snakes do, and grow fatter or thinner according to

162

how well you've chosen your new environment. You need to acquire the wisdom of the serpent, Hubert, and always, I repeat, *always* seek out the sunny positions.'

'I see. Have another on me, Ralph. Another double – that's for you. I'd better have a single. I've had more than enough. You surprise me, Ralph. I didn't think of you as a philosophising sort of fellow. Perhaps I've misjudged you. I think we ought to go back to the lounge when you've finished your whisky. It must be nearly time for supper.'

They went into the lounge. Meg and Gwyneth were talking. Alan was smoking and reading, with a glass of beer in his hand.

'Anyone want a drink?' asked Hubert, as no one apparently noticed his entrance.

'Meg? Gwyneth?'

But at this point the bell sounded for supper. The meal was a somewhat silent one and afterwards, as if by tacit consent, they did not play cards. Surprisingly early, Hubert announced that he was going to bed, adding: 'A new week tomorrow. I think we've got it pretty well planned. Think I'll turn in. I find this heat a bit fatiguing.'

No one commented.

Once in the bedroom, Hubert moved restlessly about the room, taking off no more than his coat and tie. By Meg's bed lay a book with a marker in it. He picked it up as he paced to and fro. It was a translation of the *Odyssey*. What makes her read this? God, I'm tired. Can't bother to undress. Just my shoes. I'll lie down as I am.

I hate waste, imperfection. I've always dreamed of finding the fragments of a vase as beautiful as, say, the Portland vase, and then building up its pieces into a whole, re-creating the fractured beauty. Death, the death of Patrick, left a life never brought to perfection. Few lives can be, I suppose, but Patrick had this potential. Now his life is cut off. No re-creation possible. I've no religion. I don't believe, as a devout Christian

163

would, that Patrick will grow to perfection in another world, that God 'took him' from me because his beauty of body and soul was too great for this world. I cannot believe. But these weeks among the mountains, stripped of my ordinary pre-occupations, the professional treadmill, the constant clutter-ing of my mind with fatuous details of administration and so forth, the necessity to consider others – my colleagues, my students – these weeks have been a liberation. Mountains black as the Semplegades on either side of me. Like a voyager, I have had to cast out everything, all my possessions – no, possessiveness – all I owned including ownership. I have had to cast out ... Patrick. I have had to bury him on the shore, bury him decently at last and above him, as Odysseus did for one of his companions, have placed an oar to mark his grave, fitting symbol for one who died as Patrick did by water.

And Meg ... I cannot comprehend my own madness. I only know how close I came to it. I don't know why I found myself unable to follow the course I had plotted; why I did not take out a boat; why Meg is still alive. Chance, was it? Nothing more than chance that left me without a boat on that moun-tain lake? Whose arm directs the turns and twists of chance? I cannot pursue this thought. I am a doer not a thinker. But perhaps have failed somewhere. Have held my thoughts on too tight a rein. So Meg reads the *Odyssey*. Does she think of life as a voyage? I suppose it's a common idea of which the *Odyssey* is the great, the seminal prototype. I have still some way to travel but I'm at last in clear water with a propitious wind, I believe. My mind is pragmatical so why, as I lie here longing for sleep that eludes me, why am I thinking in meta-phors and classical metaphors at that? I suppose it was odd that as an archaeologist I never went to work in Greece or Asia Minor, after that long, thorough classical education at Shrewsbury. I've never even thought about it again, yet just now, picking up the *Odyssey* from Meg's table, the tales return readily enough. I can now remember the name of the young man, youngest of Odysseus' companions, whom he buried with tears on a lonely shore and thrust his oar in the sand to mark his grave. It was Elpenor. After forty years it comes back.

I seem strange to myself. I am also weak and fatigued. I've not recovered my strength after my passage through the Semplegades, in danger of my life. Am now stripped of everything but the sails and steering oar.

When I get back to Canterbury, there will be Meg, the children – almost grown-up now. I have been given time, time to turn to my family, the family that I have created. Time to bring it to perfection, this family, fragmented by death and almost destroyed by my near-madness. If there is a God . . .

Meg came into the bedroom. She spoke to Hubert but there was no reply. He is asleep. Fast asleep. So ravishingly handsome. How can I blame women for falling in love with him? Handsome is as handsome does . . . and she smiled at her own joke.

It's cooler now. There's a breeze and the room's quite cold. I'll lay my eiderdown over him. An act of tenderness that was lacking this afternoon. Was it the last time we shall make love? Then at least let me make this gesture. As I lower the quilt over his sleeping body, I am flooded with happiness. The happiness of freedom. Liberated from sensuality, from the bondage of sexual love. Not liberated from love itself. I am thinking of my family, not Hubert. Freedom to be myself, whatever that means. But yes, it does mean something. One should find out who one is. I have played several roles and they were genuine enough and perhaps necessary in my life, but who am I and what do I want my life to be? I want to think, to be able to lower myself deep into my thoughts, to journey . . . to go on a long journey, whether in reality or in thought doesn't matter. Not to escape. No, certainly not that. The journey into the interior. That's the name of a book I've never read.

I don't believe that I shall travel in the ordinary sense,

165

though thank God I've some money of my own and could afford to if I wanted to. I'd rather travel to some part of England that I don't know. Explore it, become intimately familiar with it and make it my home, a place to which friends and my children can come. Life will flower for me too in books, all the books and poetry I have never read or have forgotten. I'll go to a good bookshop, wherever I find myself. Yes, first of all I'll seek out a good bookshop. Where? York, perhaps, and I'll buy books, masses of books, and explore my own new freedom. Maybe I'll not stay so long in York or even in the hills. Maybe I'll go further afield. To Scotland, to the Hebrides, to walk in the soft rain, always within earshot of the sea. To collect driftwood and build a fire every evening and eat bread and cheese and drink a little wine and read the evening through, the night through, if I please. Long, long books; Proust, Dostoevsky, Henry James, and long poems – *Paradise Lost*, *The Divine Comedy*. Perhaps some of them would bore me. All right, I'll let them go. No compulsions, no guilt. There's so much before me and not only books. So much to see, even on a bare, treeless island. There would be always the light, the light changing at different times of day. The shapes of clouds, the shadows of them on the sea, so much for me to contemplate, to store away in my memory for later. And it is almost time to leave for the unknown destination.

———— 20 ————

Postcard

August 28

Sorry Mum is not so well. I meant to write before but have been very busy. I can't get home yet. We'll be here another week at least. Then we go to the Prof's Institute in Kent for about a week when we leave Wales. You'll be pleased to hear I made the most important find on the whole dig. It's a sword. I'll bring some photos of it, but I expect it'll be in the papers. Look out for it. See you soon, Dad. Hope Mum is getting better.

Alan

About this week's work: Gwyneth, I want you to continue in the same trench. Alan, you will take over D trench. I'm going to work on section G which we've not touched. Ralph, Meg will drive you to the farm. We'll have to get the men back to dig new trenches in section G. I can't afford to let even that unlikely section go unexcavated. Ralph, you'll also be wanted for photography at the site, the new trenches and so on. Meg, time's getting short. We can't count on more money being available. I'd like you to help me in section G, in the new trenches.

The work went on in the usual manner for three days. A few artefacts came to light in Gwyneth's trench, rather more in

167

Alan's, but it was Gwyneth's trench that yielded the most important find since the discovery of the sickle and the scabbard: the fragments of a torc or neck-ring. Work was abandoned while the team examined the pieces. The Welsh labourers left their trenches and came over to look. They were strangers from a different farm who had not been to the site before.

'What is it, then?' they asked. 'Twisted like a rope that little bit is that you're holding, miss.'

'It *is* like a rope,' said Hubert. 'These neck-rings were placed on images of a goddess. If we could bring to light such an image here it would make archaeological history. One dares not hope for so much. This torc would imply that there *was* such an image, a small one by the size of the pieces, probably made of wood and long since perished, of course.'

'Which goddess would that be, then?' asked one of the men.

'I can't put a name to her. She's found under different names all over northern Europe.' (Really, thought Meg, he must be missing his students. He's giving an impromptu lecture to these Welshmen.) 'A mother goddess,' Hubert continued. 'A goddess of fertility, of good crops, productive beasts. Or a local goddess and spirit of the mountain and its lake. The lake that eventually became this peat bog of Gors Ddu.'

'Sacrifices would there be here?'

'Possibly sacrifices to the goddess. The twisted metal of the neck-ring was probably inspired by the twisted strands of rope that strangled the victim. At least this theory has been put forward in some quarters.'

'To think of that, in a civilised country,' muttered one of the Welshmen.

'It was a very long time ago,' said Hubert in a superior voice, certain of his civilisation and its benefits.

'We have different victims now,' observed Ralph.

'Now what exactly do you mean by that?' asked Hubert, annoyed at this interruption.

'Forget it, Prof, I won't go into it. It seems to me that there

168

are always victims in every age, often willing ones.'

'The men and women who were sacrificed to the earth goddess were chosen by lot and no doubt considered it an honour.' A sanctimonious note had come into Hubert's voice, to counter what he considered Ralph's flippancy.

'An honour, maybe,' said Meg, 'but the faces of some of those bog people in Denmark expressed terror – hideous terror.'

Hubert looked nonplussed for a moment. Meg had seen the faces. He could not argue with her. He escaped from his dilemma by rising and saying crisply: 'Back to work,' and then added, feeling himself to have spoken too much like a schoolmaster – what had happened to the inspiring leader of the team? – 'I have a strong intuition that we're on the verge of finding something even more remarkable than this torc.' It was easily said and really, what did it matter if it was rubbish as long as it restored him to his position of respected seniority?

Over their lunch, Meg suddenly asked Gwyneth: 'Have you been to Denmark? Have you seen these bog people?'

'No. It's something I would very much like to do.'

'I went with Hubert some years ago, when he was working on a site in northern Denmark. He had a sabbatical and we spent nearly the whole year there, and of course we went to the Gottorp Museum. The bodies and faces of these bog people were immensely moving. The Windeby girl, with the band still tied round her head, blindfolding her – I shall never forget her. Her ears were so delicate and her slightly parted lips, almost smiling. She didn't look terrified, I must confess. Perhaps she didn't fully realise what was going to happen to her. Perhaps there may have been some gentleness, some restraint in the way she was treated. How can we know now?'

'I remember her face from photographs,' said Gwyneth. 'And I also remember the hands and feet of these people, the veins, the lines on the palms and soles of the feet, the perfect nails. The Tollund man – you saw him, of course. The

169

extraordinary serenity of his face. I remember when I first saw a photograph of him, I thought: why so serene? He must have known. And he was strangled.'

'One of the willing victims Ralph mentioned, perhaps.'

Gwyneth said nothing for a moment. Then she murmured: 'A rag, a bone and a hank of hair. It's a quotation. Who from? Is it Yeats? I can't remember.'

But Meg was staring down at the trenches and did not appear to have heard her. They tidied up the remains of their lunch and went back to work on the site.

It was late in the afternoon, three days after, that Alan found the sword. The team stood round his trench and watched him as he slowly and carefully extracted the hilt and then the whole blade and laid it out on a long piece of cloth. For several minutes no one spoke. Then Hubert lowered himself into the trench and handled the sword, scrutinising it closely. He called Gwyneth and she too examined it. The students watched from the edge of the trench. Then Hubert spoke in a dry, practical manner from which all trace of excitement was suppressed: 'It's essential that you have more assistance in this trench, Alan. I congratulate you on this find and I'm sure that the team joins with me. You've brought the sword out from the peat with consummate skill, but we can't stop at this. The question is: are there any more important – or for that matter, less important – artefacts here? From what those labourers told the press last year, it's obvious that some things have been stolen, and probably even more were taken when peat-cutting went on regularly in the past. None the less, we must go on working in this area. Gwyneth and I will help you, Alan. The sides of this trench must be carefully cut back and every grain of peat sifted. Meg, I'd like you to work on the neighbouring trench, level with us. Ralph, you've got enough to do with your camera and your pencil. Take the students under your wing, please, and show them how these things are done.'

*   *   *

Although Hubert insisted on standing celebratory drinks all round that evening, the team were rather subdued after dinner, all of them tired. They sat in the lounge exchanging small talk. There was again no suggestion of cards.

Gwyneth went out to post a letter. Alan watched her go. He had been silent, and contributed nothing to the desultory conversation. Fate has treated me kindly, I suppose. In this team my name is going to have a special relevance. Surely this is more than chance. The Prof put me in that trench because he trusted my skills, and my skills brought to light this splendid sword. At last I feel my feet on firm ground. If I'm conscious of a slight tremor, it comes from those ancient forces that Gwyneth embodies for me. Poor Gwyneth. I haven't treated her well. She represents my romantic adolescence but reality has destroyed that.

She's just come back from posting the letter she was holding. God, how beautiful she is. Looking at you now, Gwyneth, my heart turns over. I shall never see a more beautiful, more desirable woman. But life for me is moving forward fast. I can't halt by the way. That's what the first few weeks of this excavation were for me, a pause. Now I am set on course for the career I want more – yes, more – than Gwyneth. It's a sacrifice of my ideal of woman built upon Gwyneth, but now I've found another sacrifice, two thousand years old. An offering to the gods and on it I shall build my career. Meg was right. When I need a girl, I shall find one. I'm grateful to Gwyneth. She taught me things I was ignorant of. She was no lesbian, believe you me. She knew it all. Of course, I could have learnt these things from any experienced woman. Yet Gwyneth taught me something more important, though painful at the time. She didn't really want me. She just let me have her that once, but then I was put back into my place. The outsider's place. I wasn't good enough for her. I saw clearly then that I'm an outsider in this team. The working-class lad. I'm an outsider too in my own home. I don't want any prating about local boy making good. I shan't go back there more

171

than I can help. In fact, I'd like to go abroad straight away. An outsider, a loner, gets further. I don't want any baggage encumbering me. I'll go it alone.

While Gwyneth had been gone to the post, a suggestion had come from Ralph.

'D'you remember when Gwyneth told us about Blodeuydd?' he had begun.

'Ah, Blodeuedd,' repeated Hubert. 'Yes.'

'I think we ought to have asked her to read one of those Welsh tales while we were here. If she's not too tired herself, why don't we ask her to do it tonight? There won't be many more opportunities.'

'Mmm, yes. We could ask her.'

'*You* ask her, Prof.'

'You think so? Very well, if we're all agreed.'

So I am to read to them to pass the evening. I go upstairs to fetch my *Mabinogion*. I feel like an old wise woman, humouring them. If I'm to read them a story, it shall be one that has a meaning for us all. I'll never do this again, never play the bard, but if I'm to do it tonight, by God it must get home to them, under their skins. They none of them really know me. Here we've been these many weeks, pursuing our profession, but at the same time living out our private lives, which cannot come to a halt while we excavate a peat bog. As I come down the stairs, with the *Mabinogion* in my hand, I remember my American colleague at Durham telling me that she has a grandmother still living in Virginia, who is full of old saws and snippets of down-to-earth wisdom. One of my favourites was: 'I allus aims not to want what I cain't have.' It's a good working philosophy. It amused me when I first heard it and amused me too to hear the different accents Beverly Banks could put on, ranging from Chicago to New Orleans. I shall miss her when I get back to Durham. She was only there on a year's exchange and she's gone back to the States. She would

172

have helped.

I shall forget the accents, the stories, the proverbs and wise saws. But I've good reason to remember grandmother Banks in Virginia. *I allus aims not to want what I cain't have.* OK. It sounds 'sorta comfortable', as Beverly might have said. But its wisdom is beyond the price of rubies and beyond the price of my pocket, perhaps. I consider it, scan it carefully and recognise that it's worth every penny of fortitude that I possess, yet I spend most of my reasoning power upon evasion, the evasion of the plain truth: Deborah will not come back to me. Why is it not enough, this diamond-hard truth, set as it were in the ring of Granny Banks' words? Well, I must find them a story and it must be the story of the Blessed Bran. Considering the others, just before I step back into the room ready to read, I have to surmise their experience of loss. Ralph, for instance. I have not come to know Ralph well. I've liked him better as the weeks have gone by, but he seems pretty well adjusted to the sloppy standards he sets himself and which I suppose I privately deplore, puritan that I am. If he ever lost anything or anyone, he'd drink or joke his way out. Hubert and Meg? I know of Patrick's death but little of their way of healing themselves of its pain. From the little I see of them together, I'd guess there's been no partnership in healing. Hubert, indeed, seems if anything to nurse his loss. Of Meg I'm not so certain. I simply don't know these people. I've been too self-absorbed. That's it. Not curious enough about them. If I'm to read this tale, I must wash my face and clear the grief from my eyes. The truth is ... I don't know ... simply don't know how I am going to live without you, Deborah. No comfort from Granny Banks. The wisdom will have to come from myself and not from proverbs or philosophy. I suppose if I'd taken the short way out, if I'd killed myself, I'd have ended the pain, but what a strange end – a conclusion you don't know that you've reached. No, I won't kill myself. I'll give myself a chance to ... to what? To learn a new code to live by, I suppose, having chosen so deliberately to live. Am I being pompous? I'm in pain and I don't care whether I'm pompous or not. For God's sake, I've got to *live*. And I've got to find a way how to live.

I dry my face on a tissue. Now for the lounge where they are waiting for me. Here's the story of Bran. Perhaps it is for myself that I shall read it. For myself only.

'I'd like another cup of coffee, Ralph, before I start to read. In fact, I shan't read you more than a few bits that I'll try to string together. It's getting late and the whole tale is a long and complicated one, as most of them are. It's the story of the Blessed Bran, and it's a branch of the *Mabinogion* which tells of the Three Unhappy Blows in this island. Thanks, Ralph. This is the story: it begins with the coming to Wales of an Irish chieftain, Matholwych, to fetch his bride, a Welsh princess called Branwen, sister of Bran. Unfortunately, soon after Matholwych the Irishman arrived in Wales, he was subjected to serious insults. I won't go into it all except to tell you that Bran, to wipe out the insults, gave him a precious cauldron.

"And the virtue of this cauldron," said Bran, "is this: a man of thine, slain today, cast him into the cauldron, and by tomorrow he will be as well as he was at the best, save that he will not have the power of speech."

After this, Matholwych departed for Ireland with his Welsh bride and his brother-in-law's gift, the magic cauldron. But during the next two years, the Irish came to hear about the insults that their chieftain Matholwych had suffered in Wales, and they persuaded him to avenge himself, in spite of the gift of the cauldron, by ill-treating his wife, Branwen.

The vengeance they took was to drive away Branwen from the same chamber with him, and compel her to cook in the court, and to cause the butcher after he had been cutting up meat to come to her and give her every day a box on the ear.

174

They also set a ban on all traffic of boats and coracles between Wales and Ireland so that the unhappy Branwen was cut off from her brother and her people.

Not less than three years they continued thus. And meantime she reared a starling on the end of her kneading-trough and taught it words and instructed the bird what manner of man her brother was. And she brought a letter of the woes and the dishonour that were brought upon her. And the letter was fastened under the root of the bird's wings and sent towards Wales. And the bird came to this island ... it found the Blessed Bran ... at an assembly. And it alighted on his shoulder and ruffled its feathers so that the letter was seen and it was known that the bird had been reared among dwellings.

This is a tale of revenge and counter-revenge. Having read the letter, Bran immediately summoned his host and set out for Ireland. The story says that "in those days the deep water was not wide. He went by wading".

'Inevitably the Welsh forces of Bran met with the Irish and fighting broke out. The Irish were the victors. They had the magic cauldron and flung their dead into it, whereupon they were at once brought to life again. At the end of it all, the Blessed Bran was wounded in the foot with a poisoned spear, and was left with only seven men of his host. He knew that he was dying, so he commanded his men to strike the head from his body.

"And take the head," he said, "and carry it to the White Mount in London, and bury it with its face towards France. And you will be a long time upon the road. In Harddlech you will be feasting seven years, and the birds of Rhiannon singing unto you. And the head will be as pleasant company to you as ever it was at best when it was on me. And at Gwales in Penfroyou you will be fourscore years; and until

175

you open the door towards Aber Henfelen, the side facing Cornwall, you may bide there, and the head with you uncorrupted. But from the time you have opened that door, you may not bide there: make for London to bury the head."

So they struck off the head of Bran and set out for the other side, these seven men, and with them went Bran's sister, Branwen. And when they came to land in Wales, she looked back at Ireland and said: "Woe is me that ever I was born: two good islands have been laid waste because of me!" and she heaved a great sigh, and with that broke her heart. And a four-sided grave was made for her, and she was buried there on the bank of the Alaw. The seven men went on their journey, exactly as the Blessed Bran had said, and hardly noticed the passing of time, they were so joyful, nor had they any remembrance of what they had suffered, or indeed of any sorrow in the world.

'But there came a day when one of them decided to open the door to find out if what Bran had said was true. So the tale ends:

He opened the door and looked on Cornwall and Aber Henfelen. And when he looked, they were as conscious of every loss they had ever sustained, and of every kinsman and friend they had missed, and of every ill that had come upon them, as if it were even then it had befallen them ... And that is what the tale says. That is their adventure, the men who set forth from Ireland.'

There was a long silence when Gwyneth closed the book. Then Hubert cleared his throat.

'In primitive societies,' he began pontifically and then changed his tone. 'In all of us, the ancient theme of revenge still ... er ... we talk of being civilised, but we are a part of our past. I'm not perhaps explaining this very well. One is

176

not only an archaeologist. I hope we remain human beings. Science must not be allowed to stifle our natural feelings. These people of whom Gwyneth has been reading were the contemporaries, almost, of those who threw the votive offerings into Gors Ddu, who may even have made a sacrifice to the goddess of the place. Between us is not much in the history of man. A mere moment.'

Then Meg spoke. 'The end of the story,' she observed, 'is very powerful. Knowledge of loss and suffering is a subtle and terrible punishment for opening the door upon Aber Henfelen, whatever that means. I am not sure of the meaning. I need to think about it.'

No one contributed a suggestion and the next speaker was Alan, who lit a cigarette and remarked: 'The door upon Aber Henfelen doesn't mean anything to me. In fact, I don't see the point of this story. But then, I'm not aware of ever having had a loss.'

Ralph had the last word.

'You don't know what you've missed, Alan,' he said. The words were spoken lightly but his face was serious.

Men in their generations are like the leaves of the trees. The wind blows and one year's leaves are scattered on the ground; but the trees burst into bud and put on fresh ones when the spring comes round.

Homer: *Iliad*, translated by E. V. Rieu.

There were no more finds. The work on the site was done. A visit from the landowner. Short notices in the local press. Longer but non-committal ones in the national press. A few local sight-seers. Students arriving on motor bikes. Archaeologists struggling up the rough track, anxious to see the site before it was covered up for good and to talk to the team about the finds. Welsh labourers filling in the abandoned trenches and enjoying the publicity that came their way. They had a number of theories about the finds and were ready to expound them to anyone who would listen. Finally everything found was carefully packed up for removal to the Institute at Canterbury.

Was there a sacrifice?

If Meg had drowned under the water of the lake ... it would have been ... but this victim died quickly. Maybe willingly. Perhaps a young virgin strangled to placate the goddess of fertility, to persuade her to bless their crops and beasts. The mountains, this very peat bog we have been working in, must have looked much the same as they do now to those who brought the victim along the track two thousand years ago. They would have had no thought of murder, of a wasted young life, of the grief of parents. All had an essential rightness for them. There seemed to my mind, infatuated with thoughts of revenge, the same essential rightness. A terrible justice. But I was wrong and they were wrong. Death is death. There can be no justification. The goddess of retribution whom I served is as hideous as their Celtic Astarte. What am I saying? She is more hideous, for she is one of the aspects of the psyche. She arose from deep within me. My Astarte to whom I would have sacrificed Meg, was within my own heart, obsessed with Patrick's death.

Before we leave this place to which I shall never return, near which lies the valley of the Blow of the Axe which brought back to me so vividly Phyllis, my wife, here and now let me reflect on these offerings lying buried in the peat on the mountain-side; of the victim if there was one, a victim who probably died young, and of Phyllis, who also died young. And let me weep for all waste of life and waste of joy. Who in the whole universe cares? No one. There is no one to care. It is left to us while we are alive to pay a tribute of grief. The ancient gods, if they still exist in the misty hollows of these mountains, are as silent as those standing stones on the edge of Gors Ddu.

Phyllis, I weep for you now, briefly, but tomorrow I return to life as it must be lived. There is no other way.

Alan has made this major find. If I saw him at first as a reincarnation of Patrick, this is not how I see him now. My son is dead. These weeks and the five years before them have brought me to the brink of madness and out of it in mercy has come a kind of quittance, a discharge of my debt to the Eumenides. Let Alan take over the ambition that was reborn for me in Patrick. I bequeath it to him without regret. With

179

pain, yes. That will always be with me. Alan is young and his ambition has begun to show like a beard sprouting on a young man's chin. This summer's excavation will carry him a long stride forward in his career. I wish him well. Soon I shall be back in Canterbury, in my home. With Barbara and the twins. With Meg. Not so far ahead and there will be no children living in the house with us. We shall be alone, Meg and I. It will be a new life, something we shall have to build together. I have only a few more years at the Institute. Then Meg and I ... it won't be easy. My grief for Patrick has been an ichor on which I have drunk myself into madness, but now ... a new life ... is it possible? The thing is to *plan* for it. We must make a blue-print for the future. Yes, a blue-print.

For me, the tale of Bran's severed head has had great potency. One must look one's losses in the face. I don't repudiate the past, whatever Hubert may think. I accept it. I feel like a tree. I have gone through the long cycle of motherhood and domesticity. Now it is time for my tree to shed its leaves and grow into a new cycle. To look through the open door brings a knowledge of far more than loss and suffering. Like a light playing over them comes an inner illumination. This is the gain that arises from loss, and having found it, one must store it up in the heart. Whatever the tale of Bran meant to the others, that is what it meant to me.

I am standing in the corridor and suddenly I am aware that I am not alone. At the far end stands a woman. She seems to be watching me and I have the extraordinary feeling that she is myself. She moves to a window and lowers the glass, lowers her arm outside to turn the door handle ... the door opens ...

The train came to a standstill in the drab fields of Bedfordshire. The guard hurried down the track. About half-way down, an outer door was swinging gently. A smell of wet earth from the furrows beyond the railway embankment drifted through the door.